THE DARKEST NIGHT

By *Barbara Nadel*

BARBARA NADEL

THE DARKEST NIGHT

HEADLINE

First published in Great Britain in 2024 by
HEADLINE PUBLISHING GROUP

1

Cataloguing in Publication Data is available from the British Library

ISBN 978 1 4722 9378 7

Typeset in 13/16pt Times New Roman by Jouve (UK), Milton Keynes

Printed and bound in Great Britain by Clays Ltd, Elcograf S.p.A.

HEADLINE PUBLISHING GROUP
An Hachette UK Company
Carmelite House
50 Victoria Embankment
London EC4Y 0DZ

www.headline.co.uk
www.hachette.co.uk

To Ahmet, Eser, Pat and Celeste.
Also to all the cats of Istanbul.

Cast List

Çetin İkmen – ex İstanbul police detective
Çiçek İkmen – his daughter
Samsun Bajraktar – İkmen's Albanian cousin
Inspector Mehmet Süleyman – İstanbul police detective
Gonca Süleyman – his wife, a Roma artist and fortune teller
Rambo Şekeroğlu Snr – Gonca's youngest brother
Cengiz Şekeroğlu – Gonca's brother in Romania
Rambo Şekeroğlu Jnr – Gonca's youngest son
Erdem Şekeroğlu – Gonca's eldest son
Elvis and Django – Erdem and Rambo Jnr's cousins
Inspector Kerim Gürsel – İstanbul police detective
Sinem Gürsel – Kerim's wife
Melda Gürsel – Kerim and Sinem's daughter
Sergeant Eylül Yavaş – Kerim's sergeant
Sergeant Ömer Müngün – Mehmet Süleyman's sergeant
Yeşili Müngün – Ömer's wife
Gibrail Müngün – Ömer and Yeşili's son
Peri Müngün – Ömer's sister, a nurse
Dr Arto Sarkissian – Armenian, senior police pathologist
Dr Aylin Mardin – police pathologist
Dr Fuat Kartal – pathologist
Commissioner Selahattin Ozer – commissioner of police
Ali Oğan – public prosecutor
Sergeant Hikmet Yıldız – scene-of-crime officer
Superintendent Fahrettin Uysal – incident commander

Inspector Mevlüt Alibey – organised-crime officer
Sergeant Sükran Güllü – Alibey's deputy
Constable Miray Oktay – organised-crime officer
Inspector Mehmet Görür – newly promoted officer
Sergeant Timur Eczacıbaşı – temporary officer
Dr Bülent Saka – hospital doctor
Dr Zaladin – Forensic Institute doctor
Sınan Altuğ – lawyer
Bilal Sönmez – fire chief
Mansur Nebati – lawyer
Ümit Avrant – crime boss
Atila Avrant – his son, an artist
Görkan Paşahan – crime boss, currently in exile somewhere in
    the EU
Fazlı Paşahan – Görkan's son, a carpet dealer
Sümeyye Paşahan – Görkan's daughter, engaged to Atila
    Avrant
Recep Türkoğlu – worked for Görkan Paşahan
Neşe Bocuk – mother of imprisoned crime lord Esat Bocuk
Şevket Sesler – Roma godfather
Selami Sesler – Şevket's son
Nuri Taslı – magician
Ecrin Taslı – Nuri's wife
Ali, Şevket and Alp Taslı – Nuri and Ecrin's sons
Sami Nasi – old friend of İkmen's, magician and occultist
Ruya Nasi – Sami's wife
Buyu Hanım – head of Turkish magic association
Büket Teyze – fortune teller, friend of Gonca
Sıla Gedik – horse-riding stable owner
Zekeriya Bulut – groom at Gedik riding stables
Tahir Bulut – Zekeriya's brother
Mihai and İskender – grooms at Gedik
Aslı Dölen – female groom at Gedik

Mustafa, Ece, Necip and Levent İstekli – witnesses
Zuzanna Nowak – Polish woman
Emir Kaya – ceramicist
Meryem Kaya – Emir's sister, a blacksmith
Ayaz Tarhan – community leader
Enver Yılmaz – Kerim Gürsel's neighbour
Merve Karabulut – tattooist
Xemal Shehu – Albanian shopkeeper
Madam Edith – Edith Piaf impersonator, drag queen
Kurdish Madonna – transsexual brothel madam
Belisarius – Greek coffee shop owner

Pronunciation Guide

There are 29 letters in the Turkish alphabet:

A, a – usually short as in 'hah!'

B, b – as pronounced in English

C, c – not like the c in 'cat' but like the 'j' in 'jar', or 'Taj'

Ç, ç – 'ch' as in 'chunk'

D, d – as pronounced in English

E, e – always short as in 'venerable'

F, f – as pronounced in English

G, g – always hard as in 'slug'

Ğ, ğ – 'yumuşak ge' is used to lengthen the vowel that it follows. It is not usually voiced. As in the name 'Farsakoğlu', pronounced 'Far-sak-orlu'

H, h – as pronounced in English, never silent

I, ı – without a dot, the sound of the 'a' in 'probable'

İ i – with a dot, as the 'i' in 'thin'

J, j – as the French pronounce the 'j' in 'bonjour'

K, k – as pronounced in English, never silent

L, l – as pronounced in English

M, m – as pronounced in English

N, n – as pronounced in English

O, o – always short as in 'hot'

Ö, ö – like the 'ur' sound in 'further'

P, p – as pronounced in English

R, r – as pronounced in English

S, s – as pronounced in English

Ş, ş – like the 'sh' in 'ship'

T, t – as pronounced in English

U, u – always medium length, as in 'push'

Ü, ü – as the French pronounced the 'u' in 'tu'

V, v – as pronounced in English but sometimes with a slight 'w' sound

Y, y – as pronounced in English

Z, z – as pronounced in English

It was so dark he almost couldn't see it. His eyes cringed away. There was hair, black like his daughter's, the back of a tiny head, face down. He couldn't see whether it was male or female, but it was naked.

'God!' he murmured.

A man and his two young sons had been out for an early-morning walk when they'd found the body. Nice middle-class residents of the newly gentrified district of Kağıthane, they'd come down to the creek to watch the sunrise and see what birds they could spot. Instead they'd found this. The father had called it in, a man of around Inspector Kerim Gürsel's own age, now comforting a boy of about twelve and a tiny lad probably the same age as Kerim's own daughter, Melda.

Fighting to hold back tears, Kerim said to his deputy, Sergeant Eylül Yavaş, 'ETA for the doctor?'

'I'll get an update,' she said, and took her phone out of her pocket.

It had been raining the previous night and so the ground was soft and muddy. Kerim shifted slightly awkwardly from foot to foot. Kağıthane Creek was the point at which the Kağıthane Stream fed into the Golden Horn. An area back in Ottoman times where princes and sultans came to picnic beside the famously crystal-clear stream, it had then been known as the Sweet Waters of Europe. Later, during Kerim's youth, the area had been given over to heavy industry, polluting the Golden Horn and making it stink. Now cleaned up, it had been developed into a superior housing development complete with a high-end shopping mall. People like this respectable man and his family had moved in and now the nearby waterway provided relief from the traffic-choked centre of İstanbul. A benign little patch of open space for the megacity – except that it wasn't. Kerim had recently read a newspaper article that cited Kağıthane as one of the İstanbul districts most at risk of 'soil liquefaction' should another earthquake destroy large parts of the city as it had done back in 1999. 'Soil liquefaction' meant that when the earth moved, Kağıthane would fall into a vast water-soaked hole.

'The doctor's about fifteen minutes away, sir.' Eylül put her phone back in her pocket.

'Good,' Kerim said. The sooner this child was wrapped in a blanket the better. And although intellectually he knew that warming it made no difference, because the child was dead, looking at its marbled flesh brought to mind such a lack of care and love, he just couldn't bear it.

Eylül put a hand on his arm, and Kerim gripped her fingers.

Chapter 1

The tall woman in the nurse's uniform bent down to kiss her sleeping lover. She whispered in his ear, 'Your breath stinks.'

Çetin İkmen opened his eyes and said, 'Are you going?'

'Got to be at work for eight,' she said. 'Those crystal-meth casualties won't treat themselves.'

Still sleep sodden, Çetin İkmen sat up in bed and ran his fingers through his thinning iron-grey hair. Rolling his tongue around his mouth, he realised that Peri Müngün had been right. His mouth tasted like mouldy grapes. That was the last time he was going to flirt with red wine. Brandy or rakı were his drinks. No more assignations with other alcoholic beverages even to please Peri.

He took his cigarettes and lighter off his bedside table and lit up. Then he placed an overflowing ashtray on his chest. He coughed, but persisted. Peri was nagging him to give up – not that *she* had, but then she was twenty years his junior. Much as he cared for her, İkmen thanked a God he didn't believe in that they didn't actually live together. She'd come over the previous evening for dinner and stayed as she often had during the course of the past year.

In truth, ex-inspector of police Çetin İkmen and nurse Peri Müngün had been an item since the end of 2019. But then the COVID-19 pandemic had intervened, and while Peri had fought, often day and night, to save people's lives at the Surp Pirgic Hospital in Yedikule, İkmen had been locked inside his apartment

3

with his eldest daughter and his cousin. It had been a dark time. Communicating with friends and family by phone – and, with the help of his daughter Çiçek via the Internet – had not been a lot of fun. And he'd been bored. Just the thought of it made him shudder with shame. Lots of people he knew had lost loved ones to COVID. He hadn't lost anyone. What right had he to complain of boredom?

But then that was his character. Like his addiction to nicotine, it wasn't anything he could or even wanted to do anything about. İkmen had retired from the police back in 2017, but had kept himself busy with private investigative work. However, all that had ended with COVID, and although lockdowns seemed now to be a thing of the past, his ad hoc business had yet to recover.

Using his voice to assist him, he got out of bed and wandered over to the bedroom window. On the way, he passed the mirror on his wardrobe door and briefly stared at himself. He was sixty-five now, heavily lined; his hair had thinned and he'd grown a beard, which he wasn't really sure about; and he was skinny. What on earth did a woman like Peri see in him?

His window afforded views of both the Blue Mosque and the Aya Sofya. His father had bought the enormous old apartment İkmen now lived in back in the 1960s. Although the old man was long dead, İkmen still thanked him on a daily basis for leaving the place to him. For a native İstanbullu to live at the beating heart of the Old City was a great privilege, and he knew it. And it was worth a lot of money now.

Maybe Peri wanted him for his apartment?

İkmen laughed.

Watching her made his heart bleed. Not because of what she was doing – reading her cards for the coming day – but because of what he knew she would do when he approached her. But he

4

always kissed her before he left for work. Just because she was sitting under the olive tree shouldn't make a difference, but it did.

Inspector Mehmet Süleyman took a deep breath and walked out into the frost-dusted garden. His wife Gonca looked up from her tarot card layout, spread on a red cloth on the ground, and began to rise to her feet, slowly and painfully, one hand behind her to push against the ground, her face grimacing with the effort. And although he longed to help her, Mehmet knew that she wouldn't accept help, not even from him.

'Is it that time already, darling,' she said as she stood in front of him, her arms outstretched.

He walked into her embrace and kissed her neck. 'I'm afraid so.'

Mehmet Süleyman loved his job. Like his colleague, Kerim Gürsel, he'd worked all through the pandemic, risking his life to help the people of his city avoid COVID-19 and stay safe from crime. The strain had taken its toll, and although still a handsome man, Mehmet was now greyer and more lined than he'd been before. This, however, paled into insignificance compared to what Gonca had suffered.

She held him tight. 'Love you, baby. Come home safe to me tonight.'

Gonca, like İkmen, was twelve years Mehmet's senior. An accomplished artist whose work was admired across the world, she had given birth to twelve children by her first two husbands before she met Mehmet Süleyman. As an ethnic Romani, her marriage back in 2019 to a policeman distantly related to the Ottoman royal family had scandalised both Turks and her own people. But their love had persisted, even though it had been shaken by the death from COVID of Gonca's second daughter, Hürrem.

He kissed her lips. 'I will.'

'Promise?'

He smiled at her. 'I promise.'

She'd lost much of her confidence as well as her daughter back in 2020. Every day he'd had to go to work to the sound of his wife screaming in agony at the thought of losing him too. That had now quietened to this pleading for reassurance. Until recently, even her work rate had slowed down. While she'd continued to read tarot cards for clients over the phone during the pandemic, her art had all but ceased. The only part of her that had remained entirely intact through her grief was her desire for him. As she always had done, she made love like a woman possessed, clawing at his flesh, covering his body with bites, but at an intensity he had rarely experienced before. He'd taken to inspecting his body for the wounds she inflicted so he could cover them before he went to work.

But all that was as nothing to the damage that had been done to Gonca by COVID in 2021. Apparently she'd had it mildly, but it had left her with this stiffness in her limbs that she constantly tried to ignore or hide. He knew it caused her pain, but how to even raise the subject with her when she was such a proud woman?

He let her go and walked back towards the house they shared. She'd told him she was going to work on the costumes she was creating for them to wear on Bocuk Gecesi. She would, she'd said, present as herself, a witch, while for him she was in the process of altering the Ottoman army uniform that had been worn by his great-grandfather during the Great War. He didn't really want to wear it, but he had agreed to do so because it pleased her. 'You will', she'd said, when she'd taken it out of his wardrobe, 'be my prince for the night.'

The festival of Bocuk Gecesi, said to be the darkest night of the year, was not a native İstanbullu tradition. The idea of a night of misrule came from the Thracian city of Edirne, near the border with Greece. Based around a story about a malignant family of witches, people dressed up as ghouls, ghosts and historical figures and gave each other spiced pumpkin to eat – a well-known charm against evil. Organised by a group of artists and other creatives in the trendy district of Cihangir, İstanbul's version of Bocuk Gecesi had been instrumental in bringing Gonca back to herself. She loved parties, and this was going to be a big night-time celebration featuring outdoor art exhibitions, communal feasting, and performances by street entertainers and magicians. Gonca's contribution involved a work of art based on the darkest-night theme and some in-person card reading.

As he pulled the front door of their house in Balat closed behind him, Mehmet hoped that his wife would be able to cope.

'I suppose,' Dr Arto Sarkissian said as Kerim Gürsel helped him to his feet, 'that in a city of seventeen million people, one is almost bound to see something like this once in a while.' He looked down at the tiny body he had just been examining. 'But I can never get used to it. Adults maybe. But not this . . .'

Kerim helped the pathologist brush dead grass from his overcoat, then said, 'What do you think, Doctor?'

Dr Sarkissian shrugged. The Armenian was the oldest and dearest friend of Çetin İkmen. In spite of being a year older than the policeman, however, he had not chosen to retire and was now the İstanbul police's leading pathologist.

'I don't think much at the moment,' he said. 'Until I get the poor little thing – female, by the way – back to the lab, I won't be able to tell you much, Inspector. However, there is some bruising to the back of the neck I need to take a closer look at.'

'What would you estimate her age to be?' Kerim said. 'I mean, I know I'm no expert, but she looks newborn or not much older to me.'

The doctor nodded. 'You're on the right lines there, Inspector Gürsel.' He shook his head. 'I fear we may be in the presence of a child born out of wedlock. Now that abortions have been made more difficult to obtain . . .' He let his voice trail away.

Abortion had been legal in Turkey since the 1980s, but in recent

7

years the law had been changed to make the procurement of one much more difficult. As a consequence of this, some women, out of desperation, had taken illegal routes to termination, while others had left their babies in places they hoped they might be found and taken care of by others. And while Kağıthane Creek was not an obvious place to put an unwanted child in the hope it would be rescued, this wasn't impossible. Except that it was winter, and the child was naked.

'Given the cold weather and the still sadly all-too-prevalent effects of the pandemic, I am somewhat backed up at the moment,' the doctor continued. 'Consequently I won't be able to perform the post-mortem until late this afternoon. Would five p.m. work for you, Inspector?'

'Yes, of course.'

'Thank you. I'll supervise the removal and leave you with scene-of-crime officers.'

'Thank you, Doctor.'

There was no body bag. The doctor lifted the tiny body into a blanket and then placed it in a holdall. Kerim turned away quickly and spoke to his deputy. 'We need to question the witnesses.'

'Yes, sir.'

Officers in white coveralls moved in on the site.

'What has a godfather firmly rooted in Kars got to do with us?'

Inspector Mevlüt Alibey of the Organised Crime division, a thin, grey-faced man in his early sixties, looked across the desk at Mehmet Süleyman and said, 'Seriously?'

Süleyman smiled. 'Mevlüt Bey, I am sure it hasn't escaped your notice that in spite of the fact that we have all been under threat from a deadly virus for the past almost three years now, some İstanbullus still see fit to murder each other. Just this morning my colleague Inspector Gürsel has been called out to a suspected homicide in Kağıthane. I myself am currently fighting a losing

8

battle to catch up with paperwork related to one gangland execution and a domestic murder, both more than six months old . . .'

'Mehmet Bey, Ümit Avrant is a convicted killer . . .'

'I know. He served twelve years for the murder of his brother, I recall. He's done his time.'

'Yes.'

'However?'

'Avrant's son became engaged to the daughter of Görkan Paşahan back in April,' Alibey continued. 'A huge party was held to celebrate this event at the Çırağan Palace Hotel here in the city.'

'I remember.'

Süleyman had married Gonca Şekeroğlu at the Çırağan Palace just prior to the pandemic. Back in April, when the Paşahans, one of the local crime families, had celebrated the engagement of daughter Sümeyye to Ümit Avrant's son Atila at the venue, it had been covered extensively by the kind of breathless celebrity magazines Süleyman's young niece liked to read.

'So Avrant is in the process of buying two adjacent yalıs on Büyükada and has applied for permission to demolish them both and build some sort of futuristic iteration of the Starship *Enterprise* in its place for Atila and his bride.'

Süleyman, who came from a venerable Ottoman family that still owned a creaking yalı, or summer villa, on Büyükada, a small island in the Sea of Marmara, said, 'Buildings on the Princes' Islands are protected.'

'With respect, Mehmet Bey, we both know that when it comes to crime families, particularly those in good odour with, shall we say, those with influence . . .'

Süleyman leaned back in his chair. 'Forgive me, Mevlüt Bey. While Ümit Avrant may well be in good odour, his son's prospective wife and her family are most certainly not. As I am sure you are aware, the whereabouts of Görkan Paşahan have become something of a national obsession.'

Shortly after his daughter's engagement, the crime boss had left Turkey in the wake, it was said, of a disagreement with certain people in high places. Since then he had broadcast a series of podcasts threatening to detail what he knew about the private lives of various community leaders and politicians. He had also, it was alleged, killed a Latvian prostitute. Paşahan was a wanted man, both by Süleyman and his colleagues in Homicide and by the people he had threatened to expose. So far, his whereabouts had proved elusive.

Alibey leaned forward. 'We're trying to get to Paşahan's money,' he said. 'If we can cut him off from his cash, we can possibly starve the bastard out. But there's a problem: it's all offshore. Mehmet Bey, I've come to you in order to find out what you've got on Paşahan regarding the death of this prostitute. When we can find him, maybe we can extradite him . . .'

It was clear that Alibey was under pressure from those way above his pay grade. İstanbul Commissioner of Police Selahattin Ozer was probably behind it. A friend of the ruling elites, Ozer was possibly under considerable pressure himself regarding Paşahan.

'So this isn't about Avrant at all?' Süleyman said.

'Well, it is inasmuch as Avrant appears to be moving into the city . . .'

'Possibly.' Süleyman tipped his head. 'But surely any sort of alliance with Paşahan – were that ever a reality – has to be off the agenda at the moment due to Görkan Bey's current status. I mean, I'm assuming the wedding is off . . .'

He brought up his records regarding the death of prostitute Sofija Ozola.

'Sofija Ozola was found dead by her roommate, a Polish woman, in the apartment they shared in Kuzguncuk on 1 May 2022. Death by strangulation. Suspects were customers. Three ruled out. Forensics felt the place had been cleaned post-mortem, paucity of

usable evidence. Anecdotal evidence that Paşahan was a regular.'
He looked up. 'Motive unknown. However, Paşahan did leave the
country on 10 May, and so . . .'

'If we find him, can he be extradited?'

'On what I have, it's questionable. Hearsay. The only actual
witness statement we had was later withdrawn. And while I infer
from your presence here, Mevlüt Bey, that you are probably experiencing some pressure to progress the apprehension of Paşahan,
I am not yet in that position. I will help you if I can, but my time
is already limited, and with another potential unlawful killing
today . . .'

'I understand, Mehmet Bey,' Alibey said. 'It's just . . .' He shook
his head. 'I've got my doubts about the notion of bringing him in
on fraud charges.'

'Because the money's offshore?'

'Not just that.' Alibey looked behind him. It seemed the
organised-crime officer didn't want anyone overhearing what he
was about to say next. 'Mehmet Bey, I wouldn't say this to anyone
else. But as you know, while I never liked him, I always respected
Inspector İkmen as a man of integrity, and I know you remain
close.'

'Yes . . .'

'While some of Paşahan's money, as we know, comes from
his long-term connection to the heroin trade, much of it, we
think, comes from sources some would rather didn't come to
light. Those connections he now seeks to . . . embarrass. I am,
as you have indicated, experiencing some pressure, and yet I
feel that should I find anything, it may be sidelined. Do you
understand?'

Süleyman paused, time during which his personal mobile
pinged to indicate he had a message. But he didn't pick it up.
Instead he said, 'And so a review of my evidence concerning the
death of Sofija Ozola would help, maybe?'

Alibey exhaled, relieved. 'I would appreciate it, Mehmet Bey.'

'Of course I cannot promise to come up with anything useful to you,' Süleyman said. 'And remember, we still don't know where Paşahan is.'

'No, but if you could . . .'

'I will do my best.'

Alibey wanted a deflection, something to temporarily take the heat off his department. Understandably, he didn't want to open the can of worms that was Paşahan's finances, and nor did his bosses. But he was compelled to go through the motions, and if Süleyman could tie Paşahan to the death of Sofija Ozola, then that was all to the good, because he had some grave doubts about the gangster's innocence.

When Alibey had gone, he picked up his mobile and opened the text he'd received. It was from Gonca. As well as reading her own cards every day, she also read for her husband. Süleyman didn't know whether he believed in fortune telling, but this snippet did pique his interest: *Darling, today you must beware of those who are not what they seem. I love you, Gonca.*

He responded with a heart emoji.

The İstekli family lived in one of the new high-rise apartment blocks that of late had characterised much of the Kağıthane district. On the eighth floor, the family's three-bed apartment was smart and spacious, and was also testament to the success of father Mustafa İstekli's hard work as a civil engineer. His wife, Ece, a covered woman, didn't work, spending most of her time attending to the needs of their two sons, eleven-year-old Levent and four-year-old Necip.

When Kerim Gürsel and Eylül Yavaş entered the apartment, Ece was sitting on a sofa in the apartment's huge lounge, comforting her boys.

After asking the officers whether they would like tea, Mustafa

İstekli took them to one side. 'I'll tell you what I can about this morning, but I don't know whether you'll get much out of the boys.'

'It was your younger son, Necip, who found the body, is that right, Mr İstekli?' Kerim asked.

'Yes,' he said. 'He was poking about in the water with a stick, as children do. I had my binoculars out. Levent and I were passing them between us. I'd spotted some goldfinches. The first time I realised anything was amiss was when I heard Necip begin to cry. I went over to him and asked him what the matter was, and it was then that I saw it.'

'The child's body?'

'Yes. Necip thought the baby was asleep and began to cry when it didn't wake up.'

'And your other son?' Eylül asked.

'Levent followed me over to his brother. Unlike Necip, he could see exactly what it was, the same as I could. I grabbed both the boys and took them away from the scene and then I called you.' He shook his head. 'I've always tried to protect my family, and so my children are not accustomed to such sights.'

Kerim said, 'I understand.'

'Do you?' İstekli asked. 'Inspector, I was brought up in Tarlabaşı, where death on the streets is not an uncommon occurrence. That and the sight of men dressed as women and all other kinds of unnatural practices is not what one wants to bring one's children up around. I thought that here in Kağıthane we'd be away from the seedier side of life.'

Kerim, who lived in Tarlabaşı with his wife and four-year-old daughter, didn't comment.

'So what will Mehmet do while you're reading everyone's cards?' Çetin İkmen asked Gonca.

They were drinking coffee and smoking cigarettes in the artist's studio at the back of her old Greek house in Balat. Although

13

married to Mehmet Süleyman, Gonca Şekeroğlu had been friends with Çetin İkmen for much longer. As a child, İkmen and his brother Halıl had been taken by their mother, Ayşe, a native Albanian and a witch, up to Sulukule, where the Roma had lived back in the 1960s. There he had met with Roma witches, including Gonca's powerful mother, and the many Şekeroğlu children had played with the two little Turkish boys. Çetin had always had a soft spot for Gonca.

'I mean, I may be wrong, but I can't see him going house to house offering spiced pumpkin to people,' İkmen continued.

Gonca waved this away. 'He's going to be wearing his great-grandfather's uniform. I just want him to look Ottoman and gorgeous.'

'Not sure whether having his face powdered white will enhance his appearance,' İkmen said.

'Oh, he doesn't have to do that!'

'Yes, he does. We all do. Either we're doing Bocuk Gecesi or we're not. And Bocuk Gecesi involves powdering your face white so the evil Bocuk witches think you're already dead.'

Gonca thought for a moment. 'Well, maybe a little powder, then.'

'You don't want him dragged down to hell . . .'

The cynical look on her face made İkmen clam up. These were not her traditions and so she only paid them lip service. Were Bocuk Gecesi a Roma festival, she would be taking it very seriously.

'Have you seen Şeftali lately?' he asked instead.

Gonca put up a series of large photographs of the Cihangir district on her easel and stared at them. Ornate nineteenth-century buildings nestled amongst tidy modern apartment blocks, their balconies festooned with flowers.

'No,' she said without looking at him. 'Why would I want to go and spend time in her stinking hovel?'

'Because she's your cousin,' İkmen said. 'Because Şeftali predicted the pandemic . . .'

14

'No she didn't!' She turned to him. 'That was her demon.'

Şeftali Şekeroğlu was a professional falcı, a fortune teller. However, unlike most people in her line of work, she relied on not just tarot cards or coffee grounds to peer into someone's future. She had a demon called a Poreskoro to help her. And while Çetin İkmen's relationship with his mother's world of magic and the unseen was at times deeply sceptical, he had actually seen the Poreskoro with his own eyes. If it was a trick, it was a good one.

İkmen had come to Balat to talk about the Bocuk Gecesi festival with Gonca at Mehmet's request. Although on the surface she seemed like her usual confident self, it was going to be her first professional engagement since the pandemic, and her husband knew she was nervous. As well as reading cards, she was also going to be gathering material for one of her famous collages, which would represent the darkest night. Later on in the year it would be auctioned off to the benefit of a local charity dedicated to the care of street animals.

'So how are you getting on with Orhan Paşa's uniform?' he asked her. 'And how do you feel about touching a dead man's clothes?'

Roma people believed that the property of the dead was inhabited by their spirits, which sought to remain on earth and do mischief to the living.

'It's Mehmet's, not mine,' she said. 'You gage don't believe as we do. Had he been Roma, I wouldn't have touched it, wouldn't have had it in the house. Anyway, it's not as if the old man died in it.'

'No, but he fought in it,' İkmen said. 'In the deserts of the Hejaz. Mehmet told me that when his mother gave him the uniform' there was sand in one of the pockets.'

'Well, there isn't now,' Gonca said. 'I've taken it in – Orhan Paşa was one of those champagne- and caviar-swilling princes – and I've cleaned it thoroughly.'

He imagined her performing unintelligible cleansing rituals over it.

'It will be ready for tomorrow night,' she said. 'And my husband will look fabulous.'

Ah, to be so in love, İkmen thought. He'd felt like that about his wife, Fatma, mother of his nine children, dead since 2016. They'd had a fiery relationship – he an atheist, she a devout Muslim – but they'd adored each other. He still loved her, in spite of her death, in spite of his girlfriend, Peri. And yet increasingly he thought more and more about Peri. Snarky and funny, she was good for him. He liked that she found sex both pleasurable and amusing – Fatma, in private, had always said she found the whole process hilarious too. Peri was also kind and tolerant. His children were not hers, and yet whenever they were at his place, she just fitted in with however many kids were at home at any one time. Ditto his transsexual cousin Samsun. A hard-working, if often tired, trans woman in her seventies, she pulled no punches for anyone. But Peri rolled with her sharp tongue and had finally gained her respect. İkmen's eldest daughter Çiçek had told him some months ago, 'Peri must love you very much, Dad, to put up with our family.'

He smiled to himself and saw that Gonca was smiling too. He knew that she knew exactly what he had been thinking.

'Do you remember what you were doing just before your brother found the baby, Levent?' Eylül Yavaş asked the eleven-year-old.

Ece İstekli squeezed her son close to her side. 'It's all right, Levent, you've done nothing wrong. Just answer the officer.'

The boy, who was skinny and tall for his age, pulled his arm across his eyes, wiping away a few nascent tears.

'I was with Dad,' he said. 'We saw goldfinches.'

'Was that exciting?' Eylül asked.

He shrugged. She suspected that birdwatching was rather more Mustafa İstekli's passion than that of his children.

16

'I heard my brother start crying. He's only little and so he does that sometimes,' Levent said. 'My dad went over to him, and then so did I.'

'Levent, did you see anyone walking about around Kağıthane Creek this morning?' Eylül said.

'No.'

'Are you sure?'

'I don't think so.'

'Any dogs?'

People often took their dogs to open spaces like the creek where they had space to run and play off their leads.

'No . . .'

'There was a horsey.'

They all turned to look at little Necip, tucked in on the other side of his mother.

Kerim leant in towards the boy. 'What kind of horsey was it, Necip? Was anybody riding it?'

'Black,' the boy said. 'Black horsey.'

Chapter 2

Sergeant Ömer Müngün leaned back in his chair and laced his fingers around the back of his head. Then he yawned.

Mehmet Süleyman looked up from his computer screen. 'Bored, Sergeant?'

Ömer shook his head. 'Sorry, boss,' he said. 'Not a lot of sleep last night. We're trying to get Gibrail to sleep in his own room, but he won't have it. Keeps on getting up, coming into our bedroom, jabbing me awake with his fingers and babbling at me.'

A native of a far eastern district of Turkey called the Tur Abdin, or Slaves of God, Ömer Müngün had been Mehmet Süleyman's deputy for fifteen years. Now thirty-six, he lived with his young wife Yeşili, their three-year-old son Gibrail, and Ömer's sister Peri in a small apartment in the central Gümüşsuyu district of the city. All members of an ancient religion centred on a Mesopotamian snake goddess called the Şahmeran, the Müngüns spoke Aramaic amongst themselves, and this was what Ömer meant when he described his son as 'babbling' at him. In spite of his own and his sister's best efforts, Yeşili Müngün still couldn't speak Turkish, which meant that Gibrail was basically a monoglot too. This upset Ömer, who wanted his son to blend in with other children as soon as possible. It was also a reminder of the fact that his marriage to Yeşili had been arranged by his parents. Three and a half years on from his wedding, he still was not in love with his wife.

'They're hard work when they're that age,' Süleyman said. His own son, who was now twenty and at university, had slept in his parents' bed until he was four.

Ömer shook his head. 'On top of that, nothing's jumping out at me about the Sofija Ozola case,' he said. 'Certainly not in relation to Görkan Paşahan. The girl she shared with, Zuzanna Nowak, was the only person who mentioned Paşahan's name. Not the landlady or the neighbours. Big blond Zuzanna Nowak . . .'

Süleyman shot him a disapproving look. 'Yes. But back to business . . . Nowak lived with Ozola and so she'd know more than anyone else. But she retracted her statement that she had seen Paşahan on the day of Ozola's death. Can you see if any forensics are still outstanding?'

'I can, although I doubt it.'

Prostitutes like Sofija were frequently victims of crime and sometimes murder in İstanbul. Unless they worked for one of the fast-disappearing state-run brothels, they were vulnerable to attack from unscrupulous pimps, organised-crime gangs and their customers. Sofija Ozola had been fortunate enough to share an apartment with Zuzanna Nowak, who worked as a sociology lecturer at Koç University and had apparently got to know Sofija via a local gym. Nowak had known what Ozola did for a living when she'd agreed to share her apartment with her, which had seemed odd, but the Polish woman had explained it by saying that as a liberal, she couldn't condemn Sofija for her choice of profession. Sex work, she'd told the police, was like any other job. But who would actually want to share an apartment with someone on the game? At the time, Süleyman had assumed that, like most people, Zuzanna was having trouble paying her rent. Landlords across the city had been ramping rents up for some years.

'And find out whether Zuzanna Nowak is still living in Kuzguncuk, would you, Ömer?'

'Yep.' Ömer looked up. 'Boss, are we going after Paşahan? You know he's outside the country.'

19

'Of course,' Süleyman said.

'And it's political,' Ömer continued.

'For some people, yes.'

'So . . .'

'I said I'd look into it as a favour to Organised Crime,' Süleyman said.

'Oh.'

'We're not exactly rushed off our feet at the moment, are we?'

'No. Unlike Kerim Bey,' Ömer said.

Süleyman shook his head. 'It's always bad when a child is involved.'

'Where are you going?'

'Büyükçekmece,' she said as she picked up her bag of tools and flung it in the back of the Land Rover.

Emir Kaya and his sister had lived in Cihangir all their lives. And while Emir was an artist, Meryem Kaya had taken over the family business from her father, who had belonged to a long line of blacksmiths. Today she was going out to the İstanbul mounted-police training centre in Büyükçekmece.

'They've a new horse,' she continued, 'a stallion. It's only his second shoeing.'

'Mmm.' Emir leaned against the wall of the garage. In the old days, this had been the forge where generations of Kayas had made shoes for thousands of the city's horses. Now his sister took her skills wherever they were needed, which ranged from the mounted-police training centre to riding schools, and also to the Roma, who still had a few horses in the back streets of Tarlabaşı. She scraped a living. But it was what she'd always wanted to do.

'You busy tomorrow?' Emir continued.

'I'll be here for Bocuk Gecesi,' Meryem said.

'So you're working in the day?'

'Yedikule. Man wants me to shoe his ancient horse. Poor beast's

20

got shoes as thin as paper.' She looked hard at her brother. 'What's the matter, Emir? There'll be lots of people here tomorrow night, and once they've seen your work, I'm sure you'll get some commissions.'

'Yes, but the nature of what I do . . .'

'Your work isn't attacking anyone specifically,' she said. 'It's a comment on a phenomenon everyone can see with their own eyes.'

'Maybe. But people will be coming from outside Cihangir, remember.'

He looked crestfallen, and so Meryem, his big sister by ten years, went over and stroked his face.

'Don't worry, little brother,' she said. 'Everything will be fine, I promise. I know you're still hurting, but now you have to move on. You played with fire but you got away with it. Just be grateful you're still breathing.'

The baby looked so tiny and so vulnerable. Naked on the cold steel pathology table, she seemed to embody the tragedy of death.

Dr Sarkissian and his assistants, an anonymised group wearing scrubs, surgical masks, visors and gloves, looked like characters from a science-fiction movie as they welcomed Kerim Gürsel and Eylül Yavaş into the laboratory. Similarly outfitted, the two officers sweated heavily in the unaccustomed plastic coveralls.

Arto Sarkissian, who, due to his wide stature, was the only recognisable attendee, spoke into a voice recorder held by a colleague. 'Thank you for attending, Inspector Gürsel, Sergeant Yavaş. To give you some indication about what is going to happen today, I can tell you that I will proceed with this post-mortem in exactly the same way as I would for an adult cadaver. To wit, I will make a single incision down from the base of the neck, through the thorax and abdomen, finishing just above the groin. I will then remove and examine the subject's internal organs with a view to determining cause of death. After that, I will make an incision across the back of the skull and remove the brain, again for examination as well as for the harvesting of samples for further analysis.' He looked around the laboratory. 'Are we ready, everyone?'

Kerim didn't feel ready, but he murmured his assent. The doctor took a large scalpel from an instrument tray and made a deep incision at the base of the child's neck. This was accompanied by a noise Kerim could not describe. Forcing himself to look as Sarkissian opened up a deep fissure in the tiny body, he heard the doctor say, 'Subject is a female newborn weighing 2.7 kilograms and measuring 46 centimetres in length. This is slightly underweight for a full-term infant, which may mean that birth was concluded several weeks premature. Infant has pale skin, black hair and blue eyes. Body is pliable, rigor having passed off some four hours ago. I should add here that the onset of rigor is frequently more rapid in infants. Subsequent disappearance of rigor is also generally quicker due to paucity of muscle mass in young children. Using rigor as a guide to time of death, I would estimate this to have occurred between 0400 hours and 0600 hours local time İstanbul, Republic of Türkiye.'

Kerim looked at Eylül, who appeared impassive. They had been called to the scene of the baby's discovery at 6.35 a.m., which meant it was possible that the İstekli family had just missed whoever had abandoned the child in the creek. Only four-year-old Necip had reported seeing anyone in the vicinity, but could such a young child's testimony be validated? According to his father, Necip was 'in love' with horses. They did often see them in the area – there were two riding schools locally – and so when asked whether he'd seen anyone, it was almost inevitable that he'd mention horses. This one, the child had told them, had had a rider. A lone rider early in the morning.

The first person to touch the baby's corpse had been Dr Sarkissian. It had been cold. Also the child had been lying on her stomach, which, when the doctor had turned her over, had exhibited signs of livor mortis, of blood pooling at the lowest part of the body. This could begin to become apparent one hour after death, meaning that the horse and more specifically its rider may or may not be significant. Was it possible that he or she had stayed in the vicinity of the body for as much as an hour? Had he or she gone for a ride after placing the baby? Why?

'I should state at this point that it is my belief that the contents of the lungs may well be pertinent to cause of death,' Dr Sarkissian said. 'The subject when found was face-down in a stream emanating from the nearby Kağıthane Creek.'

'Doctor, do you think that where the body was found was where the subject died?' Eylül Yavaş asked.

'I'm not yet sure,' Sarkissian said. 'Depends what I discover, or not, today, as well as on samples and observations taken by the forensic team. I hope to have more for you when I have had time to assess my own evidence and theirs.'

Melda had gone on and on when Edith had suggested an outing to Gezi Park. Of course Sinem had known why Edith had done it, and on the one hand she blessed her for it. But on the other hand, being alone was the very last thing she needed.

At forty-five, Sinem Gürsel had the kind of life many women would envy. She had a loving husband with a good job, a beautiful little daughter, and while the family lived in Tarlabaşı, one of İstanbul's rougher districts, all their friends were nearby. She even had an unofficial nanny in the shape of Madam Edith.

But all was not as it seemed. Her handsome husband Kerim, though caring and loving towards her, was actually homosexual. Unable to be 'out' in a country that had latterly clamped down hard on such lifestyles, he still mourned the death of his transsexual lover Pembe, four years previously. And while Sinem had always known who and what Kerim was, she longed for more love

23

than he could give. Then there was her health. She had suffered from rheumatoid arthritis since childhood, and one of the reasons Madam Edith – an elderly drag queen the couple both knew and trusted – came to look after Melda was to relieve the strain on Sinem.

Until recently, the arrangement had worked well. During the pandemic, Edith had actually moved into the Gürsels' apartment, time during which four-year-old Melda had fallen in love with her. The feeling had been mutual, and almost every night, Edith sang the little girl to sleep with selections of songs once performed by her muse, Edith Piaf. This was Edith's act in drag clubs and gay bars all over the city, and Melda loved it. The two of them would often go out to Gezi or breeze along İstiklal Caddesi singing 'Non, je ne regrette rien', giggling happily. Their joy had pleased Sinem too.

But then things had changed, suddenly and without warning. When the last lockdown had ended, she'd felt so happy. Kerim had taken them all out to Bebek for the day in the car, and although it hadn't been warm, they'd sat by the Bosphorus with ice creams. Bebek was famous for its ice-cream parlours and Sinem remembered the taste of her pistachio cone, which at the time had signified the victory of their survival. No one they knew had died and the world had suddenly felt clean again, the future bright.

But then a darkness she had never even imagined had descended. Out of nowhere.

Alone and afraid, Sinem hardly dared breathe.

'I still need to test liquid taken from the lungs, but I would lay money that it came from the creek,' Dr Sarkissian said. 'The bruises on the back of the neck are consistent with the child being held face down. Unlike in the case of an adult, it would not have taken long for suffocation and death to occur.'

'How can anyone do that?' Kerim Gürsel said. 'How?' He was angry. His fury enhanced by his own status as a father.

24

'I don't know,' the doctor replied. 'However, disturbing though this is, we must not be too quick to judge. While we may have consigned the practices of our ancestors to the dustbin of history, the reality is that the twenty-first century has seen an upswing in those desirous of living a more conservative lifestyle. This can bring with it a return to dilemmas of the past, to wit the young woman made unwantedly pregnant by an abuser or a lover who finds herself desperate.'

Kerim felt his eyes gravitate towards the headscarfed Eylül Yavaş.

She said, 'Sir, if you think I approve of—'

'We must most certainly not point fingers at each other,' the doctor said. 'I was merely laying out a possible scenario. And remember that some Christians approve a more punitive approach to "sin" these days too. Everyone seems to.'

Kerim said, 'I apologise, Sergeant Yavaş.'

They were sitting in Dr Sarkissian's office after the post-mortem, drinking tea.

'The people who persecute women are my enemies too,' Eylül continued.

'Yes, well at this stage of the investigation, we must concentrate upon finding the truth,' the doctor interjected. 'Whatever that may prove to be.'

Kerim Gürsel nodded. 'Indeed.'

The men who worked with Eylül Yavaş had become used to the fact that she wore a hijab. As the daughter of an elite secular family, it was solely her choice. She didn't bring her religious beliefs to work, never proselytised, and had earned her colleagues' trust and respect through hard work and diligence. However, when something like a suspected 'honour' killing happened, her colleagues still struggled with where exactly Eylül might stand on such issues. Here a dead newborn had once again brought doubts into Kerim Gürsel's mind about his colleague. Yet he also knew that ever since the birth of his daughter, he had been particularly sensitive when it came to crimes against children – especially girls. He loved his Melda so much, he always saw her face when he came across a mistreated child and he struggled to control his tears. The little girl gave his life meaning, especially in light of the fact that his old life, as a gay man, was no longer available to him. His wife and child were now his entire world, and every night he rushed out of his office and drove like a maniac to get back to them. Well, he did this most nights . . .

The doctor's voice roused him from his drifting thoughts.

'I will probably be able to confirm my findings tomorrow, hopefully in the morning,' he said.

'Thank you, Doctor.'

The Armenian took in a deep breath and got to his feet. 'And so, Inspector Gürsel, Sergeant Yavaş, with that in mind, I will return to my work. Whatever happens, I will call you tomorrow morning. Even if that is only to tell you I still have my doubts. In the meantime, I will email Commissioner Ozer with my findings so far. I know he is eager to issue a statement to the press. There's a possibility the mother is out there somewhere, very likely needing medical attention.'

Zuzanna Nowak, the Polish woman who had shared an apartment with Sofija Ozola, had moved. Just over a month after Sofija's death, she'd given up her tenancy on her apartment in Kuzguncuk and moved to Bebek on the European side of the city. More convenient for her job at Koç University in nearby Sarıyer, Bebek, like Kuzguncuk, was an upscale district, and both of Nowak's apartments, the old and the new, were large.

Ömer Müngün leaned back in his chair and chewed the end of his pen. Moving after a terrible incident like murder made sense and was common. Why would you want to live somewhere tainted by violent death? And Bebek made much more sense than

Kuzguncuk in terms of Nowak's job. What jarred was the size and appointment of her apartments. The Kuzguncuk place had three bedrooms, the Bebek apartment four; both had Bosphorus views, and in Bebek she lived alone. Why so much space for just one person? And why had she shared with a hooker anyway when she was in Kuzguncuk? If she'd been hard up for money, she could easily have downsized.

Zuzanna Nowak had stated, almost immediately, that Görkan Paşahan had visited the day Sofija had died. Although the police had been able to find no evidence of Paşahan's presence at the property, she had stuck to her story. Then she'd retracted it, and Paşahan had had his little falling-out with powerful people and left the country.

Seventy-year-old Görkan Paşahan was not a native İstanbullu. He'd grown up in a small village just outside the north-western city of Bursa. According to his own origin myth, his father, an Albanian, had been a Karagöz shadow-play master. In fact he'd been unemployed for most of his short life. His son, however, had made his money in the nearby ski resort of Uludağ, where he'd provided security services, lavish dining and entertaining and, it was said, 'female company' and heroin to the rich and famous. A staunch supporter of the current status quo, he was, or had been, a pious man, who had a connection to the now imprisoned İstanbul godfather Esat Bocuk. It was said by some in the criminal under-world that when he moved to the city in 2021, it was with a view to taking over Bocuk's crime empire on the Asian side. But then he'd got into hot water with those in high places . . .

Ömer looked over at Süleyman. 'Boss, does Esat Bocuk's old mother still live in Kadıköy?'

'I believe so,' Süleyman said. 'Why?'

'Few months ago there was a whisper that Görkan Paşahan took old Neşe Hanım under his wing when Esat got put away. Moved to the city to be close to her.'

Süleyman frowned.

'Makes sense,' Ömer continued. 'With her son and one of her grandsons inside and the other boy raving his head off in the psych hospital, Bocuk's operation fell apart.'

'I was pleased with that result.'

'Yeah, but . . .' Ömer paused. 'When Paşahan moved to the city in 2021, he bought a waterfront property in Beykoz, the Zambak Yalı. Remember Organised Crime tipped us off?'

'Yes, but nothing happened, because shortly afterwards, Paşahan left the country,' Süleyman said. 'So he bought a yalı, which he was perfectly entitled to do . . .'

'And moved a lot of his people in from Uludağ, boss.'

'Yes . . .'

'Well, I don't know where they went when Görkan Bey shipped out. Do you? The place is empty now.'

Süleyman leaned back in his chair and stuck his pen in his mouth, in lieu of a cigarette. 'Where'd you hear about Paşahan and Neşe Hanım?'

'Organised Crime.'

'What, you had a meeting with them? I don't remember it.'

'No, boss. Lad from my old mahalle joined back in March. My dad told me to look out for him. We've been out a few times together. Officer Zeynel Kösen. He's just a grunt, but he's a bright lad. He said his boss, Inspector Alibey, reckoned that Paşahan was looking out for old Neşe.'

Alibey hadn't said anything like that to Süleyman. 'How does he know that?' Süleyman asked.

'Don't know,' Ömer said. 'Can't remember. You want me to ask him?'

What would seem to Süleyman to be a piece of vital intel, Alibey had either forgotten about or chosen not to tell him. If it was the latter, that was concerning.

'Discreetly, yes,' Süleyman replied. 'Inspector Alibey is a

valued colleague. I don't want him to think I'm checking up on him.'

'No, sir. In fact . . .' Ömer looked at the time on his mobile phone. 'Young Zeynel often goes out to the car park for a smoke mid afternoon. I could go and see whether he's about, if you like.'

'Mmm, yes,' Süleyman said. 'But remember, be subtle.'

Ömer Müngün wasn't always very good at subtle and he knew it. He put his jacket on.

'Of course, boss.'

'In the meantime, I will try to find out whether Neşe Hanım still lives in that vast apartment off Bağdat Caddesi,' Süleyman said.

Before the inspector telephoned the old woman's local belediye office, he pondered upon the reading that Gonca had performed for him that morning. Someone in his orbit was not who they seemed . . .

When Kerim was a child, his family had lived in the district of Yedikule. On the European side of the city, Yedikule was the heavily populated area that clustered around the Byzantine city walls and was dominated by the Yedikule Fortress, built by the conquering Ottomans in 1458. Always a hard-working district, in the 1970s and 80s, during Kerim's childhood, it had been home to many migrants from Anatolia, who had flooded into the city in search of work alongside native İstanbullus like the Gürsels. Along with their many skills, these migrants had also brought with them what Kerim's late father had called 'country stuff'. This covered not only the way they looked, but also what they wore, what they believed and how they lived. It also covered how they got about, which, back in the seventies particularly, was often on horseback.

Kerim didn't know whether his antipathy towards horses came

from his father's assertion that nobody should be riding in a city except the army, the police and gypsies. All he knew was that they made him nervous. So when Eylül Yavaş went up to a huge beast, mercifully trapped behind a stable door, and stroked its muzzle, he shuddered.

'What do you want?'

A voice behind caused him to turn. A tall, slim woman wearing a riding hat and carrying a short whip held a hand out to him, which Kerim shook.

'Sıla Gedik,' she said. 'One of my grooms told me you're police.'

'Yes,' Kerim said. 'You're the owner of these stables?'

She smiled. 'They're called Gedik Stables, so . . .'

The Gedik Stables were the closest horse-riding establishment to the creek. But they hadn't been easy to find. There were several smallholdings in the area with which the dilapidated-looking riding establishment blended in easily.

He smiled back at her. 'I'm sorry.'

'It's OK. And you are . . .?'

Sıla Gedik was, what was the word? Disarming. Tall, slim and blond, with piercing green eyes.

'Inspector Kerim Gürsel,' he said. Eylül arrived. 'And this is Sergeant Yavaş.'

Sıla Gedik nodded at Eylül and then said, 'So what do you want to speak to me about? You know we've been established on this land for over thirty years.'

'Oh, it's nothing to do with your premises, hanım,' Kerim said. 'It's . . .' Out in the open, with the sky darkening, he suddenly felt exposed. 'Do you think we might talk inside?'

She bowed slightly, a short, man's bow, and then said, 'Of course. I'll take you to my office.' She set off at a truly alarming pace towards a building that looked as if it might collapse at the next puff of wind.

*

30

Now that İkmen had finished admiring Gonca's latest work in progress – a collage representing the notion of hüzün, that uniquely İstanbullu version of sensual melancholy – the gypsy had taken him to her salon, where her youngest daughter, Filiz, served them tea and cakes while a warm fire burned in the old Ottoman stove in the corner. The only jarring element in this cosy winter scene was the fact that Gonca had her pet boa constrictor draped around her shoulders.

İkmen was rather fond of Sara the snake. He knew that Süleyman had to steel himself to even look at it but made himself do it because the serpent meant so much to his wife. Back when Roma families like the Şekeroğlu had lived in their old quarter of Sulukule, a lot of the women and girls had danced for tourists, who had paid them. Some girls, like Gonca, had danced with snakes. Now, many years later, Sulukule had been turned into a quarter for the new pious elite, and the gypsies were either confined to the poor district of Tarlabaşı or living in tower blocks many kilometres outside the city. Gonca, however, had money, so was the exception to this. She lived in her vast house in Balat because she loved it and because her skill as an artist had allowed her to buy it.

But she still mourned her old life in Sulukule. Sara, who'd been with her back then, was both her baby and an elderly relative who required tender care.

Now she kissed the boa's snout and said, 'You've been with me since you were a snakelet, haven't you, darling.'

'And still beautiful,' İkmen said as he lit a cigarette.

'Me or Sara?' Gonca asked.

'Both.' He smiled.

She looked at him sharply. 'You're bored, aren't you, İkmen?'

'No. How could I possibly be bored around you, Gonca Hanım?'

'I mean professionally,' she said.

'Oh, that. Well, yes. I know I'm a very old bastard now, but I do object to being useless.'

31

'You're not.'

'I am at the moment.'

Gonca rearranged Sara so they could both be more comfortable.

'You should try manifesting a case for yourself,' she said.

He frowned. 'Manifesting?'

'It's what Hollywood stars do,' she said. 'They think about what they want and then it happens. There are thousands of magazine articles about it every week.'

'Isn't that just casting a spell? Do such people know how to do that?'

'No,' she laughed. 'They get things because they're rich and famous and then convince themselves the universe is dancing to their tune. I had a woman on a telephone reading last week. Very posh Şişli lawyer. I read what I saw, and she said she'd go away and work on the things she liked about my reading and then manifest them.'

'God!'

'How is a witch supposed to make a living in such a world?'

İkmen shook his head.

'A lifetime of magical practice reduced to three paragraphs in *Cosmopolitan*.'

'But tomorrow night is the darkest night of the year,' İkmen said. 'And you will be giving the people of Cihangir the real stuff.'

'Will I?'

He looked at her. Thinner than she had been in the past, Gonca was still beautiful, even though her great black eyes looked haunted sometimes – like now.

'When my Hürrem died, I lost something,' she said. 'I can't tell you what, I don't know. All I can tell you is that were it not for Mehmet, I would be dead.'

İkmen thought for a moment. 'When he comes home to you, he brings a light that breaks through your darkness. This I know, Gonca. When my son died, the only person who could touch me

32

was Çiçek. It's not a choice. I didn't cling to my daughter and she didn't cling to me. It just was – until it wasn't.'

'What do you mean?'

'One day I could "do" other people again. I wanted to be with them. It'll happen for you. One day they'll all bring you joy again – not just Mehmet.'

'I hope so. I feel as if even magic has deserted me, you know.'

'It hasn't,' İkmen said. 'You have magic in abundance, Gonca. But when my Bekir died . . .' He shook his head. 'It isn't natural to lose a child. We're supposed to go first.'

'I wished myself dead, İkmen. I wished it, I worked for it . . .' Gonca's face was tight, strained beyond words.

And then İkmen's phone rang, and when he looked to see who was calling him, he wondered whether he had inadvertently manifested.

Chapter 3

'Horses don't let you sleep in,' Sıla Gedik said. 'I'm up at five most days.'

'Doing what?' Kerim asked.

'Exercising. Around our own fields here, sometimes further.'

'Did you go further this morning?'

'No,' she said. 'I was tired, I just kept to the fields. Where did you say the body was found, Inspector?'

'By the creek.'

Sıla Gedik's office had proved to be a barn filled mainly with straw plus one desk covered in paperwork and an ancient Apple computer.

'I know that Zekeriya took Yıldırım out this morning, so he may well have gone that far.'

'Zekeriya is . . .'

'One of my grooms. He's a strong lad and often exercises Yıldırım. Not all my boys can handle him.'

Eylül Yavaş said, 'A big horse?'

'Seventeen hands.'

'That is big.'

'Yıldırım is the type of ride we only give to experienced riders,' she said. 'A Friesian stallion. I'll put him to stud next year.'

'What colour is he?' Kerim asked.

It was Eylül who replied. 'All Friesians are black, sir.'

Sıla Gedik smiled. 'Do you ride, Sergeant?'

'When I was a child, I was mad about horses,' she said. 'I haven't ridden for years, but I still love them.'

'Can we speak to your grooms, please?' Kerim asked.

'Of course,' Sıla said. 'Follow me.' She led them back out into the gathering gloom.

According to the local authority in Kadıköy, Neşe Bocuk was still resident in the apartment her son had bought fifteen years before. They even had both a landline and a mobile phone number for the old woman. And yet as far as Süleyman could remember, Neşe hadn't had any other relatives in İstanbul apart from her son and grandsons. Maybe she stayed to visit Esat and İlhan in prison, poor Ateş in the private psychiatric clinic where he battled his demons. She'd never struck Süleyman as the maternal type. She'd always supported her gangster husband and, later, her son, who'd been in the same line of work. Some believed that Neşe, a falcı or fortune teller by trade, had murdered those who opposed her family with her own hands. But there was no evidence for this even though some people believed she was the brains behind the Bocuk family business. One of those people was Çetin İkmen, Süleyman's closest friend, and when İkmen believed something, it was probably true.

Ömer Müngün returned from what had proved to be a rather long break out in the car park with headquarters' junior smokers. He didn't partake himself and so Süleyman imagined he must have got into some deep conversation – hopefully with his fellow Mardinli, Zeynel Kösen.

The sergeant sat down and put his jacket on the back of his chair.

Süleyman said, 'Nice lunch, Ömer?'

'Sorry, boss,' Ömer said. 'Took a while for me to get the lad on his own.'

'And?'

'And he overheard Inspector Alibey talking about Neşe Bocuk.'

'Talking to whom?'

'His sergeant,' Ömer said. 'Şükran Güllü. Zeynel says he sent her out to see Neşe Hanım.'

'What about?'

'He doesn't know. It was something between Alibey and Güllü. Zeynel reckons he wasn't supposed to know about it. No one else in Organised Crime has spoken to him about it and he's never heard so much as a whisper since. But there is gossip about Alibey and Güllü.'

Süleyman said, 'This is just gossip . . .'

'Yes, and I know you don't hold with it, boss.'

'It can be very destructive.'

Süleyman himself had been the subject of gossip a few times over the years – with reason. He'd had affairs with two of his colleagues before his marriage to Gonca Şekeroğlu. Now certain colleagues continued to whisper about him because when he had finally settled down it had been with a Roma woman.

'But if Inspector Alibey and Sergeant Güllü are in a relationship and they've been to see Neşe Hanım without the knowledge of Alibey's team, that strikes me as a bit wrong, sir.'

Süleyman was way ahead of him. Why had Alibey come to him for assistance in tracking down Görkan Paşahan if he was directly in touch with someone who might well know where he was? Unless of course Şükran Güllü had gone to see the old woman for another reason. But what might that be? Ever since Süleyman had arrested her son and eldest grandson for murder, the Bocuk stock had dropped dramatically. Unless rumours about an alliance between Görkan Paşahan and Neşe Hanım were true, the old woman had no value. But if she was connected to Paşahan in some way, why had Alibey not told Süleyman?

*

36

If any street in Tarlabaşı could be said to be typical of the quarter, then Feridiye Caddesi was it. A potholed road flanked by what had once been elegant nineteenth-century houses, the upper floors characterised by square bay windows. Tall, most of them, typically four storeys high, many exhibiting peeling plaster in a variety of colours including pink and pale green. Some had shops at ground level: tiny bakkals selling daily provisions, water and cigarettes, cheap clothes outlets and places flogging plastic toys from China. An old man pushing a cart walked wearily down the middle of the road, the driver of a smart Tesla car, honking his horn as he tried to get past. The ambient smell was overwhelmingly one of open fires and drains.

One building, taller and narrower than those on either side, was Çetin İkmen's destination on this dingy winter late afternoon. Like most of the houses hereabouts it was accessed via a small staircase, at the top of which was an ornate door – on this occasion some men lurked both before and behind it – which İkmen passed through to get to a desk in the surprisingly clean marble hallway.

At the desk, a lean blond transgender woman looked up and smiled when she saw him.

'Ah, Çetin Bey,' she said. 'We've been expecting you.'

İkmen smiled. 'Always a pleasure, Madonna Hanım.'

'Come with me.' She stood up and took his hand, then whispered in his ear, 'Edith is waiting for you in my apartment. I'm afraid the poor old darling is agitated.'

Kurdish Madonna, as the person who had once been a shepherd boy in the east of Turkey was now known, operated one of the most popular transgender brothels in İstanbul. Fearless and efficient, she expected the same standards from her girls as those she'd imposed upon herself when she'd still been on the game. Regular health checks, no working without a condom and no violence. Madonna and İkmen went back many years.

She led him to a door at the back of the house. In the very taste-
ful and warm salon of her private apartment sat the small figure
of the elderly drag queen known as Madam Edith. Like her muse,
Edith Piaf, she was dressed in black, lace mostly, and was smoking a cigarette. When İkmen arrived, she rose to her feet and
kissed his cheek.

'It's so good of you to come, Çetin Bey,' she said.

'Always a pleasure.'

Madonna said, 'I'll leave you two in peace. There's rakı in the
fridge and a bottle of brandy underneath the sink. Help yourselves.' Then she was gone.

'Do you want a drink, Çetin Bey?' Edith asked.

He sat. 'No thank you, Edith. Driving. So what's it about? You
sounded worried on the phone.'

'I am,' she said. 'I'll get right to the point. I'm worried about the
kiddie.'

İkmen knew that Edith helped to care for the Gürsels' little girl,
Melda.

'What about her?'

'Well, it's actually about Sinem Hanım,' she said. 'Although it's
beginning to affect Melda and I don't like it.'

'What is? Start from the beginning.'

'I'll have to have a drink first.' She went to rise to her feet, but
İkmen got there first.

'I'll get it. What do you want?'

'Brandy.'

He walked into Madonna's small kitchen and opened the
cupboard underneath the sink. Years before, when he'd been
a functioning alcoholic, İkmen had always kept his bottles
under the sink. Above his head he heard the unmistakable
sound of a man achieving sexual satisfaction. Madonna's place
wasn't for the faint-hearted. But if Edith was going to talk about
the Gürsels, she could hardly do it in their apartment. Since

COVID hit, she'd been living with the family on a permanent basis.

He found a glass on the draining board and poured a large measure of brandy. When he gave it to Edith, she said, 'Bless you.'

İkmen sat down and lit a cigarette. 'So . . .'

'It all began when the restrictions were lifted in the spring,' she said. 'We'd managed really well and we were all so pleased to be free again. Kerim Bey took us out to Bebek for the day to celebrate. But then within a week, Sinem went right down.'

'What do you mean?'

'She became listless, depressed.'

'A lot of people only realised how tough lockdown had been when it was over,' İkmen said.

'Oh, it's more than that,' Edith said. 'At first I thought that maybe her pain was getting the better of her. But she's had that for years, and even when she's bad, she still makes time for the little one. But playtime with Melda came to a stop and I began to find I was doing most of that when Kerim Bey was at work. Then she started being funny with him.'

İkmen frowned.

'Yes, the love of her life. I mean, I know it's never been easy for her, what with him being what he is, but he promised her he'd never put the family at risk and I think he's kept to it. Poor soul. I know he loves them, but he must be twisted up inside somewhere. I mean, he must think about men . . .' She sighed. 'Anyway, Sinem Hanım began pushing him away. Now they hardly speak, let alone touch. He comes home from work, plays with Melda, has something to eat and then goes to bed. They still sleep together, but quite honestly, that's because there's nowhere else for them to sleep.'

'Marriages go through phases,' İkmen said. 'However much in love—'

'And then there's how she is when I want to take the kiddie out,' Edith continued. 'She either can't bear to be alone or she's

39

pushing us out the door. It's as if she's fighting with herself all the time. And there's the clothes . . .'

'The clothes?'

'Her clothes. More often than not, I do the washing, so I should know.' She took a swig from her glass and then leaned in close to İkmen. 'They go missing. And I know this to be true because she's asked me to buy her underwear from the Sunday pazar.'

Tarlabaşı's Sunday market, a vast outdoor event that took over the whole district one day a week, was well known for selling just about everything at rock-bottom prices.

'It's underwear that goes missing?'

'Mainly,' Edith said. 'The odd thing is, I've never seen any of it in the rubbish. I mean, were she having regular accidents, I think I would know. Then I remembered about that terrible old pervert on Tatlı Badem Caddesi who used to steal women's underwear. But he's dead. So then I thought . . .' She took another swig from her glass. 'Then I thought that maybe she's seeing someone.'

'Seeing someone?'

'You know!' she said. 'What she can't get from her husband.'

'She loves him, and she's disabled, Edith,' İkmen said. 'She can barely leave the apartment.'

'Which is why someone has to be coming in!'

'Really? Who? Who gets to see her? How can anyone with bad intent know about her?'

'I don't fucking know!' Edith put her drink down and lit a cigarette. She clearly believed what she was saying, but İkmen was finding it hard. Sinem Gürsel never went out on her own. The only people who visited her were her siblings and, occasionally, her doctor. Kerim's friends and colleagues would sometimes come to the apartment with him. The only other person İkmen could think of was Kurdish Madonna, who liked to bake and would sometimes take bread round to the Gürsels' apartment.

'Have you asked her what's wrong?'

'Repeatedly,' Edith said. 'She tells me she's fine.'

'And Kerim?'

'Behaves as if it's not happening.'

'So maybe . . .'

'İkmen, it's not in my head!' Edith said. 'And here's the kicker. She's self-harming again. Tops of her arms, where she thinks I can't see. She's not done that for years, not since she was keeping her true feelings from Kerim Bey. Something's wrong, İkmen, and I want you to find out what it is.'

Long ago, when he was a child, Kerim Gürsel's mother had told him an old Turkish fairy story about a princess who married a horse. This large and fearsome stallion of course turned out to be a prince who had been bewitched by a sorceress. But he had always imagined the horse in the story to look almost exactly like the beast that now stood in front of him, Yıldırım the Friesian. Beautiful, regal and probably dangerous.

Eylül stroked the animal's muzzle. 'You're a handsome boy, aren't you,' she said.

He was, unlike his groom. Zekeriya Bulut, while well built and muscular, had a closed-off, sullen face peppered with large angry-looking spots. His eyes, out of which he looked at the world with deep suspicion, were so close together it was almost possible to ignore his nose completely.

His responses to Kerim and Eylül's questions about his early-morning ride beside the creek consisted mainly of grunts, shrugs and the occasional tic, all of which added up to the notion that he had seen and heard nothing untoward. However, such sullen behaviour was a good wall to hide behind if one had something to conceal. So when the boy had slouched away, Kerim asked Sıla Gedik if Zekeriya was always like that.

'Oh yes,' she said. 'You'll find that a lot of people who work with animals have few social skills. It's in part why they choose to spend their time with other species. Zekeriya is a good groom and an excellent rider. Quite exceptional, in fact.'

Two of the three other grooms, who all stated they hadn't been anywhere near the creek that morning, had added little to Zekeriya Bulut's story. Now, however, the two detectives came to Aslı Dölen, the only female groom on the premises and quite another matter. Cheerful, talkative and pretty, Aslı was a middle-class girl, in love with horses.

'I got here just after five,' she said.

'She's the only groom who doesn't live on site,' Sıla added. 'But she's almost always the first out in the mornings.'

'Where do you live?' Eylül asked.

'Nişantaşı.'

Of course she did. Nişantaşı was middle-class central, only two kilometres from Şişli, where Eylül lived with her wealthy parents.

'I drive here,' the girl continued. 'Traffic isn't bad at five. Anyway, I'd run through fire to get to my beautiful lady.'

'Aslı takes Badem out most days,' Sıla said. 'She's a lovely, lively little mare who needs far more exercise than you'd think just by looking at her. But then she's an Arab. Black as night, she's a real superstar.'

'Yes, but I didn't take her beyond the fields this morning,' Aslı said.

Kerim had told Sıla and her staff, in minimal fashion, about what had been found at the creek that morning. But somehow now, maybe because Aslı was a woman, he felt that he had to elaborate.

'I will be frank with you and tell you that we suspect foul play in this infant's death,' he said.

'Oh.'

'So anything you can tell us about this morning . . .'

'I can't tell you anything,' Aslı said.

'The person who found the body saw a horse in the distance.'

Aslı shook her head. 'Wasn't me.'

'Did anyone see you out with Badem this morning?' Eylül asked.

'Only the other grooms.'

From the testimony they'd given, the grooms had all seen each other.

'Zekeriya took Yıldırım out that way,' Aslı continued. 'He usually does.'

Kerim looked at Sıla. 'You didn't have any early rides booked this morning?'

'No,' she said. 'We don't do that in the winter. Most people don't want to ride in the rain. It's why my staff have to take the horses out.'

'And you've how many horses here?' he asked.

'Ten, including two Shetland ponies for the children. The grooms will sometimes take more than one horse out on exercise in the morning, but we've got two mares in foal at the moment and so we'll just let those out in the fields.'

The two officers left. Once back in the car, Kerim said, 'That place is not doing well.'

'No,' Eylül agreed.

'Horses look fine to me, but the premises themselves are really dilapidated.'

'And if she's got two mares in foal, that takes away two potential rides,' Eylül said. 'And she said she was planning to put Yıldırım to stud. But then it is winter . . .'

'Where did you go when you rode horses, Eylül?' Kerim asked.

'Kemer,' she said, naming one of the premier riding schools in the city. 'And yes, it was expensive. We had an indoor training centre as well as fields. Gedik won't be able to charge anything like the Kemer fees. Sir, did you get any sort of feeling that those we spoke to weren't telling the truth?'

He sighed. 'Not really, no. I don't know whether it's because I'm uncomfortable around horses, but I felt uneasy. I know it may well come to nothing, but could you do some digging into Gedik's finances?'

'Yes, sir.'

'Don't spend long on it. I'd just like to know a bit more.'

Zuzanna Nowak had not seen Görkan Paşahan's face when he had allegedly left the apartment she had shared with Sofija Ozola on the day of the latter's death. She'd just arrived back in Kuzguncuk and had been parking her car across the road. She had recognised him from his gait. Grey haired like Paşahan, this man had walked with the same rolling gait emblematic of the gangster. Apparently he had many years previously sustained a bullet wound to his right hip.

Süleyman read on. Paşahan, however, had an alibi. He'd been with his daughter Sümeyye at her apartment in Nişantaşı at the time of Ozola's death. And while an alibi provided by a family member was not strictly to be relied upon, both the kapıcı of Sümeyye's building and the taxi driver who had taken Paşahan to her place had vouched for him. Then of course he'd gone abroad. Firstly to Serbia, then London, and now, although no one was sure, he appeared to be in Malta. It was said he knew people in high places in the small Mediterranean island. He broadcast his bile-filled podcasts from there and yet there was no record of his having entered the country. Paşahan was now 'political', and it was well known that talks between Turkish and Maltese officials had taken place, but as yet to no avail. The Maltese still denied any knowledge of him.

Ömer Müngün had left for the day and so Süleyman was alone.

Gonca was working that night and he was in no rush to get home. When the pandemic had hit, she had taken to reading her clients' cards online, or by phone. She'd subsequently discovered that a lot of readers, particularly Roma, had been doing that for years. And as soon as word had got out that Gonca Şekeroğlu, the famous artist, was reading online, other clients had appeared. Now she read for people in Antalya, Erzurum and even Azerbaijan.

Unlike her daily readings for herself and for him, reading for others required Gonca to perform certain rituals before she began. They took her hours and were, she had told him, designed to protect her and her clients from malign forces. When he'd asked her to explain, all she had said was that it was mainly in case someone asked her to contact the dead. He'd never imagined that his wife would even consider practising necromancy – the Roma considered the dead unclean – but he also knew that one of her cousins allegedly lived with a demon. Were these apparent anomalies simply all part of the obfuscation the Roma employed in their dealings with the gage? He would probably never know. That he loved his wife with such a fierce passion in spite of this was simply further proof of the strength of his feelings. That, or love was truly blind.

His thoughts returned to Görkan Paşahan and his railing against the Turkish state. For a man who had been such a passionate advocate of the status quo, this volte-face had been sudden and violent. His life up until the previous May had been lucrative and comfortable. Then suddenly there had been a connection to a dead prostitute and everything had changed. But why? And why had Zuzanna Nowak given a statement implicating him when people like him paid off witnesses like her every day? Why then run, and even more confusingly, why not pursue Nowak and silence her? True, she had retracted her statement. Had that been the deal? Since Ozola's death, Zuzanna Nowak had not only moved, but she seemed to have actually prospered too.

*

Kerim Gürsel wasn't a drinking man. But the sight of that child's body face down in the mud had affected him. Whatever he did, whenever he recalled that image he always saw Melda's long black hair soaked in rainwater. He needed a drink.

Rather than go into his apartment block, he crossed the road to the meyhane run by Gonca Şekeroğlu's brother Rambo and sat down at a table outside underneath a patio heater. As soon as he'd lit a cigarette, he looked up to see the owner in front of him. A good-looking man in his thirties, Rambo Şekeroğlu knew Kerim and what he liked to drink. He placed a glass of rakı and a small jug of water in front of him and said, 'You look as if you've had a bad day, Kerim Bey. With my compliments.'

'Oh no, Rambo . . .'

The gypsy smiled. 'I may not be able to tell your future like my sister, but I know when a man is at the end of his patience. My pleasure.'

Rambo went back inside. Kerim poured some of the water into his rakı glass and watched the aniseed spirit turn milky.

'Kerim Bey.'

He looked up again, this time into the face of his neighbour.

'Enver Bey,' he said. 'Good evening.'

'Good evening. Do you mind if I join you?'

'No, not at all.'

Enver Yılmaz, who was probably in his forties, was tall, dark and stylish. He had moved into the apartment next door to the Gürsels just before the pandemic hit in 2020. He worked in IT, although during COVID he had worked from home. During that period Kerim had seen him from time to time, usually when both men had been picking up deliveries in the lobby.

Enver Bey sat. 'Good day?'

'No, but it's kind of you to ask.' Kerim signalled to Rambo to bring another rakı. This wasn't the first time the two men had met at this meyhane. In recent months they had encountered each other on several occasions. Kerim liked his neighbour's company and felt that he enjoyed their conversations too. He was, however, painfully aware that he found Enver Bey attractive, and so he knew he had to be guarded when they met. One slightly flirtatious blink of an eye and his career could be in the gutter.

'Anything you can talk about?' Enver asked.

'Thank you, but no.'

Enver's drink arrived. He wiped the glass with his handkerchief and lit a cigarette.

'I saw your aunt this morning as I was leaving for work,' he said.

'Ah.'

The permanent presence of Madam Edith had necessitated Kerim creating a story about her.

'I think it's nice to see traditional families like yours,' Enver said. 'Where the older generation help to look after the children. Good values.'

'With respect, my aunt is only living with us because of my wife's illness,' Kerim replied.

'Nice for your little girl, though. Your aunt looks like she's a lot of fun, the way she plays with your daughter.'

If he learned the truth, he'd be horrified. Unless . . . Sometimes when they spoke it was almost as if Enver Bey knew. But maybe that was just Kerim's fear talking. He found the man attractive and also strangely familiar, so he was always slightly on edge. Had he met him in a dark gay bar one night long ago?

Keen to deflect conversation away from himself, he said, 'Do you have any children, Enver Bey?' He'd never asked before, which was a bit odd, he now felt.

'No,' Enver said. 'I prefer to be a free agent.'

Was that some kind of code? In the frightened world of closeted gay men, this was the sort of thing that was sometimes said. Kerim had never seen any women leaving Enver Bey's apartment. In fact, he'd never seen anyone enter or leave. But then that wasn't unusual these days, not since the coming of COVID-19. Some of the most sociable people he knew had turned their homes into fortresses.

Kerim finished his rakı more quickly than he usually did. The sudden rush of strong spirit to his brain made his head swim for a moment. He had to go home. If he stayed and drank too much, anything could happen. He was an affectionate man, who needed to love and be loved to function, and these days he was beginning to think his wife was falling out of love with him. Although they still slept together, they rarely touched. In fact, if he tried to cuddle or kiss Sinem, she shrank away from him. What really hurt, however, was how cold she was with their daughter. Melda didn't understand and was beginning to think her mummy didn't like her. He'd tried to talk to Sinem, but she refused to engage with him. Was her pain now so bad it made her tetchy? She said it wasn't, but Kerim really couldn't think of any other reason for her behaviour. She had loved him ever since they'd been teenagers. Having his child, she'd told him, had been the fulfilment of all her dreams.

He stood up. 'I must go,' he said. 'Nice to talk to you, Enver Bey.'

'And you.'

Kerim headed towards his apartment. After a whole day effectively alone with Melda, Edith would be anxious to get out and meet her friends for a drink. He would play with his daughter and he'd enjoy it. But against a background of silence from his wife, it would not be what it had once been. And now he also had the vision of that dead baby in his head . . .

Chapter 4

'I'll get away as soon as I can.'

Mehmet Süleyman kissed his wife, who had just woken up. Still partially hidden deep underneath multiple duvets and bedcovers, Gonca made a sleepy grab for his neck and pulled him close.

'Oh darling, I'm sorry I was so late to bed last night. You were sleeping and I didn't want to wake you,' she said.

He smiled. 'Doesn't matter. Go back to sleep and I'll see you this evening.'

They kissed again, and then she said, 'Bocuk Gecesi . . .'

'It will be fun,' he said.

'Maybe.' She closed her eyes. 'But it's also the darkest night, Mehmet, so we must be careful . . .'

When he arrived at headquarters, Süleyman didn't go straight to his office. Instead he crossed Vatan Caddesi and went to a coffee shop that had opened recently selling what the owners claimed to be the 'best Turkish coffee in İstanbul'. Probably not *that* good, it was nevertheless excellent, and just what he needed after a night of little sleep.

Mehmet Süleyman didn't usually lie to his wife, but when he'd pretended to be asleep when she'd got into bed at around 2 a.m., it had been for a reason. Probably because he'd not been involved in anything active for a while, he had clung to his tiny corner of Organised Crime's Paşahan case like a drowning man. Usually he shied away from anything in the slightest bit political, but when faced with that or completing his paperwork, it was no contest. There was in addition something off about the whole situation, and the previous night he'd needed time to think. Now, queuing for coffee, he was thinking about it again.

'Good morning, Inspector Süleyman.'

He looked behind him and saw a slim, blond woman with a slightly crooked smile. Sergeant Şükran Güllü, Mevlüt Alibey's deputy in Organised Crime and, allegedly, his lover.

'Good morning, Sergeant,' he said. 'We all seem to have discovered this place.'

'Just what you need in the morning,' she said. 'A good hot shot of caffeine to wake up your brain – and your body.'

'Quite.'

She was flirting with him. She was famous for it. There had been other men before Alibey – and she was married. A man twice her age, it was said.

'I hear you're helping us out,' she said.

'Yes. Although I don't know that my input will do a great deal of good.'

'I'm sure it will.'

She literally fluttered her eyelashes, which was both rather amusing – did she realise what Gonca would do to her if she ever found out? – and unsettling.

Süleyman wanted to ask her about her meeting with old Neşe Bocuk, but he was aware that if he showed his hand too soon, it could be detrimental. Hearsay information like that given to him by Ömer Müngün was best held in reserve. If Alibey and Güllü were in contact with the old woman about Paşahan, he needed to find out what, if anything, connected them and why the pair had chosen to keep that encounter to themselves.

When he got to the counter, he bought his coffee and left. Sergeant Güllü watched him go.

*

Kerim Gürsel had received a call from Dr Arto Sarkissian first thing that morning, as he'd been getting into his car.

'Given that the water in the child's lungs emanated from Kağıthane Creek, and in light of the bruises on the victim's neck, I am declaring the death unlawful,' the doctor said. 'What the circumstances of said murder might be is of course your province, Inspector. All I can do is wish you success in your endeavours. For what it's worth, I will expedite DNA analysis inasmuch as I am able.'

'Thank you, Doctor.'

Kerim had called Eylül and the two of them had agreed to meet at the site in Kağıthane, where scene-of-crime officers had resumed their investigations. Kerim had extended the investigative field by a hundred metres and a team had been dispatched to the block of apartments directly facing the site. So far the İstekli family remained the only witnesses.

It was another grey, cold morning and Kerim rubbed his hands together to warm them. He'd not slept much the night before. Lying beside Sinem, who'd cringed every time he accidentally touched her, was not conducive to sleep. This on top of the row they'd had before bed about the fact that she'd seen him drinking outside Rambo's bar had produced an almost unbearable tension.

But now something happened that, while not lightening the mood, gave Kerim some cause for optimism. One of the reasons he had extended the search area around the site was to see whether they could find anything that might point towards the presence of horses in the area. One horse from the Gedik Stables, the nearest riding facility, had allegedly been in the vicinity early the previous morning. But using the previous fifty-metre radius had yielded nothing. Now, however, one of the SOC officers called Kerim over to a place only about ten metres from where the child's body had been found.

51

He pointed to a mark in the semi-hardened mud. 'It's not much, sir,' he said. 'But looks like a partial print of a horseshoe.'

Kerim peered at it. 'Just the one?'

'No, I think I've managed to make out three more, but they're poor.'

'You didn't see them yesterday?' Kerim asked.

'I photographed the whole site,' the officer said. 'But it was only when I got back to the lab and blew them up that I saw what I thought could be hoofprints.'

Kerim nodded. 'Take casts,' he said.

The djinn in the corner of Çetin İkmen's kitchen had materialised just before his wife Fatma's death in 2016. After the road accident that had taken her life, her ghost had haunted the apartment's balcony for years. And while Çetin, even as the son of a once famous Albanian witch, had never really known what he thought about ghosts, 'Fatma' had brought him comfort during his years of mourning.

Then, at the end of 2019, the sister of Mehmet Süleyman's sergeant Ömer Müngün had taken a romantic interest in him. Nurse Peri Müngün, a tall, thin, dark woman from the eastern province of Mardin, had unexpectedly kissed him at a party. Then they'd gone to bed together. After that, Fatma had vanished. But not the djinn. İkmen believed that the Islamic mythical entity of smoke-less fire represented his guilt at having 'betrayed' his late wife, even though his children told him their mother would have wanted him to move on.

Now, sitting eating breakfast at the kitchen table with his cousin Samsun, who could also see the djinn, İkmen rolled his eyes as the furry snaggle-toothed horror reared up so that its head touched the ceiling.

'I wish it wouldn't do that!' he said as he gave up on breakfast and lit a cigarette.

Samsun, who had named the thing Yiğit, or 'brave', said, 'Don't react. You know he only does it to piss you off.'

'I wish you wouldn't refer to it as "he"!'

'No woman would act like he does. Rearing, drooling and farting. Anyway,' Samsun said, 'why are you in such a bad mood? I heard Peri Hanım leaving in the early hours . . .'

'She's on nights now,' İkmen said. 'Had to go home and get some sleep.'

Samsun finished her breakfast, put the bowl in the sink and then sat down again. İkmen gave her a cigarette.

'I repeat, Çetin, why the bad mood?' she said.

He sighed. 'Someone has given me a job.'

'You're usually in your element—'

'An impossible job,' he qualified.

'Your mother would've said there's no such thing.'

'With respect, Samsun, I am not my mother.'

They lapsed into silence. İkmen's mother, Ayşe the witch, had been Samsun's aunt. She remembered her as a dazzling figure who could produce kittens for her to play with out of thin air.

When Samsun had finished the cigarette İkmen had given her, she lit another. Like most of İstanbul's older, tougher transsexual women, she smoked like a factory. She'd been living with İkmen and Çiçek ever since Fatma's death.

'Wanna talk about it?' she said.

He shook his head.

'I know you met up with Madam Edith yesterday,' Samsun persisted.

İkmen eyed her narrowly. İstanbul, although home to an estimated seventeen million souls, was not somewhere a person could easily do something and not be both observed and gossiped about. Some people called it 'the biggest village in the world'.

'Unhappy, I've heard she is,' Samsun continued. 'And not just because she's as old as time.' She leaned in closer to him. No one else was around; she was just accustomed to being secretive. 'It's said that Kerim Bey is on the scene again.'

İkmen felt his heart jolt. This was different to what Edith had told him. But then Samsun often got the wrong end of the gossip stick.

'Who says?' he asked.

'Couldn't possibly say,' she answered. 'But it wouldn't surprise me. Good-looking man like him. And you know what I always say, Çetin, once you've had cock there's no going back.'

Before Sinem had fallen pregnant with Melda, Kerim had been in a long-term relationship with a trans woman called Pembe, who was now dead. It was well known that he still mourned her.

'Well I hope you're not spreading that rumour,' İkmen said.

'Me? Never!'

The djinn hissed as if to scold her.

'Ah, shut the fuck up!' Samsun said.

İkmen had of course said that he would help Edith. She was going to take Melda with her when she went shopping at lunchtime, and so İkmen was going to have his lunch, in liquid form, at Rambo Şekeroğlu's bar, which was opposite the entrance to the Gürsels' apartment block. That way he could see who came and went. According to Edith, Sinem had been very keen for her and the child to go to the shops at midday. He didn't feel good about it. Spying on friends made him queasy. And if Samsun was right and Kerim was seeing men again, then if Sinem was having an affair, he could understand that.

'I saw Görkan Paşahan on TV this morning,' Ömer Müngün said to Süleyman, who had just walked into his office, coffee in hand.

'Oh? On which channel?'

'BBC World,' Ömer said. 'Been watching it for a bit, trying to improve my English.'

'Good. What did the old bastard have to say for himself?'

54

'Usual. Everyone's corrupt except him. Promising to release details about government ministers, head of the army.'

'So more of the same. Any names?'

'No.'

Süleyman sat down. 'He knows that if he does name names, he's a busted flush,' he said. 'I can't get away from the idea that it's all theatre.'

'What do you think he's up to, boss?'

'I don't know. Unfortunately I'm not a psychopathic gangster and so getting inside his mind is beyond me. Maybe he's trying to get one or more of his former allies to do something for him. If money hasn't attracted results, perhaps he's now turned to threats.'

Ömer shrugged.

'Have you managed to find anything else out about Zuzanna Nowak?' Süleyman asked.

'She's still lecturing at Koç University. Drives a new Jaguar.'

'Does she indeed?'

'Yeah, but boss, Nowak ID'd Paşahan. Even though she later retracted her statement, why would he reward her for that?'

'Maybe he isn't,' Süleyman said. 'You know, Ömer, between Çetin Bey and my wife, I have become quite a fan of the notion of things being not what they appear. Always look behind the curtain, or in this case, into Ms Nowak's accounts. Find out who she banks with.'

'Yes, sir.'

'Oh, and Ömer, while not breaking the confidence of your fellow Mardinli in Organised Crime, I feel it's about time we paid Neşe Bocuk a visit. We put two of her men in prison after all, so I feel we should check on the old woman's welfare.'

For a district named after an Ottoman prince, Cihangir had a lot of liberal credibility. To call someone a 'Cihangir solcusu' was, however, slightly insulting, as it implied that residents, many of whom were young, were merely flirting with socialist ideals. A lot of people in the area were not 'Cihangir solcusu'; quite a few were foreigners. However, what was difficult to deny was that the mahalle attracted a large number of writers and artists.

One example of this tribe was forty-seven-year-old Ayaz Tarhan. The son of a highly regarded and highly paid family lawyer, Ayaz had studied fine art at Mimar Sinan University. Financially supported by his father, he had developed his skills as a miniature portrait painter, opening his Cihangir atelier in 2006. Fascinated by folklore, and once resident in Edirne, he had decided to bring the Thracian Bocuk Gecesi festival to İstanbul. And while other Cihangir creatives backed the transplanted festival, Ayaz was still its main proponent and chief organiser.

Events would be happening all over Cihangir that night, but the epicentre of the Bocuk Gecesi action would be around the Firüzağa Mosque on the corner of Firüzağa Cami Sokak and Defterdarlık Yokuşu. A light green nineteenth-century structure, the mosque was surrounded by a leafy square ringed by cafés and small restaurants. It was on the street corner before the mosque that Ayaz, mobile phone forever in his hand, had just supervised the raising of the tent where famous collage artist Gonca Şekeroğlu would read tarot cards for revellers later on that night.

Now, however, he was on Dalgıç Sokak, on his way to visit Meryem and Emir Kaya. The blacksmith and her ceramicist brother were going to light a fire in their great-grandfather's forge, which now sat empty at the back of their garage.

Ayaz knocked on the garage door and Emir Kaya opened it.

'Good morning, Emir,' Ayaz said. 'Just checking that everything is ready for this evening.'

'Oh yes,' the young man said.

'Meryem in?'

'No. She's working, but she'll be back soon.'

'Good.' Ayaz pulled up a spreadsheet on his phone. 'So you've got chestnuts?'

'Yes. Two sacks,' Emir said. 'And small bags to put them in. Just hope the forge doesn't fill the place with smoke after all this time. We had the chimney swept, but . . .' He shrugged. 'Meryem's on at eight, isn't she?'

'Yes. Tales from the Forge,' Ayaz said. 'Should be popular. People love local history these days. I've also managed to get Madam Theodora out to tell tales of the old Rum Cihangir.'

Madam Theodora was one of a small group of İstanbul Greeks, or Rums, who still lived in the city. She was going to tell stories about old Cihangir in the vintage-themed Susam Café.

'Is it true that Gonca Şekeroğlu is going to be reading cards here tonight?' Emir asked.

'Yes.'

'I love her work.'

'Well, she'll be producing a new piece based on our Bocuk Gecesi,' Ayaz said.

'I'd love to meet her.'

'I'm sure you will. She's coming with her husband. He's a police officer. He helped us get all the right permissions we needed to put this on.'

He glanced inside the garage and raised his eyebrows. 'That a new piece, Emir Bey?'

Emir invited him in and took him over to a large red model house on a table. At the front was an entrance hole for the cat that would one day call this home, typical of these model houses that were produced by Emir and other artists. The upper floors of the structure were covered with a sheet of Perspex.

'Very skilful, if not beautiful,' Ayaz said.

'The current owners have wrapped glass around the top storeys. I reproduce what I see,' Emir replied.

It was well known that Emir's cat houses had a political

motivation. Through his work, which provided homes for street cats, he also commented upon how many of the Bosphorus yalıs had been ruined by unsympathetic renovations carried out by their new super-rich owners. As a native İstanbullu, he felt this was a form of desecration.

'Mmm. Not pretty, but then that's not the point, is it?' Ayaz continued. 'Where is it?'

'It's called the İskender Efendi Yalı and it's in Kanlıca. Just back from the waterfront and so easy prey for anyone who wants to really mould the place in their own image. They ripped out a nineteenth-century Ottoman kitchen inside and replaced it with a vast chrome affair.'

Ayaz put a hand on Emir's shoulder. 'Hopefully you'll do well tonight,' he said. 'Everyone knows about the cat houses of Cihangir, and animal lovers from across the city will be attending.'

Twenty per cent of everything sold was going towards a new animal shelter that was under construction in Cihangir with the help of local vets.

'I hope so,' Emir said. After being wildly enthusiastic about the project a few weeks before, he seemed subdued.

The old woman was in, but she certainly didn't want to see them.

'She told me not to lie and so I won't,' said the young maid who answered the door. 'She'd rather meet Satan than you lot.'

Neşe Hanım, mother of former gang boss Esat Bocuk, lived in a vast glass and steel apartment just off Bağdat Caddesi, İstanbul's premier shopping street. On their way to the apartment, Süleyman and Ömer Müngün had pushed their way past hordes of well-dressed people carrying Prada, Moschino and Gucci carrier bags. The cold air had reeked of Chanel No. 5.

The girl, a small, covered female, had a plain, make-up-free face but, oddly for a modest woman, a very obviously curvaceous figure.

'Well, we need to speak to her,' Süleyman countered. 'And so if she would rather do that at headquarters . . .'

The maid went away to relay this message, and when she returned, she ushered them both inside.

As well as belediye records, a man called Rauf Saraç had told them that the old woman was still in town. Previously an employee of Esat, he now, he said, made his living begging outside the many coffee shops on Bağdat Caddesi. A one-time enforcer, known for his skill with a blade, Saraç did not, Süleyman felt, just beg for a living.

That said, as soon as he'd seen the officers, he'd gone into a routine about how poor and humble he was and how Esat Bey's arrest had made him mend his ways. It was bullshit, but Süleyman had let him ramble on. When he finally paused for breath, he'd asked him about Neşe.

'Oh, she still lives here,' Rauf had said, 'but in reduced circumstances. Only goes out to visit Esat Bey when the prison authorities allow.'

Süleyman gave him fifty lira to buy his silence, knowing that old Rauf would be on the phone to Neşe Hanım just seconds after they left him.

And now here they were in an apartment that looked anything but reduced in any way. Still full of opulent sofas and ridiculous pot plants, it nevertheless now smelt very different from the last time Süleyman had visited. With Esat Bocuk and his sons gone, the aroma of the apartment reminded him of his mother's house: camphor, tobacco and lavender oil with a background note of ammonia. An old-lady smell.

Neşe Bocuk, a plump, elderly bundle sitting on the floor smoking a nargile pipe, looked up at Süleyman. 'What do you want, Mehmet Efendi? Rather, what *can* you want now that you've taken the men of my family and stripped us of our living?'

'You seem to be thriving in some comfort, Neşe Hanım,' he said.

'The business my late husband built is in ruins. All our properties sold except this one.'

Süleyman and Ömer sat down on the large sofa in front of her.

'Your son and one of your grandsons broke the law,' Süleyman said. 'As a woman of faith, you will know that when wrong-doing occurs, punishment follows.'

She said nothing, tucking her head inside her many scarves.

'However, I am not here about your son,' Süleyman continued. 'I thought it was about time we came and made sure that you were flourishing. After all, Neşe Hanım, you were an innocent party . . .'

'Don't try to flatter me, Mehmet Efendi,' the old woman said. 'You don't care about me and I don't care about you. Go to hell.'

'I'm sure I probably will.'

'Want a reading, do you?' she said. 'Oh, but you've got your gypsy wife to do that, haven't you. Never trusted the Roma. Gonca Hanım'll break you in the end, you mark my words.'

If anything was Süleyman's Achilles heel, it was his wife. Ömer Müngün saw the boss's face redden slightly.

'My private life is my affair,' he said.

'My life with my son and grandsons was private until you lot destroyed it,' the old woman countered.

This was getting nowhere and so Süleyman came to the point.

'Neşe Hanım, earlier this year a man called Görkan Paşahan bought a very lovely house on the waterfront at Beykoz, a district your son Esat enjoyed.'

'We had no property in Beykoz,' she said.

'I know. But your family had . . . influence there.'

The Bocuks had run most criminal operations on the Asian side of the city until the police had put Esat and İlhan Bocuk in prison back in 2019.

'So?'

'So, you may or may not know that Görkan Paşahan is currently wanted by both us and the security services for sedition.'

'He's the one that broadcasts from abroad,' the old woman said. 'Don't agree with him.'

'I didn't think you would. I'm asking whether you know anything about his house in Beykoz.'

Neşe Hanım narrowed her eyes. 'What do you want, Süleyman?'

He sat back and folded his arms. 'Let's call it aftercare,' he said. 'When a district – in this case encompassing most of the Asian side of the city – loses the "protection" of a powerful man like your son, other players often seek to fill that power vacuum. In the process of this takeover, those connected with the previous man or woman of power may be at, shall we say, a disadvantage.'

'Paşahan is out of the country,' she said.

'He is. Neşe Hanım, have you heard of the Internet?'

She huffed. 'Don't insult me, Mehmet Efendi,' she said. 'You may be a prince, but you don't have an empire any more.'

'I've noticed that,' he said. 'So let's be civil to one another. Paşahan has bought property in what was once your son's sultanate. Whether this, as well as a property bought by another businessman called Ümit Avrant on Büyükada, is destined for Paşahan's daughter Sümeyye and her fiancé, Avrant's son Atila, is something I don't know. Now, Atila's father, like your son and Görkan Paşahan, is ambitious. He comes from Kars but in recent years he has expressed a desire to move to İstanbul. Luckily for him, his son has apparently fallen in love with the daughter of a man who began his own move to the city at the beginning of 2020. Or maybe like me you don't believe that. Maybe like me you believe that the proposed Paşahan/Avrant wedding is purely political, a way of getting Avrant into a position of power in this city. That said, however, at the moment, *you* are my concern.'

'Me?'

'Yes. I wonder in the deep, dark hours of the night whether Paşahan – distant though he currently is – has asked you for money in order to provide protection to you and your remaining relatives. I hate to use the word extortion . . .'

'No, he hasn't.'

'You know I can look into your bank accounts.'

'Still no,' she said. 'I don't know him. I disapprove of him, and this Avrant character is unknown to me.'

Taking Ömer by surprise, Süleyman stood, closely followed by the sergeant.

'Well, thank you for your time, Neşe Hanım,' he said. He put one of his cards down on the large glass coffee table in the centre of the room. 'Do call me if you come across these men or their employees.'

'I won't.'

'Ah, well then, I just hope that if they do happen along, you may feel more confident in calling other police officers you might know,' he said.

This time it was Neşe Hanım's turn to blush.

'I don't know any of your lot,' she yelled at them as they left. 'None.'

When they got outside, Ömer said, 'Did you notice the maid, sir?'

'The maid? What about her?'

'Gorgeous figure.'

'First Zuzanna Nowak, now Neşe Hanım's maid,' Süleyman said. 'Ömer Bey . . .'

'Those little skivvies from the countryside are usually either like sticks or sacks of potatoes,' Ömer said. 'She was, well . . .'

'Ömer Bey, I am a happily married man,' Süleyman said sternly. But then he smiled. 'However, yes, I did notice her. Gonca Hanım is my world, but I'm not dead.'

Ever since COVID restrictions had been lifted in early 2022, Çetin İkmen had tried to help those around him get their businesses back up and running. This involved patronising businesses owned by people he knew, one of whom was Rambo Şekeroğlu senior. Whenever he was passing, he'd slip into Rambo's bar in Tarlabaşı and buy rakı, brandy or whatever took his fancy. Everybody knew he did this, and so when he arrived at the meyhane just before midday, no one was surprised.

As usual he sat outside underneath one of the patio heaters Rambo had purchased for his smoking clientele and sipped a glass of rough local brandy. He actually preferred it to the smoother, more upmarket French version.

Just after midday, Madam Edith and Melda Gürsel left to go shopping. In case Sinem was watching, Edith and İkmen waved to each other. Then İkmen settled in for an hour of slow drinking, smoking and observation.

The Gürsels, İkmen thought, had to have been living in their apartment block, locally known as the 'Poisoned Princess apartments', for coming up to ten years. Four-year-old Melda had been born while they had been living there, and prior to that, Pembe, Kerim's lover, had come and gone from the place on a regular basis. Briefly, just for a second, he saw Sinem Gürsel's face at the window of her fourth-floor apartment, but then she was gone. A man of about forty went through the open front door to the block, but left almost immediately after taking a letter out of one of the pigeonholes on the lobby wall.

İkmen drew his coat close around his skinny frame and settled himself in for a long period of boredom.

Chapter 5

Everything had been planned down to the last detail. The show was going to be held at the top of the open-air stone staircase known as Kumrulu Yokuşu, thus increasing the sense of jeopardy in the audience. Accurate timing and misdirection were of course of the essence. And though the team around magician Nuri Taslı practised with him every day, they all knew there was still room for error to creep in.

His principal assistant, his wife Ecrin, was a hard taskmistress who put the all-male crew, her sons, through her husband's set pieces again and again. Known professionally as Bartolomeo, Nuri had chosen this name in honour of the great Italian magician Bartolomeo Bosco, who had founded his own theatre, the Bosco, in Beyoğlu back in 1839.

After forty years in the magic business, Nuri still worked meyhanes and clubs all over the city, as well as venues out in the open like the Cihangir Bocuk Gecesi night. But he was nearly seventy, and so he was not as quick or dextrous as he once had been. This meant that those around him had to be really on their game at all times. He'd performed the illusion he was to do in Cihangir a thousand times, all over the country. But it was one of those that if it did go wrong would leave him looking like a foolish old man. And he didn't want that.

The Taslı family home was in Ortaköy, amid the many cafés and bistros down by the waterfront. One of very few wooden Ottoman houses in that area not converted into commercial

64

premises, it had been inherited by Ecrin at a time when such places were worth only a few lira. It also had a garden, which was where Nuri and his team practised in an old barn. In front of a stage area at the back of the building, two young men raised a velvet curtain in front of a locked trunk. Counting the two beats Nuri had instructed them to, they let go of the curtain to reveal their father half in and half out of the trunk, while Ecrin stood to one side, her head in her hands.

'No! No! No! No! Too quick! Two beats, for God's sake!'

She knew full well that it wasn't the boys who were too fast but her husband who was too slow. She knew this because she was the one who was supposed to swap places with Nuri and appear on top of the box while he slipped inside. But she couldn't say that even though her husband knew it was his fault. As he picked himself up off the floor, he said, 'I think we all need a break.'

'No! We must carry on until it's right!' Ecrin said.

But the boys – Ali, Şevket and Alp – were already moving towards the house.

She put a hand on her husband's arm. 'We'll put it right after lunch,' she said. 'Nuri, it's not the beats that are too quick . . .'

'I'm too slow,' he said. 'I know! I know! But I'll get better. Tonight will be perfect.'

Ecrin knew better than to argue with him. In his youth, Nuri had been a truly great magician – even, some said, greater than the famous Sami Nasi. But while Sami was actually older than Nuri, he was still fit and remained at the top of his game. Ecrin sometimes wondered whether having a wife much younger than him had energised him.

She hugged her husband and the two of them began to walk back towards the house. Later, she thought, they'd get the trick right. Later they'd come out and work hard until it was perfect.

*

65

'Did you see her blush?' Süleyman asked Ömer Müngün. 'When I mentioned her possible association with other police officers?'

They were sitting outside a tiny café in Balat owned by Süleyman's İstanbul Greek friend Belisarius. While Ömer was due to go back to headquarters, Süleyman himself was headed home. However, before that, the two men needed to discuss what had happened at Neşe Bocuk's apartment.

'Yes,' Ömer said.

'I know why Alibey has asked me to get involved in the Paşahan affair,' Süleyman continued. 'If I can find some firm evidence to bring him back here on a murder charge, it saves Alibey from the bother of pursuing an organised-crime route. But he knows me. He knows I'll look under every stone. If he's been in contact with Neşe Hanım, he knows I'll find that out.'

Belisarius arrived with two cups of thick coffee. He put them down on the table and said, 'Two Greek coffees for the police officers.'

Süleyman smiled. He always had a little to-and-fro about the origins of this beverage.

'You mean Turkish coffee, Belisarius Bey.'

'Greek.' Belisarius began to move away.

'Turkish.'

They smiled at each other, and the Greek left.

'Maybe he's been on to her about something else?' Ömer said.

'Possibly. But what?' Süleyman asked. 'Her son's in prison, ditto her grandson. The Bocuks' stock has fallen. And let's not forget that a so-called religious woman like Neşe should have no time for Görkan Paşahan.'

'Except he used to be establishment.'

'Used to be, yes,' he said. 'But not now.'

'Unless, as you've said before, boss, it's all a game.'

They both looked at each other. Then Süleyman said, 'But what game?'

*

66

It was cold. In spite of sitting directly underneath a patio heater, Çetin İkmen could feel the circulation in his legs dwindling to nothing. He moved his feet inside his shoes and stamped on the ground a few times. It hurt, but he persisted. God, getting old was a bastard! But what choice was there? It was this or lie down in a hole in the ground and rot for the rest of eternity.

So far only a few ancient teyzes had come and gone from the Poisoned Princess apartments. Women laden down with black bags full of washing, grandchildren and pots of steaming stew. Had his wife Fatma lived, she would have become one of these, but with better clothes. She'd been all about family. From the moment their eldest, Sinan, had been born, she had devoted herself heart and soul to her children and her husband. What a good woman she'd been! How he'd loved her! How he now betrayed her on an almost daily basis with Peri Müngün, a woman young enough to be his daughter! On the verge of tears, İkmen pulled himself together. Silly old bastard! Fatma had been the kindest, most loving woman he'd ever met. She wouldn't want him to be unhappy, and Peri made him happy. Quirky and imbued with that dark sense of humour only people who worked in public service had, she made his body tingle every time they touched and, perhaps more significantly, he felt safe with her. Safe and loved.

Madam Edith, Melda in tow, arrived back laden down with numerous plastic bags full of shopping. Edith looked exhausted. They'd been to the Şok market on Tarlabaşı Bulvarı, where it seemed the elderly drag queen had bought everything they had in tins.

After lifting Melda onto the chair next to İkmen, Edith sat down opposite and let her plastic bags down underneath the table.

'That was bloody!' she said once she'd caught her breath.

'Heaving with Tarlabaşı Roma all pushing and shoving, their kids running around all over the place.'

Looking in her bags, İkmen said, 'Looks like you've bought every tin of chickpeas in the city.'

'We ran out,' she said. She took a cigarette and lighter out of her bag and lit up. Melda briefly glanced up from the toy mobile phone her daddy had given her and shook her head.

'Smoking's bad, Auntie!'

'Yes, sweetheart, it is,' Edith said. 'You must never do it. Your Auntie Edith's a terrible, weak old woman.'

Melda, completely focused on her phone again, said, 'I won't tell Mummy.'

Edith and İkmen looked at each other, then the drag queen said, 'See. Secrets. Even she has them and she's only four.'

'Do you want a drink?' İkmen asked.

'I shouldn't,' Edith said. 'But a small vodka and tonic, please. Why I should abstain when she' – she pointed to the Poisoned Princess building – 'scoops down red wine, I don't know. Anyway, anything significant happen here?'

İkmen called one of Rambo's waiters over and ordered Edith's vodka, a glass of ayran for Melda and another brandy for himself.

'No,' he said. 'Teyzes mainly. One man walked into the lobby, took a letter from a pigeonhole and left again.'

Their drinks arrived and Edith helped Melda with her ayran. The glass was full, and until the little girl had drunk some, it was unwieldy.

'Then I remembered the fire escape,' İkmen said.

Edith shook her head. 'The bottom quarter rotted off during the pandemic.'

'Oh.'

There was a reason for the nickname given to the Gürsels' apartment block. Back in the 1980s, the then mayor of Beyoğlu had described the whole of Tarlabaşı as a 'poisoned princess' within his otherwise noble sphere of operations. He'd wanted to bulldoze the entire quarter, but Tarlabaşı had survived and still lifted its tattered head to the sun every morning, the appellation now retained only in a local description for a particularly shabby apartment block.

'What remains of it's covered in all sorts of shit,' Edith continued. 'People who can't be bothered to bring their rubbish down to the bins park it on the old fire escape. The rest of it'll be down soon.'

'Edith,' İkmen said, 'me sitting here looking at a door for an hour does no good. I've not seen anyone who could remotely be involved with you-know-who. Besides, even if she's seeing someone, although I don't know how, I've picked up a rumour that could mean that what she's doing is reactive.'

'What do you mean?'

'I mean our boy could be playing away.'

'No!'

'Why not? He's a handsome man.'

'My daddy's handsome,' Melda said.

Edith put a hand on her arm. 'We're not talking about your daddy, treasure.' She turned back to İkmen. 'I don't know about that, but I don't think so.'

'Can't you just ask her, if you're that worried?'

'No!'

'Auntie Edith,' Melda said, 'why is my mummy so clumsy?'

'Oh well,' Edith said, 'Mummy's got an illness.'

'I know that,' Melda said. 'Arthritis. She's told me. No, I mean the cuts on her arms. She told me she did them when she was chopping up vegetables for our dinner. She shouldn't do that, should she?'

Edith paled. 'No, sweetheart.'

But Melda was back inside the world of her phone.

Edith leaned across towards İkmen. 'How can I ask her anything if she's doing that?'

What Kerim Gürsel called 'the crazies' had started to contact the police as soon as the press put the latest news up on their Internet sites. A newborn child had been found dead near Kağıthane Creek. Police were appealing to the public for information, and also for the mother of the child to come forward to obtain medical attention.

The lines jammed early, and teams of uniformed officers began to be dispatched across the city to check out the more plausible claims. One had come from a woman who told them that one of her neighbours' daughters had been pregnant and now wasn't any more but there was no sign of a baby. Kerim's first thought about this was that the poor girl had probably miscarried.

Eylül Yavaş walked into the office they shared and said, 'Gedik Stables' finances are dire, sir. They're using their overdraft facility to pay for the animals' feed.'

'That's not good.'

'No. Although what bearing that might have on the death of the baby . . .'

'Any more sightings of a horse and rider?'

'Yes,' she said. 'From the apartments facing the creek. But nothing that adds anything to what we already know.'

'OK,' Kerim said. 'I'm going to bring that groom Zekeriya Bulut in here for another chat. Get him out of his comfort zone.'

'What about the girl, Aslı Dölen?' Eylül asked. 'She was riding a black horse that morning too.'

'She said she didn't leave Gedik's compound.'

'She said . . .'

He looked up at her. 'You don't trust her?'

Eylül smiled. 'It's not that I don't exactly trust her, sir. I just . . .

70

I know her type – horsey, privileged. I grew up with girls like her. I could have *been* a girl like her, easily. They're self-absorbed, so they don't notice anything or anyone around them. I'm not saying she's hiding something – I don't think she is. I simply feel that maybe she needs more prompting about what she may or may not have witnessed.'

The implication here was that Eylül's personal discovery of religion had, at least in part, saved her from the same life of ease and lack of responsibility Aslı Dölen had. If she did indeed have that.

Kerim said, 'OK. Let's get her in too. Shake the tree and see what falls out.'

Usually when he came home, and particularly if he came home early, he'd hear Gonca call out to him as soon as he opened the front door, 'Mehmet, darling, is that you?'

But this time the house was silent, and so even before he entered the brightly coloured salon at the back of the building, Mehmet Süleyman had begun to feel anxious. When he saw his wife curled up into a tight ball on one of their iridescent green sofas, he knew that something was very wrong. He walked over to her and squatted down, laying a hand on her shoulder. Now he was close, he could see that she'd been crying.

'What's wrong, goddess?' he asked her. 'I came home early so that we could spend some time together before Bocuk Gecesi.'

Her voice catching in her throat, she said, 'I can't go.'

He felt his heart hammer. He'd feared this would happen. 'Why not?' He sat on the sofa beside her and laid her head in his lap. He kissed her hair. 'Gonca, you're the best falcı in the city,' he said. 'People are looking forward to having you read for them.'

'I don't want their pity!'

He knew what she was referring to, but he had never thought about people's reactions to the loss of her daughter like that.

71

'No one will pity you.'

'They will!' she said. 'Look at that poor old gypsy who can't even protect her own family! Not going to have my cards read by that old fraud!'

'We'll be in Cihangir,' he said. 'People are not like that there. I don't know that people are like that anywhere, except in your head. And I know why that is, but, darling, our friends will be there too. And your family. Erdem is bringing his children, Rambo's involved in some sort of fire-eating show with his friends, then there's your sister Mihrimah, and most importantly Zeki and his girls.'

Zeki was her dead daughter Hürrem's husband, who was going to bring his three little daughters to see their grandmother.

'No. I can't.'

He turned her over so that he could see her face. It was red from where she'd been crying, and her mascara had run down her cheeks.

'You have to go for the children.'

'No!'

'Look, I know you're nervous after all this time—'

'No, you don't!' She sat up suddenly. 'You've not lost a child! What do you know? My daughter went to that hospital alone. I had to sit here screaming while those doctors put tubes inside her.'

'They did that because they were trying to save her life.'

'They failed!' she yelled. 'They failed and you wouldn't even let me into your car so I could go to her!'

He'd always known this would come one day. Hürrem had been taken to the Cerrahpaşa Hospital during lockdown. Zeki had called an ambulance because she couldn't breathe. Mehmet had gone to Tarlabaşı to make sure the ambulance arrived, and had followed it to the hospital, where of course he had been turned away. No one could go in, not even Hürrem's husband. When the doctors

72

had discovered they needed to intubate Hürrem, they had obtained his permission as her next of kin by phone. When she had died, she had been buried outside the city, with not one of her own people to mourn her.

Ever since, Gonca had lived in fear of further loss, especially that of her husband. She'd clung to him, burying herself in her desire for him, worrying herself into a frenzy every time he was late home. He pulled her onto his lap and looked into her face.

'Now listen to me,' he said. 'This is the reality. I couldn't take you anywhere unless you were sick. I carried on working because that was what we did during COVID. The police carried on, just like the nurses, just like the doctors. I wasn't allowed anywhere near your daughter in case I caught COVID. You know this! I know you want to blame someone, anyone for what happened, but there is no one to blame. Hürrem caught a deadly disease for which there was no treatment at that time. It's hard and it's cruel and I would do anything to take your pain away, but—'

'I miss her so much! She was one of my babies and I let her die.'

'No you didn't,' he said. 'It's awful, unbearable, and I am daily lost in admiration for the way you carry on. I'm not sure I could be as strong as you are if my son died. But I love you, your family love you, and none of those people in Cihangir will pity you. Yes, they will empathise. They will feel sorrow for you, but they will not pity the strong, beautiful, wonderful Roma woman I am in love with. No one can or will.'

For a moment she remained absolutely still. Then she leaned forward and kissed him.

'Baby, I'm so sorry,' she said.

He kissed her back. 'It's all right, Gonca,' he said. 'But really you must allow yourself to live now. Those little girls, Hürrem's children, love you, and I know they are looking forward to seeing you.

73

Everyone is. I spoke to Zeki yesterday and he told me that he's even bought them brand-new dresses for the occasion. They will look so sweet. And no one, no one will pity you, I promise. Everyone will just be amazed by your strength and your beauty, just like I am every day.'

Fifteen minutes north-west of Taksim Square, the district of Dolapdere, while partially gentrified in recent years, was still somewhere to treat with respect. On Mirmiran Sokak, in an apartment above a cheap clothes shop, uniform had made a gruesome discovery.

Squatting down beside duty pathologist Dr Mardin, Kerim Gürsel fought a losing battle with flies as he looked into the face of a dead woman. Twenty at the most, she had long dark red hair and a distinctly swollen belly. This could be a result of a build-up of gas post-mortem – a neighbour had reported a bad smell. Or she could possibly have given birth in the last few days.

'Any idea how long she might have been here?' Kerim asked the pathologist.

Dr Mardin was in her forties, single, pragmatic. Some of the more misogynistic officers with whom she sometimes worked joked amongst themselves that she was a lesbian – mainly because she was neither charmed by nor attracted to any of them. Those who did know her, like her boss, Arto Sarkissian, were aware that she had been in a long-term relationship with an esteemed judge for decades.

'No,' she replied.

It was hot in the tiny room where the body had been found, locked in. Kerim's officers had been obliged to break down the door.

Mardin continued. 'But if she had been pregnant, she isn't now.

I'll have to get her back to the lab. Is there anything you can tell me, Inspector?'

Kerim had spent some time talking to the neighbours, including the woman who had called the incident in.

'The family moved out yesterday,' he said. 'No one knows where. Circassians apparently. The father was called Berkan Bey, the mother Perestu. Only the parents and the girl, the neighbours say, and she hadn't been seen for some time.'

'Name for the girl?' she asked.

He looked at his notebook. Originally from what was now Russia, the Circassian people had fled to Turkey in the nineteenth century as a result of the genocide carried out against them by the tsarist authorities. Muslims, they were distinctly fair skinned and immensely proud, and many of them possessed unusual names.

'Tirimujgan,' he read.

'Mmm.' Mardin nodded. 'If she has been pregnant, I'll request comparison DNA with your Kağıthane infant. I can't see any sign of foul play, but the fact she was locked in here may point to abuse or, at the very least, neglect.'

When he left the shabby little apartment, Kerim called Eylül Yavaş.

'I'm sticking around here for a while,' he said. 'But I'll go home straight after. Can we meet at the office at seven tomorrow? I want to get over to the Gedik Stables so that we can pick up Zekeriya and Aslı Dölen.'

'Fine with me,' she said. 'And regarding Aslı Dölen, sir, she's the same age as Görkan Paşahan's daughter, Sümeyye. They went to the same school, the Lycée Notre Dame de Sion.'

'So?' Eylül was rather more fixated on Aslı Dölen than Kerim felt she should be. And, if he remembered rightly, she had attended the prestigious Lycée herself.

'Sergeant Müngün told me that Inspector Süleyman is working with Organised Crime to help bring Paşahan in.'

Kerim had heard about that, even though he hadn't spoken to Süleyman lately. 'Yes? And?'

'And sir, Görkan Paşahan was still based in Uludağ when his daughter came to school here, so she boarded with a local family during term time. Aslı Dölen's family.'

Chapter 6

While Tomtom Kaptan Sokak was not as near to Cihangir as he would have liked to park his car, Mehmet Süleyman had an old school friend who lived there. Uğur Kalyoncu now had a very nice apartment in what had once been a convent. For one night, he had given Süleyman his parking space.

As Mehmet opened the car door for his wife, he draped a large woollen scarf around her neck. 'It's freezing,' he said.

He offered her his hand as she got out of the car, but she refused it. 'I can manage.'

Tomtom Kaptan was a steep cobbled street and he worried about her falling.

'I know you can, but—'

'You know, you are far more handsome than your great-grandfather in that uniform, Mehmet.' She always changed the subject when she felt vulnerable.

She rose painfully to her feet and then pulled herself up to her full height. Back home she'd made him pose for numerous photographs, some of which she'd sent to his mother. Nur Süleyman had objected to her son's marriage to a woman she called a 'common falcı'. Gonca wanted her to know that she fully appreciated her husband's pedigree.

'He was at war when that photograph was taken,' Mehmet said. 'I don't know that I would have been as brave as he was.'

Gonca took his arm and they began to walk. He wanted to say how proud he was of her for overcoming her fears and fulfilling her obligations. But he didn't. Now that she'd made the decision to come, there was nothing more to be said.

Already they could see lights flashing over in the direction of Cihangir, and there was a smell of barbecued meat on the air. It was, however, the music that caught Gonca's attention. Although amplified almost to the point of distortion, it was very obviously a ballad, accompanied by a flute and a violin. Three women's voices rose and fell in harmonies that sounded to Süleyman rather like the French folk songs he had heard as a child at Galatasaray Lisesi. The language, however, wasn't French.

'Ladino,' Gonca said. 'They're singing in Ladino.'

And once he'd tuned into the song, Süleyman recognised the ancient mix of Hebrew, Spanish and some Turkish words that characterised the music of İstanbul's ancient community of Sephardic Jews. When the Catholic monarchs of Spain, Ferdinand and Isabella, had expelled the Jews from their lands in 1492, they were given a home in the Ottoman Empire by Sultan Beyazıt II. And while many had, in recent years, left to settle in Israel, those who remained still sometimes spoke and sang in their old language, brought with them all those centuries ago from Iberia.

Squeezing her husband's arm, Gonca said, 'I love it.'

'Sinem.'

She was pretending to be asleep. She did it a lot these days.

But Kerim Gürsel, lying down beside his wife on their bed, persisted. 'Edith has gone out with Madonna to this Bocuk Gecesi festival in Cihangir and I've just read Melda her story. I thought we might talk.'

He felt her body stiffen. 'What about?' She still hadn't turned to look at him.

Kerim swallowed. 'Sinem, things haven't been normal between us for some time . . .'

78

'Normal!' Now she did look at him, and there was fury in her eyes. 'Since when was anything in our lives normal?'

The Gürsels had been friends since childhood. They'd married ten years before when Kerim had still believed that Sinem was a lesbian and that they were both hiding what they were from their families. Then Sinem had admitted that she'd lied because she was in love with him. He'd not stopped loving her, though, and Sinem had become pregnant with their daughter. Kerim had consequently settled himself to his new life as a husband and father. But then something had gone wrong. Not with him, but with Sinem.

'We're all doing our best . . .'

'Are we?' Sinem said. 'I don't see you doing much besides reading bedtime stories and playing with Lego. Edith does most of the cooking and cleaning. You work all the time. Or do you? I never see you . . .'

'Sinem, that's not fair,' he said. 'My job isn't some office-based—'

'No, you're out there protecting us all every day.'

'I am. I try,' he said. 'Sometimes that means—'

'You were drinking outside Rambo Şekeroğlu's meyhane yesterday,' Sinem said. 'I saw you.'

'Yesterday was bad,' he said. 'A dead baby out in Kağıthane.'

For a moment her expression appeared to soften; she even raised her hand as if to stroke his face, but then pulled it away. She said, 'I'm sorry. Was it murdered?'

'Yes,' he said. 'But Sinem, I don't want to talk about that. I want to talk about us. I love you, but you won't even let me hold your hand now. I know that sex isn't always . . . well . . .'

'I don't want sex with you, Kerim,' she said. 'Who in their right mind would want to have sex with a man who has to force himself to touch them?'

Her words slapped him. Although they didn't often make

79

love, he had thought that when they did, they both enjoyed it. Sinem had even told him that whenever she had an orgasm it eased her pain.

Fighting to control an urge to scream at her, Kerim said, 'I never have to force myself to touch you. I love you. You know this.'

'I also know that you look at men,' Sinem said.

Kerim's head sank lower. 'I do,' he said. 'I've never lied to you about that. I've also promised you that I will never act upon it.'

For a moment he thought he spotted the old, loving Sinem. But then her face hardened again and she said, 'You might as well . . .'

'Sinem!'

'. . . because you're not getting anything from me. Go and find yourself a rent boy!' And she turned away from him.

The forge was finally glowing with what Meryem called a 'mature fire' – burning deeply down to the core of the blaze. For a moment she stood and looked at it, the flames tinting her face red and gold.

Emir, who had been arranging chairs, took a shovelful of chestnuts and held them over the flames. Once their skins split, he would pour them into a metal bowl beside the fire and start the next lot. Out in the street, a group of Roma boys juggled with flaming torches, and a saz player sat cross-legged on the pavement plucking the metal strings of the lute-like instrument, producing half-tones and arabesques that caused small girls in fluffy pink dresses to sway and run and dance. Almost everyone's face was powdered white to fool the Bocuk family of witches into thinking they were already dead. There would be no dragging anyone down to hell this night.

His face taut with anxiety, Emir said, 'Can I have something?'

His sister looked up from what she was doing. 'No.'

'The tension's killing me,' he said.

'Nothing's going to happen,' his sister said. 'It's over.'

'Yes, but—'

'Emir,' she dropped her voice to a whisper, 'the fact that you're asking tells me that you shouldn't have it.'

'Meryem . . .'

'You're making excuses,' she said.

'Emir Bey!' The voice came from the entrance to the forge.

Emir turned and saw that Ayaz Tarhan was standing in the doorway with a man and a woman.

'Someone would like to meet you,' Ayaz said.

Emir put the shovel down on the floor and walked towards them. As he got closer, he recognised the woman. Her face unpowdered, dressed in a long black velvet coat, her hair touching the floor . . .

'Gonca Hanım!' he said.

She held out a long, manicured hand towards him, over which he bowed.

'Emir Bey, I've been admiring your work in the streets,' she said.

'Oh, the, er . . .'

'The animal houses,' she said. She took his arm. 'I particularly loved the Beylerbey Palace. So detailed! Do you take commissions? I'd love you to make a model of my house. I live in Balat.'

'Gonca, we don't have a cat,' said the man, who was wearing what looked like an Ottoman army uniform.

She cast him a lazy-eyed look and then turned back to Emir. 'My husband,' she said. 'And he's quite right, but these little houses you make are for the street animals, no?'

'Yes,' Emir said. Finally he blurted what he'd wanted to say right at the start. 'Gonca Hanım, I've admired your work all my life. It was you who first inspired me to work with found objects. There was an article about you in *Hürriyet* where you said you collected hair from the combs your father used to groom his horses.'

'I did.'

'And the hair ribbons used by your daughters and—'

'Gonca Hanım,' Ayaz said. 'Your tent is ready.'

'Ah, yes.' She squeezed Emir's arm. 'Now, Emir Bey, would you like me to read your cards?'

'Oh, but people are waiting, Gonca Hanım,' Ayaz said. 'People who will donate to the shelter.'

She waved a hand. 'They can wait for a few minutes more.'

She squeezed Emir's arm again and he felt himself blush. Her husband, while not looking exactly fierce, was a police officer and so could probably handle himself. Gonca Hanım was flirting outrageously, and Emir couldn't believe that he could be happy about that.

If her boss didn't slow down soon, he'd end up having a heart attack. Aylin Mardin had been just about to put the body of the Dolapdere woman, anecdotally called Tirimujgan, into one of the refrigeration cabinets when Arto Sarkissian arrived.

In order, as was his custom, to deflect attention away from his own late presence in the laboratory, he said, 'Aylin. Working late?'

'Yes,' she said.

'On whom?'

She pulled down the sheet covering the body. Long red hair cascaded across the cadaver's recently stitched chest.

'Ah, the alleged Circassian woman,' he said. 'I heard about it.'

'She turned up during investigations into reports about Inspector Gürsel's dead baby. Local people reported a smell.'

Arto bent down to examine the corpse. 'Dead how long?'

'Three, four days,' she said. 'The police found her in a locked room of an empty apartment. She probably died alone.'

Arto shook his head. 'Cause of death?'

'Not entirely sure yet,' she said. 'But I don't suspect foul play. Cardiac arrest.'

'I see.'

'And she'd just given birth when she died,' Aylin continued. 'So it's possible she could be the mother of Inspector Gürsel's Kağıthane child.'

'Mmm. Child is very different, however. Black hair . . .'

'Hair colour changes, Arto.'

'I know,' he said, 'but . . .' He bent down the better to examine the face. 'Freckles. Common amongst the Circassians, absent on the child.'

'So the father wasn't Circassian. Arto, I'm not saying this is the child's mother. But I'm not saying it isn't either. When the DNA results come back, we'll know more.'

Aylin could understand why he'd said what he did. Nice, neat connections between victims rarely happened, and he didn't want anyone to fall into the trap of making convenient connections where they didn't exist. But for once she hoped his caution was misplaced. Burying the child and its mother together was something she hoped they could do.

'God, I hate this flour! Gets into every line and wrinkle!'

Çetin İkmen rolled his eyes. As far as he was concerned, his daughter didn't have lines or wrinkles and in fact looked really quite striking with her face powdered white.

'It's all right,' he said.

But before he could expand upon that and tell her that she looked lovely, his cousin Samsun butted in with 'Oh, I know. Puts ten years on me!'

In her mid forties, Çiçek İkmen was divorced, and although not exactly obsessed with the idea of remarriage, she was lonely, especially since Mehmet Süleyman had dumped her back in 2019.

'Just enjoy the festival,' İkmen said.

They were on the corner of Firüzağa Cami Sokak and Palaska Sokak, outside the tent that had been set up for Gonca's card-reading event. And while İkmen was disturbed by the way his daughter still fixated on her appearance, especially when Mehmet

Süleyman was around, he was rather more concerned about Gonca and the young man she was hanging onto outside the tent. He was very attractive, and İkmen could see that Mehmet, while outwardly genial, was fuming inside. He knew that pained jovial look of old.

He left his relatives and approached the artist.

'Gonca!'

'İkmen!'

She was alight with bonhomie, something he'd not witnessed in her for a long time. He kissed her hand. Then, while the young man was momentarily distracted, he whispered in her ear, 'You look wonderful and happy. But don't flirt too much or you'll hurt the boy.' Because they were the same age, İkmen and Gonca often used that term for Süleyman, who was twelve years their junior.

Gonca looked shocked. 'I love Mehmet with all my soul! He knows I am completely his!'

'Yes, but he's a man, and you know how we are,' İkmen said.

She looked at him. 'He would never hurt me.'

'I know. But . . .'

The young man, no longer distracted, said, 'So my future, Gonca Hanım . . .'

'Ah, yes, darling,' she said, and snuggled into his side. Then the pair of them were gone, leaving Gonca's husband and a lot of people lining up for readings in their wake.

İkmen offered Süleyman a cigarette and they both lit up. Some fireworks exploded in the sky, and a woman carrying a tray of sweet pumpkin insisted they take slices to protect their souls.

Throwing the pumpkin down his throat in order to concentrate on the cigarette, İkmen said, 'You know she's just playing, don't you?'

'Gonca? Yes,' his friend replied. 'Took me hours to get her out of the house, she was so nervous. Then we get here, she sees a good-looking young man . . .'

'It's how she is,' İkmen said. 'It means nothing. She's infatuated with you. You know this.'

Süleyman smiled.

'İkmen!'

He turned around and saw his old friend Sami Nasi and his wife Ruya.

'Sami, Ruya.' He kissed the latter's hand. 'Come to see the magic show?'

Sami Nasi had been a professional magician all his adult life. Allegedly related to the famous nineteenth-century Hungarian magician Josef Vanek, he was well known for performing his ancestor's signature trick, cutting off his assistant's head and presenting it to his audience on a silver platter.

'I've known Nuri Taslı since the dawn of time,' he said.

'That's Bartolomeo?' İkmen asked.

'Yes. He and Ecrin have been on the circuit for years. Their three boys have grown up in magic. Nuri had a bad time with COVID. They had to intubate him, he couldn't do anything for months. I'm glad he's working again. He was always a much better escapologist than I was. And what he's doing tonight, well, it'll be impressive.'

Süleyman had joined the conversation. 'At the top of the Kumrulu Yokuşu Steps.'

'It's a challenging location,' Sami said. 'No room for error. But then I've seen him do the same trick on the edge of a mountain, so this is nothing. That said, one slip and you're bouncing down a steep flight of stone stairs on your way to the Bosphorus. I sent him a text to tell him I lit a candle for him in St Antoine.'

'He's Christian?' İkmen asked.

'No, but Ecrin is. Anyway, I told him this morning we'd see them after the show. Like most of us, Nuri likes to focus to the exclusion of everything else before a performance. The municipality closed the steps this afternoon, so I imagine he's been practising *in situ* for hours. But it's still risky.' Sami looked at his wife. 'In the meantime, we need to stock up on sweet pumpkin and sahlep.'

'Mmm.' Ruya smiled. 'Oh, and chestnuts! They're roasting them over at the old forge.'

When they'd gone, İkmen said to Süleyman, 'So what do you want to do now that Gonca's working? We can go with Sami and Ruya to the forge and listen to stories of old Cihangir, or we can follow Samsun, who, like a weathervane, always points us in the direction of alcohol.' Then, noticing Süleyman's Ottoman uniform for the first time, he added, 'Suits you. But wasn't your illustrious ancestor in the cavalry?'

'Yes,' Süleyman said. 'And before you ask, Gonca did originally want me to ride here on one of her family's horses, but I refused.'

There was nothing to see, or so the boys had been told. Rambo Şekeroğlu and his cousins Elvis and Django were keen to find out what Bartolomeo and his troupe were up to behind the screens they had placed around the top of the Kumrulu Yokuşu Steps. During lockdown, Rambo had amused himself with magic tricks and had developed an ambition to be a performer himself. His cousins, who were both younger, enjoyed hanging out with him because he played with fire and the three of them were working on a knife-throwing act.

But as the three young men got close to the screens, a man poked his head out. 'What do you want?'

'Nothing,' Rambo said. 'Just looking.'

'Well, look somewhere else! We're setting up!'

The three boys walked away. Then Elvis said, 'We could go down to Lenger Sokak and come up behind them.'

Django grunted. 'Fuck that,' he said. 'I want a drink.'

Although younger than Rambo, both Django and Elvis were

married with children. Like their father, Gonca's brother Rudi, they worked as street musicians, busking with their accordions outside the church of Santa Maria Draperis on İstiklal Caddesi. They rarely had money to do much beside feed their families, and so Django's desire for a drink was a not so heavily coded message to Rambo to pay up. He was, after all, the son of the richest member of the Şekeroğlu clan. This fortunate position came with responsibilities, and Rambo knew it.

He shrugged. 'OK.'

They began to make their way towards a small bar Rambo knew was 'cool' with Roma. Called Art Central, it was, despite its somewhat pretentious name, a no-nonsense sort of place serving beer and spirits – no wine or cocktails. In spite of being in trendy Cihangir, it was the sort of place workmen would frequent, or slightly jaded people who had just got inked at the tattoo artist's next door.

But they never made it. What the boys had thought was a large doll hanging outside a shop suddenly came to life, and what looked like a demon ran cackling through the screaming crowds, its head apparently on fire. The gypsy boys hid.

Çetin İkmen also saw it. From his vantage point beside the patisserie, he'd noticed the dordelec, an Albanian charm against intruders, earlier. Now seemingly alive, it ran through the crowds, who first screamed and then laughed as it waved its head, covered in red and gold streamers, at passing children. Bocuk Gecesi was a night of misrule and so anything was possible, but it gave İkmen a cold feeling in the pit of his stomach.

Chapter 7

Time paused. As soon as the curtain fell, there was no movement, no heartbeat, no breath.

Just before the screens were removed, Gonca said to Mehmet, 'I feel cold and afraid.'

He put his arms around her and held her tight. Later, he remembered taking a breath. But not exhaling.

The crowd parted behind them and a man approached the makeshift stage. At the same time, a figure all in black, his face covered by a Donald Trump mask, bade them all welcome. His name, he said, was Bartolomeo, and he was going to move through time and space.

On the stage was a large trunk, a tall box like an upright coffin, and two chairs facing outwards. A large black velvet curtain lay on the ground.

Mehmet remembered later that for some reason he looked at Sami Nasi and saw that he was frowning. But then he looked back at the stage, where he saw a figure, could have been a man or a woman, wrap chains around the magician's body and lock them using padlocks. Two other people lifted him into the trunk, then closed and locked the lid with yet another padlock. The man who had come up from the audience got into the upright box, and one of the assistants opened a hatch so that his face could be seen. He heard Gonca say, 'Mehmet, you must save him!'

But by that time the curtain had been raised by two performers standing on chairs.

Music was playing. Ravel's *Boléro*. İkmen had a recording of it at home somewhere. His father had liked it. The curtain went up to conceal the two boxes on the makeshift stage, and smoke billowed up from the ground. How long was the curtain raised for? It looked as if it ascended and then descended in one smooth movement. But did it?

Through the smoke, it was just possible to see that the trunk remained unmoved but open, the large padlock on the outside, now undone, swinging in the night-time breeze, creaking. The upright box had gone. Completely. Only the music continued, ploughing relentlessly through the silence that was suddenly eerie in its completeness.

And then the smoke cleared, revealing no one. Someone somewhere laughed.

It was as if he were flying. Down the steps, his feet barely touching the ground. Later Mehmet Süleyman would say that he heard a voice from the bottom of the stairs. But at the time, he just ran. People above him screamed; a young woman fell to the ground. What the hell did he, and they, think was going on? His mind a blank, he looked at the rough sides of buildings to his left and right. Then he glanced behind him. Perhaps the trick was still in progress. Maybe he'd reacted too soon. It was then that he saw someone coming down after him.

'Mehmet!' İkmen yelled. He looked like a stiff-legged puppet, jolting and jerking his way down.

Through all the screaming and crying, Mehmet caught the sound of his wife as she wept. İkmen was nowhere near, and so he yelled up at him, 'Go back! Call it in!'

Call what in? But İkmen came to a halt and Süleyman saw him take out his phone. Hurtling down towards the junction of Bakraç Sokak and Langer Sokak, he tried not to be distracted by lights from the vast traffic jam on Meclis-i Mebusan Caddesi, the coastal road at the bottom of the hill. By his calculation, six people had disappeared into thin air. How was that possible? Scanning either side of the steps, he kept looking for some sign of movement. A dying olive tree vibrated and he made a grab for it; however, like the magicians and young Emir Bey, it eluded his grasp. But it did wrong-foot him, and he caught hold of one of the handrails that ran the whole length of the stairs on both sides, his knuckles white, one of his ankles screaming with pain. The shiny riding boots once worn by his great-grandfather were slightly too small, and he felt his feet jar as he started running again.

When he got to the bottom, he looked from left to right. Seeing a man begging in front of a newly restored wooden house, he ran over to him. 'Brother, have a group of people passed this way, all wearing black?'

The man, who he now noticed was nursing a bottle of rakı, just stared at him. But then why wouldn't he? A man wearing an Otto-man uniform in the middle of the night? He probably thought he was a drink-fuelled hallucination.

Süleyman ran back to the stairs and began to jog back up to Cihangir. İkmen, no longer holding his phone, was walking down towards him.

'Anything?' the older man asked.

'Nothing,' Süleyman replied.

Then they both heard the sirens.

The designated incident commander was Superintendent Fahret-tin Uysal. A short, sallow man in his forties, he didn't like Mehmet Süleyman, mainly because the latter was 'posh'. But it was now well over an hour since İkmen had called in the incident, and even

Uysal was beginning to understand why Süleyman had insisted he and his officers close Cihangir down.

The superintendent had set up a temporary incident HQ in the premises belonging to Meryem Kaya, the sister of the man who had taken part in the trick on the steps, the now missing Emir Kaya. Quiet and shocked, she answered his questions in a dull monotone.

'When was the last time you saw your brother, Miss Kaya?' he asked.

'I'd just finished my storytelling session. Everyone wanted to go and see the magic show,' she said. 'Emir had been handing out bags of chestnuts in the street. He came in to get some more and I said I'd meet him at the steps.' A lot of discarded chestnuts had been found outside the forge, some still in bags. 'But I got held up.'

'Held up how?' Uysal asked.

'One of the people who'd come to the storytelling event. Merve Karabulut,' she said. 'She was asking questions.'

'Why?'

'Wanted to know more about how our great-grandfathers came to the city,' she said.

'Who is Merve Karabulut?'

'She's a tattoo artist. Her studio is next door, between us and the Albanian shop.'

Uysal looked down at his notes. 'Shqiperi?'

'Yes.'

'So you didn't see your brother walk onto the stage and get into the box?'

'No. I'm still not sure it was Emir.'

Uysal looked at Süleyman. 'You believe it was him?'

'Absolutely. More to the point, my wife does too. She spent some time with Mr Kaya when she read his tarot cards earlier this evening.'

'Mmm.' Uysal turned back to Meryem. 'Question: if the man in that box wasn't your brother, then where is Emir?'

'I don't know,' she said.

Samsun Bajraktar wound Gonca Süleyman's big scarf tightly around the gypsy's body.

'I'd make you a valerian tea if I had any valerian,' she said. 'Good for shock. But then you'll know that.'

They were sitting together outside the Firüzağa Kahvesi, drinking tea. Çetin İkmen had corralled the women in his family, plus Gonca, when he had returned breathless from the stairs.

'I knew and I didn't say anything,' Gonca said to Samsun. 'I've not seen such a catastrophic layout since Father died.'

'This was for the young man?'

'Emir, yes,' she said. 'There was nothing in his future. It was as if he was already dead. I should've said something to Mehmet, but you know how he is about such things.'

'Why didn't you tell Çetin?'

She flung her arms in the air. 'I don't know! I was shaken. All my readings from then on were just . . . I wasn't very professional.'

'Did you tell this Emir what you saw?'

'How could I? Such a young, beautiful boy! I convinced myself it was me, that I hadn't performed the ritual correctly.' She leaned in towards Samsun. 'Mehmet came home early this afternoon. I was nervous about tonight. Since Hürrem's death, it's been difficult, going out.'

Samsun took her hand.

'But I had performed my rituals in good time. The only thing was . . . As I told you, Mehmet came home early. I was crying and he comforted me. One thing led to another . . .'

'Oh.'

'Sex isn't permitted just before a reading. But . . .' Gonca shook her head. 'So strictly I hadn't performed the ritual correctly.'

'You're a mother in mourning for your child.'

'I'm also someone people should be able to trust.'

'Honey, none of this is your fault,' Samsun said. 'And anyway, we don't know what's actually happened yet. Maybe it was some sort of prank.'

'It's been over an hour since that boy disappeared!'

'Mehmet and some others are going with Sami Nasi to Bartolomeo's house in Ortaköy,' İkmen said as he sat down beside the women. 'He's known Nuri Taslı and his family for years.'

Çiçek, who had been talking to a friend, turned around. 'They won't be there if they've kidnapped that boy.'

'Nobody knows whether they have or not,' İkmen said. 'Sami reckons the Taslı family wouldn't do anything like this. But we have to start somewhere.'

And then he saw something that distracted him, and for the second time that night, Çetin İkmen got to his feet and ran.

The small Ottoman house, squeezed between a coffee shop and a high-end boutique, was painted a subtle shade of green. As well as having a tiny front garden full of potted plants, it also, according to Sami, had a large back garden and a workshop.

'Nuri and his boys build their own equipment,' Sami told Süleyman as they approached the building.

In spite of the fact that it was gone one in the morning, the streets of Ortaköy were busy with people both arriving and leaving the many local nightclubs in the area. Reina was probably the most famous, a place that attracted a wealthy crowd plus a considerable number of foreigners. Nuri's house, situated in a tiny alleyway off İskele Sokak, was, in contrast to everything around it, dark and silent.

Süleyman had brought three uniformed officers with him, two

constables and a sergeant. There was a small passageway between the house and the coffee shop, at the end of which, according to Sami, was an entrance into Nuri Taslı's garden.

He said to the sergeant, 'You take Constable İşik to the back of the property. I'll try to gain access with Constable Yerlikaya via the front door.'

'Yes, sir.'

'What do you want me to do?' Sami Nasi asked.

'Keep out of the way.'

He stood in the street while Süleyman rang the bell and called out, 'Police!'

Some people smoking outside the coffee shop walked over to Sami. 'What's going on?'

'Nothing.'

When he refused to be drawn, they moved away.

Süleyman knocked on the door again, but got no reply. Then his phone rang.

Sami Nasi moved back towards the house. Süleyman said, 'The sergeant's found the back door open. He's coming to let us in.'

The dordelec, or rather the person inhabiting the dordelec's likeness, seemed fitter than Çetin İkmen. Wheezing and panting after it as it made its way towards Sıraselviler Caddesi, he was made painfully aware of his own inadequacy. Time was, back in the day, when he would run after retreating villains with a cigarette sticking out of his mouth, and catch them. His clothes had been perpetually mud-stained and ripped during his twenties and thirties, when he'd cheerfully hurled himself at wrongdoers on the run. Now his body was nothing more than a shambling encumbrance and he hated it. That said, he still managed to somehow keep Peri happy. Or so it seemed.

Sometimes, in dark moments İkmen wondered whether Peri was under-sexed in some way, or had just come to accept bad

94

sex as the norm. Poor girl! Not that she was unenthusiastic – she wasn't – and she was also very quick to praise his performance. She'd told him that she loved him. He didn't know what to think about that, even though he felt sometimes that he might love her too.

Having finally reached Sıraselviler Caddesi, İkmen looked up and down the street, searching for a cackling creature with red and yellow ribbons coming out of its head, but all he saw was a few drunks on their way home, a couple kissing in a shop door-way. Catching his breath, he crossed the road and stood in front of the Cihangir Pet Shop. His grandson Timur had taken him there some months before, when he'd been trying to persuade his parents to buy him a dog. In an effort to get his grandfather on side, he'd shown İkmen all the 'cute' clothes owners could buy for their dogs. It had backfired.

'Dogs don't wear party dresses!' İkmen had said when pre-sented with a rack of outfits. 'They're animals! A dog in a tutu is an abomination. How's it supposed to shit?'

Now he paused at the shop to catch his breath. Bocuk Gecesi was supposed to be a night of misrule, when the black witches belonging to the Bocuk family ran about looking for souls they could drag down to hell. So far it was living up to the hype. In spite of the police presence, the city was still loud and colourful and scary, even if his own soul was where it had always been, residing in his unwilling body.

And then there it was again. But this time it was right beside him, with its head on his shoulder.

At first there was nothing. Just blackness and silence. Süleyman pushed Sami Nasi behind him and switched on his torch. Now that the whole team was together, they proceeded from room to room, the junior men, weapons drawn, opening doors as they worked their way through Nuri Taslı's house. It was not for the

95

faint-hearted. In the first room, the salon, they found a false guillotine, while the kitchen was decorated with clown masks and playing cards.

Turning to Sami, Süleyman said, 'Is anything likely to spring out at us?'

'Like what?'

'I don't know! A rabbit out of a hat?'

Sami said, 'No one does that old stuff any more.'

A study was filled with books, both on shelves and flung carelessly across the floor.

One of the young constables hissed, 'Sir!'

'What is it?'

'There's a rat!'

Süleyman had seen the rodent before Constable Yerlikaya but had ignored it. He'd grown up in an old wooden house like this and knew that rats were just a fact of life. Also this house, like his old home, was near the Bosphorus.

'So?' he said.

The young man shut up.

They made their way up the creaking staircase in the middle of the house to where, according to Sami, Nuri had his family living room. It was as they moved towards the door into this room that they heard banging on the floor.

'What's that?' Süleyman motioned to the constables to stand each side of the door and then open it.

At first it appeared the room had been burgled. Everywhere they looked, chairs, cupboards and tables were upended. As he stepped into the room, Süleyman heard glass break under his shoes, and there was a smell of earth where numerous pot plants had been either toppled or thrown.

As they moved further into the room, this smell became stronger and more complex. There were metallic notes now, which made Süleyman shudder. The smell of iron could indicate

96

that blood was present. Then Sami saw a pair of eyes staring up at him . . .

Çetin İkmen hardly dared breathe.

'I know what you are, you know,' İkmen said when he finally got hold of himself enough to speak. 'You're a dordelec, or rather someone dressed up as a dordelec. What I don't know is why.'

The dordelec said nothing. But there was something poking into İkmen's back and he feared it was a gun. He'd been here before and so he recognised it – and his own fear.

Should he try to engage this person in conversation? Would the fact that he knew what it was meant to be make any difference to what might happen next?

He took a punt.

'My mother was Albanian,' he said. 'Dordelec can still be seen outside empty houses in that country.'

Its breathing rasped. Should he try to muster up a few words of Albanian? He couldn't think of one. Frustrated with himself, he said, 'What the fuck do you want?'

The feeling that he had a gun at his back increased and he shut up.

Whether he closed his eyes voluntarily at that point because he didn't want to watch his own viscera being blown out into Sıraselviler Caddesi, he would never know. But his eyes did close, and when he opened them again, the dordelec had gone.

They were all alive except Nuri. The metallic smell Süleyman had picked up as they'd walked into that living room had been his blood. Whoever had attacked him had shot half his head away. The eyes Sami Nasi had seen belonged to a terrified Ecrin Taslı.

Tied to metal garden chairs with wire overlaid with thick masking tape, the family had been gagged and, if Ecrin was anything to go by, beaten. Until Sami helped him untie her, Ecrin shrank away from Süleyman. Once she could speak again, she rasped, 'Sami, my boys!'

Checking to make sure that the young men were being untied, a shaken Sami said, 'They're safe, Ecrin.'

Unable to walk, she toppled forward into his arms. Then she howled, 'Nuri!'

Süleyman called an ambulance while his men freed the three boys and helped them to sit up.

Sami put his coat around Ecrin's shoulders while Süleyman called Superintendent Uysal. Sami heard him say, 'The wife and three sons were gagged and tied to chairs. I think they've been beaten. The family patriarch has been shot . . . No, he's dead. I'm going to get the survivors to hospital and secure the scene. Can you call it in and make sure the pathologist is informed? Someone needs to declare life extinct.'

Sami heaved. A small amount of vomit entered his mouth, but he swallowed it down.

'Ecrin,' he said, 'what happened?'

One of her sons, Ali, shuffled across the floor and put his arms around her.

'They were in the house,' the young man said. 'We'd been practising in the garden.'

'Did you know them?'

'No.' He looked at his mother, who was crying. 'Mum!' He started crying too.

Groans of pain came from the back of the room, where the police officers were tending to his brothers. The body of Nuri Taslı lay unfettered in front of a sofa, what remained of his head jammed against one of its legs. Had he tried to escape? Had he fought with his attackers?

Gleaning any information from his weeping family was not going to be possible at this point, and Süleyman hoped the ambulances would soon arrive to take them to hospital. Then he and others could examine the crime scene and try to make sense of what had occurred. Interviewing the victims would have to come later.

Had he not received that email from the forensic laboratory just before he got into bed, pathologist Arto Sarkissian knew that he wouldn't feel nearly as wrecked as he did. But that report on the dead baby's DNA sample had shaken him. It would shake anyone.

Devlet, his driver, still hadn't arrived. God knows what he'd been doing when he called him! And yet the man knew that his boss was on night call-out this week! Arto dressed and put on his spectacles. Devlet had probably been smoking nargile with his taxi driver friends in Tophane, telling dirty stories about local women he fancied. The man was a moron!

But as he looked out at his car, a large black Mercedes, the doctor knew for a fact that he couldn't face driving himself. While Ortaköy was only four kilometres from his home in Bebek, it was a journey peppered with nightclubs and the traffic that always accompanied such places. He'd lose his mind if he tried to drive through that. Luckily Devlet had already lost his, which meant he could do it with ease.

He put his shoes on, grunting as he attempted to bend over his ever-increasing stomach. He'd wondered about contacting Kerim Gürsel as soon as he'd read the email, but what was the point of waking him up? It wasn't as if he could do anything about it. Süleyman was in Ortaköy at this latest crime scene. He too would be interested in what the forensic laboratory had discovered.

Ecrin Taslı had wanted to see her husband.

'I need to see him so I know it's the truth,' she'd told Süleyman. 'If I don't, I will for ever have dreams that he may be alive somewhere.'

And so they'd shown her.

The crying, the screaming, the unbearable grimace on her face had stopped then. Hardly breathing, Ecrin Taslı looked like a statue as she stared at her husband's shattered head and face. A pillar of pain. Süleyman wondered whether she would have remained like that for ever had her three sons not attempted to join her. As they moved forward, she screamed at them, 'Get away!' Then, crouching like a lioness over her husband's body, 'You don't see this! You don't carry this! Your father wouldn't want that!'

They backed off. Süleyman could hear sirens in the distance, although whether they were the ambulances he had requested or the scene-of-crime team, he didn't know.

'Mrs Taslı . . .'

She took his arm and pulled him roughly out into the hallway. 'I want to talk,' she said. 'Before I forget. I want to talk now. They were waiting for us in the kitchen, at lunchtime. Six people, their faces covered.'

'Six? You're sure?'

'Listen! Let me get this out!' she said. Her eyes filled with tears, but she bit them back.

There was a chaise longue underneath the hallway window. Ecrin sat on it and motioned for Süleyman to join her.

'Six. I'm telling you. All wearing masks. Faces of politicians. Donald Trump, that one they call Boris the Turk from England, some others. They told us to sit down and shut up. I had a pot of soup on the hob and it was going to burn, so I said, "Look, can I just switch off the soup?" They said nothing, but then one of them shoved the pot over with the end of his gun and it spilt all over the floor. I shut up. That was all they said.'

'What? In total?'

'Yes. No,' she said. 'No. When they took us upstairs, they . . . No, go back, go back a bit!'

'Hanım,' Süleyman said, 'take your time.'

'There is no time!' she screamed. 'No time. Listen!'

She'd lost her mind. Süleyman saw Sami and one of Ecrin's sons looking at them. They knew it too.

'Two of them brought the garden furniture indoors and upstairs,' Ecrin said. 'They tied Ali to one of the chairs. Their guns were on us all the time. But Nuri could see they were hurting Ali. As one of them pushed me into a chair and wound wire around my legs, he tried to shove them away. They shot him. They called him a bastard, over and over, and then they shot him. I closed my eyes. I kept them closed until you came. They kicked my chair over, onto the floor. After that . . .' She began to shake violently.

Süleyman heard footsteps on the stairs. A male voice called, 'Ambulance!'

'Up here!'

Süleyman put his arms around Ecrin. Another of her sons, Şevket, came to her and took her hand.

'It's all right, Mum,' he said. 'We can tell them anything else they need to know now.'

Her eyes bulged and spittle appeared at the corners of her mouth. The paramedic, who had now reached the top of the stairs, squatted down in front of her. 'Shh, shh, breathe, teyze, breathe! I've got you now . . .'

Süleyman moved aside to let him sit next to her.

'My name is Burhan,' the paramedic said. 'You are . . .'

'Ecrin,' her son said. 'Ecrin Taşlı. She's my mum.'

The paramedic looked at her arms. 'You've got some impressive bruises there, Ecrin.' Then he showed her what looked like a plastic peg. 'Just going to put this on your finger so I can see whether you're getting enough oxygen.' He looked up at Şevket. 'Do you know whether your mother's on any medication?'

'Um, sleeping tablets . . .'

'Which?' He put a blood pressure cuff around her arm and repeated, 'Breathe. Breathe.'

'Zopiclone, I think,' Şevket said. 'She's taken those for years. Then there's the Rivastigmine, one capsule twice a day.'

The paramedic looked up. 'I see.' He smiled at Ecrin and began to pump up the blood pressure cuff. She was now noticeably calmer.

Sami took Süleyman to one side. 'Rivastigmine is given to people with early-stage Alzheimer's. Ecrin's not bad yet, but she does forget things. That was why she was so anxious to speak to you, before she forgot.'

Chapter 8

The cat looked up at İkmen and İkmen looked down at the cat. Some of the matted clumps around its neck were moving independently. Fleas. And there was some sort of gunk oozing out of the corner of its right eye.

'You look how I feel, Marlboro,' İkmen said to the cat, who rumbled a low growl.

A vast filthy tabby, feral and wildly promiscuous, this cat was the latest iteration of 'Marlboro', which was what İkmen had called all his cats since he was a teenager. İkmen was the only human the animal would tolerate, mainly because he fed it decent food.

It had been a long, long night and when İkmen had finally returned to his apartment it had been half past five. No point going to bed, and so he had sat out on his balcony wrapped in a blanket, smoking. Then the cat had jumped onto his lap. Now stroking the beast's ragged head, İkmen said, 'So what was all that about, we wonder? Disappearing boys, a dead magician, a dordelec? I have to say, Bocuk Gecesi rather over-delivered last night.'

Marlboro pummelled his master's chest and then slumped down on his lap.

After his experience with the dordelec, İkmen had returned to the tea garden, where he'd found Mehmet Süleyman handing his car keys over to his wife. He was about to go to Ortaköy with Sami Nasi – an enterprise that had resulted in the discovery of the Taslı family and the dead body of its patriarch.

'I've given Gonca my keys,' he'd told İkmen. 'Can you drive her home once she's been questioned?'

'Of course.'

Süleyman had begun to walk away. 'And drive yourself and your family home too,' he said. 'I'll come and pick the car up whenever I manage to get away.'

Now the great white BMW sat next to İkmen's ancient Mercedes. Unlike the Merc, the BMW didn't smell of mould and wasn't littered with empty cigarette packets. İkmen hoped no one stole it.

He'd been home for less than an hour when Süleyman had called to tell him the news about the Taslı family. It seemed that persons unknown had taken their place at the Bocuk Gecesi event. These people, it would seem, had been the ones who had kidnapped that young man. But why? And why use such lethal force against a little family of magicians?

Süleyman had been of the opinion that whoever had done this was making some sort of statement. About what and to what end was still unknown. But it made İkmen squirm. Nuri Taslı's head had been all but blown off for this.

'Are you sure?'

Kerim Gürsel had arrived at his office early that morning. He'd found headquarters on high alert due to the events of the previous night over in Cihangir. Apparently one man had been abducted while another had been killed, but he knew no details. Mehmet Süleyman had been involved, but he wasn't in yet. Dr Sarkissian had been called out to the death, but that wasn't what he wanted to talk to Kerim about now. He had another tale to tell.

'It's like this: human beings inherit fifty per cent of their genetic material from their mother and fifty per cent from their father,' he said. 'Where seventy-five per cent of the overall hundred per cent is identical, what this tells us is that the child's parents are closely related. The mother and father were, say, brother and sister or father and daughter.'

'So incest?'

'Indeed.'

'God.'

'You've never come across it before, Inspector?' the doctor asked.

'Well, yes, but only as a sort of rumour. There was a family from our mahalle when I was a child. They all had red hair and didn't mix with anyone. People used to say the parents were brother and sister, but no one actually knew.'

'I've discovered a few cases in my time,' the doctor said. 'In my experience it's something that is more likely to happen in rural families. Usually involves a father and daughter. Always comes as a shock. And in this case there's something extra.'

'Something extra?'

'Yes, a positive match on the convicted criminal database.'

'Who?'

'Görkan Paşahan would appear to be our unknown baby's father,' the doctor said.

Stunned, Kerim shook his head. 'But he's out of the country.'

'He wasn't nine months ago,' Dr Sarkissian said. 'He has a daughter, doesn't he?'

'Yes. Sümeyye Paşahan.'

'Then you'd better go and see her, Inspector.'

Kerim sighed. 'I would,' he said. 'Except her last known location was London, England.'

Mehmet Süleyman had finally arrived home at 8 a.m. He'd taken off his great-grandfather's now bloodstained military uniform in the laundry room and, after briefly showering, got into bed beside his wife. He was due at headquarters at midday. In the meantime, Ömer Müngün would keep in contact with scene-of-crime officers and the pathologist. Fortunately, when Süleyman had called Ömer at 6 a.m., he'd already been up, by the sound of it, soothing his baby.

'So does this mean that our reappraisal of the death of Sofija Ozola is at an end then, boss?' the sergeant had asked.

'Not quite,' Süleyman had replied. 'Speak later.' To explain what Dr Sarkissian had told him back at the Taslı house was just not possible, even though it haunted him.

Now Gonca wound herself around him like an opulent blanket and, her eyes only half open, said, 'Baby, are you all right?'

He stroked her hair. 'I am now.'

She kissed his mouth and then laid her head on his chest. Being with her always made him feel better. But after what İkmen had told him, he couldn't sleep.

He knew why Gonca hadn't told him about Emir's card reading. He'd never made a secret of the fact that he found what she did hard to believe. Thinking back on the events leading up to the illusion in Cihangir, he remembered that his wife had been tense. When the young man had entered that box, Gonca had pleaded with Mehmet to save him. But he'd not taken it seriously. With no knowledge of what had gone before, why would he? Later, she'd told İkmen. Of course she had. He inhabited her world in a way Mehmet knew he never could.

She stirred, and he held her close. Sleepily she said, 'They didn't get you, the Bocuk witches. I would not have it. The boy was enough. The boy was more than enough.'

'Gonca, the Bocuk witches did not take Emir Kaya.'

She knew better than to argue with him. Instead she stroked his shoulders, which were tight with tension.

'You're full of anxiety.'

'Go to sleep, Gonca,' he said.

'But I can take that away for you, baby.'

His eyes were so sore, he could barely keep them open. 'Darling, were I capable of making love to you . . .'

Ever since she'd started doing her readings remotely at night, she'd been late to bed and had taken to waking him up for sex in the early hours of the morning. Most of the time he was just as enthusiastic as she was, but not always.

'Oh no,' she said. 'You're exhausted. No, I was thinking I would maybe pour lead for you.'

'No.'

Pouring lead was a divination technique prevalent in the Balkans, in which molten lead was poured into water. The idea was that the lead would form into a shape that would predict the client's future. The water could then be used as a drink thought to calm anxiety and depression. The source of the lead was usually a bullet.

'Why not?'

'Gonca, I cannot give you a bullet from my gun. I have to account for every one. My superiors would not be amused.'

'Oh.' She settled down again.

But it was difficult for her not to feel hurt. Pouring lead was just something the Roma did in times of trouble. And although she knew that the gage rarely did it, she had hoped that Mehmet would let her help him. Sometimes the differences between them were hard to bear.

'Atila!'

It wasn't the first time Atila Avrant's house on Büyükada had been searched by the police, and so when Kerim Gürsel, Eylül Yavaş and four uniformed officers arrived, he wasn't surprised.

His house was modest to the point of being shabby. It had been bought for him by his father, Ümit, while he waited for planning permission to redevelop two nearby Ottoman yalıs for his son and prospective daughter-in-law, Sümeyye Paşahan. When Görkan Paşahan had left the country, Atila's house had been one of those the police had searched.

'Again?' he asked.

He hadn't come down to open the door. Instead he'd popped his head out of one of the upstairs windows. A self-described artist, Atila Avrant wasn't a bad kid, according to one of the uniformed officers who'd been on the last team to search the place. During their journey by police launch over to Büyükada, he'd told Kerim Gürsel that the young man wasn't a typical gang boss's son. 'Paints and draws and wanders about in old tracksuits,' he'd said. 'Not a Ferrari in sight.'

Kerim called up. 'I've a warrant, Mr Avrant. And we want to talk to you.'

'OK.'

Atila came down and opened the front door. Medium height, with lots of unruly brown hair, he wore a paint-spattered dressing gown.

Kerim held up his warrant as his officers entered. 'Sorry if we disturbed you,' he said. 'I am Inspector Gürsel. This is Sergeant Yavaş.'

'What's it about?' the young man asked.

'Let's go inside and then we can talk.'

Atila led Kerim and Eylül through to a large lounge while the uniformed officers began their search upstairs. The room was dominated by four easels on which stood canvases, two of which looked like photographs. One was a view of the Aya Sofya, the second of the Bosphorus Bridges, while the other two appeared to be just colour washed.

Seeing the officers looking at them, Atila said, 'My style is hyper-real. The aim is to produce something that is beyond the photographic.'

'They're beautiful,' Eylül said. 'Must take a lot of work.'

'They do. What's this about?'

'May we sit down?' Kerim asked.

'Oh, yeah.'

Atila cleared some books off chairs and onto the floor next to paintbrushes laid on rags and tubes of oil paints.

'Do you want tea?'

'No,' Kerim said as he and Eylül sat. 'We've come about Sümeyye, your fiancée.'

'What about her?'

'It is thought that at the moment she is residing in London.'

'Yeah.'

'However,' Kerim said, 'in light of a telephone call I made to the Metropolitan Police, it would seem that is incorrect. They have no record of a Miss Sümeyye Paşahan entering the United Kingdom.'

'Oh.'

'Oh? Mr Avrant, we're talking about your fiancée. I would imagine that you'd at least be a little alarmed by this.'

Atila put his head down for a moment, then said, 'Firstly, Inspector, if Sümeyye isn't in London, I don't know where she is. I was told she'd flown to see her family over there months ago. Don't take this the wrong way, but I think she was fed up with all the media attention she was getting – as well as questions from yourselves about her father. In fact, ever since he left Türkiye, she's tried to keep herself to herself.'

Kerim could easily see how her reticence might also effectively hide her pregnancy.

'So I've not seen her for months,' Atila went on. 'I can understand why your men are searching here, me being her fiancé and everything. But they won't find anything. Me and Sümeyye, we were arranged. The first time I met her was the week before our engagement party. As you know, both my dad and Görkan Bey are businessmen. They wanted an alliance between our families.'

'So it wasn't a love match?' Eylül asked.

He smiled, looking at her headscarf. 'No. It happens, as you know.'

'How did you and Sümeyye feel about that?' she continued.

He sighed. 'To be honest, I was OK. As long as I can paint, I'm happy. My dad wants to create this massive new house for us, but I don't really want it. It'll be for Sümeyye, she likes those kinds of things. Designer labels, cars. When we met, I told her she could have all that, but I wasn't interested. She was fine with it. We get on.'

'You get on as, I suppose, friends . . .'

'Yes. My dad said that love will come. She's pretty.'

She was. Kerim had seen photographs of Sümeyye Paşahan. At twenty-three, she was small and slim, with what looked like enhanced breasts and bottle-blond hair. She'd had a lot of Botox and fillers. She would, he felt, look very out of place alongside this scruffy lad who was three years her junior.

Getting to the point, Eylül said, 'Atila, how was Sümeyye with her father? Are they close?'

He frowned. 'Well,' he said, 'that was a bit of a worry for me, actually.'

Information was still coming in from Cihangir regarding the disappearance of Emir Kaya. Kumrulu Yokuşu Steps were cordoned off and witnesses were still being questioned. Ömer Müngün was at the Acıbadem Hospital in Taksim interviewing the late Nuri Taslı's sons, Ali, Şevket and Alp. Like their mother, the three young men were about to be discharged and were only waiting on the antibiotics they had been prescribed.

'They must've had keys,' Şevket said in answer to the sergeant's question about how their assailants had got into the family's home.

'How'd they manage that?' Ömer asked.

'It's easy enough,' Ali said. 'Our house is old, and so there are no elaborate modern locks. All you have to do is get hold of say the front-door key, take an impression in some plasticine and you can create your own key.'

'But how would they get the key in the first place?'

'Steal it,' Şevket said.

'From one of you.'

'Yes.'

'Does anyone outside your family have access to a key?'

'Only dad's sister, Auntie Bulbul.'

'Where does she live?' Ömer asked.

'Bulgaria. She married a Bulgarian,' Alp said. 'They come about once a year, usually. But because of the virus we haven't seen them since 2019.'

'Could your aunt have given the key to anyone?'

'We can call her and check,' Şevket said. 'But it's unlikely. Sergeant, whoever did this to us, they were fellow magicians. I'd like to say that if someone picked my pocket I would know, but if whoever did it was skilled enough, I wouldn't. I know this because I can do that myself. We all can.'

'You keep your house keys in your pockets?'

'Mostly, yes. I think men generally do.'

Alp said, 'Mum keeps hers in her handbag.'

'If you're skilled enough, you can take the key, make an impression and put it back in a matter of seconds,' Şevket said. 'It's a common trick, Sergeant. Me and my brothers used to do it to each other for fun.'

'Did you get any kind of idea about who these people might have been?' Ömer asked. 'I imagine that magic is a small world . . .'

'It is.'

'What I'm trying to find out is whether your family was at odds with any other groups of magicians.'

'What, you mean like the beefs rappers have with each other? No.'

111

'People are competitive,' Alp said. 'But . . .'

'Everyone loved Dad,' Ali said.

This reflected what Sami Nasi had said about Nuri Taslı. He had been highly respected and liked in the magic world.

'Inside magic he was legendary,' Ecrin Taslı said. 'Not outside, though.'

Şevket took his mother's hand.

Ömer Müngün had been warned that Ecrin Taslı was in the early stages of Alzheimer's. Süleyman had told him she had been very keen to get her memories of the attack out while she still could.

'Ecrin Hanım?' he said.

'Sergeant, I need to speak to you alone.'

'Misdirection on a night of misrule . . .'

'What are you mumbling about?' Samsun asked Çetin İkmen.

They were sitting outside on the balcony, watching the fog lift slowly off the Aya Sofya and the Sultanahmet Mosque. At the moment, neither building appeared to possess a central dome, and it was disquieting.

'Samsun, do you know anything about an Albanian shop in Cihangir?' İkmen said as he lit a cigarette.

'Shqiperi,' she said. 'They sell tat. You know: double-headed eagle flags, honey, those ashtrays they make over there in the shape of wartime bunkers . . .'

'Is it Albanian owned?'

'Owned I don't know about,' Samsun said. 'It's run by an old man called Xemal and two grandsons. Xemal is definitely Albanian. We have talked in the past. He's from Durrës and he's a proud Gheg, like us.'

'Like you,' İkmen said. 'Remember, my father was Turkish.'

Samsun said, 'Do you want to know about this shop or not? Anyway, the two boys, the grandsons, handsome little devils, they're involved in something.'

112

'In what?'

'I don't know, I don't ask,' she said. 'But word on the street is that they get things for people, you know.'

He did. Although not part of the Albanian community – he didn't even speak the language – he was aware that they, like every community, had their 'fixers'. People who arranged things like planning permission, local bribes and even passports. 'Getting things' was about much more than just dealing illegal cigarettes. It was usually shorthand for gang activity.

'Did you see the dordelec hanging outside that shop last night?' İkmen asked.

'No. Why would it be there? That shop's occupied.'

'It was a person dressed up,' İkmen said. 'I don't know how or when it lowered itself to the ground, but when it did, it proceeded to run about among the crowd.'

'Oh, that!' Samsun said. 'Gypsy boys called it a demon.'

'I followed it,' İkmen said. 'Up onto Sıraselviler Caddesi. It appeared behind me at the pet shop. I had the feeling it, or rather he, had a gun.'

'It's a bad omen,' Samsun said.

Exasperated, İkmen responded, 'No it isn't! The thing was a distraction, a misdirection made flesh, and I'm wondering why!'

'Why?'

'Yes, why! Oh never mind!' İkmen stood up. 'I know it's not what I usually do, but I think I need to go out and walk about for a while. Alcohol may be consumed.'

'My father was called Nikos Ballasakis,' Ecrin Taslı said. 'He was a Byzantine Greek from one of the last families to live in this city. My mother was Turkish; it was the first time any of my father's family had married a non-Greek.'

'This is very interesting, Ecrin Hanım,' Ömer Müngün said, 'but—'

113

She put a hand on his arm. 'Bear with me,' she said. 'Our house, or rather *my* house in Ortaköy is worth a lot of money. My father's family were employed by the sultans over many generations. The house I live in now was a gift to my great-great-grandfather Konstantinos from Sultan Abdülhamid in recognition of his help in improving the quality of the sultan's stables.'

'He was an architect?'

'No,' she said, 'a horse breeder, like his father and grandfather before him. Konstantinos improved His Majesty's horse stock and was given what was once a country house in Ortaköy as a reward. My house, Sergeant, is not only one of the oldest houses in Ortaköy, it is also one of the few that possesses a large garden. I know that it's worth a fortune. Nuri knew that too. But not once over the years we were together did he ask about selling it. Then he caught COVID and nearly died, and about a year after that he began to talk about it.'

'Selling the house?'

'Yes,' she said. 'I told him no at first and that was the end of it. The TAPU is in my name after all. But then at the beginning of this year he began talking about it again. I thought maybe he was worried about paying for my care. And yes, I do know that I have Alzheimer's.'

'Mrs Taslı—'

'Allow me to finish. So I sold some of my mother's jewellery. I made a large sum of money from it. My mother had some very nice pieces. But Nuri still worried, still wanted to sell the house. I began to wonder whether someone was trying to force him to sell.'

'And were they?'

'Yes,' she said. 'And I know you're probably thinking that I may be an unreliable witness, due to my illness. And when I tell you that the boys don't know, it will make you even more suspicious. But Nuri admitted this to me.'

114

'Did you ask him who they were?'

'Yes. But he didn't tell me. I begged him! But he wouldn't. All he would say was that if I didn't want to sell the house, it wouldn't be sold. He said he'd find another way to get these people off his back.'

Chapter 9

'Sümeyye and her father are close,' Atila said. 'To be honest, I was surprised when he left the country without her.'

'By close, what do you mean?' Kerim asked.

'Well, you know she's got a brother, Fazlı. He and his father barely speak. Everything is about Sümeyye. What she wants, she gets, and she loves her father very much. I don't know how I'm supposed to compete. Maybe I'm not. I won't insult your intelligence by pretending to not know what my father and Görkan Bey are. This is a marriage of convenience for them. I wouldn't be surprised if Sümeyye stayed with her father after we're married, to be honest. I expect you think that's strange, don't you, Inspector? How can I agree to such a thing? I expect you married for love.'

'My wife and I were in love when we married, yes,' Kerim said.

He could have just said 'yes', but he hadn't. And amongst those who didn't know him, this small exchange would have gone unnoticed. But Eylül Yavaş did know him, and his wife and baby, and the fact that he'd used the past tense alarmed her. Kerim Bey hadn't been himself lately. Easily distracted, he also looked tired all the time and he'd lost weight. Eylül knew that there were rumours about him. But she wasn't one for gossip, and so she tended to ignore those who speculated about her boss's sexuality. She liked him and they worked well together, and that was all that mattered.

'I know the cliché of the businessman's child is that of the spoilt brat hanging onto a gold mobile phone and wearing a Rolex. And that is Sümeyye on one level. But I think she's got a good heart. I think that eventually we'll be all right.'

It wasn't exactly a confident prediction, but Atila seemed to be sincere about it.

'Fazlı's different,' he continued. 'He just consumes – cars, jewellery, clothes, everything. As you can probably tell, I want a quiet life. But one thing I am going to be strict about is him.'

'Fazlı?'

'I don't want him near us,' he said. 'There's something unnatural about him.'

'Hi, Meryem.'

She'd left the door to the garage open and the woman had just walked in. Merve Karabulut was a small person. Dressed in metres of black gothic lace, she had piercings through her nose and eyebrows, and dragons tattooed down each arm. Like Meryem, she was no longer young.

'How are you?' she asked as she put a hand on Meryem's shoulder.

'OK.' She wasn't. Her brother was missing and she had no time for doing deals. 'I'm out,' she added.

'Oh.' Merve looked disappointed for a moment, but then she said, 'I'm actually here about Emir. Do you know—'

'No. We don't know anything.'

The police had told Meryem to keep her phone with her at all times and not to leave the area. But now she wanted to go and see them. If she told them everything . . .

'You've always been so close,' Merve continued. 'You must really be missing him.'

'Yes.'

'Must be hard having the police around the place.'

Meryem, who had been staring down at her phone, looked up. 'What do you want, Merve?'

'I just came to—'

'I told you, I've got nothing.'

'Did you have—'

'I was out before the police came,' she said. 'And of course in view of Emir, I won't be able to do anything for a while.'

'Mmm. And I suppose you'll just have to hope that nobody speaks to them about—'

'Merve, I repeat,' Meryem said. 'What do you want?'

Merve sat down on a battered old armchair beside the forge. 'They came to see me, the police.'

Meryem remembered she'd told them that it had been Merve who had held her up the previous evening.

'Yeah. I had to tell them why I didn't see the magic show. We were talking.'

'Yes.' Merve paused. 'I told them nothing,' she said. 'About you . . .'

'What I do is irrelevant.'

'Is it?'

Meryem looked at her. 'What do you mean?'

'I mean you've been playing with fire, haven't you, Meryem?'

'You don't seem to mind.' Was the woman threatening her? If so, why?

Merve stood. 'Oh well, I'm just saying,' she said. 'I mean, I think it would be unwise of you to mention me again, or anyone else for that matter.'

She turned and left.

Incest was a dark crime, perpetrated in secret, touching the most primal parts of the mind. Süleyman's first wife, Zelfa, a psychiatrist, had once described it as 'pure id'. Though not a Freudian, she had sometimes used his theories to describe what she discovered in the minds of those she treated. The id, the most primitive and reactive part of the psyche, was pure desire, unfettered by social norms or standards. Let loose without the mediating influence of the ego and superego, it was a wild and dangerous force with no concept of consequence.

The id of a gangster didn't bear thinking about. But Mehmet Süleyman was compelled to think about it. In all probability Görkan Paşahan had made his own daughter pregnant. In addition, that daughter had possibly killed the child.

Not that he was at this moment being paid to think about that. He was on his way to Cihangir to see what his scene-of-crime team had come up with and to coordinate the search for Emir Kaya. Ömer would meet him there.

The missing man's sister was to be his first port of call. Just after the abduction, she had claimed that her brother had no enemies, but then she'd been in shock. In the clear light of day, hopefully she would have more to tell. Emir Kaya was an artist specialising in ornate houses for street cats. A quick search of the Internet had brought up pictures of many of his pieces, as well as some commentary Süleyman had found disturbing. An environmentalist also concerned with heritage, Emir Kaya had produced work that was a direct challenge to the way some members of the elite, as well as rich foreigners, had renovated and developed certain historic buildings in the city. Copying them in miniature, in all their steel and glass glory, he gave them names like 'the Yalı of the Oligarchs' and 'Princess Instagram's Palace'.

What the owners of these properties made of this did not seem to be available online. Only a few – acolytes of these people, he imagined – made any sort of comment, usually along the lines of the artist being jealous of the owners' wealth. Support for Emir's work was, however, all over the net. He was praised for 'telling it like it is' and admired for his 'sneaky subversion'. He could be a target for those he opposed, but he was a small fish. A humble artist was no danger to the city's elite, criminal or otherwise. And why abduct him in such a theatrical manner?

At 3 p.m., Süleyman was due to meet someone called Buyu Hanım, who was apparently a representative of İlluzionist Derneği, the Society of Turkish Magicians. Apparently she knew everyone currently working in the city and might have some idea about possible rivalries between performers. This didn't give him long in Cihangir, but Buyu Hanım's assistant had been very clear that her employer had little time to spare.

Süleyman put his foot down.

Arto Sarkissian usually worked alone, with assistance from laboratory staff. But on this occasion he had welcomed input from his colleague Dr Aylin Mardin. While it was very clear to see what had killed magician Nuri Taslı – a catastrophic gunshot wound to the head – he wanted her to confirm his findings with regard to tissue discovered in the man's stomach and intestines.

'He didn't have long,' Aylin Mardin said. 'Must've been in quite a bit of pain.'

'Bloods are outstanding,' Arto said. 'We'll see whether we can deduce what type of pain control he was taking when they come back. He must've known he had cancer, given its advanced state.'

'I can't see how he couldn't have done,' Aylin said. 'Irrelevant, however.'

'Maybe.' He shrugged. 'I agree that the cancer didn't kill him, but maybe his terminal diagnosis meant he became involved in something . . .'

Aylin put a hand on his arm. 'We're not police officers, Arto.'

He smiled. Once they'd sewn Nuri Taslı's body together again, they went and got washed and changed. Back in Arto's office, they drank tea and talked.

'Any more on your body from Dolapdere?' the Armenian asked.

'Well, we now know there's no way the Kağıthane baby can be related to her,' Aylin said. 'Incest! I mean . . .'

'It happens,' Arto said. 'Even amongst those who point the finger at their one-time allies here at home, people they accuse of immorality. This is why we must keep this information amongst ourselves for the time being. When it gets out, all hell will break loose. I assume you know that Inspector Gürsel has been assigned to that case to the exclusion of everything else?'

'Yes. The Dolapdere investigation is now in the hands of someone called Inspector Mehmet Görür. He's new, I'm told.'

'I don't know him,' Arto said.

'Well, he's very enthusiastic,' Aylin replied. 'Convinced the girl's parents locked her in that room.'

'He may be right.'

'He may. But whether he's right or not, if he does find Berkan and Perestu Ramazanov, I do hope that someone has the sense to hold him back.'

'Why? Is he some kind of maniac?'

'I don't know about that,' she said. 'But he's built like a bull and, so I'm told, has zero tolerance for anyone who isn't an actual Turk.'

Arto cleared his throat. 'I had better watch out then, hadn't I?'

It had been an old friend of Çetin İkmen's who had talked about the different levels upon which İstanbul manifested. Max Esterhazy, occultist turned murderer, had spoken at length about the way the physical city was layered in physical space and time. It was between these layers that the intersections with other dimensions existed. It was why, he'd said, from time to time people went missing in the city only to reappear later somewhere else. Looking at his officers move from house to apartment block to church searching the vicinity of the Kumrulu Yokuşu Steps in Cihangir

121

brought this home to Mehmet Süleyman. Each building was like a maze – cellars and sub-cellars, rooms added on top of buildings, most without planning permission and in various states of disrepair. Then there were the rumours that had always dogged almost anywhere in the city, of secret underground tunnels.

He turned to the tall, muscular woman sitting opposite. 'Meryem Hanım, I have become aware of the fact that your brother frequently made miniature copies of buildings in the city that could be regarded as contentious. Did he ever have any kickback from their owners?'

'No, why should he?' she said.

'Because some of those owners are powerful people, unaccustomed to having their properties given offensive names.'

She smiled. 'Emir's a young man, Inspector. He enjoys a joke.'

'I don't think the owners of these properties are the sort of people who tolerate jokes at their expense.'

'My brother had no trouble,' she said. 'Emir is popular round here. You've met him. He's very charming and handsome.'

'And yet he doesn't have a girlfriend.'

'He prefers cats. What can I say? I'm not married either and I'm ten years older than he is. Our parents died when we were young and I brought Emir up. We're close. I continued my father's business when he died, partly because I love working with horses, but also to allow Emir to do what he wanted.'

'That's very noble.'

'It's what you do when you love someone,' she said. 'If you have children, Inspector, I'm sure you want them to do what they love.'

He did. Patrick, his son with Zelfa, was a very clever boy, now studying at Trinity College, Dublin. Both his parents had wanted the boy to train as a doctor, but he'd chosen to read psychology because he wanted eventually to become a stage magician like his idol, the English illusionist Derren Brown.

'Point taken,' he said. Then he changed tack. 'Tell me about your business Meryem Hanım.'

'My family have been blacksmiths here in Cihangir since the beginning of the twentieth century,' she said. 'Before us the forge was owned by a Greek family called Ypsilantis. My great-grandfather bought this building and all its contents from the previous owners. Ottoman princes used to come here to have their horses shoed. But with the coming of cars, our business diminished. Now I go out to riding clubs, your police training school and other places to do my job. For a while the gypsies still used to come here, but now, like everyone else, I go to them.'

'I see, and do you have any problems with competitors?'

'No,' she said. 'Blacksmiths are few in İstanbul now. If anything, we help each other. Do you know the story about the blacksmith and the devil, Inspector?'

'No.'

'I ask because I know that your wife is a Roma woman. She may have told you.'

Süleyman was aware of the fact that, İstanbul traffic or no İstanbul traffic, he had to be in Eyüp at three. But he was intrigued.

'What is it?' he asked.

'Well,' she said, 'the story goes that there was once a Romani blacksmith who was visited by a gentleman who said he would like him to make him some shoes. The blacksmith was taken aback, as you can imagine. But when he looked at the man's feet, he saw that he had hooves. So this is the devil, he thought. I bet he knows a lot of secrets about fire. But how can I make him tell me them? So he made the devil his shoes and nailed them to his hooves, but also to the floor. Now trapped, the devil was forced to answer all his questions about the secrets of fire until finally, when the blacksmith was satisfied, he was released. And this is why the Roma are such good blacksmiths: they understand the magic of fire.'

123

'And yet the Roma employ you,' Süleyman said.

'Ah well, yes,' she said. 'But then what I failed to tell you was that the great-grandfather who bought this business was a Romani.'

Süleyman smiled. 'You tell a good tale, Meryem Hanım. No wonder so many people came to hear you talk last night.'

'Sergeant Yavaş!'

Çetin İkmen had been drifting around Sultanahmet for several hours when he spotted Eylül Yavaş coming out of the Aya Sofya. Irritated by Samsun's unquestioning superstitiousness, he'd been looking at the great monuments, talking to people he knew, and had only stopped once for a brandy at the Mozaik. Now here was another friendly face.

As he drew level with her, he said, 'I thought you'd be at work.'

'I finished early,' Eylül said. 'I don't often get to perform the Salatu-l-Asr prayer, and I've never prayed in Aya Sofya since it was reconsecrated. It's an amazing experience.'

İkmen, who had been against the reconversion of what had been a museum to a mosque back in 2020, said, 'I'm happy for you. Any particular reason you chose today to come here?'

She looked down at the ground, and when she looked up, he saw that her face was grave.

'It is auspicious to pray here,' she said. 'I wanted to pray for someone I know who is unhappy.'

'Well, that's very kind of you,' İkmen said. 'Thoughtful.'

'Thank you.'

If Çetin İkmen had learned anything in his sixty-six years of life, it was how to spot someone who needed to talk to someone else about a problem they were having.

He bowed slightly. 'Eylül Hanım, would you do me the courtesy of taking tea with me?'

*

124

Kerim Gürsel looked at the photographs the Forensic Institute had taken of the casts they'd made of the hoofprints from the crime scene in Kağıthane. In the accompanying email, certain features had been pointed out relating to the probable weight and height of two horses. There was also what looked like an Orthodox cross on the left-hand side of each print. This, the email explained, was probably a blacksmith's mark, something that distinguished this person's work from that of others. It would seem to suggest that the blacksmith involved was an Orthodox Christian, Armenian or Greek. But there weren't that many of those in the city, and so he'd have to ask Sıla Gedik in the first instance. These prints had most likely come from her horses.

However, for the moment he was in pursuit of Fazlı Paşahan, brother of Sümeyye Paşahan, the supposed mother of the dead baby. Atila Avrant had described Fazlı as 'unnatural', but he had refused to say what he meant by that. It could be code for almost anything – homosexuality, adultery, addiction, even incest. Kerim sighed. Sinem's behaviour was pushing him away – possibly in the 'unnatural' direction of Enver Yılmaz.

The way their neighbour looked at him made Kerim almost certain that Enver Bey was gay. Years of being obliged to pick up on the slightest hint had made him very sensitive to such phenomena. The Turkey of 2023 was not the Turkey of 2014, when İstanbul Pride had attracted over 100,000 people. Back then, Kerim had dared to hope that things would get better, and while he would never wish either Sinem or Melda away, he longed for those heady days when he'd bought a rainbow flag to give to his lover Pembe.

Now, not only was Pembe dead, but his wife was seemingly throwing him into the arms of other men. Sinem had loved him so much! She'd known what he was all along, but she'd stuck with him and he'd stuck with her, because loving her had been easy. Melda, their daughter, had been born of that love, and they both worshipped the little girl. What had changed?

He couldn't keep on thinking about it. The department had a lot of information about Fazlı Paşahan, mainly because of his father. Apparently Fazlı was a carpet dealer in Çemberlitaş. His shop, which was called Azure, was on Vezirhan Caddesi, near the famous Çemberlitaş Hamam. There was a photograph of him on the shop's website. Apparently in his twenties, he was short, slim and had veneers on his teeth. A lot of people had that now. Veneers covered up less than perfect teeth and gave those who had them pure white smiles.

Kerim wondered whether Fazlı Paşahan was as oily as he looked in his photo.

Because it was said to be the burial site of the Prophet Muhammad's standard bearer, Eyüp el-Ansari, the İstanbul district of Eyüp was a place of pilgrimage for pious Muslims. It was also the site of a vast graveyard for those who wanted to be buried alongside el-Ansari and the mosque, the Eyüp Sultan Cami, which had been built in the standard bearer's honour. This same mosque had also, back in Ottoman times, been the place where new sultans were girded with the Sword of Osman, the empire's version of the lavish coronation ceremonies that took place in Christian Europe. It was not a place either Mehmet Süleyman or Ömer Müngün associated with stage magicians. And yet here in a small white house on Ballı Baba Sokak, overlooking the vast graveyard, lived Buyu Hanım, one of the city's most experienced magicians.

'Don't know whether I'd be able to put up with all these tombs,' Ömer said as they stood on the doorstep of the white nineteenth-century house. 'Bad enough my sister coming home every night telling us about people's septic pressure sores.'

'One thing the dead can't do is hurt anyone,' Süleyman said. Then he added, 'In my experience.'

'Oh, I don't know about that,' Ömer said. 'Our Peri's seen some things looking after the dying . . .'

The wooden door snapped open and a tall woman said, 'Yes?'

The officers introduced themselves and were taken into a large room, where the first thing that caught their eye was a guillotine. As they approached, the blade came down, severing the head of a straw-filled dummy below. A tiny woman wearing a dinner jacket and fishnet stockings then stepped from behind the device to shake their hands. Buyu Hanım possessed a Venus-like figure made up of dramatic curves and smooth limbs; her face, however, was that of a sun-dried elderly teyze, wearing a long blond wig. It was quite a look.

Smiling, she completely ignored Ömer Müngün and turned to Süleyman. 'So you want to know about our members, do you?'

Süleyman came straight to the point. 'As I told your assistant, we are investigating the death of Nuri Taslı, known as Bartolomeo. He was shot sometime yesterday by persons unknown, who, we believe, disguised themselves as Mr Taslı's troupe in order to kidnap a young man at the Cihangir Bocuk Gecesi festival last night. As yet, we don't know why this young man was abducted.'

'Why do you think any of our members were involved?'

'Because the replacement magic troupe performed the trick they used to cover the kidnap of the young man well.'

'Says who?'

'Says a magician who was in the audience,' Süleyman said. 'Sami Nasi.'

Buyu Hanım pulled a face. 'Professor Vanek, to use his stage name, is an occultist, not a stage magician.'

'He's both,' Süleyman said. 'The point is, Buyu Hanım, that Sami Nasi knows how that particular escape illusion is achieved. And with the exception of the surprise appearance of the man in the tall box, it was achieved to perfection. So much so that during the seconds it took myself and my officers to react, the perpetrators and their hostage seemingly got clean away.'

She shook her head. 'They didn't.'

'What do you mean?'

'Let's go and sit in my salon. It'll be more comfortable there.' She called out to her assistant, 'Handan! Tea in the salon for three!'

'He seems so unhappy,' Eylül said.

Muffled up in overcoats, Sergeant Yavaş and Çetin İkmen were drinking tea, and in İkmen's case a brandy on the side, outside his favourite bar, the Mozaik in Sultanahmet. They were talking about Kerim Gürsel.

'How long would you say he's been unhappy, Eylül Hanım?'

'A couple of months now,' she said. 'He's lost weight too. I don't want to pry, his business is his business, but I respect him so much and I hate to see him like this. I've even wondered whether he is ill.'

Kerim had chosen Eylül from a large cohort of fast-track university graduates. The ban on police officers wearing hijab had just been lifted, and in spite of some resistance from his colleagues, he'd taken her on to work with him. A to-the-letter-of-the law officer, she was intelligent, moral and fiercely loyal to her boss. For a while Çetin İkmen had wondered whether she was attracted to Kerim – he was a man many found appealing – but she claimed she wasn't and he believed her. As far as he knew, Eylül was not aware of Kerim's sexuality.

'Then today something happened,' she continued. 'He was questioning a man in connection with our dead baby case and he alluded to the fact that his wife had, past tense, loved him when they married. I wouldn't have taken any notice had he not had such an unbearably sad expression on his face. Don't get me wrong, Çetin Bey, I know that all marriages have their problems. I don't live in fairyland.'

He smiled.

'But whenever I've seen him with his wife and little Melda, they always seem so happy. And I know it can't be easy for any of them because Mrs Gürsel is often in pain. Kerim Bey works so hard and it's all for them, his family! You know I come from a wealthy family, Çetin Bey. I go home to my parents' centrally heated apartment in Şişli. We have servants to cook our meals and clear up after us, and my bedroom alone is about the same size as Inspector Gürsel's whole apartment.'

'Eylül Hanım, you can't feel guilty,' İkmen said. 'One is born into what one is born into. My ancestors were peasants, but because my father was a clever man who chose to become an academic, I own this huge apartment here.' He pointed upwards at his building. 'You serve your country, you have nothing to be ashamed about. As for Kerim Bey . . .'

'I want to help him, but I don't know how,' she said.

İkmen himself was at a loss. He'd tried to find out whether Sinem Gürsel was seeing another man, but so far that had come to nothing. And yet if Eylül's assessment of Kerim's state of mind was correct, maybe he needed to try a bit harder.

'Talk me through your experience,' Buyu Hanım said.

'From my perspective, a person got into a large trunk,' Süleyman said. 'His assistant padlocked him into it and then stood behind it. The upright box beside it contained the missing man, Emir Kaya. Two other assistants raised a curtain in front of both boxes. Then there was a puff of smoke, the curtain was dropped and all that remained was the trunk.'

'Not the upright box?'

'No. That had gone completely.'

'And what happened just before the illusion?' Buyu Hanım asked.

'There was some sort of commotion involving a person dressed as what a colleague told me was an Albanian character called a dordelec,' Süleyman said. 'Some sort of spirit entity that is supposed to protect buildings. I didn't take much notice, to be honest. Just thought it was all part of the festival. And anyway, my wife was talking to me at the time. She was worried about the young man who was being placed in the tall box.'

'Why?'

'She felt that he was an unwilling participant.'

'Why?'

He sighed. 'My wife, Buyu Hanım, is a Romani woman. She was reading people's cards yesterday night. She read them for the young man and was disturbed by what she saw.'

'Mmm.' She nodded. Then she looked at Ömer Müngün. 'And you? What did you see?'

'I wasn't there, hanım.'

'I see.' She leaned back in her chair and steepled her fingers underneath her chin. 'Well, here's what I know,' she said. 'Firstly, that illusion isn't hard. The principal skills you need for it are physical speed and misdirection. I could teach that to performing monkeys.'

'Sami Nasi—'

'Sami Nasi does things his way and I do the same things mine,' she said. 'Inspector, what were you expecting to happen when you watched this illusion?'

He frowned. 'I think I was expecting the magician in the box to either appear outside the apparatus or in the upright box, possibly being replaced in the trunk by the young man. Or his assistant. But then again, the whole troupe were dressed identically in black and so it would be difficult to tell. Maybe the young man would materialise at the back of the crowd—'

'Did these performers say anything before the trick?' she interrupted.

'A few words of greeting. Ravel's *Boléro* was playing, but nobody spoke.'

'And so with a strange spirit jumping and yelling amongst you, as *Boléro* played, with people dressed in uniform black and no

130

expectations about what you were about to see . . . And then smoke . . .' She raised her hands, circling 'magic' movements in the air. 'Then nothing!' She clicked her fingers. 'As I said, misdirection. Maybe a little hypnosis . . .'

'Hypnosis?'

'Ravel's *Boléro* is thought to induce that or a similar state in some people,' she said. 'Inspector Süleyman, I have to tell you that you're not necessarily looking for magicians. I know, I would say that. We are a small community, we look after each other. But I would tell you if I had my suspicions about anyone. This is murder, after all, and Nuri Taslı was a popular member of our organisation. Like all of us, he suffered financially during the pandemic – no performances and then he caught COVID. He was lucky to survive. And almost as soon as he was through that, his wife began exhibiting signs of dementia. Poor Nuri.'

'Did his colleagues know about his wife's diagnosis?'

'Yes,' she said. 'He had a lot of support. But . . .' She shrugged. 'I was so happy for him when he got the gig in Cihangir.'

'Sami told us he and the family practised hard for it,' Süleyman said.

'Nuri was no longer young, and I think he and his wife would have had to rely upon their sons to do this well,' she said.

When the two officers got back in Süleyman's car, Ömer Müngün said, 'So what do you think, boss?'

On the way over to Eyüp, the sergeant had told his boss what Ecrin Taslı had said about how Nuri had been leaned on by someone to sell their house.

'Ecrin Hanım was worried I wouldn't take her word for the situation with the house because of her illness,' he continued now.

'And yet it would seem that Buyu Hanım and other magicians were concerned about Nuri's finances,' Süleyman said.

'Do you think that whoever killed Nuri wanted to get him out of the way so that they could negotiate directly with Ecrin? I

131

mean, she seems quite normal to me, but I imagine that given her illness, she could be vulnerable.'

'Possibly,' Süleyman said. 'I think we need to delve into the Taslis' finances.'

'Yes, boss.'

'While not forgetting the outstanding plight of Emir Kaya. Maybe we should start looking at possible connections between Emir and Nuri Taslı . . .'

Chapter 10

The Azure carpet shop in Çemberlitaş was one of those retail outlets that didn't know what it wanted to be. Housed in a tall nineteenth-century stone building close to the Çemberlitaş Hamam, the lower facade had been ripped off and replaced by a vast sheet of plate glass and a flashing neon sign. One large Ottoman court carpet was showcased in this window; behind it could be seen a rather dingy shop with several men sitting on piles of small kilims.

When Kerim Gürsel entered, one of the men got up to greet him while the others just watched him with suspicion, especially after he showed them his badge. After a short wait, he was taken to see Fazlı Bey in his office – a minimalist place consisting of a desk, two chairs and a computer.

As soon as Fazlı had ordered tea, he said, 'I suppose this is about my father.'

'No,' Kerim said. 'Your sister. Do you know where she is?'

In the flesh, Fazlı Paşahan was much pudgier than in his photographs online. Also his teeth were even whiter than Kerim had ever imagined teeth could be.

Fazlı shook his head. 'I don't know who put you on to me, Inspector, but I don't really "do" my family.'

'What does that mean?'

'It means I don't have much to do with them,' he said. 'It's been like that since my mother died five years ago. And just to be clear, and in line with what I've told every police officer since my father

133

left the country, I don't know where he is. I don't like him, we don't get on and I am totally at odds with what he says in his podcasts. When he talks about pious community leaders indulging in gambling, womanising and financial malpractice, he's describing himself, not them.'

Kerim was unimpressed by the young man's protestations of political conformity. 'Did you know that your sister was alleged to be with some of your relatives in London?'

'No,' he said. 'I didn't.'

'You attended her engagement party last year,' Kerim said.

'There are certain occasions one has to go to. Anyway, that was before my father lost his mind.'

'So your father's disappearance has damaged your family?'

'Of course!' Fazlı said.

'You condemn your father very readily.'

'I know him. And so do you. He's a gangster. I've made it very clear to your people and the press where I stand.'

'But he's your father.'

'We don't choose our parents, Inspector.'

'What about your sister? Where does she stand on your father?'

'She loves him. She's like him. Anything for money. Anyway, if she's in London—'

'She isn't,' Kerim said. 'According to UK immigration, she hasn't entered that country. I should also add that our own records do not show her leaving this country.'

'Then I'm at a loss . . .'

'Do you know any of her friends? Might she have left the city?'

'I don't know,' Fazlı said. 'Doesn't her fiancé know?'

'No.'

'Then I can't help you. If she had left the country, I'd say she was probably with my father. But she hasn't, and so I don't know.'

Their tea arrived, and after the assistant had served them and gone, Kerim said, 'Mr Paşahan, can you tell me about your sister's relationship with your father?'

'I've told you, she supports him. They were always close. When our parents divorced, she took his side even though my mother's subsequent death was partly down to him.'

'In what way?'

'He terrorised her,' Fazlı said. 'Threw her out on the street. She had to come and live with me. I came home from work one day and found her dead in my bathroom. She'd swallowed a whole packet of tranquillisers. She was so humiliated she didn't want to live any more.'

'I'm sorry.'

Fazlı Paşahan had tears in his eyes when he described his mother's death. It was difficult to interpret his impassioned diatribe as anything but genuine. But when Kerim left the Azure carpet shop, he still wasn't convinced. Atila Avrant, Sümeyye Paşahan's fiancé, had been very clear about how he felt about Fazlı. He had described him as 'unnatural', and, while Kerim hadn't felt anything like that emanating from the man, it put a question in his mind about whether Fazlı Paşahan was protesting against his father too much. Also he had got no further forward in finding Sümeyye.

He looked at his phone and saw that it was almost eight o'clock. He should, he knew, go home. But would he?

'I heard about it,' the old man said. 'But I wasn't here. The shop was shut.'

'Why was that?' scene-of-crime officer Sergeant Hikmet Yıldız asked. 'Surely the festival would bring more money your way.'

'Why? Our shop is Albanian, like us. Bocuk Gecesi is a Thracian custom. We're not Thracian.'

'No, but—'

'We were shut,' repeated the old man, Xemal Shehu.

135

Inspector Süleyman had told Yıldız about the dordelec – about how it had run through the crowds just before the magic show at the top of the Kumrulu Yokuşu Steps.

'If a dordelec is hanging outside a building, it means that building is empty,' the old man continued.

Yıldız said, 'It got down and ran about screaming.'

'Then it wasn't a dordelec, it must've been someone dressed as a dordelec.'

'Any idea who?'

'Someone who wants to discredit Albanians? I don't know. But that's possible. I'd look at people who call us "scum" and "primitive" if I were you. You'll be spoilt for choice,' Xemal Shehu said gloomily.

Yıldız let him go. Scene-of-crime officers had minutely investigated the Kumrulu Yokuşu Steps and uniform had interviewed hundreds of people both in person and by phone, and still they had no idea about the whereabouts of Emir Kaya. Like all the old İstanbul districts, Cihangir was a maze. Now it was dark and also spitting with rain, and so Yıldız decided it was time to call off the operation for the night. Everyone was exhausted.

Çetin İkmen had two surprises that evening. The first was the appearance of Peri Müngün at his door, and the second, half an hour later, the arrival of his friend Mehmet Süleyman.

Peri, who worked at the Surp Pirgic Hospital in Yedikule, had managed to swap shifts with a colleague and had turned up to spend the night with İkmen, who had been delighted. She'd been lying beside him on his bed when Süleyman had arrived.

When İkmen answered the door, Süleyman said, 'I'm sorry to just turn up, Çetin, but I need to speak to you. Hope I'm not disturbing you . . .'

He stepped inside. People did that when they visited the İkmen apartment. They knew they'd never be turned away.

'Not at all,' İkmen said as he followed his friend into the living room. 'Tea? Something stronger?'

Samsun, who was embroidering a piece of cloth and watching television, said, 'Mehmet Bey.'

'Samsun Hanım.'

'You know he's got his lady friend over, don't you?' Samsun said.

Süleyman turned to İkmen. 'Oh Çetin! If you'd rather I went . . .'

While Ömer Müngün wasn't totally entranced by the idea of his older sister dating a man twenty years her senior, most of İkmen's friends were delighted. His wife had died back in 2016 and he'd been alone for a long time when he got together with Peri in 2020. And everyone liked Peri. Sharp, witty and clever, she was a perfect match for the 'old man'.

'Oh, it's no problem, dear boy,' İkmen said. 'Sit down. I'll get the rakı.'

At that moment, a slightly bleary-eyed Peri walked into the room. 'Hello, Inspector Süleyman.'

'Peri Hanım . . .'

'You know you boys are going to have to go and talk about death on the balcony,' Samsun said. 'Can't expect Peri Hanım and me to sit out in the cold. Anyway, there's a new Alp Navruz dizi coming up and I'd rather die than miss it. When you get to my age, all you can do is look at handsome young men.'

Peri sat down beside Samsun and looked at her embroidery. 'That's good!' she said.

İkmen came out of the kitchen carrying a tray containing a rakı bottle, a water carafe and two glasses. He bent to kiss Peri on the head and said to Süleyman, 'I'm sorry about Samsun, Mehmet. But she's right, the TV is her domain and there is no way I'm going to risk my beloved Peri catching a chill outside.'

'Oh, I am so delicate! So precious!' Peri said sarcastically.

İkmen opened the door to the balcony. 'You are to me, my darling.'

Once settled outside, Süleyman got straight to the point.

'Çetin, how well do you know Sami Nasi?'

İkmen frowned. 'You don't suspect Sami, do you?'

'No, but . . .'

'But what?'

Süleyman breathed in. 'I've been speaking to Buyu Hanım, the head of the Society of Turkish Magicians. I wanted to sound her out about what happened last night. She was emphatic that none of her members would do such a thing.'

'She would be,'

'Of course. But she also told me that last night's illusion was simple. The way she put it, she could train monkeys to do it. Sami Nasi told me one would have to be an experienced magician to pull the trick off. Now I'm not saying Sami is wrong . . .'

'Sami isn't a member of any society as far as I'm aware,' İkmen said.

'Buyu Hanım described him as an occultist,' Süleyman said. 'And not in a positive way.'

İkmen laughed. 'Sami's difficult,' he said. 'He guards everything he does very jealously. He'll have you believe his tricks aren't tricks at all but "real" magic, and I for one don't know whether he's right about that. I've had too many . . . experiences, shall we say. And I know there are those, not all of them mad, who believe he may very well have done a deal with the devil.'

'Çetin, Nuri Taslı was worried about money. Both his wife and Buyu Hanım told us this. He lost a lot of work during COVID and now his wife has early-onset dementia. One can still converse with her, but of course there is an issue around reliability. However, she told Ömer that Nuri was being leaned on by someone to sell their house in Ortaköy. It's Ecrin Taslı's ancestral home and so Nuri wouldn't sell.'

'If, as I think, you're suggesting that someone killed Nuri for his house, I have to ask why,' İkmen said. 'There are lots of old Ottoman houses for sale these days.'

'I did ponder on that,' Süleyman said. 'I came up with its vast footprint. Ecrin's house is historically important inasmuch as it belonged to her great-great-grandfather, who was in charge of the horses at Yıldız Palace when Abdul Hamid II was sultan. It looks from the front like a lot of the other nineteenth-century houses in Ortaköy. It's only when you get round the back that you realise how big the plot actually is. The garden, while narrow, is a good hundred metres in length, and at the bottom it opens out into a small field, which is where Nuri had his workshop. You could build a lot of property on that site without even touching the house. And in today's climate of mass building programmes, it would be quite a prize.'

'You couldn't build a tower block in Ortaköy,' İkmen said.

Süleyman raised an eyebrow. 'You or I wouldn't, Çetin,' he said. 'It would totally destroy the slightly bohemian atmosphere of the place. But we both know that there are people who would, and some of those people would find ways around any planning restrictions that might apply.'

'Mmm.' İkmen nodded. 'Your missing artist Emir Kaya had something to say about that, didn't he?'

She couldn't eat. Until she knew where her brother was, her stomach just wouldn't allow her to do so. And that conversation she'd had with Merve Karabulut earlier in the day was still haunting her.

Of an age, Meryem and Merve had been friends when the tattooist had first moved into Cihangir. Merve was a very skilful artist, which had meant that she'd got close to Emir too. After about a year, it came to Meryem's attention that sometimes her brother would tell Merve things he wouldn't tell her. Like about his relationships. It made sense. Meryem was his sister and he was embarrassed talking about women to her. And he was shy.

However, by this time, she had worked out that Merve had a serious addiction problem. Sometimes, if her usual dealer couldn't get her anything, she couldn't work. It was also then that she could get spiteful and aggressive. But then Meryem had her own small problem with addiction and had taken to small-time dealing to fulfil her needs. Sometimes she helped Merve out. Meryem usually had something for her, but one day four months earlier she had not. Which was when Merve told her about Emir.

'You do know that your brother has a little habit too, don't you?' she'd said in a fit of frustrated vindictiveness.

Meryem, who hadn't known this, had been appalled. She'd always kept her little brother away from such things. Had Merve introduced him to drugs?

She'd denied it, of course. But then she'd come out with something else that had hit Meryem like a truck. Emir's habit, it seemed, emanated from his latest girlfriend, who according to Merve was a drug dealer and was involved in organised crime. Meryem had almost lost her mind when she'd found out the woman's name. It was then that she'd begun giving Emir some of her own stash, to stop him going to see his girlfriend. However, mercifully, the relationship had soon finished.

But now Emir was missing. Meryem lay down on her bed and curled herself into a ball.

'I'm not doing any readings tonight,' Gonca said as she put a plate of lamb chops, pilav and peppers down in front of her husband.

'Good.'

He looked down at the food and smiled. Gonca's sister Didim had been at the house most of the day and she had almost certainly cooked this. But he didn't say anything.

Gonca poured water for them both from the bottle on the kitchen table and then drank.

'Aren't you having anything to eat?' Mehmet asked as she sat across the table from him.

'Didim made me eat lunch with her,' she said. 'I can't have two meals a day, I'll get fat.'

He shrugged.

'You affect a casual attitude, Mehmet Bey Efendi,' she said. 'But if I turn into a huge barrel of grease you will turn your eyes elsewhere.'

He reached over the table and took her hand. 'I will never leave you, goddess,' he said. 'I love you, and you can do things to and for me that no one else can.'

She smiled. This little conversation was all part of the enduring proof of his love for her that she needed to survive. Sometimes she needed it on a daily basis. But satisfied now, she changed the subject.

'I let Sara out today,' she said.

Alarmed, her husband said, 'Let her out where?'

'In the house.'

'Again!'

'She can't be in the terrarium all the time, Mehmet,' she said. 'It was being cooped up that gave her bad skin before.'

'That was before the pandemic,' he said. 'Since then, she's always out! And you know what happens? One moment we have a large boa constrictor quietly lying underneath a radiator, and the next thing we know she goes into hiding for a week!'

'Oh, don't be such a child!'

He stood up, his meal unfinished. 'You know I can't relax if she's on the loose, especially at night. I know you love her, but I don't, and the thought of waking up with her in our bed . . .'

He ran up the stairs to the salon at the top of the house – a favourite haunt of the serpent in the past. Gonca got to her feet and followed him. She could hear him muttering. Didn't he understand that Sara would never hurt him because she loved Gonca? He thought the snake was entirely insentient, which irritated her.

When she got to the second floor, she saw that Sara was curled around the banister. Mehmet must have run straight past her. Gonca removed the snake and draped her around her shoulders. Then she walked up to the fourth floor.

She saw him at the top of the stairs looking out of one of the many windows she'd had fitted to give spectacular views of the city. He had his back to her and appeared to be staring at something.

'I've got her, Mehmet,' she said, but he didn't reply. It was then that she saw there was a large fire across the Golden Horn, possibly in Beyoğlu. Sirens blared across the city.

'Meryem!'

Emir?

Meryem Kaya's eyes flew open and she saw her brother standing at the bottom of her bed. Then he was gone. Had it been a ghost? Did that mean he was dead? But then her bedroom door closed with a bang and she heard the key being turned in the lock. A man's voice said something, and she heard her brother scream. This time she found her voice.

Hurling herself out of bed, she threw herself at the bedroom door. 'Emir!'

A gunshot outside made her freeze, then she began to tug frantically at the door handle, but to no avail. Someone had locked her in.

She ran to her bedroom window and pulled the curtains open. There was nothing to see outside, only the darkened back yard.

'Emir!' she yelled again. But nobody answered. Returning to the bedroom door, she tried once more to open it, but to no avail. She went back to the window, which was when she saw smoke coming out of the garage, the one-time family forge.

The house was on fire and she was locked in her bedroom! Why? And what had her missing brother been doing there? Questions made themselves noisy in her brain, preventing her from thinking. She made a thin, whining, frightened noise, like a confused elderly person. It wouldn't do!

She put a hand up to her head. Think! There had to be a way out of here. She knew that! She just couldn't think what it was . . .

Kerim had known that if Sinem looked out of their living-room window, she would see him having a drink outside Rambo Şekeroğlu's bar. What he hadn't counted on was that he would be joined by his neighbour Enver Yılmaz again. And if Sinem saw *him*, she'd accuse Kerim of wanting to sleep with him. He did, but he wasn't going to.

When he finally climbed the stairs to his apartment, however, his worst fears were quickly realised. He opened the front door onto a scene that was both strange and distressing. Madam Edith was holding Sinem's arms by her sides while his wife screamed.

'You!' she shouted when she saw her husband. 'Drinking with men! Laughing!'

'Sinem, you'll wake the kiddie!' Edith said.

Kerim moved towards his wife, who said, 'Don't touch me!'

'Sinem . . .'

Breaking free from Edith's grasp, Sinem pushed her husband out of the way and made for their bedroom. Before she went inside, she said to him 'You sleep on the sofa tonight!' and then she shut and locked the door behind her.

Now alone with Edith, Kerim flung himself down on the sofa and buried his head in his hands. Edith sat beside him and put her hand on his neck.

'I'm sorry,' she said. 'She saw you out of the window . . .'

'I couldn't face coming home,' he said. He looked up at her, his eyes wet with tears. 'I'm not doing anything with that man, I swear! I'm not doing anything with anyone! How could I? I promised her I wouldn't, and when do I get a moment to myself anyway?'

Edith went into the kitchen and poured him a glass of rakı. 'Here,' she said, 'drink this.'

He took the glass and she offered him a cigarette.

'Not allowed to smoke indoors,' he said.

'Melda's asleep and I don't think Sinem is going to come out of the bedroom any time soon, do you?' Edith said as she lit up.

Kerim joined her.

'I don't know how much more I can take,' he said when he'd finished one glass of rakı and then poured himself another. 'I swear to God I'm not being unfaithful, and yet she won't believe me. Sometimes I think she actively doesn't want to, that she's pushing me away. What can I do?'

'I don't know, sweetheart,' Edith said. 'All I can tell you is that she's reasonably normal with me and the kiddie when you're out. She only kicks off like this when you come home. That said, she's always unhappy these days. Sometimes she almost pushes me and Melda out the door.'

He frowned. 'Why?'

Edith didn't want to tell him about the suspicions she had about Sinem, and so she just said, 'I think she wants to be on her own.'

'She does that sometimes when her pain is too much to bear.'

'I know, love,' Edith said. 'And we're used to it. This unhappiness is new, and I can't fathom it out any more than you can.'

Kerim lowered his voice. 'You know, Edith, I wonder sometimes whether Sinem might be losing her mind. I wonder whether *I've* made her lose her mind. This strange life we lead . . .'

'She loves you, Kerim,' Edith said. 'Always has. Maybe you're right and she is ill in ways we've not come across before. Maybe her mind isn't well.'

Kerim shook his head. 'Question is, how do I get her to a doctor

144

when she hates me so much, and how do we keep this from Melda?'

His phone rang. Mehmet Süleyman kissed his wife one more time and then grabbed it off his bedside cabinet.

'Süleyman?'

'It's Buyu,' an elderly female voice said. 'I've been thinking about your Bocuk Gecesi problem and something has occurred to me.'

He sat up. 'Yes?'

'Do you have any video footage of the illusion in Cihangir?'

'Some,' he said. 'All amateur camera phone footage, quite bad. Why?'

'I was thinking about the nature of time,' she said. 'As I recall, you told me that you saw the curtain rise and fall in one movement.'

'I did.'

Gonca beside him, kissed his chest. They'd just finished making love and she was still sex-drunk.

'Mmm. And yet with all the smoke and the hypnotic music, I wonder whether you actually did,' Buyu said.

'What are you getting at, hanım?'

'I'm wondering whether the curtain was first thrown up,' she said.

'Up? But I would have seen that. And surely if the curtain was thrown upwards, we would have seen the trunk and the box.'

'With smoke pouring out or with a curtain that was overlong for the task you wouldn't,' she said. 'This was an illusion, Inspector, anything is possible. And while such a thing would only add at most a second to the time, that would have given those performing the trick an advantage. How long was it before you ran down the steps?'

He frowned. It had felt as if he'd done that immediately. But of course he hadn't. First of all he'd had to register what he was

145

looking at, then he'd reacted to the shock of those around him, and Gonca had said something . . .

'Maybe five seconds,' he said. He wasn't really sure.

'So enough time for these people to melt into the streets and yards of Cihangir,' she said.

'We searched them.'

'Immediately?'

'Well, not exactly . . .'

'Inspector, if you could get hold of that footage for me, I might be able to help you,' she said. 'Can you meet me this morning in Cihangir?'

He looked at his watch. Yes, it would be 'this morning' . . .

'Of course,' he said. 'I've got to go over there anyway. Can we make it about eleven? That will give me time to organise the footage for you.'

'Excellent,' she said. 'Meet you at the top of the steps.'

Süleyman put his phone back on his bedside table and turned to face his wife. 'Sorry, goddess.'

She smiled. 'If magical women didn't call you up in the middle of the night, I would wonder what was wrong with you,' she said.

Süleyman's phone rang again.

Arto Sarkissian sighed. He hated cases involving fire. Not only was one obliged to work around acrid smoke, but there was also all the water that remained after the fire was out, not to mention what felt like a thousand hoses to trip over.

He'd been called out at 5 a.m. This time his driver, Devlet, had been asleep, but he roused quickly and they arrived in Cihangir just after six. The police had already been called, and Arto soon found himself speaking to a very pale and slightly scruffily dressed Inspector Süleyman.

'So,' he said as he approached the yawning policeman, 'a body in a burning building, eh?'

146

'Yes, Doctor.'

He shook his head. 'God, I hate them!' he said. 'Almost as bad as drowning victims. You have to be so careful not to break bits off a poor soul burned to a crisp.'

'Well you'll be happy to know that this poor soul is not burned to a crisp,' Süleyman said.

'No?'

They began to walk towards the smoking ruins of the Kaya blacksmith's shop, treading carefully over coiled hoses as they did so. Firefighters directed them away from the forge, which was in danger of collapse, and led them into the smoking house.

The fire chief walked over to what remained of the stairs. 'We found him down here. We didn't know whether he was alive or dead at first, and so he's wet through.'

'How do you know it's a he?' Arto asked.

'Not burned to a crisp,' Süleyman said as he led the doctor towards the body.

When he saw it, however, Dr Sarkissian frowned.

'Have I gone mad, or has he been shot?' he asked.

'He has,' Süleyman answered. 'He is also, if I'm not mistaken, our missing Emir Kaya.'

Chapter 11

'Those hoofprints are definitely from the Kaya blacksmith's,' Sıla Gedik said. 'Meryem uses the original equipment her family got when they took over from the Greeks who were there before them, hence the crosses.'

'And you use the Kaya blacksmith's?' Kerim asked.

'Yes,' she said. 'A lot of stables in and around the city do.'

Kerim put his phone away. 'These casts were taken near to the site where we found the dead child,' he said.

'Oh.'

'I'll need to talk to your grooms again.'

'All of them?'

'No,' he said. 'Just the two who were riding black horses yesterday. Aslı Dölen and Zekeriya Bulut.'

He saw Eylül flinch at the girl's name. She had a problem with privileged girls. He'd have to watch that.

'Ah, Mehmet Bey . . .'

The thin, grey face of Mevlüt Alibey looked up at him.

'Mevlüt Bey.'

'I hear you're fully occupied again,' Alibey said.

They'd met in the corridor outside Süleyman's office. He'd had to come back briefly in order to speak to his superior, Commissioner Ozer.

'Yes, which means, I'm afraid, that any further work on the

148

Sofija Ozola case is currently on hold,' Süleyman said. 'As I'm sure you know, the situation centred around Cihangir is very much a live investigation.'

'I heard you found a body in a burning house?' Alibey asked.

'Yes.'

'Arson?'

'Not sure yet, but the victim was shot rather than incinerated.'

Then he remembered Kerim Gürsel. He hadn't seen his colleague for a few days now, but he knew that he was still working on the Kağıthane dead baby case – and that Mevlüt Alibey's nemesis, Görkan Paşahan, was involved. However, there was no time to go into that now, because he had to get back to Cihangir for his meeting with Buyu Hanım.

'Regarding Görkan Paşahan, however,' he said, 'you may find it useful to liaise with Inspector Gürsel.'

'Why? Isn't he working on an infant death?'

'He is,' Süleyman said. 'But there's a connection you may find enlightening. Call Kerim Bey. I'm sorry, I have to go.'

He ran towards the stairs and the back exit into the car park.

Peri Müngün looked across the kitchen table at Çetin İkmen. 'We should go away for a few days.'

'Should we?' He lit a cigarette.

'Now we can travel freely again,' she said. 'I mean, I know COVID is still out there. We're still seeing the unvaccinated at work. But we're vaccinated and so why not?'

'Did you have anywhere in mind?' İkmen asked.

He'd made them a very substandard menemen for breakfast. He couldn't help noticing that Peri wasn't eating. He wanted to apologise for his culinary uselessness, but he knew she'd just tell him to stop being hard on himself.

'East,' she said. 'Mardin, maybe.'

Peri and Ömer's parents lived in Mardin, and İkmen knew that neither of them had seen the old couple for over two years. How could he refuse?

'I've not been to Mardin for decades,' he said. 'That would be wonderful. However, if we're going to see your parents, how will you introduce me?' With a twinkle in his eye, he added, 'You're not intending to propose, are you, Peri Hanım?'

She smiled, and then reached across the table to take his hand. 'You will be my very best friend,' she said. 'Because you are.'

He got up from his seat and kissed her. 'I thought I'd got lucky there,' he said.

'I like us just the way we are, don't you?' she said.

'Of course I do.'

And he was being entirely sincere. İkmen knew he'd never be able to replace his dead wife. Fatma always had been and remained the love of his life. But he also loved Peri, albeit in a different way. He knew that, like him, she needed her freedom and her space. Maybe one day they might try living together, but . . .

'What are you doing today?' she asked.

'Ah, well I'm over to see Sami Nasi first, and then possibly I'll be in Tarlabaşı for a bit.'

'No point my asking why?' she said.

'None whatsoever. And you?'

'I'll go home, probably attempt to teach my nephew some more Turkish and then go to bed. I'm on at six tonight.'

'Gibrail's Turkish is still shaky, I take it.'

'If only his mother would learn, it would help,' Peri said. 'Sadly, a Suriani woman has moved into our building, and so now Yeşili has someone else with whom she can speak Aramaic.'

'What does your brother say about it?'

She shook her head. 'Ömer's given up. He's really good at looking after the kid, but Yeşili might as well be invisible as far as he's concerned.'

150

'Do you think he—'

'I don't speculate,' Peri said. 'But it was an arranged marriage, and so . . . Let's put it this way, I think there's a reason why Yeşili hasn't got pregnant since she had Gibrail. That's all I'll say.'

Later, they caught the tram together, parting when İkmen got off at Karaköy to take the Tünel funicular railway up to Beyoğlu. Sami Nasi didn't know he was coming – which was the way İkmen wanted it. Süleyman had been uneasy about some of Sami's opinions about the Bocuk Gecesi event, and İkmen wanted to find out why that might be.

The girl, Aslı Dölen, said, 'What's that got to do with anything?'

Eylül Yavaş had asked her about her relationship to Sümeyye Paşahan. The girls had been to school together, Notre Dame de Sion, and Sümeyye had lodged with the Dölen family while her father still resided in Uludağ. The question was fair, given the parentage of the dead baby, but Kerim Gürsel also felt that Eylül's method of questioning was harsh – and personal.

'Just answer the question,' she said.

'I rarely see her,' Aslı replied. 'I went to her engagement party last year. I've seen her maybe twice since. She visited me here a long time ago. Why?'

Kerim had told Eylül not to talk about the parentage of the dead child. Now Eylül clammed up.

Kerim said, 'Our scene-of-crime team took casts of hoofprints close to the site where the dead baby was found.' He laid out photos of the casts for her to see. 'Your employer Sıla Gedik told me that it is very possible these prints came from her horses.'

Aslı looked up and stared at him.

He pointed to the small cross on one of the casts. 'This mark, I am told, indicates that the horseshoe was fitted by the Kaya black-smith's in Cihangir,' he said.

He'd heard there'd been a fire at the blacksmith's last night, but

151

he didn't know any details. He needed to seek out Mehmet Süleyman and talk to him.

'You probably already know that Miss Gedik uses the Kaya blacksmith's,' he continued.

'No.'

'Really?' Eylül said.

Kerim put a hand on her arm.

'Very well. Now, the witness who found the child's body the day before yesterday saw a black horse, with rider, moving towards the Gedik Stables, having passed the crime scene. My understanding is that there were two black horses being exercised that morning: your horse Badem and Zekeriya Bulut's mount Yıldırım.'

'I didn't go down by the creek, I told you!' Aslı said. 'I don't know about Zekeriya. Ask him yourself.'

'We will. But in the meantime, we're speaking to you,' Kerim said. 'Miss Dölen, are you absolutely certain you didn't ride down by the creek yesterday morning?'

'I'm sure! Ask Mihai and İskender, they were in the field with me! Ask Sıla Hanım!' She shook her head. 'I didn't go to the creek and I haven't seen Sümeyye – although what all this has to do with her, I don't know.'

Sami Nasi's apartment in Çukurcuma was situated at the top of a tall nineteenth-century building with no lift. Consequently, Çetin İkmen had to climb up four flights of stairs to visit the magician. Such a climb rarely ended well, and when Sami opened his front door, he found İkmen leaning against his doorpost, wheezing.

'The smoking really has to go, you know,' he said as he allowed İkmen to tumble inside.

Sami's hall opened out into a large living room scented with burning frankincense. Elderly velvet-covered chairs and sofas vied for space with vast glass alembics and tables covered in retort

152

stands upon which sat bubbling flasks perched on glowing Bunsen burners. His interests extended beyond stage magic and occultism to alchemy.

'So,' İkmen said as he sat down on one of the sofas, 'found gold yet, have you?'

The magician huffed. 'You know that isn't what it's all about, İkmen. Don't be a silly old fool.'

İkmen smiled. He was well aware that alchemy, in the occult sense, wasn't about making gold from base metals but about perfecting one's soul.

'What do you want?' Sami asked.

'I want to speak to you about Nuri Taslı.'

He sat down. 'What about him?'

'I've heard he was hard up for money,' İkmen said.

'Who isn't? None of us performed during the pandemic.'

'Mmm. So I imagine that competition for the Bocuk Gecesi performance must have been intense.'

'I don't know,' Sami said.

'Why not?'

'I wasn't involved.'

'I would have thought you would have been,' İkmen said. 'What with Ruya being pregnant.'

'Who told you that Ruya was pregnant?'

'When we all met up in Cihangir, I could tell. I hope you're not going to tell me I'm wrong.'

'Of course not!' Sami snapped. 'It's just that . . . This thing you have where you know these things about people is . . . disconcerting.'

'Says the magician.' İkmen smiled. 'I don't know how it works. All I know is that it's something I have inherited from my mother. There's a look, a smell pregnant women have . . .'

'Spare me!' Sami raised a hand. 'I repeat, İkmen, what do you want?'

153

'Well, firstly I want to know why you didn't put yourself up for the Bocuk Gecesi gig.'

Sami sighed. 'Mainly because of the organiser. Ayaz Tarhan, he's called, and he's one of those who is sniffy about the unseen. Stage magic is one thing; what I do is beyond the pale to him.'

'Why?'

'I don't know. Maybe he's a fanatical secularist. There are still a few.'

'You know this for a fact?'

'I've met him, İkmen,' Sami said. 'It did not go well. Anyway, I was happy when Nuri got the gig.'

'Because he was hard up?'

'Yes.'

'More than others in your circle?'

Sami thought for a moment. 'I'm getting the distinct impression you know more than you're saying.'

İkmen smiled. 'Sami, do you know who was leaning on Nuri to sell Ecrin's house?'

'No.'

'Why do I get the feeling you're holding something back?'

Cihangir was not the sort of place where one routinely saw lots of police officers. Consequently some of the locals were looking distinctly nervous. However, when Mehmet Süleyman went to a small coffee shop at the top of the Kumrulu Yokuşu Steps to purchase drinks for himself and Buyu Hanım, he was told there would be no charge.

'Is it right you've not found Meryem Hanım yet, Inspector?' asked the owner, a small man in his forties.

Mumbling platitudes about not being able to comment, Süleyman gratefully took the drinks and then sat down with Buyu Hanım outside. He wanted to talk to her for a little while before they went to the steps. Should the body or indeed the live form of

154

Meryem Kaya suddenly turn up, his officers would know where to find him.

He handed the magician his phone and said, 'These are the best images we have of the illusion. Tell me what you think.'

Today Buyu Hanım was dressed from head to foot in black fake fur. It was an arresting look, although in Cihangir people were too cool to stare. After watching the video for a few minutes, she said, 'Interesting.'

'Meaning?'

She looked across at him and smiled. 'Let's go to the steps and I'll explain.'

He offered her his hand, which she took as she rose to her feet.

'You're quite the gentleman, aren't you, Mehmet Bey,' she said as she picked up her coffee cup. 'The polar opposite of Gonca Şekeroğlu's first two husbands.'

'I didn't know them, Buyu Hanım, and so I can't possibly comment.'

'Oh, they were thugs,' she said as they began to stroll across the road. 'The first one wasn't even good looking. Ugly and ill mannered. I've not seen Gonca for years, but I'm happy for her. And you.'

He smiled.

'Gonca is a remarkable woman. Her magic, unlike my own, is real.'

They both looked down the steps, and then Buyu Hanım said, 'So, it's like this . . .'

'Yes.'

Zekeriya Bulut, it seemed, tended towards the monosyllabic. Having slept very little for two nights in a row, Kerim Gürsel wasn't in the mood for young-man angst.

'Yes what?' he snapped. 'Yes, I saw Aslı Dölen and her horse Badem out by the creek the day before yesterday while taking part in the morning ride, or yes, I can confirm she was actually in the Gedik field the whole time.'

Zekeriya shrugged.

'Well, what's it to be, boy!' Kerim yelled. 'It must be one! It can't be both!'

Eylül Yavaş put a hand on his arm to calm him.

'She was in the field to start off with,' Zekeriya said.

'Well of course she fucking was!' Kerim was beginning to sound more like İkmen by the day. 'You all started there! You always do!'

The boy said nothing.

Kerim leaned across the table that separated them. 'Look, kid,' he said, 'it's like this: my forensic investigators have told me that two sets of hoofprints have been found near the Kağıthane Creek crime scene. One set indicates a heavy horse while the other set, I am told, comes from a smaller, lighter mount. It is the heavier prints we are particularly interested in because they are closer to the place where we found the dead baby. We have a witness who reports seeing a black horse and its rider moving away from the crime scene.'

'You said you had two sets of prints.'

'We do, and believe me, I am working on that apparent anomaly,' Kerim said. 'But that in no way lets you off the hook.'

'I didn't do it,' Zekeriya said. 'I might have passed by the crime scene, but I didn't see anything.'

'So you were definitely there?'

'I've never said I wasn't. But I saw nothing.'

'And yet the estimated timing of the child's death would suggest you were nearby at the very least,' Kerim said. 'The manner of death means that whoever did it would have been *in situ* for a few minutes only. However, and crucially, he or she would have to go to the site with a live, possibly crying, baby. But you are telling me you saw and heard nothing?'

156

'Yeah.'

'All I can tell you is what Nuri told me,' Sami said. 'The agreement was between him and them. And no, I don't know who they are because he never told me. All he said was that if he agreed to not doing the show, they'd stop pestering him about the house. He felt bad about it, which was why he didn't tell his family. He told me they had assured him they would make it look as if the family had been attacked. They'd tie them up, perform, and then be out of his life for ever. I went to the performance because I was supposed to lead the police to the house, where they'd find the family safe, if a little shaken. Finding Nuri dead was not something I expected. I tell you, keeping my composure in front of the Taslı family and Mehmet Süleyman was no easy task.'

'You should have told Süleyman all this,' İkmen said. 'Why didn't you?'

'How could I? In front of Nuri's boys, not to mention poor Ecrin!'

'Look, I know you don't live in the same world as the rest of us on a full-time basis, but surely even you realise that whoever these people are, they're not going to leave the family alone.'

Sami frowned.

Exasperated, İkmen went on, 'Nobody but a criminal would do such a deal. Nuri was dealing with criminals.'

'Yes, but—'

'And the young man those people took away, where is he? There was a fire in Cihangir last night and I heard people on the street talking about it being at the Kaya blacksmith's, where the young man lived. Now, Sami, I've not had a chance to speak to Mehmet Süleyman yet, but I suggest you contact him and tell him what you know right now.'

'. . . you don't run away, you stay where you are,' Buyu Hanım concluded.

157

'What do you mean?'

Süleyman and Buyu were looking down the Kumrulu Yokuşu Steps. Still closed to the public, the site was being investigated by scene-of-crime officers wearing white coveralls and plastic boots. There was a look of a 1950s invaders-from-space film about the scene.

'I mean that while I can see that the people in charge of the curtain and therefore in charge of the illusion threw the rail holding it up into the air before letting it fall to the ground in order to buy an extra second, nobody was going very far anyway.' She smiled at Süleyman's confusion. 'What did you do when you first realised something was wrong?'

He thought for a moment. 'I looked around to see what other people were doing. My wife was distraught. Just prior to the illusion, she had said she wanted me to save him.'

'The boy?'

'Yes. She called out my name, and then I ran,' he said. 'Down the stairs, looking from left to right as I did so. An ex-colleague, Çetin İkmen, followed me, but I told him to go back.'

'And do what?'

'Nothing. No! I told him to call the incident in. Also, he's older than I am, I didn't want him to fall and hurt himself. I nearly fell myself. I ended up on Lenger Sokak. I saw a beggar outside a house, but that was all. Nobody else. A couple of cars passed . . .'

'Did any of them stop?'

'I don't know. I asked the beggar whether he'd seen anything, but he was too drunk to answer. I ran back up the stairs. Oh, and when I ran down, I thought I could hear a voice at the bottom of the stairs. Sorry . . .'

'OK,' she said. 'My contention is this: your magicians and the young man were actually behind the banisters on either side of the steps.'

'I would've seen them!'

'Would you? What did you do once the initial shock had passed? You ran, downwards. Your eye was drawn towards Lenger Sokak because that was where you expected to see something.'

'Yes, but what about all the other people at the top of the steps? What about my wife?'

'They were watching you,' she said.

They had been. Gonca in particular, scared for him. He thought about it for a moment. 'Yes, but I looked, side to side . . .'

'You were moving,' she said. 'You didn't look, you took in impressions. Like the beggar. You said he was drunk, but was he? Did you go back and question him?'

'I . . .'

'You didn't,' she said.

He shook his head. 'But if all this is true, why didn't the young man call out if he could see me?'

'Maybe he *didn't* see you. Maybe someone had a gun to his head. Maybe he was immobilised in some way.' She turned back to the roads leading away from the top of the steps. 'Look at this.'

'At what?'

'Here we have one road crossing the top of the steps, the café we met in across the road and two small streets running on either side of it. Either side of the steps are buildings, lots of them. It's enclosed. One could even say claustrophobic.'

He frowned. 'I have to admit, I thought it was rather a small space in which to perform an illusion. The Rainbow Stairs would have been more appropriate, thinking about it, because there's more space for an audience.'

The Rainbow Stairs were a Cihangir institution. A much longer iteration of the Kumrulu Yokuşu Steps, they were about half a kilometre away. They were also contentious in some people's eyes, being identified with İstanbul's LGBT community.

Buyu Hanım smiled. 'And there you have lighted upon a very

159

important issue, Inspector,' she said. 'In order for a large outdoor illusion to work, the audience must be limited.'

'Really?'

'Really,' she said. 'This is because you can only hope to control or misdirect so many people's perception of an event at a time. You want to "disappear" the Topkapi Palace? You can. But unless you do it on TV, you can only do it in front of a small number of people. Magic, my dear Inspector, is about mind control, and none of us can do that with very many people or for very long without help.'

'Inspector Gürsel.'

Kerim was out in the car park, smoking, when Inspector Mevlüt Alibey approached him. Neither Zekeriya Bulut nor Aslı Dölen had deviated from their story about what they had been doing the morning the Kağıthane baby had died. Eylül Yavaş was still convinced that Aslı, at least, was lying and had suggested reviewing CCTV footage from Gedik and in the vicinity of her home as a way of proving, or not, that she had not interacted with Sümeyye Paşahan in recent times. But Gedik's CCTV system was faulty, and anyway Kerim felt this was pointless. Plus where did that process stop? Would they become involved in an operation to look at every piece of CCTV footage at every location where the two women might have met across the entire city? Eylül's antipathy towards Aslı puzzled him, and yet at the same time it alerted him to the notion that something might be wrong with the young woman. Eylül did not take against people for no good reason. Or did she?

'Kerim Bey?'

Finally roused from his reverie, he said, 'Oh, Mevlüt Bey . . .'

The organised-crime detective smiled. 'You looked a little distracted there, Kerim Bey,' he said. 'Problems?'

Kerim offered him a cigarette, which Alibey took. 'Thinking about . . . Doesn't matter. What can I do for you, Mevlüt Bey?'

160

'Inspector Süleyman has told me that you might have some information pertaining to Görkan Paşahan,' he said. 'Some connection with your current investigation?'

'Oh, well . . .' As far as Kerim knew, Görkan Paşahan's parentage of the dead baby was not as yet common knowledge. That said, Alibey was the officer tasked with bringing Paşahan in, by whatever means. 'DNA evidence points towards Paşahan as the father of the Kağıthane child.'

'Really?'

'Really.'

'And yet Görkan Bey is out of the country,' Alibey said. 'Hence my current enquiries . . .'

'Nobody is saying that Paşahan killed the child,' Kerim said. 'But there's something else too.'

'Where Paşahan is involved, there usually is something else, Kerim Bey.'

'The mother of the child,' Kerim said. 'We think it's his daughter.'

There was a moment of almost complete silence. Alibey's mouth gaped.

'And so considering the fact that you've been working on Paşahan and his organisation for some time,' Kerim continued, 'do you know where Sümeyye Paşahan might be now? We thought she was in London, but there's no record of her having entered the United Kingdom. In fact we have no record of her leaving this country, Any ideas you might have would be greatly appreciated.'

Chapter 12

Fire Chief Bilal Sönmez had two great passions in life. One was the care and welfare of his ninety-year-old mother Rabia; the other was fire investigation. One of the reasons he'd originally joined the fire service was because he'd witnessed a terrible house fire as a child back in his home province of Batman in the far southeast. Two entire families had been wiped out in a conflagration many thought might have been arson but no one could prove.

Spurred on by this formative experience, Bilal had become not only a fire chief but also one of the best fire investigators in the country. Leading scene-of-crime officer Sergeant Hikmet Yıldız up the stone staircase that led from the Kaya forge to the residential rooms up above, he said, 'Place is a bit of a maze. Not your normal apartment.'

'In what way?'

'Building's mid-nineteenth century and hasn't changed a whole lot since then.'

Yıldız shrugged. 'Not entirely uncommon, but ... Anything turn up about a second occupant?' He meant Meryem Kaya, who was still missing.

'No. But what I'm about to show you may mean she's still alive.'

At the top of the stairs, Sönmez took Yıldız into a heavily blackened room.

'This the seat of the blaze?' Yıldız asked.

'No, that's out in the hallway.'

'Arson?'

162

'Oh yeah. But this bedroom was locked from the outside. I fully expected to see a body in here. I mean, why lock a door from the outside unless you want to keep someone in, right?'

'I guess so . . .'

'Window's out, as you can see. But that would've blown due to the blaze. By that time, anyone left in the room would have been overcome by smoke.'

Sönmez walked to the back of the room and tugged on what looked like a charred door handle.

'What's that?' asked Yıldız.

'Cupboard.'

'So . . .'

'Or is it?'

The fire chief stepped inside the cupboard and invited Yıldız to join him. The smell of charcoal was almost overwhelming, until Bilal opened another door, which led into a room almost completely untouched by the blaze.

He smiled. 'Little mystery for you, Sergeant,' he said. 'False cupboard. No idea why. People having an illicit affair back in the old days? But if Meryem Kaya was locked in that bedroom, this is how she got out.'

Madam Edith had called İkmen just as he was leaving Sami Nasi's apartment.

'Sinem has asked me to go and get her medication from the pharmacy,' she'd said. 'Insisted I take Melda with me.'

As if on cue, İkmen had heard the child cry out, 'Park first, Auntie Edith!'

'Via Gezi Park, as you can hear,' Edith continued. 'Although God help me, the pharmacy is a mission on its own. Crowded with all the dead and half-dead of Tarlabaşı. Generally takes me an hour just to get the medication. So if you want to see what madam might be up to during that time, Çetin Bey . . .'

163

So now İkmen was in Tarlabaşı, in the Poisoned Princess apartments, breathless after climbing four flights of stairs and looking at the Gürsels' closed and silent front door.

'Where?' Süleyman asked the front desk officer as he entered headquarters.

The officer, an older man who sat down a lot on account of a bad back, had called Süleyman over with news that 'some Arab' wanted to see him. Said Arab had turned out to be magician Sami Nasi. After being scolded by İkmen for withholding information about the late Nuri Taslı, he'd come to confess everything to Mehmet Bey.

Up in Süleyman's office, Sami told the inspector what he'd told İkmen.

'I didn't want to mention Nuri's deal in front of his family,' he said. 'Rightly or wrongly, I thought it would have just about finished Ecrin.'

'I take your point,' Süleyman said, 'but you should have come to me straight after. Had I known about this "arrangement", I could maybe have altered the focus of my investigation to take it into account. However, now that I do know, I have to decide what happens next.'

Ömer Müngün was leaning back on his chair with one foot on his desk. 'We'll have to speak to the Taslıs again, boss.'

Sami said, 'Oh . . .'

'We have no choice,' Süleyman said. 'We only have your word, or rather Nuri Taslı's word, that they didn't know about his arrangement with these people. Are you sure you don't have any idea who they were?'

'None,' Sami said.

'Were they Turkish? Do you know what part of the city they came from?'

'I don't know,' Sami said. 'When the character who was

164

supposed to be Nuri came on stage and spoke, he did it in that comedy Italian accent Nuri had stopped using years ago. But that means nothing.'

'Anything else?'

'No! I know nothing, Mehmet Bey! To be honest with you, I didn't want to know. And Nuri was fine with that. He even told me that the less I knew, the better.'

'And yet he wanted you to lead us to his house after the event.'

'He did.' Sami shrugged. 'We were both magicians. We know how to lie. Maybe I shouldn't say that to you, but . . .'

'No, maybe you shouldn't.'

'The fact that I wanted things to work out for Nuri so much blinded me to the danger he was in. But I honestly thought it was OK.'

'Sami, do you know when Nuri was awarded the Bocuk Gecesi job?'

'Some time ago.'

'Years? Months?'

'When we came out of lockdown last year.'

'And do you know when he received this offer from persons unknown?'

Sami thought for a moment. 'Recently. Two, three weeks maybe.'

'Did you get any indication from him as to why?'

'I told you—'

'No, not why the offer was made, but why at that time?'

He paused to think again and then said, 'I got the impression these people had a problem. They needed Nuri to help them solve it.'

A problem involving the now dead Emir Kaya. But what could that be?

Once Sami Nasi had gone, Süleyman said to his deputy, 'The organiser of the Bocuk Gecesi event . . .'

'Ayaz Tarhan,' Ömer said.

Süleyman nodded. 'Miniature artist. Invite him to come and see us, will you, Ömer?'

Nothing happened. İkmen lit a cigarette and leaned against the wall in the corridor outside the Gürsels' apartment, positioned so that if Sinem looked through the spyhole in the door, she wouldn't see him. Whatever she was doing, she was doing it quietly. İkmen wondered what she'd do if she suddenly opened the door and found him lurking outside. But then she wouldn't do that because Sinem Gürsel was slow, her movements inaccurate and painful.

Unbidden, a horrible thought entered his mind. Who would want a woman who was crippled by pain much of the time? Pretty though she was, Sinem's lovely face was frequently twisted by agonies that just, as he understood it, got worse with age. Kerim loved her and so his perception was mediated by that. But for someone to have an affair with her . . .

Maybe Samsun was right and it was Kerim who was being unfaithful to Sinem. It would account for her sadness, her retreat into self-harm. Did she periodically want Edith and Melda out of the way so that she could indulge her need to cut? But what of the missing underwear? Did she use that to maybe clear up the blood that flowed afterwards? But if that was the case, why not use kitchen towel or paper tissues, which could be more easily disposed of? Her behaviour made no sense. Was she having a breakdown, maybe?

Then he heard a voice. Low and deep. He couldn't make out what was said, but there was anger behind it. Deep, whispered and cold. He moved closer to the door, but the voice didn't come again. Silence washed in.

Had it sounded like Sinem Gürsel? No, her voice was light and a tiny bit husky. Had it been a man's voice?

And then suddenly there *was*, unmistakably, Sinem Gürsel's voice, screaming.

166

'No! No!'

And Çetin İkmen found himself with a choice.

To smash his fist on that door – or not?

Eylül Yavaş looked away from her computer screen. 'Sir, just got a message from Inspector Görür about the dead girl in Dolapdere. You're copied in.'

'Am I?'

Kerim Gürsel had been thinking about the fruitless interviews with Zekeriya Bulut and Aslı Dölen. He couldn't shake the conviction that what they were saying wasn't entirely true. It was near the truth and he had no reason to wholeheartedly believe it wasn't the truth, but . . .

'Says a man answering the description of Berkan Ramazanov has been apprehended trying to cross the border into Syria at Nusaybin,' Eylül said. 'Inspector Görür is on his way down there.'

Now that the Tirimujgan Ramazanov case had passed to the young and eager Mehmet Görür, the sight of that horribly bloated dead girl in Dolapdere had largely left Kerim's mind. But now it was back.

'Didn't Ramazanov have a wife?' he asked Eylül.

'Yes. Perestu,' she said. 'No mention of her.'

'Well I wish Görür good fortune,' Kerim said. 'Whatever the outcome.'

'Yes, sir.' She paused. 'Sir . . .'

But Kerim held up a hand to silence her. 'Sorry, Eylül,' he said. 'Just had a message from Mehmet Bey asking whether we can meet him in his office at about five.' He looked up. 'That convenient for you?'

'Yes, sir.'

Kerim messaged Süleyman back, muttering, 'No idea what it's about . . .'

'Sir?'

'Eylül.' He looked at her again and smiled. 'You were about to say?'

'Sir, given that we now know our baby was fathered by Görkan Paşahan on his daughter, I can't shake the conviction that Aslı Dölen knows more than she's saying. To start with, she was in the vicinity when the baby was dumped and killed. Secondly, the Dölen family must know the Paşahans well. Sümeyye lodged with them for years. Also, if Aslı and Sümeyye were close, did they share a love of horses? Aslı admitted that Sümeyye had visited her at Gedik. Did she do so to ride, or was it just to see Aslı? I know you're not entirely convinced . . .'

'Eylül, I'm sorry, but to me it feels as if you are rather fixated on this girl.'

'Only because I think there's something wrong here, sir. I completely understand that I have a personal antipathy towards girls like Aslı, because I grew up with them. I *was* one of them for a long time. But I still think she has some tough questions to answer. For instance, if she and Sümeyye were good friends in the past, what changed that? Sümeyye visited Gedik once at least, we know. Was she maybe looking at the place with a view to leaving her baby there when it was born?'

In the absence of Sümeyye Paşahan and her father, finding new avenues to pursue was difficult. As yet the parentage of the baby was not common knowledge, and the investigative team wanted it to stay that way.

Eventually Kerim said, 'All right, Eylül, set up a meeting with Sıla Gedik. Let's see what she says. Based upon that, we may be able to interview the Dölen family.'

But he still wasn't convinced. Two riders of black horses had been out that morning, and somehow, Aslı Dölen, with her connection to Sümeyye Paşahan, felt a little too obvious . . .

*

'Sinem Hanım! It's Çetin İkmen!' He banged on the door again. 'Are you all right?'

There was a pause. 'Yes, yes. It's just . . .' He heard her grunt. 'I have to get to the door . . . What do you want?'

'I heard you cry out,' he said.

'Oh, it . . . My pain . . . I'm sorry . . .'

Slowly she opened the door. Her face was flushed and she was leaning on a walking frame.

'Come in,' she said.

While he took his shoes off, he looked around. There were four doors off the small hall, leading to the living room/kitchen, two bedrooms and the bathroom. All were shut. The overwhelming smell of the place was of damp. Whoever the landlord of the Poisoned Princess apartments was, he didn't do much maintenance, it seemed.

'Sinem Hanım,' İkmen said. 'Are you—'

'The pain has been bad today,' she said. 'Edith is out with Melda getting my prescription made up.'

He knew this of course but said nothing.

'Come into the living room. I'll make us some tea.'

He let her go first, her walking frame clicking slowly across the scuffed parquet floor.

The living room, which had a small kitchen in one corner, was neat and clean, if battered by time, which had not been kind to the family's second-hand furniture. İkmen had noticed the old-fashioned soba heater in the hall, and though it put out some heat there, none of it seemed to reach the living room.

'Sit down,' Sinem said as she walked towards a samovar on the kitchen counter.

İkmen sat on a velvet-covered wing chair that had seen happier times. 'I'm sorry to have disturbed you.'

'Oh, that's OK,' she said. Then she asked him something he had not anticipated. 'What did you want, Çetin Bey?'

Chastising himself for not having formulated a cover story while he lurked outside this woman's apartment, he said the first thing that came into his mind.

'I want your advice, Sinem Hanım,' he said.

'Oh?'

He heard a noise and looked towards the glazed door leading to the balcony. Was he right in thinking he saw a figure behind the thick net curtains? He stood up. Sinem, pouring tea from the pot into a glass, said, 'Is everything all right?'

'A noise outside . . .' He began to move towards the door.

'Pigeons,' she said. Was there a level of panic in her voice. 'Edith feeds them with Melda every morning. They won't stop coming.'

'They won't if you feed them,' İkmen said. 'Even I get them, and I've got a cat.'

As he pushed down on the handle of the door, he heard Sinem yelp.

'Ow!'

'What is it?'

'Scalded myself!'

The look outside he managed to take before he went to help her was brief but revealing.

After he'd bathed Sinem's scald, they talked about how İkmen would at some point like to propose marriage to Peri Müngün. He swore her to secrecy. What he'd seen out on the balcony now stored silently inside his head, he knew he would only be able to get it out and look at it when he was with Süleyman.

Süleyman hadn't expected Ayaz Tarhan, the Bocuk Gecesi festival organiser, to come to headquarters as soon as he was summoned, but here he was. Clearly regarding himself as a spokesperson for the people of Cihangir, he said, 'We're all absolutely devastated by the death of Emir Kaya. He was one of our most significant artists. Inspector, have you found any trace of Meryem Kaya?'

'No, I'm afraid not,' Süleyman said.

Tarhan shook his head. 'If she did escape the conflagration, she must be somewhere. Wandering around confused, I shouldn't wonder.'

'Or scared?'

'Well, of course! That too after such a terrible fire!'

'I mean scared of who set the fire,' Süleyman said. 'Because they're still out there.'

'At the moment, yes. But I'm sure you'll catch them, Inspector.'

'Are you?' Süleyman leaned back in his chair. 'Ayaz Bey, have you always lived in Cihangir?'

'Er, no. Why?'

'Where did you live before?'

'Why—'

'Please answer the question, sir,' Süleyman said.

'I was born and brought up in Besiktas. My father still lives there; his legal practice is based there.'

'And you moved to Cihangir . . .'

'In 2010.'

'So you've been there for over a decade.'

'Yes.'

'You must know it well to be able to engage so many people and businesses in your Bocuk Gecesi venture.'

'Cihangir is full of people like me,' Ayaz said. 'Artists, academics, creatives. We all know each other and we know our neighbours, who are generally business people involved in hospitality and the antiques trade. A lot of Turks, but some foreigners too.'

Ömer Müngün, sitting behind Ayaz Tarhan, could tell that his superior was getting to the nub of his interrogation. Tarhan's shoulders tensed.

'And what about protection?' Süleyman said.

171

Ayaz frowned. 'Protection?'

Süleyman smiled. 'Mr Tarhan,' he said, 'Cihangir is a wealthy and popular part of the city. And while resident artists like yourself may not make a fortune from your pursuits . . .'

'We don't.'

'. . . business people, those who run coffee shops, bars and high-end antique emporia, do.'

'What are you getting at, Inspector?'

'Organised crime,' he said.

Ayaz Tarhan frowned. 'In Cihangir? Inspector, Cihangir is not Gaziosmanpaşa.'

'No. But if you think organised crime doesn't operate, in one form or another, right across this city, then you are sadly mistaken.'

'Yes, but—'

'Sir, we have reason to believe that your Bocuk Gecesi festival may have been used as a cover for illegal activities including kidnap and arson,' Süleyman said. 'Now I want you to tell me how this festival was organised and with whom. In addition, anything you know about the Kaya family may also be useful to us.'

His phone rang. 'Excuse me,' he said, and took the call. It was Arto Sarkissian.

'It's like trying to walk with a broken leg.'

Büket Teyze, the falcı, shook her head.

'And the doctors say it's due to that COVID thing?' she asked her friend Gonca.

They were sitting in Gonca's colourful salon in Balat, drinking coffee. Büket, a long-time friend of the gypsy's, had come to visit unexpectedly, with news. But for the moment they were talking about the stiffness Gonca had suffered from ever since she'd caught coronavirus.

'Yes,' Gonca said. 'Some post-viral thing, apparently. Might go,

172

might not. But as you can imagine, with a lusty younger husband to satisfy, this is not what I want.'

'Of course not!' Büket lit the cigarette Gonca had given her. 'What do you do?'

'Oh, he still makes me hot,' Gonca said. 'But I have to ignore the pain when things get a bit . . . well, physically challenging.'

Büket put a hand on her knee. 'Poor darling,' she said. 'Have you told him?'

'And have him go elsewhere for more athletic fun? No.'

'Oh Gonca, Mehmet Bey would never leave you! He's a good man, and anyway, he's older now himself.'

'Not too old that women don't still follow him about with their tongues hanging out!' Gonca said. She shook her head. 'Anyway, Büket Teyze, you didn't come here to talk about my problems. What's the matter, and how can I help?'

Büket Teyze crossed her arms over her considerable bosom. A woman in her early seventies, she'd known Gonca since the latter was a child. They were friends, and Büket trusted and believed in Gonca's magic completely.

'I want a curse, girl,' she said. 'One of your darkest.'

Gonca let out a long stream of smoke from her generous painted lips. 'On whom, and why?'

Büket drew closer and looked behind her as if checking for someone who might be listening. 'As you know, Gonca Hanım, I don't mind having rivals . . .'

'In your work?'

'Yes. In and around İstiklal Caddesi there are too many falcıs to count. I know that! I accept that! But next door?'

'You've another falcı setting up business next door?'

Büket hugged herself furiously. 'Bitch!'

Büket Teyze had worked as a fortune teller at the Kervansaray café on Galıp Dede Caddesi in Beyoğlu for decades. She had a good reputation and many loyal clients, which was just as well,

173

because she had no pension and no husband, and relied upon her falcı work to pay her rent.

'So who . . .'

'Some witch from Antakya,' she said.

Fortune tellers from the south-eastern city of Antakya were thought to be especially gifted in the art of divination.

'You know who?' Gonca asked.

'No. But whoever she is, she's got money. It's said in the mahalle that she's bought that building next door.'

'Really?'

What had once been a music shop next door to the Kervansaray had been empty for years. Like a lot of older İstanbul real estate, it was rumoured locally to be the subject of an ownership dispute.

'It's also said that this woman has friends in high places,' Büket continued.

'What high places?'

She threw her hands in the air. 'I don't know! But if she's bought the music shop, she must have real money. You know how property prices have gone up in the last few years. The whole thing is mad! Rents, too. Gonca, if she's got celebrity clients – actors in dizis, politicians – she'll put me out of business.'

'You have loyal customers . . .'

'I know. But what if she has stars like Selen Öztürk or Haluk Bilginer going to see her? My clients will think that if people like that go to her then maybe they should too.' Büket shook her head. 'Gonca, you've got to help me! You know my apartment in Tarlabaşı. Shithole though it is, there are worse, and I can't bear the thought of moving at my time of life.'

'How was it funded?'

Now that his call from Dr Sarkissian was over, Süleyman was talking to the Bocuk Gecesi organiser again.

174

'The way we always fund activities in Cihangir,' Ayaz Tarhan said. 'Via the community committee.'

'What's that?' Süleyman asked.

'A consortium of local business people, artists and residents. We set it up in 2012 when the district started to become really vibrant.'

'Were you one of the founding members?'

'Yes.' Ayaz nodded. 'We're all like-minded people. We want the best for Cihangir. This includes preserving our heritage, keeping the place clean and tidy. The Bocuk Gecesi event was arranged in aid of a new shelter for street animals. My family hail originally from Thrace, so it was my idea. I've been going to Bocuk Gecesi celebrations in Edirne for most of my life. Cihangerlis enjoy things like that. Turkish Halloween, what's not to like? I reckoned on lots of people attending, and I was right. Came from all over the city. You were there.'

'I was,' Süleyman said. 'With my wife.'

'So you'd know how it was funded, Inspector.'

'I know that my wife agreed to a fifty-fifty split on receipts for her tarot card readings, yes.'

'Mrs Süleyman was most generous,' Ayaz said.

'How did you make money from the shops, cafés and bars?'

'They donated a fee in order to take part. In return, we gave them a sticker to put on their store front and listed them in our programme. In spite of what happened later, they all did well, as I knew they would. Well worth their donations.'

'And what about the magicians?' Süleyman asked.

'Ah, we paid them up front.'

'Why?'

'Performers suffered more than most during the pandemic, and so we as an organisation committed ourselves to paying such people in advance. Had we hired a theatrical troupe it would have been the same. We get donations to cover such eventualities.'

175

'I see.' Süleyman nodded. 'What do you know about the Kaya family, Mr Tarhan?'

'Not much. I know they have been in Cihangir for over a hundred years. I suppose you could say they are local royalty, inasmuch as the forge is a Cihangir institution. Meryem is greatly sought after for her blacksmithing skills and Emir was an artist, as you know.'

'An artist of works some would deem controversial . . .'

'Cat houses?' Ayaz shook his head. 'Yes, well we all know what they represent, but he was also a very fine artist. I only ever heard praise for his work.'

In the sometimes rarified atmosphere of Cihangir, that was probably the case.

'Ayaz Bey,' Süleyman said, 'to go back to crime in Cihangir . . .'

'There's very little.'

'I know. But sir, let's be frank with each other, a bohemian community like yours is not vice free.'

'People drink . . .'

'And smoke cannabis. I smelt it on the air myself during your festival, and it isn't the first time. When I was single, I lived on Sıraselviler Caddesi and it was a common occurrence. Now, strictly speaking, cannabis is illegal in Türkiye. Our narco teams regularly raid premises all over the city, including Cihangir.'

'I don't know anything about that,' Tarhan said.

'Of course not, but you have to know that it happens.'

'What? People smoking dope? Yes, but—'

'Drugs do not, as I am sure you are aware, just appear,' Süleyman said. 'They originate either in this country or abroad and are transported to customers by dealers. Some are small-scale, people who deal as "hobbyists", you might say. But many dealers are big, and are backed by organised crime.'

'I've told you, nothing like that happens in Cihangir!'

'Then tell me what does happen,' Süleyman said. 'We both

know that drugs exist in Cihangir, a place close to the territory of a man who is a very big player in the drugs world.'

'I don't know any dealers!' Ayaz Tarhan said, desperate now for this interview to be over. 'I know people take drugs, but . . . Look, all I know is . . . this is hearsay . . . a couple of men . . .'

'Which men?'

'I don't know.' He looked around the room helplessly. 'Mehmet Bey, I think it's probably better if I speak to someone else.'

'Who?'

And then suddenly Süleyman knew. He sighed. While giving him an insight into a culture radically different from his own, his wife's presence in his life sometimes threw up difficulties he had never experienced before.

'Mr Tarhan,' he said, 'are these men by any chance Roma?'

Tarhan would not meet his eyes.

Eventually Süleyman said, 'I see.'

Chapter 13

Sıla Gedik couldn't come in to headquarters because she'd just called the vet out to one of her horses.

'Yıldırım has a puncture wound,' she said. 'The vet's just arrived but it'll take him a while to dress it. Can you come here?'

Eylül said that she could. However, this would mean that she would probably miss Süleyman's meeting at five. Kerim told her he'd fill her in later.

When she arrived at the stables, she found Sıla Gedik outside Yıldırım's stall.

'He picked up a nail in his left back fetlock,' Sıla said.

Eylül asked, 'You know where?'

'No. I have our field scrutinised for such things on a weekly basis, but of course Yıldırım does go beyond Gedik. What do you want, Sergeant Yavaş?'

'Is there anywhere we can talk more privately?' Eylül asked.

Sıla looked at the vet. 'I'll be in the barn if you need me, Dr Ergül.'

Once again in Sıla's straw-filled office, Eylül said, 'Sıla Hanım, do your employees ever bring friends or relatives to the stables?'

Sıla frowned. 'Why?'

'Just answer the question, please.'

Eventually she said, 'Sometimes.'

'Why?'

'Why? Various reasons. The boys live away from their homes and so sometimes their parents come. They're young, it's natural.'

'You don't mind?'

'No.'

'And friends?'

'That doesn't happen often, and to be honest with you, I don't encourage it. If the boys want to see their friends, they can go into the city and meet them on their days off. Unless those friends want to ride, of course.'

'And what about Aslı?' Eylül asked.

'What about her?'

'Does she ever bring her friends to the stables?'

Sıla thought for a moment. 'Only if they want a ride.'

'And do you know who any of these people are?'

'No.'

'Well would you have a record of—'

'No . . . It's unlikely. Casual riders, pay cash, you know . . .'

Eylül took a photograph out of her handbag and showed it to Sıla Gedik.

'Do you know this woman?' she asked.

Sinem was worse than ever – shaking, sweating, almost in tears. Once Melda had been placed in front of the television, Edith sat beside her and said, 'What's the matter, darling? Are you ill?'

White as chalk, Sinem said, 'I think I may have a stomach bug.'

'Oh lovey! Let me get you some peppermint tea to sip.'

'No. No, it's all right. I just . . .'

İkmen had told Edith what had happened when Sinem had admitted him to the apartment earlier in the day; about her pain, about the fact he'd heard her crying. He'd also said that he had a theory about what might be going on with her, but he wasn't prepared to say what that might be yet.

Sinem wiped her eyes. 'Of course, peppermint tea. That would be lovely. Thank you, Edith.'

Edith patted her knee and stood up with a grunt. Sinem hadn't said anything about İkmen . . .

'Your knee bad, Edith?' Sinem asked.

'Oh, just a bit of old-lady arthritis.' Edith walked to the kitchen and switched the kettle on.

'Just over a hundred milligrams, so one dose basically,' Süleyman said in answer to Ömer Müngün's question.

'Found on Emir Kaya's body?' Ömer wanted to make sure he got his facts right.

'Yes,' Süleyman said. 'Brown powder in a small plastic bag, according to Dr Sarkissian. Leads me to think he was probably going to chase the dragon. Maybe I'm wrong, but I imagine that old practice is somewhat more acceptable in Cihangir.'

'Why do you think that, boss?'

Süleyman smiled. 'Prejudice. I hold my hands up. I'm afraid I see people in alternative, outré places like Cihangir with opium pipes in their mouths. More romantic than shooting up in some restaurant toilet.'

Ömer frowned. 'Do you think it might've been planted on him?'

Süleyman shrugged. 'So far the fire service haven't found anything else of that nature at the forge, but they're not finished and so . . .'

'So what?'

'If Meryem Kaya knew there was smack on the premises, it would explain why we can't find her.'

'We sure there's no other body in there?'

'As sure as we can be,' Süleyman said. 'Which is why I've given the order to circulate her description. If she or her brother or both were dealing while Sesler was moving into Cihangir, I don't have to tell you how dangerous that might be.'

Ömer shook his head. Şevket Sesler was the pre-eminent Romani godfather of İstanbul. Operating out of down-at-heel

Tarlabaşı, he controlled most of the drugs circulating in the Roma community and all the significant fleshpots. As a young wife and mother, Mehmet's wife Gonca had been sexually threatened by a teenage Şevket Sesler. It was an encounter neither of them had forgotten. Sesler was, however, unaware of the fact that Gonca had told her husband about it when she became ill during the pandemic.

'We don't know that those Roma Tarhan heard about were Sesler's men,' Ömer said.

Süleyman gave him a look. 'Cihangir could be a lucrative market for him,' he said. 'People tend to think he will always confine himself to Roma districts, but Sesler doesn't discriminate. And don't forget it's not far from Tarlabaşı. People there have money.'

'Mmm.'

'Anyway, it's something else we will discuss with Kerim Bey when he gets here. He lives in Tarlabaşı, so he may know more than we do. And Sesler, as we know, isn't above acts of violence if someone crosses him.'

'You think Sesler may have kidnapped Emir Kaya?'

'I think it's possible,' he said.

Everything was lost – her home, her business, her baby brother. Even her clothes had gone.

Meryem Kaya sat on a bench beside the Bosphorus at Besiktas in her pyjamas and tried to ignore the stares she was getting from people going to and from the ferry port. She had hoped that her dishevelled appearance would simply mark her out as just another homeless person, but people seemed to think she was some sort of anomaly, which she was.

It wouldn't take the police long to catch up with her, and then what? Unless everything had burned to the ground in the fire, she was looking at some serious prison time.

The blacksmithing business hadn't broken even for years. For a while she'd relied on bank loans; then when she'd been unable to service those, she'd briefly got into destroying dodgy firearms for people whose names she didn't know. Only then had she branched out into narcotics, mainly because smack was her own drug of choice. Her little 'brightener' that had come about when the financial problems had become too much.

She'd never dealt from home. Only on that one occasion that she now regretted bitterly. When the tattooist Merve Karabulut had moved into the shop next door, Meryem had let her guard down. Merve was her sort of person: alternative, liberal, enjoyed a joint. Unfortunately she had also enjoyed something a bit stronger too, and so, in the fullness of time, Meryem had helped her out.

It had been one of her clients who had first given her heroin. A very rich woman who had what she described as a 'ranch' out at Polonezköy on the Asian side of the Bosphorus. Meryem had gone to shoe two of her horses one hot August day, and had broken down in tears when the woman had offered her lemonade. She'd kept all her anxieties about money to herself for so long. That day, they had all come flooding out. The two women had chased the dragon together, and Meryem had felt much better. That was how it began.

However, the product wasn't cheap – not after that initial free trial – and so Meryem began to fund her habit by dealing to some of the Roma over in Tarlabaşı. Before Meryem came on the scene, it was in Tarlabaşı that Merve had obtained her supply – from a different group of Roma. Meryem's product was cheaper, though, and so Merve never went back to her original dealer. And that was where things had taken a dark turn.

Rumour had it that for some months, Romani men had been spotted in Cihangir. Anecdotally, according to Merve, they were dealing smack. She had recognised one of them and was frightened. What if they'd come to take revenge for losing her business? Meryem had her own problems with her brother at the time and so she'd not taken it as seriously as she should have. Emir's entanglement with organised crime still obsessed her. And now here she was, alone, with nothing, facing the possibility of Merve, no doubt completely paranoid now her supplier had gone, flapping her mouth to the police. It was hopeless. Unless of course she used the one person she might possibly have power over . . .

Did Sıla Gedik react when Eylül showed her the photograph of Sümeyye Paşahan? If she did, Eylül didn't catch it.

'No,' she said. 'Should I know her?'

'Not necessarily.'

'Who is she?'

Two of the grooms came into the office, one of them Zekeriya Bulut.

'Sümeyye Paşahan,' Eylül said to Sıla Gedik. 'She's a friend of Aslı Dölen. Aslı told us she's been here.'

'Oh . . .'

'Sıla Hanım . . .'

Both Sıla and Eylül looked over at Zekeriya. For some reason, it made him step backwards.

He said, 'Vet's going now, Sıla Hanım. Wants to see you.'

'Oh.' She looked at Eylül and smiled, 'Sorry, I'd better go.'

'Of course.'

As she left, along with the other groom, Zekeriya's eyes followed her.

Eylül held up the photograph of Sümeyye Paşahan and said, 'Have you seen this woman on these premises lately?'

Kerim Gürsel had just put his jacket on in preparation for going to see Mehmet Süleyman when their superior, Commissioner Selahattin Ozer, called him.

'Can you come to my office, please, Inspector Gürsel?'

When he arrived, he found that Inspector Mevlüt Alibey was also there. The two men sat down.

'I want to speak to you both about the Paşahan situation,' Ozer said. 'Dr Sarkissian came to see me this morning and told me about his findings regarding this dead infant in Kağıthane. He is of the opinion that Görkan Paşahan is the child's father.'

'Yes, sir,' Kerim said. 'Although I'd disagree about that being his opinion. Dr Sarkissian has DNA evidence that confirms the child was conceived as the result of an incestuous relationship between Paşahan and his daughter.'

'Mmm. How low can these criminals stoop, eh?' Ozer said. 'Kerim Bey, you believe that Sümeyye Paşahan is still in Turkey, is that correct?'

'Yes, sir. I contacted the Metropolitan Police in London, where Sümeyye was rumoured to be living, and they have no record of her entering the country. There's also no record of her leaving this country.'

He saw Alibey looking at him with a slight smile on his face.

He continued. 'We are following every lead we have so far . . .'

'And yet it doesn't seem to have occurred to you that Sümeyye Paşahan may have left this country on a false passport,' Ozer said.

It hadn't, and Kerim suddenly felt cold. He knew he wasn't thinking straight. He wasn't sleeping, and his every encounter with his wife was like a knife to the heart.

'No, sir,' he said. 'An error on my part.'

'Which is why I think your team should in future liaise with Organised Crime,' the commissioner said. 'Paşahan is a divisive figure whose aim as far as I can tell is to spread disinformation about our political and military leaders, and for that he is a wanted man.'

Kerim, like most people, had never known why Paşahan had fallen out with his erstwhile allies. It was one of those questions that never seemed to be asked, much less answered. Why was that? He decided he would try to find out.

'Sir,' he said, 'do we know why Paşahan turned against his former friends?'

There was a silence.

Kerim Gürsel had not turned up to Süleyman's meeting. He'd been called into Ozer's office and so there was little to be gained by waiting around. Mevlüt Alibey was in there with them, and Süleyman imagined their meeting probably concerned Görkan Paşahan.

As they walked through the streets of Tarlabaşı towards the lap-dancing club owned by Şevket Sesler, Ömer said, 'I'd've thought that given how Görkan Paşahan is public enemy number one, the incest story would be plastered all over the Internet.'

Süleyman used the side of his foot to push a dead rat into a gutter filled with cigarette butts. He said, 'No statements have been made. I don't know. Logically you'd think information like that would encourage people to want him brought in all the more. But . . .' He stopped as they reached the club.

'Whaddya want?'

There was almost always one or more henchmen outside Sesler's place of business. This one was short, with a shaved head, a broken nose and thick rings on every finger. He clearly didn't know Süleyman and Ömer, and so the former showed him his badge.

The man peered at it.

'Police,' Süleyman said. 'Come to speak to Şevket Bey.'

'Well you can't,' the man said. 'He's busy.'

'No he isn't,' Süleyman said. 'Tell him Mehmet Bey has come to see him. I think you'll find his diary is suddenly empty.'

Eylül Yavaş walked back to her car, where she spent a few moments looking at the photograph of Sümeyye Paşahan she'd shown Sıla Gedik and Zekeriya Bulut. They'd both been very sure of the fact that they'd never seen Sümeyye before, and yet Aslı Dölen had welcomed her to Gedik on at least one occasion.

Like a lot of young women with money, Sümeyye Paşahan had spent much of it on cosmetic procedures. 'Enhanced' breasts and bottom gave her the perfect hourglass figure, while hair extensions produced long multi-hued locks that reached almost to her waist. Her face, which had always been pretty, had changed a lot in recent years, mainly due to the application of fillers and Botox, plus truly enormous false eyelashes. To Eylül's way of thinking, Sümeyye was still attractive despite these enhancements. However, one of the side effects of all this 'work' was that she now looked like a lot of other women her age. Mostly. One thing that set her apart from her peers was her very unusual eyes. The corners sloped downwards, giving her a slightly sleepy look. Clever use of eyeliner could lessen this effect, but it couldn't get rid of it. It was so distinctive, it wasn't something that could easily be overlooked.

Sıla Gedik and Zekeriya Bulut might not have seen Sümeyye Paşahan up close, but if the young Romanian groom Mihai, who had spoken to Eylül on her way out of the stables, was to be believed, one of them at least must have glimpsed her at some point.

When she'd shown him Sümeyye's photograph, he'd said, 'She came here sometimes until about two months ago.'

'Did she come with Aslı Dölen?' Eylül had asked.

He'd said that she had. However, he'd also said that he'd seen her at night.

'At night? Where?' Eylül had asked.

The boy had shrugged. 'Walking about outside.'

'When was this?'

He thought for a moment. 'Near Christmas, so December.'

'And she was on her own?'

186

'Yes. Although I did see someone following her one time. I don't think she knew she was there.'

'Who was there?' Eylül had asked.

'Sıla Hanım.'

Şevket Sesler had put on weight since the last time Süleyman had seen him. He'd never been slim, but he'd also never been the man with three rolls of fat round his middle that the inspector saw now. COVID lockdowns had not been kind to the Roma godfather.

Without being asked, Süleyman sat in front of Sesler's large dark desk and lit a cigarette. Ömer Müngün stood behind his boss like a bodyguard.

Sesler got straight to the point. 'What do you want, Mehmet Bey?'

'A glass of tea would be very welcome on this cold evening, Şevket Bey,' Süleyman said.

Sesler tipped his head at his henchman, who left the room.

'Well?'

'Well, Şevket Bey, you and I have not seen each other for a while. You look prosperous.'

'Cut the Ottoman crap,' Sesler growled. 'Why are you here?'

'Heroin,' Süleyman said.

'What about it?'

'Some of your boys offering to serve it up in Cihangir.'

'Says?'

Süleyman shrugged.

'Well whoever is saying it is wrong,' Sesler said. 'Cihangir's full of pot-heads, not junkies, you know that.'

'I know drug addiction of any kind doesn't discriminate on the basis of class.'

Sesler took a cigar out of a wooden box on his desk and lit up. He looked at Ömer Müngün. 'What do you think, kid?'

'I think Mehmet Bey is right, sir,' Ömer said.

'Course you do.' Sesler shook his head. 'You'd say black was white if he told you to.'

The henchman came in with a glass of tea, which he set down in front of Süleyman.

'I'm not interested in Cihangir,' Sesler continued. 'They're not my kind of people.'

'I thought anyone with money was your kind of person,' Süleyman said.

'I don't do religious fanatics and I don't do liberals, Mehmet Bey. On top of which, I don't do smack.'

Süleyman took a sip from his tea glass. 'Don't insult my intelligence, Sesler. You and I can and do co-exist because we are honest with each other. I know you supply.'

'So why don't you arrest me?'

'Because you are the devil I know,' Süleyman said. 'If I put you in prison, I wouldn't know your replacement like I know you, would I?'

Mehmet Süleyman wasn't picking up, and so İkmen sent him a text. From the mail pigeonholes on the ground floor of the Gürsels' apartment block, he'd discovered that their neighbour was called Enver Yılmaz.

When he'd gone out onto the Gürsels' balcony earlier in the day, he had noticed that their only adjoining neighbour had the door to his own balcony open. He'd heard a man's voice in the Gürsels' apartment, he was sure of it. He'd heard a man's voice when Sinem Gürsel was supposed to be alone, then he'd heard her crying. And when he'd gone out onto the balcony, Sinem had very conveniently scalded herself.

He sat down in the broken, blanket-covered mess that was his chair to think. Marlboro the cat jumped onto his lap and began purring loudly.

Why would Sinem Gürsel have an affair with her next-door

neighbour? In spite of everything, she loved Kerim, they had a child together and she wasn't a well woman. It didn't make sense. What did make sense, however, was what İkmen had blurted out when she'd asked him why he'd come to visit her.

First thing that morning, when Peri had told him they ought to go away for a few days, he'd joked that perhaps she intended to propose to him. She'd said that she preferred them to remain just as they were and he'd thought at the time he agreed with that. However, the way he'd so easily and speedily chosen the subject of a possible proposal to Peri when he'd been obliged to give Sinem an excuse for his presence at her apartment had made him think. He realised that he hated it when she left him to go home. He always wanted her to stay.

But it was too late to do anything about that now. And he had to admit that what he probably loved most about Peri was her independent spirit. Then again, if Sinem betrayed his confidence . . .

'Look, I don't expect you to tell me whether you're dealing smack in Cihangir,' Süleyman said. 'And quite honestly, at the moment, that's not my concern. I want to know who killed Emir Kaya and who burned down the family's forge. I'd also like to know whether those were the same people who kidnapped the boy and killed Nuri Taslı.'

'How should I know?' Şevket Sesler said.

'Because I have a hunch that if you're scoping out Cihangir for future business opportunities, you might know the dark side of the place rather more thoroughly than I do.' Even if he wasn't, if the Roma seen in Cihangir dealing heroin were simply opportunists, he would know more than Süleyman did.

Sesler leaned back in his chair and puffed on his cigar.

'Assuming I know anything, Mehmet Bey, why should I tell you?'

Süleyman smiled and leaned across the desk. He knew he didn't have to say anything. After what had happened all those years ago, when Gonca had rejected his advances, Şevket Sesler was afraid of the powerful witch – and by extension, her husband. If Gonca Hanım put a curse on you, you knew you were cursed and so did everyone else in Tarlabaşı.

Sesler sighed. 'All I know is that what's happened is way above my head,' he said.

'What does that mean?' Süleyman asked.

'Whatever you want it to mean. I don't have names, and even if I did, I wouldn't tell you. All I know is that I was warned off.'

'By whom?'

Sesler just glared at him.

'What were you doing or planning to do in Cihangir when you were warned off?' Süleyman asked.

Sesler smiled. 'Out of your own mouth, some Roma were witnessed dealing in Cihangir,' he said. 'That won't happen again, Mehmet Bey. But it won't not happen due to anything you may or may not have done. If you want answers, don't look down in the gutter at your wife's people. Look up.'

Chapter 14

'Sir, I think that's a mistake,' Kerim said. He was shaking with both fear and rage and he knew the other two men could see it. 'Sümeyye Paşahan has had a crime committed against her by her father. In addition, and I'm sure that Dr Sarkissian has made you aware of this, she may need medical treatment. And then there's the issue of the child. Did she kill it? We don't know!'

Ozer sat motionless in his chair. 'Inspector, I understand your concerns—'

'I don't think you do!'

Mevlüt Alibey put a hand on Kerim's shoulder. 'Kerim Bey—'

'Get your hands off me!'

Alibey withdrew his hand. Ozer said, 'Becoming overwrought helps no one. I'm not saying that your search into the whereabouts of Sümeyye Paşahan should stop. I am simply taking over this endeavour with the help of the Metropolitan Police in London. If Sümeyye Paşahan travelled to the United Kingdom on a false passport, we will find her.'

'All right,' Kerim said, 'but let me look for her here too.'

'No one is stopping you,' Ozer said. 'But discreetly, Inspector. In light of the notoriety of her father and the threats he has made to public officials, I am obliged to keep the investigation here low key.'

'Obliged by whom?'

'It doesn't matter. Not to you.'

The office became quiet. Kerim had started circulating

Sümeyye Paşahan's photograph to forces across the country. Eylül had taken one with her to the Gedik Stables. What did continuing in a 'low-key' way mean? And why were those presumably way above Ozer's head so worried about what might happen were the truth about Sümeyye Paşahan's relationship with her father to move into the public domain? More immediately, how were Kerim and Eylül going to work alongside Mevlüt Alibey and his organised-crime team? Inspector Alibey was a charismatic officer who demanded, and received, absolute loyalty from his troops. In return, he gave them his unwavering support, even when, it was rumoured, said troops crossed ethical lines.

Working against and for organised crime were two very different things – most of the time. But with Alibey and his team, it was rumoured that sometimes that wasn't the case.

Zekeriya Bulut didn't go out socially with the people with whom he worked. The girl, Aslı, didn't live at Gedik – plus she was posh, and being seen with her wasn't a good idea. Besides, he had a girlfriend. The other boys were only interested in getting drunk whenever they went into the city, especially the Romanian, Mihai.

Zekeriya showered and changed his clothes. He was putting on his boots when Sıla Gedik entered the bunkhouse.

'Where are you going?' she asked.

'Into the city.'

'What for?' She sat down beside him and attempted to stroke his hair. Zekeriya pulled away from her.

'I'm meeting my brother,' he said.

'I hope you're not—'

'I told you, no!' he said.

'All right! Don't lose your temper! You know what the deal is, and the police are still sniffing around.'

'I'm going to see my brother Tahir,' he said.

'So you'll be back tonight?' She reached out and massaged his thigh.

'No,' he said. 'Tahir wants me to go with him to visit Mum.'

'Wrong answer,' Sıla said.

'Yes, but—'

'I don't care how demented your mother might be, you don't need to visit her at night,' she said. She kissed the side of his face. 'She'll be asleep. But I won't . . .'

Mehmet Süleyman looked at his wife's latest work in progress. 'What is it?'

Annoyed by his lack of vision, Gonca pointed at the collage and said, 'Well, that's a white-powdered face, and down here are the Bocuk witches. I used bark from a tree on Tomtom Kaptan . . . Mehmet, it's not finished. Not even halfway.'

'Oh.' He looked at her and smiled. 'I'm sure it will be wonderful . . .'

'Don't lie,' she said, but she was smiling too, and then she kissed him. 'How your ancestors built all those wonderful palaces with no appreciation of art is beyond me.'

'We had "people" for that,' he said. Sitting on the large battered sofa in the middle of her studio, he pulled her down onto his lap. They kissed again, and then he said, 'So were you working all day, goddess?'

'Most of it,' she said. 'Büket Teyze came round for a curse.'

'A curse?'

Mehmet understood Gonca's card-reading activities. He didn't understand her art, but it wasn't a bone of contention between them. However, her status as a witch was something he couldn't always appreciate. Love spells were one thing, but curses?

'You're such a kind person, darling. I can't understand why you would do such a thing.'

'Büket is my friend,' she said. 'She's hit hard times. Not only has business been slow, but her landlord has put up her rent, and we all know how the cost of food has risen. All she has is that tiny apartment in Tarlabaşı and her falcı work. Now she says a new falcı has taken possession of the old music shop next door to the Kervansaray café.'

'There are thousands of falcıs all over the city . . .'

'Yes, but this one comes from Antakya, and you know how a lot of people rate them very highly. Poor Büket fears she will take her customers, particularly if this new woman has celebrity clients.'

'So wait and see,' Mehmet said. 'It may not happen.'

'I agree. But Büket is old and she was really upset, so I told her to find out the woman's name and let me know.'

'So you can curse her?'

'Yes.'

He sighed. 'I will never understand.'

'You don't need to. Now what about you? How was your day, love of my life?'

He smiled again. She knew he didn't often talk about his work when he got home. If he did, she got what he described as 'the redacted version'. Today, however, he'd been to see Şevket Sesler, and so every Roma in the city would know. He said, 'I went to see Şevket Bey.'

She loosened his tie. 'I know.'

'So why did you ask?'

'I wanted to see what you'd say, darling.'

She undid the buttons on his shirt.

'Gonca . . .'

'So Şevket Bey . . .'

'Nothing for you to worry about,' he said.

'No, but if it concerns the Roma, then maybe I can help you.'

'You can't,' he said. 'Or rather you can, by not asking me any questions about it.'

194

She stroked his chest. 'Come to bed.'

'And if you think you're going to get round me that way . . .'

His phone rang. It was İkmen.

'Sümeyye Paşahan came to the stables a lot until about two months ago, according to Mihai Albescu,' Eylül said.

Kerim Gürsel, who had been walking home to his apartment when he got the call, was now sitting outside Rambo Şekeroğlu's meyhane opposite his apartment block. Rambo came and put a glass of rakı and some water in front of him. Kerim mouthed, 'Thank you.'

'Mostly, according to Mihai, at night,' she continued.

'So not with Aslı Dölen.'

'Seems not,' she said. 'And one night, Mihai saw her outside being followed by Sıla Gedik.'

'He was sure it was Sümeyye Paşahan he saw?'

'Recognised her photograph.'

'So Sıla Gedik has been lying to us.'

'Yes, sir.'

Kerim sighed. He didn't want to go home, but he didn't want to go out to Kağıthane either. But what choice did he have? 'Eylül, we need to get out there.'

'I know,' she said.

'Also I need to speak to you about a meeting I had with Ozer this afternoon. Can you pick me up from outside my apartment building?'

'On my way,' she said.

Gonca was usually pleased to see Çetin İkmen. But on this occasion, she just let him into her house without a word and then disappeared. Once inside her colourful salon with her husband, İkmen asked, 'What's the matter with Gonca? Anything I should know about?'

Mehmet embraced his old mentor. 'Nothing of any importance.'

It was a remark that, had Gonca heard it, would have enraged her. She had been about to take her husband to bed when İkmen had called, and that was no trivial matter.

İkmen sat down. He'd given Süleyman the gist of his story about the Gürsels on the phone. What he needed to discuss was what to do with what he knew, and didn't know, so far.

'I was aware he hadn't looked well for a while, but I didn't want to address it with him in case I was wrong or he resented my intrusion,' Mehmet said. 'Kerim's private life isn't easy to talk about at the best of times.'

'I know. But when first Edith came to me and then Sergeant Yavaş . . .'

'So what are you thinking, Çetin?'

'I'm thinking I'm making what could be an erroneous supposition,' İkmen said. 'When I was outside the apartment, I heard a man's voice, couldn't make out any words, and then Sinem Hanım screamed "No! No!" I eventually managed to get her to open the door and I could see that she'd been crying. She told me everything was all right. The apartment appeared to be empty, and she offered me tea. While she was in the kitchen, I went out onto the balcony, which was when I saw that the balcony door of the neighbouring apartment was open. Then Sinem Hanım screamed that she'd scalded herself and so I rushed back inside.'

'And had she scalded herself?'

'Yes, although whether she'd done so on purpose . . .' He shrugged. 'Mehmet, I cannot say whether the neighbour was in the Gürsels' apartment. The open door may just have been a coincidence. But when I went out onto that balcony, it appeared to fluster Sinem Hanım. Does the name Enver Yılmaz mean anything to you? I mean, it's not an uncommon name . . .'

'In terms of crime, do you mean?' Süleyman asked.

'Yes.'

196

'Then no. I'll run it through our system for you gladly, but don't hold your breath.'

İkmen nodded. 'And there's something else.'

'Oh?'

Gonca arrived with tea, which she put down on the table between the two men.

Süleyman said, 'Thank you, darling.'

She left without a word.

'So it's not just me then?' İkmen said.

Süleyman leaned across the table. 'She intends to curse someone and made the mistake of telling me. I always knew this marriage would not be straightforward, but . . .'

'She loves you and you love her, it'll be fine,' İkmen said. 'Anyway, you don't believe in curses, so forget it.'

He smiled. 'Of course. So what was this something else?'

İkmen sipped his tea. 'There's a rumour, unsubstantiated, that Kerim Bey is back on the gay scene.'

'Really?' Süleyman frowned. 'What the situation might be between him and Sinem Hanım, I don't know. But he would never do anything, directly or indirectly, to jeopardise his daughter.'

'As I said, unsubstantiated,' İkmen said. 'But if it's true, maybe Sinem Hanım is taking her revenge.'

'She adores him!'

'Not at the moment she doesn't. According to Madam Edith, she won't let him anywhere near her.'

It was so sad; neither man felt as if he could add anything more to what had apparently become a domestic tragedy.

Eventually İkmen said, 'So no more involvement with the Görkan Paşahan investigation for you then, Mehmet?'

'No. The Cihangir situation has all my attention. Thanks to Sami Nasi, nudged I know by you, I have a clearer picture of the situation. Nuri Taslı was dealing with some serious people. No idea who.'

'Mmm. Pity in a way that you were taken off Paşahan's possible connection to the death of that prostitute.'

'Sofija Ozola,' Süleyman said. 'Why?'

'I always felt there was more to that than met the eye.'

'Like what?'

'Don't know exactly. I just found it odd that the woman who lived with Ozola accused Görkan Paşahan of being at the apartment at the time of her death and then failed to accurately identify him. Then she retracted her story. In effect, it gave Paşahan time to get away.'

'Witnesses often get confused.' Süleyman leaned back in his chair. 'However, I take your point, and Zuzanna Nowak, Ozola's flatmate, did seem to prosper after the event.'

İkmen nodded. 'Follow the money, Mehmet.'

'If I get a chance to revisit that case, I will bear that in mind.'

'Sümeyye Paşahan is Aslı Dölen's friend, not mine,' Sıla Gedik said.

She lived in an old wooden house on the edge of her property. Smelling of damp and in need of some serious renovation work, it was lit by candles, which, while romantic, was also, Kerim felt, eerie. Pictures of long-dead men riding horses in Ottoman uniforms lined the walls.

'Miss Dölen has told us that she only brought Sümeyye here a few times, some months before this alleged sighting,' Eylül said.

'When was it?' Sıla asked.

'December, around Christmas,' Kerim said. 'You were following her outside.'

'Where outside?'

Mihai hadn't told Eylül exactly where, but it would seem to have been near the stable block. She told Sıla this.

'What would she be doing wandering around the stable block?' Sıla said. 'I may well have been there at the same time, because I sometimes go and see the horses before I go to bed. But I can tell you now, I didn't see her! Who told you this nonsense anyway?'

'We can't say.'

'Oh? Really?' she lit a cigarette. 'Well I'd lay money it was the Romanian. I'll dismiss him.'

'On no evidence? That seems unfair,' Kerim said.

'Not your judgement to make,' she snapped back.

Eylül said, 'Where are your grooms this evening? I can see no lights on in the bunkhouse.'

'They have the night off,' she said. 'They'll be back in the early hours and hung-over tomorrow morning. I'm a tolerant employer.'

'But not a wealthy one,' Kerim said. 'I notice that though you burn candles, you do actually have electric light bulbs and sockets.'

She shrugged. 'Cash flow. I hope to get the power back on soon.'

'How?'

'When my stallions go out to stud.'

Kerim glanced at Eylül, then said to Sıla Gedik, 'You can earn a lot of money that way?'

'My horses can,' she said.

On their way back into the city, Eylül and Kerim discussed what had happened.

'Seems Sıla Gedik doesn't like Mihai Albescu,' Kerim said as they drove down Kennedy Caddesi through the Byzantine city walls. 'Racism, you think?'

'Maybe,' Eylül said.

'All those pictures of Ottoman ancestors lining the walls could point at a tendency to Turkish exceptionalism.'

'Or not,' she said. 'You know, sir, I also briefly questioned Zekeriya Bulut about Sümeyye Paşahan, showed him her picture . . .'

'And?'

'He said he didn't know her, just like Sıla did. Not sure I believed

199

either of them, but one thing I did feel was a connection between them.'

'What kind of connection?'

'When Sıla left us, he followed her with his eyes.'

'In a sexual way?'

'No,' she said. 'And yet it was intimate. I don't know. He seemed to me to exude rage.'

'You know that Roma would never burn down a blacksmith's forge, don't you?' Gonca said as she got into bed beside her husband.

'How . . .'

'I know everything,' she said. 'Don't forget it.'

Süleyman put his arms around her. 'Why wouldn't Roma burn down a forge, Gonca?'

'Because blacksmiths are wizards,' she said. 'They know things, about fire. It's said that a Roma blacksmith captured the devil and made him give up his secrets about flame. We respect blacksmiths.'

He kissed her. 'One thing I can tell you is that Sesler told me to look up if I want to find the culprit. I take that as a reference to social class. Someone who has power.'

'He's probably right,' she said. 'Those with the most money can do the most damage.'

'But who?'

'That's for you to find out.'

He sighed. 'Why would someone with a lot of power risk their liberty to murder a young boy who makes slightly obscure jokes about the bad taste inherent in conspicuous consumption via the medium of ceramic cat houses?'

'Because they feel protected by those they have allied themselves with?'

'True,' he said. 'But it still strikes me as excessive. You'd have to really hate someone to kidnap them, in a very public way, then kill them and burn their premises down. They would have to have done something terrible to you. Killed your child or raped your wife . . .'

She draped an arm across his chest and sighed contentedly. He smiled.

Eventually looking up at him, she said, 'All I know for certain is that I want you, Şehzade Mehmet. And if Çetin İkmen calls you again, I will throw your phone out of the window.'

Zekeriya wasn't used to the upmarket cafés of Bağdat Caddesi. As he sat down underneath the patio heater outside the Cafe Cadde, he wondered whether he smelt of horse. He'd tipped half a bottle of aftershave over his face and up his arms, but he still wasn't sure. The leaves of the tall green plants dotted around the patio moved slightly in the chill evening breeze. When he looked up, she'd arrived.

'Hi.'

He stood up. 'Hi.'

As usual, he couldn't really see her. She wore a headscarf and niqab even though her clothes were ordinary – a long dress underneath a long coat. She sat and so did he.

'How are you?' she asked.

They didn't touch, even though he longed to.

'The police keep coming round,' he said.

'I'm sorry.'

'Not your fault.'

'And Sıla Hanım?'

He rolled his eyes. 'I don't think I can stand it much longer.'

She looked down at the menu on the table. 'Do you want to eat something?'

'Not really.'

She looked up at him. 'I'm having spaghetti bolognese.'

'I'd like a beer,' he said, and she frowned. 'Perhaps not . . .'

A waiter came over and the woman ordered spaghetti bolognese and two cappuccinos. When he had gone, she leaned forward and whispered, 'Would you like to go somewhere afterwards?'

'I can,' he said. 'But I'll have to go back to the bunkhouse tonight.'

'You will,' Sümeyye Paşahan said.

'It's Merve. Merve Karabulut.'

A blowback of silence hit her from the other end of the call. Merve, almost crying now, said, 'Is that you, Selami Bey? Is it? Please, if you're there, can you answer me . . .'

Then a voice, thankfully familiar said, 'I've got tattoos already.'

'It's not about tattoos,' she said. 'Selami Bey, you promised me . . .'

Another pause. Then she heard him say to someone, 'Taking this outside.'

A few seconds later he said, 'My dad was in the room. What do you want?'

'I need something.'

'I'm not in the business any more,' he said.

'The Kayas' place burned down.'

'It's a shame.'

Merve began to feel hot, then cold. 'Don't give me that!' she said. 'You knew what she was doing! I saw you and that older man who works for your father in Cihangir.'

'Walking around,' he said. 'Not illegal as far as I know.'

'I didn't know you were going to do . . .'

'Do what?' he said.

She didn't know what to say. She wanted to say, 'You said that if I told you who I was buying from you'd see me right.' But she didn't. If she said the words she'd make them real, and she didn't want that.

In the end she said, 'I want to buy.'

'I haven't got anything,' he said. 'Like I said, I'm out of that business.'

His calmness infuriated her. She was desperate!

'I could tell the police.'

Silence again, and then he said, 'Where's your proof, Merve Hanım? Think about it. And think about what the police might do to you. Whatever happened at the Kayas' place had nothing to do with us. And for your information, the police have already been to see my father. They left empty handed.'

Chapter 15

'Enver Yılmaz is forty-six, single, a Muslim born in Amasya, and has a record for multiple speeding violations,' Süleyman said.

İkmen, at the other end of the phone said, 'And?'

'And he's dead. Died back in 2019.'

'Oh.'

'However, although it is only ten a.m., I have been busy on your behalf, Çetin. While Kerim Bey's landlord is largely absent, he does have an agent who was very helpful. Enver Yılmaz, now forty-nine, still single, still a Muslim born in Amasya, lives in the apartment next door to Kerim. Apparently he works for a company called Mahzur IT Solutions.'

'He's taken a dead man's identity?'

'It's possible, although with such a common name, it may also be a coincidence. Given your suspicions, what do you intend to do?'

İkmen sighed. 'A good question. I think it unlikely Sinem Hanım will tell me anything. I'll be honest, I've been trying to work out why this man may be doing this, and I've come up blank. Sinem Hanım is an attractive lady, but she's very often ill and bedbound.'

'Çetin, you and I both know that there are certain individuals who prey upon such people.'

'Yes, but why her?'

'Why not her? Though you don't actually know he's done anything, do you?'

'This is true,' İkmen said.

'Anyway, where are you?' Süleyman asked.

'On İstiklal. Following the man in question.'

Süleyman sat forward in his chair. 'How? Do you know what he looks like?'

'Couldn't sleep last night,' İkmen said, 'so I headed out to your brother-in-law's meyhane in Tarlabaşı. When I'd had enough brandy, I joined a very nice young man called Zeki, who regularly uses the space underneath the stairs up to the roof in the Poisoned Princess apartments as a bed. Chemical engineer and he can't get a job, I don't know what's happening to this country!'

'Çetin!'

'What?'

'You slept rough . . .'

'Sort of.'

Süleyman rolled his eyes.

'Anyway,' İkmen said, 'Mr Yılmaz left his apartment at nine and is now sipping coffee outside a place called Coffee Lab in the old Narmanlı Han. Not that you'd know it. So chi-chi! I preferred the Narmanlı Han when it was full of cats and that crazy old man who used to shout at everyone.'

'You would!'

While not actually against modernisation, Çetin İkmen found that as the years passed, he preferred things the way they were before everything became overly clean and horrifically shiny.

'He's a good-looking man,' he said. 'Shouldn't have any problem getting himself laid. But what do I know? However . . .'

'What?'

'Something I do know is that shortly after Mr Yılmaz left his apartment, Kerim Bey put his head out of his front door. I'm fairly certain he didn't see me, but what do you think *that* means?'

*

205

The Romanian boy had told her that Zekeriya hadn't slept in his bed. She hated that strange foreign lad, he was a snitch, but Sıla Gedik had to admit that he was right about Zekeriya. Where was he?

Not that she had time to look for him. She was the only other person who could ride Yıldırım, and he needed exercise. As she mounted up, Aslı Dölen moved alongside her riding Badem.

'Good morning, Sıla Hanım!' the girl twittered in that jolly posh voice of hers.

'Good morning, Aslı,' Sıla managed to reply. It wasn't easy.

'Where's Zekeriya?' the girl asked.

'I don't know.'

'Oh.'

Sıla kicked Yıldırım's flanks to get him to walk on.

But as soon as he started to move forwards, Mihai appeared again, waving his arms and shouting, 'Sıla Hanım, I've found Zekeriya!'

'Boss.'

Süleyman looked up. 'Ömer?'

'Just got details regarding Neşe Bocuk's finances,' the younger man said.

'Yes, well we've moved on from that for the time being.'

'She's broke,' Ömer said. 'And I mean broke. Used up her over-draft last year.'

Süleyman frowned. 'So what's she living on?'

'Cash, I imagine. She didn't look half starved when we went there, did she? Still got a maid.'

'Clearly she has some income stream that is bypassing her accounts.'

'Like I said, cash. Boss, are we completely done with her now?'

'For the moment, yes,' Süleyman said. 'And that includes her maid.'

'I was only looking . . .' Ömer muttered.

'Ömer, take it from one who knows, there is no "only looking". Your private life is your own affair and I will never criticise you for it. But equally I don't want you to make the same mistakes I did.'

Many years of sexual infidelity had taken their toll on Mehmet Süleyman. He had even once, long ago, been at odds with Ömer Müngün over a woman. That Gonca Şekeroğlu had tamed him was still something many who knew the couple failed to believe.

He changed the subject. 'Have we had any sightings of Meryem Kaya?'

'No, boss.'

He shook his head. 'I got in early this morning, which gave me time to read the fire department's report on the forge. They'll finish with the site today and I'm keen to get down there.'

'Did they find any more smack?'

'A small amount in the kitchen, taped underneath the sink, which I thought apt for people I envisage as very minor players.'

'Not so minor that other people weren't interested in their operation,' Ömer said. 'Burning the place down, I mean.'

'We don't know whether heroin was the reason the forge was burned down,' Süleyman said. 'We've only got Ayaz Tarhan's word for any interest from supposed Roma boys, which Sesler denies. And before you say anything, yes of course he will deny it, and I am, as ever, unconvinced by him. But there's something here we're not seeing, something other than heroin. Meryem Kaya is still missing and we need to know more about her. Get your coat, we're going to Cihangir.'

Status had never featured heavily in Kerim Gürsel's life until now. He'd always been ambitious, but he'd also taken direction from those more senior than himself with good grace. Now, however, the status of Mevlüt Alibey as his effective superior stuck in his

207

craw. Although nobody knew that his home life was a silent war zone, his emotions in turmoil, he knew that he was having a nightmare keeping his resentment of the organised-crime team off his face. Eylül stood by his side, impassive.

He'd left home really early that morning. Were he honest with himself, he'd been trying to catch a glimpse of Enver Bey when he heard him leave for work. Maybe the two of them could have walked down to their cars together. But he'd just stuck his head out of the door and then gone back inside. How juvenile!

The words 'Sümeyye Paşahan' brought him out of his reverie.

'We need to find her, but we can't go in with our boots on,' Alibey was saying. 'We don't know what her father has in his arsenal – all lies, of course – but it's our job to keep this incest under wraps until we can get our hands on him, or intel on his finances.'

Güllü and the rest of the team nodded gravely.

Kerim, who had barely slept and knew that he looked like death, said, 'While acknowledging that we need to establish how the baby died and why, and possibly get Sümeyye to a doctor.'

No one spoke, and then Alibey said, 'You make a good point, Kerim Bey. The woman may well be a murderer and we cannot lose sight of that.'

'She may be sick.'

'Yes, she may be, however it is my belief that to move forward with this investigation we need to find those people Paşahan moved into the city when he left Uludağ. I've emailed you all a list of names of those we need to speak to as a matter of urgency. Last-known addresses are included where appropriate. Some are well known to us, particularly those who have served time, and some are not. I've assigned the task of making contact with Paşahan's latest partner in crime, Ümit Avrant, to myself and Sergeant Güllü. I believe you, Kerim Bey, have met Ümit's son Atila.'

'Yes.' Kerim's voice wavered as he spoke and he hated it. When he'd told Eylül about their effective secondment to Organised Crime, she'd given no opinion. She knew one of the team, Constable Oktay, another hijabi officer and a new recruit. He'd seen them sitting together in the canteen a few times.

'So maybe a return visit is in order,' Alibey said.

'I don't think there's a lot to be gained by interviewing him again,' Kerim said.

'I do.' Alibey looked at Eylül. 'Sergeant Yavaş, I'd like to partner you with Constable Oktay. I think Miray Hanım will benefit from your considerable experience.'

Eylül smiled. Kerim felt as if he'd been punched in the guts.

The police arrived in the shape of three uniformed officers – a sergeant and two constables – from Kağıthane police station. The sergeant, a thin man in his thirties, hunkered down beside the body and said, 'Can't see anything obviously suspicious . . .'

'He was twenty-three!' Sıla Gedik, shaking, spat through tears. 'He was a horseman! He was fit!'

'Anyone can die, hanım,' one of the constables said.

Sıla Gedik wanted to slap him, but instead she began crying again.

Mihai Albescu had found the body of Zekeriya Bulut around the back of the bunkhouse, where tables and chairs were laid out on a small patch of ground, catering to those who wanted to smoke. Flat on its back, it was wet from early-morning rain and the face was contorted into a frightening, teeth-exposing grin, the effect of rigor mortis on the facial muscles. There was no blood to be seen on or around the corpse, although there was the sharp smell of ammonia where Zekeriya had presumably wet himself as he fell.

Eventually the sergeant rose to his feet. 'I'll arrange transport to hospital. Anyone know about next of kin?'

Sıla, pulling herself together, said, 'His mother and a brother live in Üsküdar. If you come to my office I can give you an address.'

The sergeant nodded.

'What can you tell me about drug dealing in this area?'

Merve Karabulut said, 'Nothing.'

Süleyman had caught up with the Kayas' neighbour as she was outlining a Turkish flag on the tricep of a woman who looked as if she might be a bodybuilder. When he had shown Merve his badge, the woman had gracefully agreed to come back later. Now alone with this small, dark, heavily tattooed female, he noticed that in spite of the coolness of the day, she was sweating.

'Are you sure?'

'I thought you were investigating the fire next door,' Merve said.

'We are. Tell me what you know about drug dealing in this area.'

'I've told you, nothing.'

Years ago, Süleyman had been taught by İkmen to always give suspects a chance to confess when they were being interviewed. It saved a lot of bother later, he said, by which he meant the processes of personal and premises searching.

Süleyman held up the search warrant he'd been granted that morning, and Merve Karabulut sat down on her work stool and put her head in her hands. He gave her a few moments and then said, 'Do you have your supply taped underneath your sink too?'

She looked up and nodded.

While Ömer watched the woman, Süleyman went to the kitchen, returning with two small plastic bags containing brown powder. He put them down in front of her. 'You know that underneath the sink is a cliché, I take it? We found some rather larger bags of heroin underneath the sink in the Kayas' kitchen.'

Merve said nothing.

210

He continued. 'You know, we've been hearing whispers about drug dealing here in Cihangir, over and above the odd bit of weed, for a while now. Is that you, Miss Karabulut? Did you supply Meryem Kaya?'

'No!'

'Then did she supply you?'

She put her head down again.

'I'll take that as a yes.'

'I don't know where she got it,' Merve said. 'I swear.'

'How long have you been dependent upon heroin, Miss Karabulut?'

'About five years.'

'And did Meryem supply you for all that time?'

'No,' she said. 'Just the last year.'

'Where did you get your supply from before?'

'Tarlabaşı,' she said. 'Don't know who they were.'

'Does the name Şevket Sesler mean anything to you?'

'No.'

'Are you sure?'

'Yes.' Then she added, 'I had nothing to do with the fire.'

'I didn't think you did,' Süleyman said. 'Why would you attack your dealer? Why would you put your own premises at risk? But if you do know who might have done this, it is in your interests to tell us. Because had the fire department not managed to get the blaze under control as quickly as they did, your premises could have caught light too. These are serious people, not above killing others to achieve their goals.'

Watching a middle-aged man drink coffee and type things into his laptop was not something Çetin İkmen found exciting. Enver Yılmaz had been doing this for well over an hour. In that time he'd consumed two lattes and smoked three cigarettes. But then he wasn't alone. Other men and women sat at other tables doing

211

exactly the same thing. As a self-confessed dinosaur, İkmen knew he didn't understand modern working practices. All he did know was that there was no substitute for getting out and about if one was involved in policing.

In spite of the fact that a considerable number of traffic violation notices were now issued using CCTV evidence, he disapproved on principle. The cameras might be very efficient, but those using them just sat about looking at screens all day and, so he'd heard, putting on weight. How could anyone work like that?

He ordered himself another espresso and lit another cigarette. Every so often Yılmaz looked up briefly, consulted one of two mobile phones for a moment and then returned to his laptop. Did he know that İkmen was observing him? Apparently the company he claimed to work for, Mahzur IT Solutions, had an office in Maslak, and a website. İkmen had read it twice and still couldn't fathom what they did. The business had been started by a man called Mahzur Yılmaz. Whether he was a relation wasn't clear, and there was no mention of Enver Yılmaz.

What was he trying to achieve anyway? The address of the office in Maslak was on the website, and so in all probability it existed. He looked at the page again, and it was then that he spotted an apparent anomaly. While a lot of businesses used mobile numbers these days, companies who actually had offices still used landlines. So why only a mobile number? There was an email address, but nothing to indicate that Mahzur were on any social media platforms. Again, unusual these days.

İkmen called a waiter over and paid for his drinks, then walked away from the café and called Mahzur's number.

Merve Karabulut was shaking. Süleyman asked her whether she was cold and she said that she wasn't.

'I'm afraid,' she said as she looked around the grey walls of the interview room. 'You people frighten me.'

212

Merve and her lawyer, a man provided for her by her wealthy parents, sat across a table from Süleyman and Ömer Müngün, who were recording their conversation.

Süleyman continued. 'You were found in possession of two hundred milligrams of brown powdered heroin, a controlled substance, which was discovered in two small plastic bags taped to the underside of your sink. This you obtained from your neighbour, Meryem Kaya, who you claim has supplied the drug to you for the best part of a year.'

Merve looked at her lawyer, who nodded.

'Yes,' she said.

Given the Karabulut family's standing in legal circles – her father, Süleyman had discovered, was a judge – she was probably being advised to cooperate, up to a point, pending some sort of deal. He didn't do those unless leaned on from above, and even then it wasn't something he took lightly. He wondered whether Merve Karabulut knew this.

He leaned back in his chair. 'What do you know about Roma dealers moving into Cihangir?'

'Nothing,' she said.

'But you used to buy your smack from dealers in Tarlabaşı.'

'I don't know whether they were Roma. I've told you this!' she said.

'So if I asked you whether you were worried about rival dealers, possibly Roma, moving into the area, what would you say?'

'Well, it's always possible . . .'

He leaned towards her across the table. 'Miss Karabulut, I've been doing this job now for a very long time, and in that time I have come to believe I have a good instinct for when someone is holding information back. Do you understand me?'

She looked at her lawyer, who almost imperceptibly shook his head.

Süleyman tapped on the table to command her attention, and

213

then said, 'People have died. Emir Kaya at his home in Cihangir, magician Nuri Taslı at his home in Ortaköy. Meryem Kaya is missing. I have no reason to believe these events are related to each other – and no reason to believe they are not. Emir Kaya was kidnapped and then killed by people impersonating the Taslı magicians, and though I cannot prove beyond reasonable doubt that those people also set fire to the forge, I think it highly likely. And while I know, with help from eminent stage magicians, our pathologist and the fire department, how these things happened, I do not know why or who may be involved. Miss Karabulut, I cannot make the charge of possession go away. Get that out of your head right now. But if you care about anyone in Cihangir, including yourself, you must tell me everything you know, even if you think some of those things are completely unconnected to these crimes. Do you understand?'

When had he become that person who just rolled over and gave up? Had it only been since Sinem had suddenly rejected him, or had he always done it?

Kerim Gürsel sat alone in his office looking at a photograph of Sümeyye Paşahan on his computer screen. Was that the face of a murderer? It was certainly the face of someone who had been abused by her father – not that this picture showed anything more than an apparently carefree young woman wearing a low-cut shiny one-piece swimming costume. Her skin was honey coloured and perfect, her eyelashes unnaturally long, ditto her hair. She looked like hundreds of other overprivileged crime-lord kids, and yet Sümeyye Paşahan had been damaged in ways her peers could not comprehend. Or could they?

Mevlüt Alibey had not so much clipped Kerim's wings as removed them. With no role in the operation to seek out and question Paşahan's associates in the city, he'd been left alone at headquarters – a 'point of contact', apparently. Eylül had gone off with Constable Oktay without a word to him. But then what else could she have done? Alibey was in charge now, and he knew far more about Paşahan's organisation than Kerim did. Not that this fact meant that Paşahan's men still in the city would tell him and his team anything. But then maybe that was the point. Obfuscate the investigation until Paşahan's location could be confirmed, and then find out what he knew and about whom. It was a dangerous strategy, aimed only at protecting those who, it had to be faced, might be as guilty as Paşahan himself. It made Kerim feel tainted.

His phone rang.

'Inspector Gürsel? It was a woman's voice.

'Yes?'

'It's Aslı Dölen, from Gedik.'

'Oh, hello,' he said. Suddenly the investigation at the Gedik Stables seemed like a long time ago. 'What can I do for you, Aslı Hanım?'

He heard her take a breath.

'Zekeriya Bulut is dead,' she said.

The groom had been a picture of health.

'They think he had a heart attack,' she continued. 'They've taken the body to the Forensic Institute.'

'Really?' Someone, possibly the doctor, did not think this death was entirely natural.

'Sıla Hanım is in bits,' Aslı said. 'I don't know what to do with her. She just keeps screaming.'

Kerim shuffled one arm into his jacket. 'I'm on my way.'

'It's got nothing to do with drugs,' Merve Karabulut said. 'Well, not directly.'

'Tell me,' Süleyman said.

She looked at her lawyer, who tipped his head to one side, apparently giving her permission to speak.

'Emir was a lot younger than Meryem,' Merve said. 'His

215

parents died when he was young and so Meryem brought him up. He'd always been a sensitive boy. He liked history and he was personally upset by all the changes that had been happening to buildings in the city.'

'Hence his cat houses.'

'Yes. He was a brilliant artist.'

'But?'

'But he was an unworldly boy,' she said.

'Girlfriends?'

'That's the point,' she said. 'Emir never had girlfriends. He was shy around women.'

Süleyman remembered how Gonca had taken so quickly to the handsome young man, and how flattered he had been by her attention.

'When he fell for someone, he was going to fall hard,' Merve said. 'Which was what he did.'

'I see.'

'For a while Meryem didn't know who this girl was. She knew there *was* a girl, because Emir was out a lot more and seemed distracted. She tried to look at his phone, but he caught her and they had a huge row. He said that what he did was his business, that he was in love and he didn't want his sister messing things up. Meryem backed off for a while, until she noticed how unhappy he was.'

'Why was he unhappy?'

'He told her this girl came from a problematic family,' she said. 'Her father didn't want her seeing him any more. Meryem imagined some religious type furious at Emir having taken his daughter's virginity, but it wasn't that. It was worse.'

'In what way?' Süleyman asked.

'Firstly, according to Meryem, Emir hadn't slept with this girl. I know she didn't buy it, even though he swore he hadn't. What he did do was share with her the heroin he occasionally bought from

216

me. The boy was so nervous, Smack helped him to relax. I know I did wrong to supply him, but he was such a sweet boy and all he ever wanted was to make a life of his own. Meryem treated him like a child! We fell out over it, Meryem and me, especially when Emir told us who the girl was.'

'And who was this girl, Merve Hanım?' Süleyman asked.

'Sümeyye Paşahan,' she said. 'That motormouth Görkan Paşahan's daughter.'

Chapter 16 ·

Kerim Gürsel had thought that Aslı Dölen might have been exaggerating when she said that Sıla Gedik was screaming. She was, loudly and without let-up. What did one do in such circumstances? Not only were her staff upset, but the horses were becoming agitated too.

Kerim bent down and put a hand on the woman's shoulder. She was lying on the floor of her office, beating her head against the ground.

'Sıla Hanım . . .'

She turned her head briefly to face him and then began screaming all over again. The Romanian groom Mihai Albescu came forward. 'What can we do?'

Kerim took hold of the woman's shoulder again and said, 'You get round the other side and let's lift her onto a chair.'

Although she resisted, the two men managed to haul her into an ancient office chair, still screaming. In the movies, someone would slap a hysterical person around the face. But Kerim knew it didn't work like that. He also didn't fancy being accused of brutalising a member of the public. Instead they all waited, and when there was finally an exhausted lapse in her pain, he said, 'Tell me what's wrong, Sıla Hanım. You can't go on like this, you're upsetting your staff and your horses.'

'Don't you know about Zekeriya?' She was still yelling, but at least she was forming words now.

'Yes,' he said. 'I am so sorry.'

218

'They took his body away to cut it up!'

'Shh! To the Forensic Institute, I know,' he said. 'I need you to be calm. Do you know why they did that, hanım?'

She went to speak and then turned her head away and resumed screaming and clawing at her own face.

Mihai tapped him on the shoulder. 'I know,' he said.

It hadn't been easy making an appointment with someone to talk about something one didn't understand, but somehow Çetin İkmen had pulled it off.

He'd watched Enver Yılmaz pick up his call. 'Mahzur IT Solutions,' he'd said. 'How can I help you?'

İkmen, by that time hidden around the corner from the coffee shop, had asked him a generic question about Mahzur's services and products. There had been a short but perceptible silence, after which Yılmaz had gone off on some sort of IT-speak tirade. He might as well have been speaking Mandarin Chinese.

At the end of that abomination, İkmen had said, 'That sounds very interesting, bey efendi. May I make an appointment to visit your team at your office?'

Again the almost imperceptible silence, and then, 'We tend to go out to our clients, er . . .'

'Halıl Tatar.'

When being someone else, İkmen always used his older brother's first name plus the surname of Halıl's first wife, Deniz Tatar.

'Halıl Bey . . .'

'I'd prefer to come to your office,' İkmen said. 'I feel that in order to do business in a professional manner, it is important that it occurs in a professional setting. Don't you agree?'

'Ah, yes . . .'

İkmen looked at the notes he'd jotted down about the company. 'I see you are in Maslak. Near the Hilton.'

'Yes, but—'

'Shall we say ten thirty?' İkmen said.

'Halıl Bey, we don't normally see clients at our office,' Enver Yılmaz said. 'We are a digital operation.'

'I understand that, but I hope you will understand that I am the sort of person who likes to see what kind of company I am entrusting my money to. So, to recap, ten thirty in Maslak.'

'Both Meryem and I knew that Emir was playing with fire,' Merve said. 'Paşahan may be out of the country, but he still has clout. And hooking his daughter on smack was not a good idea. Maybe he thought if he loosened her up a bit, he'd get her into bed. But then I don't think he was like that. He was an unhappy boy, Inspector Süleyman. I don't know about the girl, but I imagine her position is not as secure as it was before her father turned on his allies.'

Knowing what he did about Sümeyye Paşahan, Süleyman could see why she might be tempted to try something that would make her problems temporarily dissolve. He knew that Kerim had been going all-out to find her. He also knew that his evidence so far had been turned over to Alibey at Organised Crime.

'Did you ever meet Sümeyye Paşahan, Merve Hanım?' he said.

'No. As far as I know, they didn't meet in Cihangir. According to Emir, it all finished anyway.'

'When?'

'Couple of months ago. He was very sad. I know nothing of the circumstances, but I was glad. If old man Paşahan had found out what his daughter was doing, it may have attracted attention to Meryem and her side hustle. It's been the only thing keeping her business afloat this past year. She needed to keep it quiet.'

Which begged the question: if Emir and Sümeyye had split up, why would Görkan Paşahan come after him and his sister? Paşahan's people could have burned the forge down, but why kidnap the boy first in such an elaborate way? And why burn the forge anyway if the affair was over? If it was over . . .

Süleyman called for a break and went outside into the car park to have a cigarette. He needed to speak to Kerim Gürsel, but when he tried to ring, he just got voicemail. He left a message.

Mihai Albescu took the cigarette Kerim offered him. 'I found him.'

'Zekeriya?'

'Around the back of the bunkhouse there are some tables and chairs for smokers,' he said. 'He was lying on the ground. I thought he was asleep until I tried to rouse him.'

'What happened then?' Kerim asked.

'I told Sıla Hanım, but she just lost it and so I called the police. They came from the Kağıthane station.'

'They called the doctor?'

'Yeah.'

'Do you know where from?'

'The public hospital. He was with the body for quite a while. He said he thought Zekeriya had had a heart attack.'

'And yet he sent his body to the Forensic Institute.'

'Yeah.'

They smoked in silence for a few moments, and then Kerim said, 'Zekeriya and Sıla Hanım, were they close?'

He could still hear her, whimpering now.

Mihai looked around and then moved closer to Kerim.

'Truth is, they were sleeping together,' he said. 'But don't tell her I told you.'

'Do the other grooms know?' Kerim asked.

'I think so. Oh, except that posh girl, Aslı. She doesn't live here. I don't think she knows.'

'It was you who told my sergeant that you saw Aslı Dölen's friend Sümeyye Paşahan here at night,' Kerim said. 'Sergeant Yavaş told me that on one occasion Sıla Hanım was following her.'

221

'Yes, that's right.'

'And yet Zekeriya Bulut and the other grooms said they'd never seen Sümeyye Paşahan.'

Mihai shrugged. 'Maybe they didn't. But then her father's some gangster, maybe they wanted to keep clear of it. I'm a foreigner, so it doesn't matter to me. I don't know why she was here. I don't know why Sıla Hanım was following her.'

Sıla Gedik did certainly appear to be a woman labouring under the weight of a terrible loss. But so what if she was having sex with Zekeriya? Unless she'd killed him, that was her business. And if he did die of natural causes, it was nothing to do with the police anyway. It was Sümeyye Paşahan's alleged presence at Gedik that niggled, and Kerim didn't even have Eylül to talk it through with.

He took his phone out of his pocket and switched it on. There was, predictably, nothing from the organised-crime team. But there was a message from Süleyman. He'd deal with it later.

Recep Türkoğlu had the appearance of a man who had been inflated. His apartment, which overlooked the waters of Lake Küçükçekmece, was less a home and more a gym. Full of weights, benches, kettle bells, running and rowing machines, it was the home of someone obsessed by his physical fitness. And like most of the men who had worked for Görkan Paşahan – and maybe still did – Recep Türkoğlu was fanatical about keeping in shape. Even when Eylül Yavaş and Miray Oktay managed to find wooden kitchen chairs to sit down on, Mr Türkoğlu continued to lift weights, staring fixedly at his own biceps.

'Yes, Görkan Bey gave me some work in the past,' he said to the officers. 'But not lately. I don't hold with what he's doing now. I don't believe what he's saying.'

'About those he formerly supported?' Eylül asked.

'That's right,' he said. 'Do you?'

222

A cold grey light reflected off the lake and into the room. The district of Küçükçekmece, on the European side of the city, abutted the shores of the Sea of Marmara. Flat and low lying, it had in recent years been heavily developed in terms of high-rise apartment buildings, like the one where Recep Türkoğlu lived. It was said they had been constructed quickly, using substandard materials, and Eylül was aware of an unpleasant smell she interpreted as faulty sewage disposal. But it was a nice location. The lake was a destination for those involved in water sports.

'What I think is irrelevant,' she said.

Her young partner, Constable Oktay, looked at her with a mixture of surprise and admiration.

'What exactly did you do for Mr Paşahan?' Eylül continued.

'Security,' he said.

'Indeed. Armed?'

He stopped pumping iron. 'I have a licence.'

'Can I see it?'

Wordlessly he went to a cupboard and took out a piece of paper, which he gave to Eylül. He wasn't lying; he did have a gun licence. She gave it back to him.

'Sir, I will come straight to the point. We need to find Görkan Paşahan as a matter of urgency. I would therefore urge you, if you know where he is, to tell us.'

'I don't know,' he said. 'You think I wouldn't tell you people if I did? It shames me to have worked for such a person. The man is a snake!'

'Do you have any theories about where he might be?'

'No. I didn't know him, as in know him. I worked for him for a while, before he started this shameful business, that is all.'

'Do you know why he pursues this "shameful" course of action?' she asked.

It was well known that he'd fallen out with his former allies – over some lucrative building contracts, it was thought.

'No.' He paused. 'He had contacts in Italy. I was once assigned to protect him on a trip to Reggio Calabria.'

'What sort of trip? Whom did he meet?'

'A business trip. I don't know who they were. Görkan Bey was very satisfied at the end of it. Kissed all the big Italians goodbye.'

When the two women left, Constable Oktay having barely spoken a word, Eylül was full of questions. Why they had been assigned by Alibey to question Türkoğlu confused her. To send a senior investigator like her to question a man who had been a very infrequent and low-level member of Paşahan's organisation struck her as odd. Alibey had given her the impression he thought she was a valuable member of his team, so why put her up against a thug? That said, Türkoğlu had mentioned something she did find interesting, and that was Paşahan's visit to Italy. She knew that Reggio Calabria was the centre of operations for the southern Italian Mafia organisation known as the 'Ndrangheta. They were not widely known about in Turkey, but in Italy they were notorious. They dealt in drugs and human trafficking, and were rumoured to be close to power in that part of the country. If the 'Ndrangheta godfathers didn't get what they wanted, people started dying.

Was Görkan Paşahan now on their payroll? And was he maybe somewhere in Italy?

Sıla Gedik, once she had got control of herself, led Kerim away from the stables towards her house. A mishmash of permanent concrete construction with an older wooden core, it had probably been a gecekondu long ago. Put up in the 1950s and 60s, gecekondu dwellings were the places migrants from the countryside built to live in when they first came to the city. If an individual or family could put up four corner posts and a roof in the space of one night, they could legitimately carry on construction and live on the land. Thousands of gecekondu properties remained, although their numbers were dwindling.

She offered him a chair and Kerim sat down. Sitting opposite, she said, 'I loved him, what can I say? He was thirty years younger than me. It was ridiculous. But I loved him.'

She began to cry again. Kerim let her. This wasn't an unusual story. Older woman with money falls for younger man without. Except that Sıla Gedik didn't have any money. Maybe Zekeriya Bulut had really loved her?

Calm again, she said, 'I expect you think that Zekeriya went with me because I was his boss. Maybe I bullied him into my bed . . .'

'Did you?'

'No,' she said. 'And for your information, I am broke, my business is in debt. I don't know what Zekeriya saw in an old woman like me, but we worked. Running a stables is a relentless business. If you don't take things day by day, you'll go under. I didn't think about the future.'

'I know my sergeant asked you this question, Sıla Hanım, but I'm going to ask you it again,' Kerim said. 'Does the name Sümeyye Paşahan mean anything to you?'

She held her breath, then released it. 'He became besotted with her. He said he wasn't. He said he was just using her to get money.'

'Who was besotted by whom?'

'Zekeriya was besotted with Sümeyye – and I think the feeling was mutual. I knew it the first time I saw them together. She was a friend of Aslı's – if you can call someone like Sümeyye a friend. She came here at night after Zekeriya, like a bitch on heat!' Her eyes blazed. 'He told me he was just stringing her along. Said he'd found something out about her he could use. But he loved her, he . . .'

'Do you know where Sümeyye Paşahan is now, Sıla Hanım?' Kerim asked.

225

'No,' she said. 'When he went out last night, I asked him whether he was going to her and he said no. His mother has dementia, lives with his brother in Üsküdar. He said he was going there. But he was probably lying, and now he's dead.'

'Are you saying you think Sümeyye Paşahan killed him?'

'Who knows!' Her eyes filled with tears again. 'Little whore!'

Kerim's phone vibrated. He excused himself to Sıla Gedik and played the message. He'd left a message himself for whoever was dealing with Zekeriya Bulut's case at the Forensic Institute. Now they'd got back to him. A Dr Zaladin asked that he visit him at the institute as soon as possible.

Putting his phone back in his pocket, he said, 'I'm afraid I have to go, Sıla Hanım. I will be back . . .'

'We need to find Meryem Kaya,' Süleyman said. 'As far as I can deduce, the Kayas have no other family members in the city.'

'They were Roma originally,' Ömer Müngün said. 'There must be others somewhere.'

Süleyman shrugged. 'That was, if my understanding is correct, a long time ago. What about clients?'

'Kerim Bey was working with one of them, that baby death in Kağıthane.'

'Yes, but Kerim Bey isn't getting back to me,' Süleyman said. 'I imagine Inspector Alibey is keeping him busy. No, I'm thinking about the people she was supplying with drugs.'

'You think she may have gone to one of them?'

'I don't know.' He leaned back in his chair. 'Maybe. Also, if Meryem was dealing smack, she must have got it from somewhere. If indeed she was frightened of Paşahan finding out she was indirectly dealing to his daughter, then I doubt whether any of our high-profile dealers are involved. Also she dealt small amounts – relatively speaking. Most of her records were destroyed in the fire, but anecdotally she had clients all over the city. Riding schools, some Roma in Tarlabaşı, our own equestrian training school, possibly a few wealthy people with horses.'

'That's a lot of people, boss, and if she is with one of them, they're not going to tell us, are they?'

'No, but her competitors might,' Süleyman said. 'There are very few blacksmiths in the city now. It's a small world, and in small worlds, people tend to know each other. Search for blacksmiths and talk to them. Impress upon them our fears for Meryem Kaya's safety.'

'Yes, boss.'

'We have Merve Karabulut in custody for possession and so it's possible she may have more to tell us, but we can't be sure of that.'

Chapter 17

There were lots of barely legitimate companies all over the city. There were a lot of barely legitimate companies everywhere, especially in the wake of the virus, which had seen so many people apparently working from home. That Kerim Gürsel's neighbour, Enver Yılmaz, worked for a company that could be one of those was possible but not unusual. It didn't make him a bad person, any more than the fact that he shared a name with a dead man made him an identity thief. That said, Çetin İkmen couldn't get away from the idea that he was wrong in some way.

Was it just the fact that his balcony door had been open when İkmen had visited? He'd heard a man's voice in the Gürsels' apartment just before he'd hammered on the door. And unless some other man had been hiding in the apartment, who else could it have been?

And yet how could he prove that without involving Sinem Gürsel – and her husband. Simply going to see this man at his supposed office in Maslak wasn't going to achieve anything except perhaps confirm that a physical office didn't exist. So what?

İkmen smoked and looked out at the darkening streets of Sultanahmet. He spent a lot of time on his balcony these days. He'd got into the habit back in the days when the ghost of his wife would come to visit. But that was a long time ago, before he became involved with Peri Müngün. Fatma had left on the very day İkmen had first kissed Peri, and she hadn't been back since. Unlike the djinn in the kitchen. Would that horror ever leave? Or was its continued presence some sort of punishment for loving another woman?

His phone rang. It was Peri.

'Çetin, is it OK if I come over this evening?' she asked. 'Provided my brother gets home before midnight.'

'Come after midnight if you like,' İkmen said. 'Come whenever you want.'

İkmen knew that Ömer Müngün often worked late. It was his way of managing to live with a marriage he had never wanted.

'My sister-in-law is done in,' she continued. 'Gibrail is just nonstop at the moment and I don't want to leave her alone with him. She needs to sleep.'

'He's still not sleeping?'

'Never,' she said.

'Bülent was like that,' İkmen said, referencing one of his sons.

'I don't think the way Gibrail behaves is normal,' Peri said. 'I'm no expert in paediatrics, but in my opinion, Yeşili gives him too many sweets. She does it to placate him, but what he really needs are playmates. The fact he can hardly speak Turkish doesn't help. Ömer and I try, but it's a losing battle.'

İkmen sighed. 'Well, anyway,' he said, 'come when you can. You know I always want to see you.'

The trick, if it could be called that, resided in having the ability to vault the electronic entry gate just as the ferry was about to pull away from the pier.

Meryem Kaya was a fit woman, but a couple of nights without sleep, in the cold, plus her overwhelming anxiety, had left her feeling weak. But what she lacked in strength she made up for in determination. She would have made it had a strong hand not pulled her back.

'Hey!'

She found herself looking into the face of a uniformed

229

policeman. The ferry was still pulling away from the shore. She could make it if only she could get away from him. She twisted away, attempting to pull his hand off her shoulder.

'No ticket, no journey!' He clung on and then grabbed her round the waist. Facing away from him, Meryem used her free arm to elbow him in the guts. He fell to the ground and she prepared to run, but then found herself in the arms of another cop.

'Where do you think you're going, lady?'

Meryem tried to reach his face, to spit or bite, but he was too tall and so she just punched him. It didn't do a lot. Unlike the first officer, this man was middle aged and solid. He pinned her arms to her sides and called to his colleague, now back on his feet.

'Cuff her,' he said.

Meryem wanted to protest. But then her position was now one of extreme weakness. Not only had she tried to get onto a Bosphorus ferry without paying, she was wearing pyjamas, carrying no ID and was probably on some sort of police missing list.

She stopped struggling and let them take her away from the Karaköy pier towards a police car.

'Crystal meth, I've got a nose for it, as it were,' Dr Zaladin said. 'The attending doctor did too, which is why the body's here.'

The doctor had come to meet Kerim Gürsel in the reception area of the Forensic Institute.

Kerim said, 'What does it smell like?'

'Ammonia mostly,' he said. 'Of course, most corpses piss themselves post-mortem and so you have to make sure. But this man, Bulut, he reeked. If I had to speculate, I'd say he was a cook.'

'He produced methamphetamine?'

'Maybe.'

'So his death . . .'

'You want to know whether he was murdered?' the doctor said. 'Can't find any sign of violence or foul play. Not yet anyway. Just another meth fatality. Do you mind if we go outside? I need a cigarette.'

They stepped out into the damp evening air. Both men lit up.

'Strictly a death like this comes under Narco,' Kerim said. 'I've been involved with the stables because we found the corpse of a murdered baby near the premises.'

'I heard about that,' Zaladin said. 'Any connection to narcotics?'

'No. Doctor, I get the impression there are a lot of meth fatalities in the city.'

'There have been casualties for years, but in the last six months it's ramped up. Ask your colleagues in Narcotics.'

'I will.'

'Personally, I think it's inevitable, given the circumstances.'

'What do you mean?'

Dr Zaladin looked around to make sure no one was listening. 'When people can't eat or pay their rent , they can become desperate. Sometimes they turn to drugs, taking them or producing them or both.' He looked Kerim up and down. 'You're a policeman, you must know what I mean. You must have days when you look at what you earn and what you need to spend to live and wonder what you're doing. I'm a doctor and I feel that every fucking day.'

Kerim nodded.

'I often wonder why I do this job, elbow deep in dead people's blood, shit and piss, when I could cook up a bit of meth and earn twice as much. Not saying I'd do that. I'm too afraid of you lot!' Zaladin barked a laugh. 'What did Zekeriya Bulut do?'

'He was a groom, took care of horses,' Kerim said. 'Dr Zaladin, you need to pass your findings on to Narcotics.'

'I know.'

'Tell them you've contacted me,' Kerim said.

'Found outdoors, wasn't he?' the doctor asked.

'Yes.'

'Any idea where he'd been?'

'Into the city, but I don't know where,' Kerim said. Then, realising he still hadn't asked what had actually killed the groom, he went on, 'So what is the official cause of death?'

Dr Zaladin scrunched his cigarette butt out with his foot. 'Cardiac arrest brought about by methamphetamine overdose. If he was cooking it and taking it at the same time, he was a fucking idiot.'

'Can you ride horses, boss?' Ömer Müngün asked when Mehmet Süleyman returned to his office.

'Mmm?'

The inspector was distracted. His wife had called him, and he'd disappeared to take her call – for a long time.

'Horses?' Ömer repeated. 'Can you ride them?'

'Oh, er . . .' Süleyman sat down, still looking at his phone, and then looked up. 'Yes. One of my uncles had horses at his summer house in Tarabya. I learned there.'

Some of the old Ottoman families had retained their property when the empire collapsed. Summer houses along the Bosphorus in places like Tarabya were things they used to take for granted. Few had them in the twenty-first century.

'Why?' Süleyman asked.

'Because I've found more riding schools and businesses using horses than I imagined,' Ömer said. 'I mean, putting the Roma aside.'

'Why would you do that?' Süleyman said. 'The Kayas were originally Roma themselves.'

'Yeah, but surely Meryem Kaya wouldn't have bought smack from them?'

'Why not? Just because Şevket Bey says his people aren't dealing outside Tarlabaşı doesn't mean it's true.'

'Yeah, but why would Merve Karabulut buy from Meryem

232

when she admits she was buying from Tarlabaşı before the black-smith got hold of the cheaper stuff? If Meryem got her heroin from Tarlabaşı . . .'

'Maybe they gave her a discount,' Süleyman said.

'Boss!'

'I don't know! But we don't rule out anyone. Anyway, I have to go home.'

Ömer knew better than to ask whether there was a problem. Süleyman's wife had lost a daughter to the pandemic, and although most of the time she coped well, he knew there were times when she didn't.

Eylül Yavaş had been trying to contact Kerim Gürsel for much of the day, but without success. Now he called her to tell her that Zekeriya Bulut was dead.

'The pathologist at the Forensic Institute told me there's been an uptick in crystal-meth deaths in the past six months.'

'Yes, sir,' she said.

'I wasn't aware of it.'

He'd just about managed to keep on top of his own work in the last few months. But how had he missed something so fundamental?

Mirroring what Zaladin had said, Eylül continued. 'First the virus and now with everything costing so much, people are struggling. Those that know how are cooking up meth like never before. It's cheaper than coke and it makes you feel good. But if Bulut died from an overdose of meth, it's got nothing to do with us, sir.'

He told her about Zekeriya and Sümeyye Paşahan. 'And of course I'm now wondering about the black horse little Necip İstekli saw when he found the baby's body,' Kerim said. 'Was the rider Sümeyye Paşahan?'

'Or Zekeriya Bulut?' she said. 'After all, that wasn't his baby.'

'But did he know that? If he was having some sort of affair with Sümeyye . . .'

'Why would he kill a child he thought was his own?'

'Because of who Sümeyye's father is?'

They both went silent for a moment, then Eylül said, 'You're right, we can't overlook that. I went to interview a minor soldier of Paşahan's today over in Küçükçekmece. A bodybuilder called Recep Türkoğlu. Told me basically nothing except that Paşahan had a meeting with businessmen in Reggio Calabria, Italy. That's where the 'Ndrangheta have their headquarters. So it could be argued that if Bulut thought he was the baby's father, he might want to kill it in view of what Görkan Bey might be involved with. Apparently Paşahan was very tight with the Italians.'

'We're assuming Zekeriya didn't know the truth – or did he? Until we find Sümeyye . . . Sıla Hanım says she has no idea where she might be. But I'm heading back to the stables now in the hope that Bulut's brother and mother may have arrived. Zekeriya told Sıla Hanım he was going to visit them last night, but she suspected he was going to see Sümeyye. Maybe they know something.'

'Well, sir, I'm in your office if you need me. Inspector Alibey has called a meeting of the team for seven.'

'A meeting about what?'

'Today's operation. As far as I know, we're no further forward. I've already emailed him my suspicions regarding the 'Ndrangheta.'

'Did he respond?'

'No. Just called this meeting.'

'Did he mention me?'

'No, sir,' she said.

The woman wouldn't speak. Maybe she was a foreigner? And she was filthy. No ID, and stank like a camel. Sergeant Cihan Çelebi began trawling through missing persons mugshots. Outside his window, the traffic on Tarlabaşı Bulvarı was stationary, and he was constantly disturbed by the sound of horns blaring. He'd just got to a picture of missing blacksmith Meryem Kaya when his phone rang. He picked it up.

'Custody.'

'My name's Inspector Görür from headquarters.' The voice was young, and Cihan Çelebi began to build a picture in his mind of a baby-faced graduate with perfect hair. 'I understand you've picked up an unknown woman this evening.'

'That's right.'

'So no ID?'

Çelebi rolled his eyes. If they'd found ID on her, she wouldn't be unknown. 'No. And she won't talk.'

'Ah. Well you see I'm looking for a woman called Perestu Ramazanov,' Görür said. 'She's Circassian and might not speak Turkish.'

'What's she look like?'

Çelebi heard the young man shuffle around with a keyboard. He looked at his own screen. The woman in the cells could be Meryem Kaya, but it was difficult to tell. Same colour hair, and the woman had been strong like he imagined a blacksmith might be. But it stopped there and so he stopped looking.

'Inspector?'

'Um, no photograph, just a description from neighbours,' Görür said. 'Tall, pale skinned, she covers . . .'

'This woman's a hundred and seventy-five centimetres,' Çelebi said.

'Ah, so that's about right. She's aged forty or so.'

Çelebi brought the picture taken of the unknown woman up on his screen. 'Could fit.'

'I want to come and see her,' Görür said.

'If she don't speak Turkish, do you speak her language then?' Çelebi asked.

'Very few people speak either of the main Circassian dialects,' Görür said. 'But I do speak Russian, which she may well do too. A lot of Russian speakers, including Circassians, came here when the Soviet Union collapsed.'

Çelebi lit a cigarette and scowled at a constable who indicated he should put it out.

'So what? You want to come and see her?'

'I said I did. Yes,' Görür said. 'Now.'

Tahir Bulut was a lot older than his late brother Zekeriya. He and his silent mother had finally arrived at Gedik Stables just ten minutes before Kerim Gürsel returned from the Forensic Institute.

Using Sıla Gedik's makeshift office, Kerim sat the man down and told him what he was allowed to. He also had questions of his own.

'Did you see your brother at all last night, Mr Bulut?'

'No.' Tahir had a gruff voice, often indicative of one who worked outside in all weathers for long periods of time.

'Did he call?'

'Said he might be able to spend a few minutes with our mother, but I never expected him to.'

Tahir Bulut was an expressionless man. Maybe looking after his mother had robbed him of his social skills. The old woman, apparently unaware of what was going on, sat on a wicker chair in a corner of the office, her feet covered in oats and straw.

'Why not?' Kerim asked.

'Üsküdar's a long way from here.'

He was right. It was. However . . .

'Mr Bulut,' Kerim said, 'Sıla Hanım, who runs this place, has told me that the grooms, including your brother, usually went into the city once a week.'

Tahir shrugged. 'Never come to us once a week.'

Kerim cut to the chase. 'Do you know whether Zekeriya had girlfriends?'

236

If anything, the man looked even more morose now. 'Mum wanted a match between my brother and the imam's daughter. But then her brain went, and who'd want their girl to marry someone whose mother just sits and says nothing. It's not normal. Imam must've thought if his girl married my brother she'd have broken children.'

It was always both sad and infuriating to hear such views still espoused in the twenty-first century. But Kerim was aware that Tahir Bulut was not alone in his belief that dementia could somehow be inherited.

Then out of the blue Tahir Bulut said, 'I think he had tarts.'

'Excuse me . . .'

'Tarts, prostitutes,' he said.

Did he mean actual sex workers, or just liberal women?

'I see him down that Bağdat Caddesi where they all go,' he continued. 'Tarts. Think they can cover their heads while they show their arms and legs like whores.'

'Your brother was with covered women?'

'Woman,' he said. 'Shameless. And he never come to see Mum.'

Üsküdar, where the Buluts lived, was a long way away from Bağdat Caddesi, which ran between the districts of Göztepe and Bostancı on the shores of the Sea of Marmara.

'He never visited us from the end of one year to the next,' Tahir added.

The sighting on Bağdat Caddesi, however, did not prove that Zekeriya Bulut was visiting Sümeyye Paşahan. His brother knew of no girlfriends in Zekeriya's life. As it stood, Kerim only had Sıla Gedik's word that the affair between Bulut and Paşahan had ever happened.

He looked at his watch. It was 7.10. He wondered how Eylül was getting on in Alibey's meeting.

*

237

Gonca was inconsolable, which made her husband feel helpless and useless.

She had tried to tell him how she felt when she'd called him at work. But she'd just ended up frightening him. She'd said, 'If I can't do things for myself then what is my purpose? I want to die!'

He hadn't wanted to go home so quickly, but he'd been afraid not to. He knew how much she still mourned her daughter, how the post-COVID stiffness in her limbs drove her to distraction. He'd had such high hopes for the Cihangir Bocuk Gecesi event; he'd thought that some hands-on falcı work where she met people would help to encourage her. But the way things had shaken out, Gonca had simply ended up feeling responsible for Emir Kaya's death.

When he arrived, he found her in the kitchen, coat on, vast pashmina around her shoulders, a suitcase by her feet as well as Sara's basket. The boa was curled up, asleep. Ignoring the snake, he went to his wife, got down on his haunches and took her hands.

'Gonca . . .'

'It's best I go,' she said. 'You can have the house, I don't care.'

'Gonca, you are my goddess, why would I want you to go? I'm nothing without you.'

She stroked his face. 'I fell over in the studio this afternoon. I couldn't get up.'

'Are you hurt?'

'No.'

'Are you sure?'

'Yes!'

'But you're here now. How did you—'

'I pulled myself up using my easel. I broke it,' she said. 'My latest work, *Hüzün*, is all over the floor. Ruined!'

'Oh, goddess!' He kissed her, but she pushed him away.

'Baby, I'm not getting any better. Even walking wears me out. What if it gets worse? What if I end up not being able to walk at all?'

'That won't happen.'

'It might!'

'Well, if it does, we'll deal with it,' he said.

'I don't want Didim or my daughters coming in to do everything!'

'Gonca, we will see other doctors. I don't care what it costs. We'll go abroad if we have to. Maybe when Patrick comes here in the summer, we can go back to Ireland with him and see a doctor there.'

'What will an Irish doctor do that a Turkish one can't?' she asked.

'I don't know. But we'll find out.'

She shook her head. 'I can't be like this, Mehmet.'

'You won't be,' he said. 'You're going to get well.' He stroked her face. 'Please, baby, don't walk out on me. I love you so much.'

'Büket Teyze came today,' she said. 'With the hair and the name of the woman she wants me to curse. I took it, but I couldn't do it. Not knowing how you feel about it. You'll hate me if I do that!'

'I won't hate you,' he said. 'I could never hate you. It's just . . . we're different, sometimes it's hard. We have to accept . . . I know you have no love for the police.'

'I can't hurt you, Mehmet,' she said. 'But I have to be myself. I don't know what to do.'

'Nor I . . .'

He began to cry. Gonca felt herself tremble.

Alibey had said nothing about the 'Ndrangheta and neither had Constable Oktay, although to be fair, she maybe hadn't made the possible connection between Görkan Paşahan and the Italian Mafia. And there was something else that had occurred to Eylül after her phone conversation with Kerim Gürsel. She raised her hand to speak.

'Sergeant Yavaş?' Alibey said, smiling.

'Sir, although Constable Oktay and I didn't manage to get much out of Recep Türkoğlu, I should like to highlight something he said.'

Oktay had given her account of the meeting already. She looked at Eylül with wide eyes.

'Türkoğlu hinted at a connection with Italian crime syndicates,' she said. 'I sent you an email about it.'

'Oh?' Alibey frowned. 'I think I may have glossed over that . . .'

'He accompanied Paşahan on a trip to meet some businessmen in Reggio Calabria,' Eylül went on. 'This is the city from which the 'Ndrangheta operate. One of the most dangerous syndicates in the world.'

Alibey nodded. 'Did Türkoğlu say that Paşahan had a meeting with the 'Ndrangheta? Did he mention names?'

'No, sir—'

'No, he didn't,' Constable Oktay cut in.

'Then that is conjecture,' Alibey said.

Sergeant Şükran Güllü smiled at her. 'There's no evidence that Paşahan has any connection to any foreign crime organisation.'

'Except that given to me by Türkoğlu,' Eylül said.

Alibey and Güllü looked at each other, then the former said, 'I'll follow it up. Leave it with me. Good work, Sergeant Yavaş. OK, everyone . . .'

The team began to break up, but Eylül still hadn't finished.

'Oh, and sir . . .'

Alibey heaved a sigh of annoyance – as did many around him.

'When we were in Türkoğlu's apartment, there was a smell,' Eylül said.

Güllü, now straight faced, said, 'So? Those apartments are on the shores of a lake.'

'I know, but—'

'That's all,' Alibey said. 'Please God we will get closer tomorrow.'

The team filed out of Alibey's office. When they had gone, Eylül remained behind with Alibey and Güllü.

Alibey looked at her. 'Sergeant? What do you want?'

'I want to tell you about the smell in Türkoğlu's apartment,' she said. She turned to Güllü. 'You shut me down.'

'Yes, because it's irrelevant,' Şükran Güllü said. 'Those lakeside properties in Küçükçekmece are notorious for damp and rot.'

'I didn't smell damp and rot. I smelt ammonia.'

'Poorly installed toilets,' Alibey said.

'Yes, that's what I thought at first. And then I was reminded that there's a big crystal-meth problem in the city right now. And I think, sir, that we've all smelt enough of that in our time to know that a big component of meth is ammonia.'

Chapter 18

Whatever language this officer was using most certainly wasn't Turkish. Nor did Meryem think it was French. It sounded Slavic, if she were honest. Clearly he thought she was some sort of foreigner, and so if she just kept quiet, maybe they'd just put her back on the streets on account of being too much bother. Police did that sometimes, people had told her. Then again, maybe they'd deport her if they thought she was foreign. But if they did that, where would they deport her to?

She'd caught that this officer had come from headquarters, and she was glad they'd not sent Süleyman. But if she continued to be detained, then the chances of coming up against him or some other cop who recognised her became more likely. And she'd assaulted one of their own, which did not play well with the police.

She sat and listened to this young man go on in a language she didn't understand. He was quite attractive if you liked that sort of thing – shaven headed, muscle bound. But Meryem had other things on her mind. She'd been caught, and unless she got very lucky indeed, she was soon going to be recognised.

As a victim of what could only be construed as attempted murder, she would attract sympathy. Yes, but the heroin . . . She had no reason to believe they had found that. She had no reason to believe that Merve had betrayed her. She was just a woman whose property had been burned down, whose brother had been shot, who knew things . . .

Could she trade what she knew for a blind eye being turned to any smack they found? After all, that was irrelevant, wasn't it?

But then if she did tell them, she wouldn't be safe. Not that she'd been safe before the fire. She hadn't.

When the young man paused for breath, she spoke. 'It's all right, you can stop that now.'

Gonca had gone to sleep. As he looked around their bedroom, Süleyman took in her now open suitcase and the basket containing Sara at the bottom of the bed. He hoped the snake was asleep, but even if she wasn't, a bridge had been crossed. When he'd finally managed to get his wife upstairs, he'd carried the basket himself, placed it down at the end of the bed and told her that Sara was to be allowed in the bedroom in the future. Anything to make her stay.

Then they'd made love. He'd wanted her, but he also knew it was the only way he could prove to her how much he loved her. She'd clawed him, pulling him inside her, and he could see blood on the sheets. But for the moment she was reassured and was no longer threatening to leave. Now all he had to do was make good on his promise to get her medical treatment.

Some people called what Gonca had 'long COVID' – a post-viral syndrome that so far was only sometimes treatable. Just the thought of it made him cold with fear, and he held her closer. She'd shown him what had happened to her latest work, which as far as he could see was salvageable, though he'd have to mend the easel.

She said his name in her sleep and he smiled. He was so lucky. Kerim Gürsel had been right. If you found the love of your life, you had to hang on tight. Poor Kerim. He'd lost his love, Pembe, and now it seemed the wife he cared for almost as deeply was rejecting him. No wonder Çetin İkmen was so keen to find out what was behind Sinem Hanım's unhappiness.

And then he remembered the curse Gonca had tried, and failed, to perform. Forgotten in the midst of their passion, there was an envelope on the table beside the bed. She'd very deliberately taken it out of her bag and placed it there. She generally performed her darkest magic at night, and so she was probably planning to get up and curse this woman when he was asleep. Was there something belonging to the woman inside? He reached over Gonca's body and picked it up.

'Eylül!'

Ömer Müngün pulled a chair over for his guest and Eylül Yavaş sat down. She was as white as chalk.

'What are you doing here?' he asked. 'Do you want tea or coffee? I have to say, Eylül Hanım, you don't look well.'

She shook her head. 'I saw the light on in Mehmet Bey's office. I hoped one of you was still working.'

'Boss has gone home,' Ömer said. 'Do you want a drink?'

'No,' she said. 'Or rather, I'd like some water.'

He found a glass in his desk and poured water into it from his bottle.

'Thank you.' She drank greedily.

Ömer smiled. 'Thirsty?'

Eylül smiled back. 'Ömer,' she said, 'I need to speak to someone I can trust. I've just come from a meeting Inspector Alibey called with his organised-crime team.'

'I heard you and Kerim Bey had been seconded.'

'Orders from on high dictate that the Paşahan affair be kept low key,' she said. 'Which I understand. He is a divisive figure, and even if the things he says about those at the top of society are not true, he puts doubt in people's minds. On the other hand, he was once one of them himself and we still don't really know what happened to change that status quo.'

'Something to do with building contracts, I heard,' Ömer said.

'Me too, but I don't know. Kerim Bey has been out at Kağıthane for much of the day, at the riding stables near to where the body of the Paşahan baby was found . . .' It was the first time she had alluded to the child as 'the Paşahan baby', but what else could she be called? 'A groom we had our suspicions about died last night, seemingly from a crystal-meth overdose. This young man, Zekeriya Bulut, lied to us. A friend of Sümeyye Paşahan also works at the stables and she told us that she'd taken Sümeyye there on several occasions. Bulut denied all knowledge of her. But according to the owner of the stables, Sıla Gedik, he was having an affair with her.'

'I see.' He wondered whether he should tell her about the other alleged relationship Sümeyye Paşahan had had – with Emir Kaya. He decided to leave that until after she'd told her tale.

'Bulut was also having an affair with Sıla Gedik, but . . . Ömer, I was out today at the apartment of a man called Recep Türkoğlu – a small-time Paşahan soldier . . .'

She told him about the possible link she'd discovered between Paşahan and the 'Ndrangheta, and about the smell in his apartment.

'Alibey said a connection between Paşahan and the Italian mob was tenuous, but I'm not so sure,' she said. 'He and Güllü just dismissed the smell in the apartment. And again they may be right, but I'm uneasy.'

In imitation of Süleyman, Ömer steepled his fingers underneath his chin.

'I know the boss doesn't trust Alibey,' he said. 'When he came to Mehmet Bey and asked him to revisit a possible murder charge against Paşahan, he was suspicious of his motives.'

'Do you know why?'

'Not really. But I do know that Organised Crime have in the past been accused of getting too close to those they investigate. Taking bribes, looking the other way. And Alibey and Güllü are romantically involved . . .'

245

'I know,' she said. 'And that always brings with it vulnerability.'

'Yeah.' Although as Ömer knew from personal experience, not getting involved with colleagues was sometimes easier said than done.

Eylül took a deep breath in. 'Ömer, I feel out of my depth. I'm convinced there's something in this and I think Kerim Bey is too, but . . . I don't know whether you've noticed but he's, well, not himself lately. I'm not sure what's wrong. I've tried to call him but his phone is switched off, it often is. You know I trust you, and it's no reflection on you, but I was hoping to speak to Mehmet Bey . . .'

Ömer nodded. He knew what she meant. He picked up his phone.

'He went home earlier, but I'll see if I can speak to him. Then we'll talk more.''

Peri had called him while she had been doing the washing-up.

'I've rung him twice,' she said into the phone she had propped against her ear with her shoulder. 'Same story, too busy to come home.'

'Then maybe he is,' Çetin İkmen said. 'You know as well as I do that Mehmet Bey is a demanding man.'

'I know. But he's not a demanding man all the time. Çetin, it's Ömer. He doesn't want to come home and I feel trapped by him. Why shouldn't we see each other? I'm single and so are you. You know there are days when I resent him so much, I want to leave!'

He paused for a moment. 'Move in here. This apartment used to hold eleven people, now there are only three of us. We've space. You could even have your own room if you wanted.'

He could hear her internal struggle.

'Çetin, you know I'd love to live with you,' she said. 'But how can I leave Gibrail alone with those two? They barely speak to each other. It's not right!'

'It's also not your responsibility,' İkmen said. 'Do you know whether Mehmet Bey is in his office with Ömer?'

'I don't,' she said. 'Anyway, I'm going to bed now. Gibrail is still up. I'll try and get him to sleep and then I'll attempt to get some rest. I'm so tired I could weep.'

She put the phone down. İkmen, alone on his balcony, brought up Mehmet's mobile number.

He received three phone calls in quick succession. He'd only just managed to get into his car.

'Süleyman.'

He'd thought about waking Gonca before he left but had decided to leave a note instead. If he didn't, she'd worry.

'Sir, this is Custody Sergeant İpek. We've a woman just come in with Inspector Görür, claims to be Meryem Kaya. She wants to talk to you.'

Süleyman sighed with relief or tiredness or both. If it was Meryem Kaya, that was a breakthrough.

'Thank you, Sergeant,' he said. 'I'm actually on my way in now.'

He put his phone down on the passenger seat and was about to turn the key in the ignition when Ömer Müngün called.

'Boss, I'm sorry to disturb—'

'I'm on my way in,' Süleyman said.

'Oh . . .'

'It seems Meryem Kaya has been found and is in custody. I'll need you if . . . You're still in the office?'

'Yes, boss. I'm with Sergeant Yavaş. She needs to talk to you urgently.'

'What about?'

'Organised Crime,' Ömer said.

'Not our business at the moment. She's seconded, same as Kerim Bey.'

'Yeah, but sir that's the point,' Ömer said. 'She needs to talk about Organised Crime, but not to them.'

Süleyman realised what he was saying.

'All right,' he said. 'Let me verify Kaya's identity and then I'll be with you. After that, I want you in on her interrogation.'

'Yes, boss.'

The phone rang again.

'Fuck!'

He picked it up and said, 'What?'

'Mehmet?'

'Çetin, what is it? I'm losing my mind here! Custody, Ömer, now you! What do you want?'

'Nothing,' İkmen said. 'It can wait.' He hung up.

Süleyman put the car into gear and left for headquarters. Whether he'd get his own discovery onto what was clearly a packed agenda, he didn't know. But he had to try, because it was important.

It was cold, but if he didn't sit outside to drink his rakı, he couldn't smoke, and he needed to. The bar he'd drifted into was in Sultanahmet, which was stupid, because if he intended to drink seriously he was a long way from Tarlabaşı. And he had his car. But he was really past caring. He didn't want to go home, and if that meant he had to sleep in the car in his clothes, so be it.

And yet . . . Why had Zekeriya Bulut died in the way he had? Most people who cooked meth might not do that in their own home, but if he hadn't been cooking at the stables then where had he been cooking? Across the Bosphorus somewhere? If Bulut had indeed crossed the Bosphorus at all. There was so much hearsay. Now that Bulut was dead, how could Kerim know for sure whom he was sleeping with? Who had been riding outside the orbit of the Gedik Stables on the day the baby's body had been found? And why had Bulut died in the way he had? What did the appearance of crystal meth even mean in this context? And what did Kerim's own demotion to Alibey's subordinate mean?

Paşahan was still being protected. He knew why, but that knowledge didn't make it any easier. The man had committed a sexual crime with his own daughter and there was a good chance he was going to get away with it. And if he had people like the 'Ndrangheta on his side, then he still had power even if his clout in Turkey had diminished. What he had revealed, and what he hinted at revealing, about those in control had the ability to shock and disgust. Kerim's old boss, Çetin İkmen, had always steered clear of politics on the basis that it was a dirty game that frequently got in the way of justice. Would that happen this time?

The baby's death had affected Kerim profoundly. In a way he felt that if he managed to provide justice for that child, it would challenge all the awful things Sinem was saying to him. He was a good man who provided for his family, who had given up an entire way of life to give Sinem and Melda the security they needed. So he looked at men? He only looked, although every time he denied his true nature, it hurt that little bit more.

'Kerim?'

He glanced up and saw Çetin İkmen looking down at him.

'What are you doing so far from home?' İkmen asked.

Had Kerim unconsciously strayed into İkmen territory when he'd stopped here on his way back from Kağıthane? He didn't know and he didn't care.

'I was just going to the Mozaik when I saw you sitting here. Tell me if you'd rather be alone . . .'

'I would,' Kerim said. And then, feeling himself blush at his own rudeness, he shook his head. 'Sorry.'

But İkmen just smiled. Briefly he put a hand on Kerim's shoulder – which nearly made him cry – then walked on to the Mozaik.

*

Süleyman sat down behind his desk and booted up his computer. Ömer Müngün knew better than to interrupt him. Signalling to Eylül Yavaş to remain quiet, he watched what his boss did.

Perusing the screen while periodically typing in pieces of information, Süleyman frowned, then said, 'There used to be a music shop on Galıp Dede Caddesi, near the top, next to the Kervansaray café. Either of you remember it?'

Ömer shook his head. But Eylül said, 'They used to sell instruments. Saz, ud . . .'

Süleyman looked at his screen again. 'Remember what it was called?'

'No, sir.'

'Mmm.' Then suddenly he looked up at Eylül and smiled. 'Sergeant Yavaş, you wanted to speak to me.'

Eylül looked at Ömer, then back at Süleyman. Then she gave him the same account she had given Ömer, concluding by saying, 'A connection with the 'Ndrangheta could explain how Paşahan managed to get abroad and then disappear so easily.'

Süleyman nodded. 'Any connection to Mafia organised crime has to be taken seriously. We've enough problems with our home-grown gangsters without importing from abroad. And the Italians are experts. But Inspector Alibey dismissed this, you say?'

'He appeared to, yes, sir,' she said.

'What does Inspector Gürsel think?' Süleyman asked.

Eylül told him how Kerim had been called out to Gedik Stables in connection with the death of Zekeriya Bulut. Halfway through her account, when she mentioned Zekeriya Bulut's alleged relationship with Sümeyye Paşahan, Süleyman frowned.

'So you can see why I thought you should come in, boss,' Ömer said.

'I do indeed.'

This time it was Eylül's turn to frown.

Süleyman said, 'Our Cihangir victim, Emir Kaya, was also

allegedly having an affair with Sümeyye Paşahan.' The room became silent for a moment. 'I need to find out who bought the old music shop next door to the Kervansaray café as soon as possible.'

'Why?'

'Because I have reason to believe Neşe Bocuk bought it.'

'But she's got no money!' Ömer said.

'Possibly because she bought the old music shop,' Süleyman replied. 'But this is hearsay, and so I need confirmation.'

Eylül said, 'But sir, if Neşe Bocuk did buy the music shop, so what?'

'By her own admission, Neşe Bocuk only has the apartment she lives in now that her son is in prison. There have been rumours of an alliance between Bocuk and Paşahan for some time. Unless she's mortgaged her apartment, I want to know where she got the money from to buy the music shop. Because if it came from Paşahan, what did she have to give him in return? But for now . . .' he stood, 'we have a woman to interview.'

The big lump of a detective had disappeared, replaced by some boy in uniform who wouldn't look at her. Meryem knew what was coming, and that was Mehmet Süleyman. The thought of what she knew he would ask her made her shudder. Emir had once tried to tell her what the ultimate consequences of his actions could be, but she'd dismissed his fears. How stupid could you get?

The door to the interview room swung open and three people entered. First Süleyman, then two younger officers, one of whom was a woman. They all sat down, and once the younger man had switched on the recording equipment, Süleyman asked Meryem to confirm her name, date of birth and last address.

'I have Sergeants Müngün and Yavaş with me for the course of this interview,' he said. 'You have been charged with assaulting a police officer and are entitled to legal representation, which I have been told by Inspector Görür you have declined.'

'Yes. You don't want to speak to me about that, do you?' she asked.

'No,' he said. 'Although I am bound to point out to you that legal representation would be to your benefit.'

'I don't want it!'

Weirdly, given the seriousness of her situation, all Meryem could think about now was how filthy and stupid her sunflower pyjamas looked under the harsh neon lighting of the interview room. Her mother, were she still alive, would have died of shame.

Süleyman said, 'Your choice.'

'Yes, it is.' She was becoming aggressive and that would not help, so she added, 'Inspector.'

Briefly he smiled, then he said, 'Meryem, I want to talk about heroin.'

Madam Edith looked at her watch. Even by his standards, Kerim Bey was late. Usually he came home in time to read Melda her bedtime story. The little girl looked forward to 'Daddy time' and had finally gone to bed, an hour later than usual, with tears in her eyes. Edith had tried to call him four times, but each time it had gone to voicemail. What was he doing?

She knew there were rumours about him. That he was back on the scene again, even that he had something going with the man who lived next door. She didn't believe any of it. But in spite of that, she felt she had to call up some of her contacts, just to make sure. In the old days, when Pembe had worked at Kurdish Madonna's trans brothel, Kerim had been in and out of there all the time.

She knew Madonna would be busy – her girls worked all night and she had to make sure they didn't come to harm – but she phoned her anyway.

'Edith?' Madonna said as she took the call. 'Fuck! What do you want? I've just had to kick some caveman in the balls. It's like hell in here!'

'Darling, I'm sorry,' Edith said, 'but have you seen Kerim Bey this evening?'

'Kerim Bey? No. Why would I?'

'Oh, I don't know. He's not come home, and little Melda's been crying her heart out.'

'Ah,' Madonna said. 'Things still bad between him and Sinem Hanım?'

'Awful.'

Pausing only to tell someone to 'fuck off and never come here again', Madonna said, 'I'll ask around. But you know he's been a good boy lately, which is why I can't understand what Sinem is getting so vexed about.'

'None of us can understand that,' Edith said.

'I mean, if I had Kerim Bey in my bed I'd be doing cartwheels to keep him,' Madonna said. 'And I say that as a woman with a hiatus hernia. Such a sweetheart.'

'Everything was spiralling downward. The business, my brother . . . I don't even have a relationship to keep me going.'

'And so you turned to smack,' Süleyman said.

'I know it's ridiculous,' Meryem said. 'I'm an adult. When I was offered it, I should have just said no, but by that time, eighteen months ago, I didn't give a fuck. I also thought I could make some money out of it.'

'Who offered it to you?'

She looked Süleyman dead in the eyes. 'No way, man. I took it, I sold it, this is down to me.'

'It would go better for you if you told us,' Ömer Müngün said.

Meryem sat back in her chair and crossed her arms. 'I taped a couple of bags underneath the kitchen sink. This is hardly the drugs bust of the century. Can we talk about my brother?'

253

She'd made her mind up to do this thing, even though the thought of it made her want to scream. She could die for what she was about to do. But so what?

Süleyman must have noticed how much she was sweating. 'We can. But first of all, Miss Kaya, I'm assuming you're in the throes of withdrawal.'

'I've been in the throes of withdrawal for days,' she said. 'What the hell would my going to see a doctor now achieve?'

'A doctor could prescribe a sedative.'

'No.' She shook her head. 'Fuck it! Look, my brother was in love with Görkan Paşahan's daughter, Sümeyye. He met her at Tarlabaşı Sunday market. He liked it over there and used to take a selection of his cheaper cat houses for sale. He never sold many, but he enjoyed the buzz. Then Miss Paşahan appears and he's obsessed.'

'What was Sümeyye Paşahan doing in a place like Tarlabaşı?' Süleyman asked.

'How would I know? Some of these rich people like to slum it.'

'When was this?'

'Last year, eight months ago.'

'What happened?'

'He started to spend a lot of time with her,' she said. 'Told me it was love, blah, blah, blah. I didn't like it, because of who she was. I have no love for any politicians, but what Görkan Bey did was dangerous. I didn't want Emir around that. Then he told me she was pregnant. I went berserk.'

'How?'

'I smacked my brother around the head with a branding iron. I didn't hit him as hard as I could've done, but I'm not proud of it. I took him to our doctor. Then we talked.'

'About?'

'He gave me some story about how the baby wasn't his, how he'd never touched her like that. I told him to tell his story to

254

someone stupid and he shut up. It was months before he told me the truth.'

'Which was?'

'I could hardly believe it,' she said. 'Still not sure that I do. Sümeyye, he said, had been made pregnant by her father.'

The three officers looked at one another.

Meryem said, 'You know, don't you?'

None of them answered her. She put a hand up to her head and laughed. 'Fuck! It's true then! I've spent months fearing a knock at the door, finding Emir's dead body in the back yard. And all that talk about how he loved her without sex . . . I thought he was trying to fool me.' She stopped.

Süleyman sensed what might be going on in her mind. 'But the forge burned down and your brother is dead.'

The room fell silent, and then Meryem said, 'Emir gave her up – or so he told me. As far as I'm aware, for the last two months he has not crossed the Bosphorus.'

Eylül Yavaş said, 'You're saying that Sümeyye Paşahan lives on the Asian side?'

'Yes. That's what he told me. He said he'd finished with her. He even invented a story about her being involved with someone else.'

Süleyman frowned.

'I know, sick,' she said.

'Do you know who this other man was?' Ömer Müngün asked.

'Didn't you hear me? He made it up!'

'How do you know that?' Süleyman asked.

She shrugged. 'I don't. But to me it sounded a bit convenient, you know? Also she was pregnant. And if she really was pregnant by her own father, who but my stupid, soft little brother would want to be involved with that?' She began to cry.

'Meryem Hanım, do you know where Sümeyye Paşahan is now?' Süleyman pressed.

She pulled herself together. 'I don't. I've never known. On the Asian side is all I know. I never met the woman. But when the forge was set on fire, I knew it was Paşahan. I don't know why, because Emir was out of it by that time. Or was he? Merve, my neighbour, said he was probably lying.'

'So Ms Karabulut knew about Emir and Sümeyye?'

'Yes. Emir told her,' she said. 'She worried about it because involvement with Paşahan might bring the police to my door and disrupt her supply of smack.'

Süleyman nodded. 'Miss Kaya,' he said, 'you work sometimes for Gedik Stables in Kağıthane.'

'Yes.'

'Do you know a groom there called Zekeriya Bulut?'

For the first time during the interrogation, she smiled. 'What? Sıla Gedik's toy boy? Yes.'

A look passed between the three officers again, and then Süleyman said, 'Miss Kaya, according to Miss Gedik, at the same time Zekeriya Bulut was having an affair with her, he was also sleeping with Sümeyye Paşahan.'

'But she was pregnant? Or was she?'

'Oh, she was pregnant,' he continued. 'The body of her baby was found in Kağıthane. Now, as well as your brother, Zekeriya Bulut is dead too. If you know where Sümeyye Paşahan is, you must tell us. People tend to die around this woman, and I want to know why.'

Chapter 19

Once she was sure that Melda was asleep, Madam Edith left Sinem in the Gürsels' apartment and hit the streets of Tarlabaşı in search of alcohol. She didn't have to go far. Rambo Şekeroğlu's bar, opposite the Poisoned Princess apartments, was still open, mainly now patronised by hardened alcoholics. She sat down at a table outside, lit a cigarette and waited for someone to come and take her order.

After a few minutes, Rambo himself appeared.

'I'll have half a bottle of rakı, please,' Edith said.

The gypsy went back inside and returned with a small bottle of the anise spirit, a bottle of water and a glass. Edith asked him to join her, and when she'd poured herself a drink, he did likewise.

'I don't suppose you've seen Kerim Bey this evening, have you?' she asked.

'No,' he said. 'But that neighbour of yours has been in. Briefly.'

'Enver Bey?' she said. She had seen the man in the hallway outside the apartment a couple of times. He had always been polite to her.

'That's him.' Rambo took a drink. 'Don't like him. Don't know why he comes here.'

'What do you mean?'

'Madam Edith, I'm Roma, I know when people don't like us. I've had plenty of practice and that man doesn't like Roma.'

'Maybe he comes here because it's close,' she said.

'Nah.'

'Why do you say that?'

'Only comes if he sees Kerim Bey sitting outside. Why he didn't stay earlier. No Kerim Bey.'

'Really?'

'Mmm. Always wipes his glass with his handkerchief before he drinks. Can't have Roma sweat getting into your rakı, can you?'

'You really think he's a racist?' Edith asked.

'Lay money on it. Not that I think Kerim Bey knows that. But then he doesn't see the way Enver Bey looks at me, how he drops money into my hand without touching my flesh. I've seen it all before, Madam Edith. Trust me.'

'Kerim Bey wouldn't want to be involved with someone like that!' Edith said.

'Like I say, he doesn't know,' Rambo said. 'And he fancies him.'

Mehmet Süleyman had told Ömer Müngün to go home. But it was already 3 a.m., and so Ömer felt there was little point. In any case, he didn't want to go home. Gibrail, if he slept at all, rarely did so beyond four. Also, he was thinking – mainly about Neşe Bocuk.

If the old woman had paid for the music shop on Galıp Dede Caddesi herself, then where had the money come from? When Görkan Paşahan had moved into the city, when he'd been riding high with those in power, there had been rumours that he'd taken the old woman under his wing. Whether as a favour to her son Esat wasn't known. Esat was still in prison, and most of his assets had been seized long before Paşahan came on the scene.

Neşe and Paşahan had certainly met. Organised Crime had, after some persuasion, reported a meeting outside the Galıp Paşa Mosque on Bağdat Caddesi at the beginning of 2022. What had passed between the pair was unknown, as was whether that meeting had been followed up by other more discreet appointments. Both of them were known for their ruthlessness; neither did anything for anyone out of the goodness of their hearts. So if Paşahan had given the old woman money to buy the music shop so she could set up in business as a falcı, he had to know he was going to get something out of it. Ömer had already checked the recent transactions on Neşe Bocuk's bank account. There was no sign of someone else putting money into the account, and certainly no property purchase.

When Esat Bocuk and his younger son had been arrested just before COVID, he'd left Neşe and his elder son, Ateş, to fend for themselves. Ateş had subsequently entered a psychiatric facility, which had left the old woman alone in the family's Bağdat Bulvarı apartment. And yet she'd maintained a reasonable lifestyle.

Ömer frowned, and Süleyman said, 'What's the matter?'

'I was thinking about Neşe Bocuk's maid, boss.'

'Mmm.' Süleyman was drowsy now and so he didn't berate the younger man for lusting after the maid this time. 'What about her?'

'Well, you know gangsters don't ever do anything for anyone without an ulterior motive?'

'In the main, yes,' Süleyman said. 'What's your point, Sergeant?'

It was then that Ömer formulated a theory he could in no way prove or disprove.

'You have to be sure, Mehmet Bey. And I don't think you are.'

Selahattin Ozer was a tall, slim man in his sixties. Genuinely pious, he was well known to practise an austere form of Islam that included fasting over and above what was required from the faithful. He wasn't a man given to appreciation of alternative lifestyles, but Süleyman knew that he was also a person upon whom a lot of pressure was exerted. It was, in addition, 5.30 in the morning and he'd not long ago been roused from his bed.

'With respect, sir, how can I be?' Süleyman said.

Just before he'd been called into Ozer's office, he'd smothered himself in aftershave to cover up the smell of cigarettes. Now it was wafting up at him and he felt he had probably overdone it.

'Until we can ascertain where the money came from to buy that building in Neşe Bocuk's name,' he continued, 'we can't confirm or deny Paşahan's involvement.'

'Organised Crime are currently interviewing Paşahan's contacts in the city—'

'We need to find Sümeyye Paşahan,' Süleyman interrupted. 'We know she bore her father's child.'

'Yes, but we don't know the circumstances, Mehmet Bey,' Ozer said. 'Maybe she tempted him.'

Süleyman slumped back in his chair as if he'd just been hit. He knew that some people believed the nonsense put around about victims of sexual abuse being complicit in their own suffering, but he hadn't reckoned on Ozer sharing such views. Though to be fair, he could see that his superior was sweating and also failing to look at him.

'Sir, that's not how it works,' he said. 'I can't believe that you think that's the case.'

Neither of them spoke for a moment, and then Ozer said, 'Mehmet Bey, we are obliged to keep anything to do with Paşahan under the radar. The things he's saying may cause panic, lack of trust . . .'

'We need to find his daughter,' Süleyman said. 'We need to find her in connection with her child's death, the death of Emir Kaya and possibly that of Zekeriya Bulut. We have it on good authority that she was involved with both of those men.'

'Organised Crime—'

'No!'

'I beg your pardon, Mehmet Bey?'

Süleyman was entering a place he knew he could possibly not come back from. He took a breath.

'Organised Crime are doing a very good job of speaking to

low-level associates of Paşahan in the city,' he said. 'I understand that there is a political dimension. But I'm only interested in the fact that people, including a baby, have died.'

'That is Inspector Gürsel's case.'

'It is connected to mine, and I believe that Sümeyye Paşahan is the connection. I don't know whether she personally has killed or whether she's paid others to do so, and I have no idea whether her father is involved. But I need to bring her in and talk to her and I need to do it now.'

Ozer maintained eye contact with Süleyman for as long as he could bear, and then said, 'I will speak to the public prosecutor later this morning about obtaining a warrant.'

'With respect, sir, I need it as soon as possible,' Süleyman said.

Ozer kept his voice level. 'You will get said warrant as and when it is convenient and proper for Ali Bey to grant this to you. You should also, I believe, alert your colleague Inspector Gürsel, if for no other reason than out of courtesy.'

It was one of those dreams where he was somewhere he knew but couldn't put a name to it. He was with people he didn't know and there was a feeling of dread.

'Kerim Bey!'

Who was that? Whoever it was sounded awful, harsh, like an ancient crow with a bad throat.

'Kerim Bey!'

God, he was rattling around like he was in an earthquake. He heard himself gasp, and then his eyes shot open to reveal a terrible old woman pushing her face into his.

'Kerim Bey, your phone!'

Samsun Bajraktar was wearing a stained nylon housecoat, her long grey hair hanging in rats' tails by the sides of her face. She thrust something into his hand and said, 'Well answer it, man!'

He swiped to take the call and looked around the room. It was

261

small and dingy and there were football posters on the wall. Galatasaray.

'Hello?'

'Kerim Bey, where are you?'

It was Mehmet Süleyman.

'Um.'

He attempted to sit up. The room swam in front of his eyes and he lay down again. Then he saw a man in a ragged dressing gown walk into the room with a cigarette between his fingers. İkmen.

'I'm with Çetin Bey at his apartment,' he said.

'I need you here. It concerns your murdered baby. I've applied for a search warrant.'

'For . . .'

'Just get here as soon as you can.' Süleyman ended the call.

'I'll drive you to headquarters in your car,' İkmen said. 'I don't suppose you'd pass a breath test.'

Samsun said, 'You couldn't even stand up when Çetin brought you in.'

'Yes, well . . .' İkmen said. 'Samsun, would you go and get Kerim Bey a glass of tea?'

When she'd left, İkmen sat down on the bed beside Kerim. 'When you've had your tea, have a shower and get dressed. I've cleaned your shoes.'

'My shoes?'

'You vomited over them.'

'Oh God! I'm so sorry!'

İkmen smiled. 'There's aspirin in the bathroom cabinet. Help yourself.'

Public Prosecutor Ali Oğan had been in with Commissioner Ozer for nearly two hours. Ömer Müngün and Eylül Yavaş watched Süleyman pace his office floor like a captured tiger. Flicking ash out of the open window of his office, he'd long since given up even a pretence of calm.

Eventually pointing towards Ozer's office, he said, 'The longer this goes on, the more likely it is that someone else gets involved.'

'Who do you mean, boss?' Ömer asked.

'Alibey,' Süleyman said. 'I don't trust him.'

'We don't know—'

'Ömer Bey, what Organised Crime had me doing was not helpful,' Eylül said. 'Inspector Alibey tried to make me think that it was, but it was pointless. While I can't level charges of collusion against Alibey, at the very least he's not serious about Paşahan. He completely dismissed my fears about possible Mafia involvement.'

'To be fair, he's walking the approved line,' Ömer said.

Süleyman sat down. 'Protecting people like Paşahan is not our job. I don't care who he's got dirt on! I don't care what people may think!'

Ömer, his head lowered said, 'Boss, you know that's not how things work.'

'Well they should!' Süleyman yelled.

They all descended into silence. As a member of a sometimes reviled minority, Ömer Müngün knew that what Süleyman was railing against was something only those with privilege could afford to question.

Eylül Yavaş tactfully changed the subject. 'Sir, is Inspector Gürsel on his way in?'

'Yes,' he said. 'I will have to brief him when he gets here. Why don't you two go and get some breakfast. You've been up all night and I don't want either of you fainting on me.'

Ömer stood. 'Sounds good to me. Eylül Hanım?'

'Yes,' she said. 'But, sir, you will call us . . .'

'I'm not doing any of this on my own, Sergeant Yavaş,' he said.

'And thank you, both of you. Ömer Bey, whatever happens, your contribution has been key to this case. I appreciate it.'

Çetin İkmen was on the tram back to Sultanahmet when Madam Edith called. A vast man with a vast tartan washing bag at his feet had his fat elbow in İkmen's ribs while a covered woman on his other side shoved her considerable bottom against his leg as she attempted to make more room for herself. Rush hour on any form of İstanbul public transport was a trial, and despite the chilliness of the day, proximity to so many bodies was making İkmen sweat.

Grunting as he slid his hand into his overcoat pocket to retrieve his phone, he apologised for touching the now outraged woman and looked at the screen.

'Edith?'

'Kerim Bey didn't come home at all last night,' she said.

'I know. I've just taken him to work,' İkmen said.

'He spent the night at your place?'

'Not exactly. There's a bar called the Rose in the alleyway beside the Mozaik. He spent most of it there, with a bottle of rakı.'

The man with the tartan bag pulled a disgusted face. İkmen said, 'So? If you eavesdrop, you'll hear things you don't like.'

The man looked away.

'I took him back to my apartment and put him to bed,' İkmen continued.

Edith told him what Rambo Şekeroğlu had said to her about Enver Bey and Kerim. She said, 'I'll be honest, I thought that was where he might be. I even put a glass up against the wall between our apartment and his, but I didn't hear anything.'

'Well, he wasn't there,' İkmen said. 'I've just taken him to head-quarters and I think something big's happening. Mehmet Bey called him this morning and it sounded urgent. But don't worry about Enver Bey, I'm on to him.'

'Are you?'

264

'Oh yes. You came to me with a problem, Edith, and I am in the process of solving it for you. I'll say no more, and not a word to anyone.'

'Of course not!'

İkmen didn't even try to put his phone back in his coat pocket. It was too much effort. When he returned to his apartment, he'd have to change into a clean shirt to go and meet Mr Enver Yılmaz or whatever he called himself. He'd not given the man the chance to tell him his name when he'd watched him take his call from afar. Of course, he might not even turn up. But whatever did or didn't happen, İkmen knew his day would be interesting.

Mehmet Süleyman had just finished telling Kerim Gürsel about Ömer Müngün's suspicions regarding Neşe Bocuk and her maid when Commissioner Ozer knocked on Süleyman's office door and walked in. Both men stood.

'Sir?'

Ozer told them to sit and then took what was usually Ömer Müngün's chair. His cold grey eyes gave nothing away, but he held a piece of paper in his hands that he now looked at gravely.

'Prosecutor Oğan has decided, after consultation with other interested parties, that whatever the political fallout might be, we cannot risk this woman, Sümeyye Paşahan, possibly killing again . . .'

'Yes!' Unable to contain his delight, Süleyman punched the air.

'. . . and so a warrant has been issued that will allow you to search the premises owned by one Neşe Bocuk. Further, as per your request, you may make entrance with a full scene-of-crime cohort, including forensic investigators. The strong smell of ammonia in Bocuk's apartment that you reported to me, was, however, what finally convinced Prosecutor Ogan to permit this action. If at least some of the methamphetamine that has been flooding this city originates from there, it will be a good result for us. However . . .'

There was a caveat. Both men leaned forward.

'Organised Crime have a legitimate reason to be included in this raid,' Ozer said. 'On the basis that they are actively pursuing Görkan Paşahan.'

'Sir!'

He held up his hand. 'Don't try to argue against this, Mehmet Bey. I have no idea what the issue between yourself and Inspector Alibey might be, and I don't want to know. If it helps, you will take the lead on this operation, and so the success or failure of it rests largely with you. For your information, Inspector Alibey is not convinced the operation is necessary.'

'No, I don't suppose he is,' Süleyman said.

'What do you mean by that, Mehmet Bey?'

He thought fast. 'I mean, sir, that Inspector Alibey is rather more sensitive to the possible political ramifications than myself or Inspector Gürsel.'

Ozer looked over at Kerim, who had now reached the shivery stage of his hangover. 'Quite.' He stood and placed the warrant on Süleyman's desk. 'Assemble your team, and if God is merciful, you will be successful.'

Everything was unbalanced now that Zekeriya was dead. Not only did Sıla Gedik not have him to warm her bed, she was now the only person capable of riding Yıldırım.

She and her grooms mounted in silence in the stable yard before heading out to exercise the horses. Aslı Dölen, one-time friend of that whore who had taken Zekeriya away from her, averted her eyes when she passed Sıla on Badem. Silly little bitch! As she rode away, Aslı's phone rang and she answered it. Sıla had always told the grooms to switch their phones off when they took the horses out. But the way she felt right now meant she couldn't be bothered to say anything.

Heading towards the creek, she urged Yıldırım on to a gallop, leaving Aslı and the other grooms to exercise their mounts in the field belonging to the riding school.

In spite of the cold weather, it felt good to be out on her own with Yıldırım. Unlike her other horses, he could gallop fast and with abandon, which was why his rider had to be strong. Even so, she struggled at times to master him. She told herself it was because Zekeriya's death had weakened her, and then she began to cry. Eventually she had to dismount and just howl into the wind while Yıldırım cropped the grass and Sıla wondered why the loss of her toy boy was so devastating. Was it because she had felt all along that he was her last chance at happiness? If so, what a fool she'd been.

She pulled herself together and let Yıldırım have his head again before she walked him back to the stables. As they approached, she saw that Badem was already in her stable. She asked one of the grooms why.

He said, 'Oh, Aslı had a message or something, had to go home.'

It was possible. The girl had taken that call before they'd ridden out of the yard. But then maybe she'd left because she knew that Sıla was furious with her.

Chapter 20

Places like the district of Maslak were what Çetin İkmen called 'anti-İstanbul'. By this he meant that it was one of those areas where vast modern steel and glass office and residential blocks had arisen around wide grey boulevards. Constructed largely within the last twenty years, such places were peopled mainly by the business community and students at the nearby İstanbul Technical University.

İkmen walked up the steps from the İtü-Ayazağa metro station onto Büyükdere Caddesi accompanied by a lot of young people with rainbow-coloured hair carrying books. He looked at the old map in his hands and tried to figure out where the building he was looking for might be. The whole thing appeared to be a mystery, and so he took a punt and crossed the road in front of him. He'd never been able to master the route finder on his phone and so he found that a lot of people were staring at him as he wrestled with his map – turning it upside-down and sideways.

Eventually, driven half mad by his own incompetence, he walked up to the security guard of the building he was standing in front of and, pointing to the address he'd jotted down in his notebook, said, 'Do you know where this is?'

The guard, a man in his forties rapidly running to fat, said, 'Seriously?'

'Do I look as if I'm joking?' İkmen said. 'I'm having a breakdown. This place is a nightmare!'

'Well, breakdown no more, uncle. This . . .' the guard pointed behind him, 'is that very building.'

İkmen sighed. 'Well, they don't make it easy, do they?'

The guard pointed to the name of the building above his head. 'Sorry, uncle. I understand it gets a bit hard when one reaches your age. God bless you.'

Resisting the urge to tell the man to fuck off, İkmen walked through the revolving door into the building and went straight to reception. A very smart young woman, deep it seemed in communion with a switchboard, eventually looked up and smiled.

'Can I help you, sir?'

İkmen gave her the benefit of his most disarming smile and watched her blush. He still had it with women, in spite of his appearance. Charm.

'I do hope so,' he said. 'I am looking for the offices of Mahzur IT Solutions. I have an appointment with Enver Yılmaz.'

She smiled at him. 'Let me see, sir.'

He waited. There was a Starbucks over in one corner of the vast reception area. Not something to İkmen's taste, but he did think that when he left, he might check out whether they served Turkish coffee alongside all their other beverages.

The young woman looked up, but this time she didn't smile.

'I'm really sorry, sir, but I'm afraid we don't have a company of that name in this building. Is it possible you may have got the wrong address?'

İkmen smiled and said, 'No. Can you please check again?'

'Of course.'

But he knew it was pointless. Enver Yılmaz, or whoever he was, had lied to him.

It was 11 a.m. by the time Süleyman, Kerim Gürsel and Mevlüt Alibey assembled their team. Consisting of one police van and two cars, six detectives and ten scene-of-crime officers, including

269

forensic support, they left headquarters car park for the Asian side of the Bosphorus. The timing was hardly ideal – traffic across the Bosphorus Bridge particularly would be nose to tail. Sirens would help, but there was a limit on how much progress they would make even with sirens blaring out. Besides, what Süleyman was looking for in Neşe Bocuk's huge apartment was not one- but twofold.

If they found even just traces of crystal meth they could arrest Neşe Bocuk and lean on her. And both Süleyman and Ömer had smelt ammonia in there when last they visited. At the time they'd dismissed it as the smell of an old woman with continence issues – and that could still be the case, but Süleyman was increasingly sceptical. He glanced at Mevlüt Alibey sitting next to him in the back of the car, which was being driven by Ömer Müngün. The organised-crime officer looked smug. Not that it meant anything; he always did. If a channel of communication existed between him and Güllü and Neşe Bocuk, the old woman was going to be on her own when they arrived, making Alibey's confidence well placed.

But what if, as Commissioner Ozer had pointed out, the old woman's maid wasn't Sümeyye Paşahan? What then?

His phone beeped to indicate he had a text. He glanced at it, noted it was from Gonca and then switched the phone off. It was probably just her daily card reading. He didn't want Alibey to see it.

Çetin İkmen tried to ring the number on which he'd first contacted Enver Yılmaz and found it was unobtainable. Then he looked up the Mahzur IT Solutions website and discovered that there was now a new mobile number for the company. Quick work. But he didn't call that number because what would be the point? Mr Yılmaz was clearly doing something less than legal, and his very obvious pursuit of him would not, he felt, help.

He sat down on a low wall outside the office building he'd just visited and lit a cigarette. A couple of smartly turned-out bearded businessmen looked down at him with disgust, but İkmen was unaffected. These men, he thought, should count themselves fortunate that he'd not told them to fuck off.

So if it was a given that Yılmaz was doing something financially questionable, where did the Gürsels figure in all this? He suspected Enver Bey was having non-consensual sex with Sinem Gürsel. Further, he also appeared to be following Kerim Bey's movements to some extent. It was almost as if he were torturing them. But why? Well, he supposed, the simple answer was that Kerim was a police officer. Sometimes İkmen himself had experienced abuse from those he'd arrested when they got out of prison. Sometimes they'd ended up back in prison because of their behaviour. But it was rare. He was just about to call Süleyman to talk about this very point when he received a call from Mehmet's wife.

'İkmen,' she said. 'Where are you?'

'Maslak.'

'Maslak! What are you doing there?'

He didn't want to explain. 'Nothing.'

'Oh, have it your way,' she said. 'Mehmet went into work in the middle of the night and I can't seem to raise him.'

'Then he's busy. He wouldn't just leave you for no reason.'

Ever since she'd become ill, she'd worried more about her husband.

'I sent him my reading for today and he hasn't responded,' she said. 'He always responds! I'm concerned. Last night I tried to leave him.'

'What?'

'It was all too difficult,' she said. 'The way I am now, the situation with Büket Teyze . . .'

'Büket Teyze? What about her?'

271

'She asked me to curse some woman over in Bostancı, an Antakya falcı who's setting up in the old shop next to Büket's place. Mehmet didn't like it.'

'Well, you know he doesn't—'

'Yes, yes, but I have to be myself, I told him! Anyway, he ended up in tears and now I don't know where he is.'

İkmen took a deep breath. 'He's working, Gonca,' he said.

'Maybe. But why won't he respond to my prediction?'

This was becoming a circular argument. İkmen said, 'What was your prediction for him?'

'Oh, it was a strange one,' she said. 'It was basically that he has to follow the money. But he follows killers, doesn't he? He's not involved in fraud or—'

'Sometimes, in fact very often, killers also have financial interests,' İkmen said. And as he said it, he felt something niggle at the back of his brain. He'd told Mehmet to do just this, to follow the money, not that long ago . . .

There was only one way into the penthouse owned by Neşe Bocuk and that was through the front door. When the building had been constructed fifteen years before, it had a fire escape, but that was long gone. After informing the building's kapıcı that they had a warrant to enter the premises belonging to the old woman, the officers got into both lifts that serviced the block and ascended to the eighth floor.

Süleyman knocked on the door and rang the bell simultaneously. 'Police! Open up!'

For half a minute nothing happened, so he knocked and yelled again.

Kerim Gürsel, at his side, had dry-heaved in the lift and now looked grey again. He'd admitted to Süleyman that he'd got drunk the previous night, but he'd not owned up to how drunk.

At last they heard the unmistakable sound of slippers slapping on the floor as the old woman came to answer the door. The old woman and not the maid . . .

She opened the door and smiled. Süleyman held up the warrant and said, 'We have a warrant to search this property.'

'Oh? Why?'

'Get out of the way, Neşe Hanım, and let us do our job.'

She flattened herself against the wall of the corridor, a smile still fixed on her face. As the officers pushed past her to gain access, she said, 'I hope you find what you're looking for, Mehmet Bey.'

The Kervansaray café was empty save for the ancient cigarette-scented barista and Büket Teyze, the café's resident falcı. Resplendent in many multicoloured scarves, her wrinkled eyelids plastered with bright blue shadow and thick black eyeliner, she was drinking from a small bottle containing clear liquid when İkmen approached.

He sat down at her table. 'Rakı, vodka or gin?'

The old woman looked at the bottle. 'Vodka today.'

'I applaud your fortitude,' İkmen said.

She laughed. 'What do you want?'

'Coffee would be a good start.' He called to the barista, who took his order with a scowl.

'I've heard from Gonca this morning,' İkmen said.

'Oh, poor girl,' Büket said. 'Not herself, and now she's worried she'll lose her man because of it. I told her, I said, "Mehmet Bey will never leave you", but she won't listen.'

'I've said much the same myself,' İkmen replied. 'But Büket Teyze, I don't want to speak to you about that. I want to speak to you about the curse you asked Gonca to put on Neşe Bocuk.'

She frowned. 'She tell you about that?' she asked.

'She did, and I'm glad she did.'

'Oh.'

273

The barista placed a tiny cup of Turkish coffee down in front of İkmen and said, 'It's sweet. We only do sweet.'

'Yes, I know.' İkmen turned to Büket. 'You do know who Neşe Bocuk is, don't you, Büket?'

'She's a falcı from Antakya,' she said. 'People reckon they're really good. Load of nonsense, but if I begin to lose business to her, I'll end up on the street.'

'Her son is Esat Bocuk,' İkmen said. 'In prison now, but he was the most powerful godfather on the Asian side for quite some years.'

'I know who her son is.'

'And it is said that Neşe then got in with Görkan Paşahan . . .'

'That bastard!'

'Equally unavailable because he is abroad,' İkmen said. 'But although I can't tell you any details, Büket Teyze, I can tell you that the name Paşahan is now of great interest to the police in this city, so proceed with caution.'

'Never met the woman!'

'But you gave Gonca a piece of her hair,' İkmen pointed out.

Büket Teyze reddened. 'Went through her bin.'

'Did you. You do know that her building houses a lot of people, don't you?'

'Yeah. Not people like her, though. Gonca show it to you, did she?'

'No, she called me.'

'White it was, the hair,' Büket said. 'Thin old-lady hair. Anyway, didn't go through the bin myself, paid some sick street kid to do it.'

İkmen raised his eyes.

'What?'

'The kid could've given you anything,' he said. 'From cotton to cat fur.'

'I watched him,' Büket said. 'It was hair. He lives behind those bins, he knows which one is hers. She's got a maid who gives him

274

scraps sometimes. She came down just after the kid gave me the hair. He told me to hide when he saw her, said if she knew what he'd been doing, she'd stop giving him food.'

'And did she give him food?' İkmen asked.

'Yeah, she did, then she left,' Büket said. 'Off down Bağdat, taking off her headscarf as she went.' She laughed. 'Covered woman, my arse! The kid didn't even eat the food. But like I say, sick, poor little bastard.'

'There are three bathrooms and one kitchen,' Süleyman said to the scene-of-crime officers. 'Swab every flat surface, plus the insides of cupboards and the floors.'

They went about their business wordlessly.

Suddenly at Süleyman's side, Neşe Bocuk said, 'What are you looking for, Mehmet Bey?'

There was a twinkle in her eye that he didn't like.

'Methamphetamine,' he said. 'Probably known to you as crystal meth.'

'Oh?'

'We think that you or someone on these premises has been cooking.'

'Cooking?'

Süleyman leaned down. 'Don't play dumb, Neşe Hanım, you know exactly what I mean.'

'Do I?' She smiled. 'Mehmet Bey Efendi, I am an old woman with arthritis and a leaky bladder. I don't get out much.'

If meth were to be found on the premises, was she going to plead she didn't know because she herself smelt of ammonia?

She said, 'Old age is a curse. I was once very lovely, you know. But now I walk with a stick and smell of piss.'

He looked at her. Of course she was going to use that defence.

'Boss!' Ömer Müngün came out of the main bedroom carrying a plastic bag. Süleyman walked over to him.

'What have you got there?

'Tylol,' he said. 'I've counted twelve boxes so far, each containing six sachets.'

Neşe said, 'I get a lot of colds.'

'Well I suggest you be careful when you take Tylol,' Süleyman said. 'All that pseudoephedrine might make you feel bad.'

Pseudoephedrine was a decongestant present in a lot of cold remedies. It was also a major component of methamphetamine.

She turned away. Süleyman whispered to Ömer Müngün, 'Where are Alibey and Güllü?'

He shrugged. Kerim Gürsel joined them. 'I think I saw them leaving the apartment.'

'Checking the dustbins,' Eylül Yavaş cut in.

Methamphetamine, as well as being potentially lethal, created a lot of toxic waste while in production.

One of the scene-of-crime officers, who had been close by during this conversation, said, 'We're supposed to be dealing with the bins, Mehmet Bey.'

'Go down and tell them to stop,' Süleyman said. 'Tell them that I am the lead on this operation and I am forbidding them to continue.'

'Yes, sir.'

Kerim Gürsel said, 'I'll come with you.'

Neşe Bocuk was still apparently amused by what was going on. 'What a forceful man you are, Mehmet Bey Efendi. I wonder how long Gonca Hanım will be able to keep you under her spell?'

A lot of people felt bewildered, or at least vaguely unsettled, by Süleyman's marriage to Gonca. Many of them justified what they saw as the 'pollution' of a Turkish aristocrat by a Roma woman as an act of sorcery. And although he was used to it, this attitude still made him angry. His wife was his Achilles heel, and he hated it when those who opposed him used her name as a weapon.

'Neşe—' he began.

But he was interrupted by a scene-of-crime officer holding a small piece of paper up in the air and calling out, 'Positive!'

This was followed shortly by other officers who had obtained the same result.

It wasn't often that Kurdish Madonna asked to meet anyone away from her own place in Tarlabaşı, and so Madam Edith was rather anxious about her friend as she walked towards their meeting place, Coffee Lab, in the old Narmanlı Han off İstiklal Caddesi. She feared some man had broken her heart again. Madonna liked straight-acting men far more than she should and tended to favour those who were in denial about their sexuality.

As she approached the outside table where Madonna was sitting, she felt her heart sink. She'd been very obviously crying. The two women kissed and then Edith sat down. A waiter came over and she ordered a cappuccino. When he'd gone, she said, 'So who is it this time?'

But Madonna shook her head. 'Oh, it's not men,' she said. 'Or rather, it is, but not like that.'

'Then what is it like, honey?' Edith asked. 'I can see you're really upset.'

Madonna leaned across the table, her long blond hair extensions framing her slim, aquiline face.

'You know when I was young, back in the village . . .'

'What, you mean before recorded time began?' Edith lit a cigarette. 'We all have *that* kind of past, darling. Hiding what you were, waiting for your father to find out and kill you . . .'

'I had a son,' Madonna said. 'I was married and I had a son with my wife. Lokman, we called him. I left when he was two. Not because I didn't love him.'

'I know why you left, you don't have to explain all that to me,' Edith said. 'And you're not the only one with kids. Matmazel Gigi

277

has two daughters. One she sees, the other won't come anywhere near.'

'Lokman wants to meet me,' Madonna said.

'How did he find you?'

'Online of course. Sometimes I think it's as if the Internet has blown off every door in the world, revealing all our secrets, exposing us to people and events that are best left in the past. I want to see him . . .'

'So see him then!'

'Oh, it's not as simple as that.' She slumped back in her chair and stared into her tea glass.

Not knowing what to say next, Madam Edith looked around at their fellow coffee drinkers, which was when she saw Enver Bey from next door. Feeling her hackles rise, she glanced away quickly. She wanted to confront him. How dare he pursue Kerim Bey! She knew very well what it was like to want a man and not be able to have him. That had happened to her countless times. But she'd always steered well clear of married men. Why couldn't this bastard?

'Lokman is married and has two children of his own, a boy and a girl.'

Edith looked back at Madonna. 'So you're a grandmother!'

But she spoke too loudly and she saw Enver Bey look over at her. He smiled, and Edith made herself respond to him in kind. But doing it made her shudder.

Madonna, oblivious to this exchange, ploughed on. 'They live in some village outside Gaziantep. The back of beyond! And he's a car mechanic. The wife is covered, for God's sake! I mean, I want to see him, but what if he turns up here and beats me up?' She reached across the table and took one of Edith's hands. 'Oh sweetie, what am I going to do?'

Edith gently stroked Madonna's hair. She had no answers for her. She had a point about her son. He might just want to meet her

278

to take revenge or take her money. But Madonna still loved him and Edith could understand that. But what could she do? In the meantime, Enver Bey was still watching her and smiling.

'Where's the girl? The maid?'

Neşe Bocuk shrugged. 'I don't know. You know what those country girls are like, Mehmet Bey, here today, gone tomorrow.'

'Except she wasn't a country girl, was she?' Süleyman said.

Now back at headquarters after the old woman had been arrested for using her premises for the production of a banned substance, Süleyman had finally got around to asking about the maid.

'Girls from the countryside don't generally have plastic surgery,' he went on. 'Particularly not breast and bottom augmentation.'

'Oh you'd be surprised,' Neşe said. 'Men are men and they like big chests and bottoms. Maybe her husband had it done to her, I don't know.'

'What's her name, Neşe Hanım?' Süleyman asked.

She looked at her lawyer before answering, then said, 'Canan.'

'Canan what?'

She shrugged again. She was playing with them. 'Like I say, here today—'

'How did you pay her?' Ömer Müngün asked.

'Cash. Girls like that only understand cash. You know how it is: have to send money home to the old parents in Anatolia, they don't have a bank account . . .'

'Neşe Hanım, your son Esat Bocuk was at one time a very powerful crime boss,' Süleyman said. 'I do not see someone like you simply taking in a young woman you know nothing about.'

'Help's very expensive now, Mehmet Bey,' she said.

Süleyman leaned back in his chair. 'Ah yes, money,' he said. 'You've got none, I understand.'

'No. You putting Esat away . . .'

279

He pushed a piece of paper across the table towards her. 'So if you've got no money, how do you explain this?'

Neşe and her lawyer both looked down at the document. Süleyman wasn't sure the old woman could read, so he said, 'This TAPU, issued by Beyoğlu Belediye, states that you are the legal owner of a property on Galıp Dede Caddesi in Beyoğlu colloquially known as the old music shop.'

Even though she was pale already, Neşe Bocuk's face became white.

'Now, we know that no money for this purchase came from you, Neşe Hanım,' he continued. 'We've been into your bank account and it is, as you say, empty. And while I am prepared to believe that you are and have been living on cash, I find it inconceivable that you happened to have sixteen million Turkish lira just lying around, even if you were cooking up meth in your penthouse for a year.'

For a moment, Süleyman stared at Neşe Bocuk and she stared at him. Then, finally sure that he was reading her correctly, he said, 'You didn't know that this property had been purchased in your name, did you? You thought that whoever bought it for you had done so under an alias. Unluckily for you, the fortune-telling community in this city knew it was you. Word had got out.'

A look passed between Neşe Bocuk and her lawyer, and then he said, 'Inspector Süleyman, I'd like to call for a break.'

'No.' Süleyman leaned across the table towards the old woman. 'Where is Sümeyye Paşahan, Neşe Hanım? Who bought this property in your name? Was it Sümeyye or her father?'

She said nothing. Her lawyer tried to call for a break again, and then Neşe Bocuk asked him to leave. When he'd gone Süleyman said, 'If we don't find out who has been cooking meth in your apartment, you will be charged. And much as you believe I will be unable to tie your meth operation to the accidental death of a man called Zekeriya Bulut – one of Sümeyye Paşahan's boyfriends, for your information – there is also the issue of the sick boy we found around the back of your building. Just a street kid, but if my colleagues in the medical profession are right, he could well be suffering from chemical burns to his eyes and skin, probably caused by by-products from the manufacture of methamphetamine. He could die.'

Alibey and Güllü had come across the boy when they had been searching the bins behind Neşe Bocuk's building. Kerim Gürsel and the scene-of-crime officer who had been sent down to inform them that they should return to the penthouse had found them shouting at the child to go away. The officer had called an ambulance while Kerim had gone back inside to speak to the kapıcı about obtaining CCTV footage from outside the building. It would be interesting to see what the boy had to say once his doctor allowed him to be interviewed.

'Now where is Sümeyye Paşahan?' Süleyman said.

'I don't know,' Neşe said.

'You are lying.'

'I'm not.'

Süleyman brought his fist down on the table in front of the old woman. 'Sixteen million lira! Who would give you sixteen million lira? Who would you allow to set up a meth lab in your own apartment? Big players, Neşe Hanım, big people like your son used to be. I bet you couldn't resist it! People always used to say that you were the brains behind Bocuk, and I think they were right.'

And then she laughed.

Chapter 21

Eylül Yavaş put a large paper coffee cup on her superior's desk and then sat down beside him.

'Anything?'

'No.'

Kerim Gürsel was looking at CCTV from the back of Neşe Bocuk's building. It mainly consisted of footage of the residents' staff putting rubbish in the bins and then leaving, often after a crafty smoke. They'd started with the night before last, on the basis that they wanted to spot Bocuk's maid before she left. They had no idea when that might have happened, and so they were erring on the side of caution. And although they didn't have a picture of the girl, they did have one of Sümeyye Paşahan, which might or might not support Omer's theory.

They'd seen the young boy who appeared to live behind the bins. They'd also seen a covered woman, whose face was turned away from the camera, give him food. So far they'd seen two other covered women put things in the bins, but neither of them had fed the boy.

Random people used the alleyway behind the block to get to and from other small streets in the area, but in the depths of the night, these were few. And so it was a surprise to see a woman, on her own, walk up to the boy living behind the bins and shake him awake at 3.06 a.m.

Kerim paused the footage and looked at his colleague. 'Interesting.' Now just about over his hangover, he was wide eyed and clearly on his second wind.

'She looks quite old from the back,' Eylül said.

'Mmm. Let's see what she does.'

He pressed play, and they both watched as the women bent down to speak to the boy and then appeared to press something into his hand. He moved with difficulty, and so she helped him up, and in the process of pulling him to his feet, she looked at the camera. Kerim once again froze the screen.

'Well, that's not Sümeyye Paşahan,' Eylül said.

'No.'

He pressed play again and they watched as the boy, unaided by the woman, tipped the contents of one of the bins onto the ground.

Eylül said, 'Is that Neşe Bocuk's bin, do you think?'

'All bins look the same to me.' Kerim paused the action once more and looked closely at the screen. 'Inspector Alibey discovered waste that's been analysed for toxicity in a bin like this – and look, plastic bags. The suspect material was in plastic bags. What's he looking for?'

They carried on watching. The elderly woman had her back to the camera again as the boy rifled through a couple of the plastic bags and then held up what looked like a ball of string. A conversation ensued, and then the woman took the string from the boy and put it in her bag before turning to the camera again, smiling.

Kerim paused the action once again. 'I recognise her.'

'I do too, but I don't know where from,' Eylül said.

'I think she may have paid the boy to go through the bin. Why?'

'If we knew who she was . . .'

They looked at each other, and then Kerim said, 'I've a notion – I don't know why – that she's Roma. I'll mark it and we'll move on, for now. Maybe I'll ask Mehmet Bey when he's free.'

Could things get any worse? Sıla Gedik knew the answer to that. The stables had been losing money for years, but in all that time she'd never before had reason to believe that her staff were crooked. But now the petty cash, which was kept in an unlocked drawer underneath her computer, had been taken. Or rather most of the notes had. There were still a lot of coins, but then they were worth next to nothing now that inflation was so high.

A float of around two hundred lira was generally kept in the drawer, mainly for riders who paid in cash. Only twenty remained, and some assorted coins. She'd asked all the boys about the money and none of them had owned up. She liked to think the Romanian, Mihai, had taken it, but that, she knew deep inside, was simply a reflection of her own innate dislike of eastern Europeans. She remembered when thousands of them had come to İstanbul in the wake of the collapse of the Soviet Union – selling shoddy tat on the streets and begging. The only reason she'd employed Mihai was for his language skills. He could speak five languages besides Romanian, including Turkish, Russian and English. He it was who gave lessons to most of the foreign riders who came to Gedik.

It wasn't Mihai. Had he still been alive, Sıla would have thought it was Zekeriya. He had stolen from her in the past, probably viewing the theft as payment for sexual favours. Shit. And then she remembered that Aslı Dölen had left early, apparently called home because of some sort of crisis concerning her father. He was old and had been ill for years.

But why would Aslı, the rich girl, steal money? She always wore the latest riding kit, was expertly made up and wore posh perfume – mainly, so she'd told Sıla, Jo Malone, which was expensive. Two hundred lira would be nothing to her. Maybe she'd needed to fill up her car in order to get home? But again, why? Why come out without any cash? More crucially, why come out without her ATM card? Everyone had an ATM card.

Thinking about Aslı made Sıla frown. It had been Aslı who had brought Sümeyye Paşahan into their lives, Sümeyye who had taken Zekeriya away from her. The bitch had said she didn't know anything about that, but she had to have done. What was she,

284

blind? Sıla had wanted shot of her as soon as she'd found out about Zekeriya and Sümeyye, but she'd held off, not knowing how Zekeriya would react to the dismissal of his lover's friend.

Now, however, things were different, and Sıla had nothing to lose by messing up the girl's life. Zekeriya was dead and she couldn't reach Sümeyye Paşahan – no one appeared to be able to do that. The other grooms had let her search their lockers, and although she knew that didn't necessarily absolve them from theft, it was good enough for Sıla. She was grieving, she was insolvent, and Aslı's friend had humiliated her. She called the police.

'That is Büket Erkek,' Süleyman said as he looked at the frozen image on Kerim Gürsel's screen. 'Known as Büket Teyze, she is a falcı. She's also one of Gonca Hanım's oldest friends.'

Kerim Gürsel and Eylül Yavaş shared a look. This was awkward. Süleyman had come to Kerim's office during a break in his interview of Neşe Bocuk. Ömer Müngün had accompanied him, but he sat quietly behind his superior.

'It was Büket Teyze who told my wife that another falcı had bought the place next door to her premises on Galıp Dede Caddesi.'

'The old music shop,' Ömer put in.

'Quite so.'

'So why would Büket Teyze get the kid to go through the bin for her?' Kerim asked. 'I don't know what that is he gives her – looks like cotton.'

'It's supposed to be Neşe Bocuk's hair,' Süleyman said. 'Although having seen it myself, I think it's probably cat fur.'

Eylül Yavaş frowned. 'You've seen it, sir?'

'Yes. I'll tell you why in a minute. Kerim Bey, you said something else happens in this footage?'

'Yes.' Kerim pressed play again.

They all watched as Büket Teyze and the boy had a short

conversation. Büket put what he'd given her in the pocket of her skirt and was just turning to leave when the boy suddenly looked panicked. Putting one arm out to the falcı, he beckoned her towards him and then helped her duck down behind a dumpster just as a covered woman wearing a long black coat appeared with a large bin bag in one hand and a plate of food in the other. She gave the plate to the boy, who smiled, and then put the rubbish bag in the bin he had just been rifling for Büket Teyze. The boy and the woman talked and appeared to share a joke. As she laughed, the woman turned so that the camera picked up her profile, and it was here that Kerim paused the footage again.

He said, 'Sümeyye Paşahan, I think.'

Süleyman squinted. 'You could be right.' The picture wasn't that clear, but he could see that the woman had down-sloping eyes, just like Sümeyye Paşahan.

Kerim said, 'When I press play this time, you'll see that she takes her headscarf off just after she leaves the boy to head down Bağdat Caddesi. Then I think you'll be more sure about her identity. I certainly am.'

They watched until the woman left and Büket Teyze emerged from behind the dumpster.

They all let out a collective breath. It had to be Sümeyye Paşahan.

Süleyman looked at Ömer Müngün. 'Your observations about the maid seem to have been justified.'

Neither of them spoke about why her face had made so little impact upon them when they had originally gone to Neşe Bocuk's apartment.

'But,' Süleyman said, 'now this leaves us with the problem of where Miss Paşahan may have gone.'

'There's her brother,' Kerim said. 'Claims he has nothing to do with her, but he could have been lying.'

'Her fiancé on Büyükada,' Eylül said.

286

'Who is, I understand, the son of Ümit Avrant,' Süleyman said.
'Atila,' Kerim said. 'He's an artist.Typical arty kid, nice enough.'
'Mmm.'

'And her friend,' Eylül added. 'Aslı Dölen'

Kerim frowned. 'There may be others, but we don't know about any of them.'

Süleyman sighed. 'We have addresses?'

'Yes.'

'So we'll need three search warrants,' he said as he stood up and put on his jacket. 'Much as I do not believe there is anything I could do to Neşe Hanım to make her tell me more, I do need to go back and try. Kerim Bey, Commissioner Ozer has moved on the Paşahan case, as you know. Can you . . .'

'I'll go and do it now,' Kerim said.

The two senior officers left the room. When they'd gone, Eylül Yavaş said, 'Mehmet Bey said he was going to tell us about the falcı.'

'Not really relevant to Sümeyye Paşahan,' Ömer said. 'Anyway, I've got to follow the boss.'

'Oh . . .'

But as he left the room, he leaned towards her and lowered his voice. 'Between you and me, he knows what he knows because of Gonca Hanım. Apparently Büket Teyze wanted her to curse Neşe Bocuk.'

Çetin İkmen really wanted to speak to Mehmet Süleyman, firstly to tell him about Büket Teyze and secondly to ask him whether he'd found out anything about Enver Yılmaz. But he couldn't raise him or Ömer Müngün. He eventually got through to Eylül Yavaş, who told him that they were all now involved in what appeared to have resolved into a hunt for the same person. She didn't give any details. But she did ask him whether she could help in the absence of Mehmet Bey.

'I'm trying to find out about a man called Enver Yılmaz,' İkmen said. 'I'm wondering whether you and Kerim Bey have ever come across this name professionally. To clarify, Eylül, I don't want Kerim Bey to know about this.'

'Is it something to do with what we spoke about in relation to Kerim Bey?' she asked.

'Indirectly,' İkmen said. 'I would ask that this remains just between ourselves.'

'If you think it's best . . .'

'I do. So . . .'

'That name means nothing to me,' she said. 'Can you tell me anything about him?'

İkmen described Enver Yılmaz.

'Does he work?' Eylül asked.

'Yes, or rather I think he might be involved in some sort of scam.'

'Oh?'

'He purports to work for a company called Mahzur IT Solutions, based in Maslak.'

For a moment she didn't answer.

'Eylül Hanım?'

He heard her sigh, then she said, 'I'm not sure, Çetin Bey. That company . . . Look, we're waiting on paperwork at the moment. I don't know when, so I can't really devote much attention to this. Give me some time to check my records and get back to you.'

'But the company is familiar to you?'

'I don't know,' she said. 'As I say, there could be something . . .'

'OK,' İkmen said. 'I'll leave it with you.'

Neşe Bocuk's attorney, a man called Sinan Altuğ, had clearly decided that his client shouldn't say anything more to Mehmet Süleyman. When the inspector and Ömer Müngün attempted to

288

rekindle the interview they had started earlier, they found that Mr Altuğ's client had been apparently struck dumb.

Eventually Süleyman said, 'As a strategy designed to possibly allow Sümeyye Paşahan to get as far away from the city as she can, I applaud your advice to Neşe Hanım, Sinan Bey.'

'Do not ascribe motive to my actions, Inspector Bey.'

'No, of course not,' Süleyman said. 'However, I should tell you and your client that photographic evidence of Sümeyye Paşahan's presence at Mrs Bocuk's apartment building is now in our possession.'

'May I see?'

'Of course,' Süleyman said. 'I will arrange it.'

'You . . .'

'No, I don't have it with me, Sinan Bey,' Süleyman said, 'because I would like someone else to see it first and find out what he thinks.'

'Who?'

'A young boy Neşe Hanım probably doesn't know about,' Süleyman said. 'Someone Sümeyye Paşahan knew.'

The moment froze. The woman's deep-set eyes fixated upon Süleyman's face. He felt the whip end of a shudder and wondered whether this was why Antakya falcıs were so feared.

He stood. 'Well,' he said, 'I will leave you to ponder, Neşe Hanım.'

Now she spoke. 'You can't hold me, Inspector Bey Efendi.'

'I can for the moment,' he said with a smile. 'As I'm sure Sinan Bey will tell you.'

Public prosecutor Ali Oğan, or 'the Dinosaur', as some people dubbed him, was a short, thin man in his mid sixties. Some people said he resembled Çetin İkmen, although the latter strongly disagreed with this. What İkmen didn't disagree with, however, was that the Dinosaur, like him, was a man who moved largely against the current grain. A liberal secularist, Ali Bey refused to espouse any branch of any religion while at the same time keeping his head well below the parapet. It was a balancing act of staggering proportions, giving rise to many theories, including that he had friends in high places and knew dark things about those people.

Commissioner Selahattin Ozer, a pious Muslim, had a somewhat vexatious relationship with Ali Bey. He also, from time to time, used the Dinosaur's existence as an excuse to do things those above him might not like. That Oğan had allowed or disallowed something politically charged gave Ozer a personal get-out clause. And while Oğan had been initially opposed to any overt pursuit of Görkan Paşahan, Kerim Gürsel's argument in favour of pursuing Sümeyye Paşahan had his full attention.

After Kerim had gone, when he was alone with Ozer, Oğan said, 'He made a good argument, I think.'

'You know there are rumours about Gürsel,' the commissioner responded.

'There are rumours about everyone. Even the dead don't get a free pass now. You and I have known each other for many years, Selahattin. And while you come from the opposite end of the political spectrum, I think you can agree with me that there has never been such a time for gossip and misinformation.'

'The Internet.'

Ali Oğan didn't ask whether he could light a cigar, he just did it. The commissioner coughed. The prosecutor raised his eyes, then said, 'You must know nobody can keep a lid on the Paşahan situation for all time. And quite frankly I don't know why you want to. So he claims to know explosive things about certain people, so what? Those who love and revere those people won't believe what he says anyway, and those who hate them will believe but will simply fester impotently.'

'Disrespect of society's leaders is a cancer. It spreads.'

'It's also human nature,' Oğan said. 'We can't stop people

finding out that Paşahan is a sexual abuser – and nor should we. What he has done discredits him. I don't care what he knows or doesn't know about people of note. I know you have your instructions, but this situation is now bigger than all of us. People have died.'

Ozer's face gave nothing away.

'I'm going to issue the warrants Gürsel and Süleyman have requested,' Oğan said. 'I take full responsibility. We can't have gangsters killing and kidnapping at will across this city. And if by acting now we also manage to at least curtail our current crystal-meth problem, then that is a bonus.' He stood. 'I know you agree with me, even if you won't say so. I know you can't.'

He was moving towards the door when the commissioner said, 'Ali Bey, I give you my word that I will support this investigation. It would seem it is the will of God.'

Oğan smiled. Now that Ozer had framed what had to be done in his own terms, he would not stand in the way of Gürsel and Süleyman. 'Thank you, Selahattin.'

What had she been thinking? Two hundred Turkish lira was nothing out in the real world, even if for Sıla Gedik it was the difference between eating and not eating. The Kağıthane cops had laughed at her. The owner of a shabby riding stables making a complaint about a girl who lived in a posh apartment in Nişantaşı! And all over two hundred lira. The officer she'd spoken to had told her to 'sort it out yourself', and so now she was doing just that.

It took Aslı a long time to answer, which wasn't unusual. Much of the time the girl seemed to live in a world of her own. It was just lucky she loved horses so much. She'd do anything for them – and she was quite a good rider too. She was also the snake who had brought her friend into Gedik and ruined Sıla's life.

Eventually a small voice said, 'Sıla Hanım?'

'Aslı, where are you?'

'I'm at home. I'm sorry . . .' She began to cry.

This irritated Sıla, who said, 'Did you take two hundred lira out of my petty-cash drawer this morning?'

It took a moment for the girl to get a hold of herself, and then she said, 'Two hundred lira?'

'Yes. Missing from the drawer in my office. Did you take it?'

'No! Who says I—'

'So why did you fuck off without telling anyone where you were going?' Sıla asked. 'Badem missed out on her exercise this morning.'

'I took her tack off and put her in her stable.'

'But you didn't take her out!' Sıla said. 'What did you—'

'I got a call,' Aslı said, and she began crying again.

Sıla shook her head in irritation. 'From?'

She heard the girl gulp back tears. 'My dad died this morning. The call was from my mum.'

Chapter 22

Mehmet Süleyman was joint owner, with other family members, of an ornate Ottoman yalı on the island of Büyükada in the Sea of Marmara. Originally constructed by one of his imperial ancestors, it was now empty except for the summer months, when various Süleyman relatives made use of its dusty accommodation and antiquated seawater swimming pool. Mehmet had taken his son to the yalı several times, and had spent a week there with Gonca the previous summer. He wasn't accustomed to visiting Büyükada in the winter, much less arriving by police launch as opposed to the much slower islands ferry.

With a warrant in his pocket to search the premises belonging to Sümeyye Paşahan's fiancé, Atila Avrant, Süleyman disembarked from the launch in company with the four uniformed officers who would help him conduct the search. The senior officers involved in the investigation had been obliged to split up in order to cover all three known Sümeyye Paşahan contacts.

It was beginning to get dark by the time Süleyman arrived at Atila Avrant's scruffy old house. If Kerim Gürsel hadn't told him that Ümit Avrant's son lived in such a modest place, he would have been surprised. Crime lords' progeny usually led extravagant lifestyles.

Once served with the warrant, the young man led Süleyman through into his cluttered studio. Surrounded by paintings that looked like photographs, mainly of landscapes, Süleyman asked him when he'd last seen Sümeyye Paşahan.

'Like I told Inspector Gürsel, not really since our engagement,' Atila said.

'Your engagement was arranged?'

'Yes. But I do like her,' he said.

The four uniformed officers began their search upstairs in the bedrooms. A loud crash from above alerted Süleyman to the fact that he'd not explicitly told his men to be careful. Excusing himself to Atila Avrant, he called up to them, 'Be careful! Mr Avrant is not a suspect! You break anything and you'll have me to deal with!'

Returning, he said, 'You were saying . . .'

The activity on the first floor became much quieter.

'We talked, at the time, Sümeyye and me,' Atila said. 'She's nice. She said if all I wanted to do was paint, that was all right.'

'Meaning?'

He pulled his fingers through his thick, tangled brown hair. 'Our fathers want things from us, you know? Like grandchildren and involvement in their businesses. Sümeyye is into all that, but I'm not. I mean, I'd like to have children one day, but . . .' He shook his head. 'Sümeyye's dad, well, we all know what he's like now. I never liked him or her brother.'

'Fazlı Paşahan?'

Atila shook his head. 'He's weird. I feel like when we do marry, I don't want him around.'

'Why not?'

He shrugged. 'Don't know really. He just . . . creeps me out. Inspector, why are you searching for Sümeyye? I thought she was in London.'

'Apparently not,' Süleyman said, but he was distracted.

He walked over to a painting resting on an easel and examined it closely.

'I told your colleague I don't see my sister any more,' Fazlı Paşahan told Ömer Müngün.

'Why not?'

'I told him that too!' Fazlı Paşahan's jowls began to shake as he lost control of his temper.

'Can you—'

'She's too close to our father!' the carpet dealer said.

Ömer had arrived with four uniformed officers and a warrant to search Paşahan's business premises and his apartment.

'You don't like your father?' he asked.

'No,' Fazlı said. 'But only because he doesn't like me. All over her . . .'

'Your sister?'

He nodded.

'Been grooming her to take over his businesses for years,' he said.

Ömer shuddered at the use of the word 'grooming'.

'Arranged a marriage between her and Ümit Avrant's soft son. One big happy crime family! Atila Avrant's only interested in his painting, so Dad and Sümeyye could just carry on as usual.'

'What does that mean?' Ömer asked.

Fazlı shrugged. 'Her living in Daddy's pocket,' he said. 'Like always, like them doing their little secret things away from me.'

'What secret things?'

One of the officers began throwing folded kilims carelessly down onto the floor from their shelves.

'Ah! Ah! Don't . . .'

Ömer put himself between Fazlı Paşahan and the officer.

'Put those kilims back!' he yelled. 'We're looking for a woman, not a carpet! Put them back – tidily!'

He looked at Fazlı expectantly. 'Well? Did your father and your sister have an inappropriate relationship?'

Fazlı coloured. 'Oh no! No, I don't think that! No, he just likes her more than me. They share jokes and spend lots of time

295

together – or they did before he left. Call me resentful if you must, but that's how I've always seen it. Anyway, why do you think she's here?'

'Because she must be somewhere,' Ömer said. 'And you are one of her very few contacts here in the city.'

'Contacts?' Fazlı laughed. 'If I were on fire, she's the last person I would call to put me out. Contrary to popular belief, I built this business myself. It was my way of breaking free of those bastards. You can look at anything and everything in my shop and at my apartment, but you won't find my sister, Sergeant.'

'I do have to look, Fazlı Bey,' Ömer said.

'Yes, I know,' Fazlı Paşahan said. 'Do what you have to, just make sure your gorillas don't damage anything, or I'll sue you.'

'I don't know her name,' Atila Avrant said when he saw Süleyman looking at the portrait.

Süleyman frowned. 'I thought it was a photograph.'

'Hyper-real is what I do,' Atila said. 'Apart from giving the mind of the viewer a reality workout, it's always really difficult to do because you have to capture everything. Every tiny wrinkle, every unwanted hair. Difficult for sitters and so I usually work from high-res photographs.'

'You are extremely skilled.'

'Thank you,' he said. 'I actually painted that from a picture taken at my engagement party. She, this woman, reflected how I felt at the time.'

Süleyman looked at the painting again. 'She looks . . . sad?'

'Maybe it was the blond hair, but to me she looked as if she didn't belong,' Atila said. 'I felt like that too. As I say, I wasn't worried about marrying Sümeyye, I just felt disconnected, if you know what I mean.'

'Not really, but . . . Do you know who she is?'

The uniformed officers were now searching the outbuildings behind the house.

'No,' Atila said. 'I think she might have been a friend of Sümeyye's. I didn't know half the people who came to that party. Her brother was there – Fazlı, we don't get on – so maybe that woman was his girlfriend or something.'

'Why don't you get on with Fazlı?' Süleyman asked.

He shrugged. 'I don't know really. Him and Sümeyye have a strange relationship, like they hate each other and love each other too much.'

'A sexual relationship?' Süleyman asked.

'I've never wanted to think about it. I don't intend to start now.' Atila paused.

'Inspector,' he said, 'my father once told me that if you want to get to the truth about the Paşahans, you need to speak to Görkan Bey. But now he's gone, I suppose we'll never know the truth.'

The apartment had been full of relatives; now it was still full of relatives, but they had been joined by the police. The girl's mother, Sabiha Dölen, took the officers to the small room that had been her late husband's study and then went to get her daughter.

Kerim, slightly overawed by the number of books the Dölen patriarch had owned, said, 'Given the circumstances, we'll need to keep this as brief as possible, Eylül.'

'Yes, sir.'

Shaking his head, he added, 'Muharrem Dölen was interested in absolutely everything.'

The door opened and Aslı entered. Her face was white and tear stained and she was visibly shaking. It was Eylül who went to her and sat down by her side.

Kerim, standing, said, 'We are very sorry for your loss, Aslı Hanım. May you live long.'

She appeared to ignore him. 'Is this about Sıla Hanım's money? I've told her, I didn't take it.'

Kerim and Eylül exchanged glances. 'We know nothing about that, hanım,' Kerim said. 'We're looking for Sümeyye Paşahan. It's urgent. We wouldn't be disturbing your mourning were it not.'

'I've not seen her, I've told you.'

'I understand that, but we do have a warrant to search these premises.'

'Oh God!'

'I'm sorry.'

'I don't know where she is. Whatever she's involved with, it doesn't concern me. I only became friends with her because she protected me at school. I was unpopular, but if I was with Sümeyye, people left me alone. She came to live here because she wanted to. I didn't ask her!'

Eylül said, 'Did she bully you?'

Aslı swallowed. 'I didn't tell my parents because she was always so nice to them and because . . . she knew things about me. She does that. She finds out things about you and then uses them against you.'

'What did she know?'

'I don't want to say!'

Eylül, who had previously disliked this girl, squeezed her hand. 'It's OK.'

'Your officers can search, but she isn't here,' Aslı said.

'Do you have any idea where she might be?' Kerim asked. 'Do you know any of her friends?'

'No. She never introduced me. Apparently I smelt too much of horse.'

'And yet you took her to Gedik.'

'Only because she wanted to go,' Aslı said. 'I was terrified that she'd mess things up for me there, and of course she did.'

'Zekeriya Bulut?'

'She has to have every man she takes a fancy to. It's what she does.'

Kerim Gürsel didn't know much about how incest affected the behaviour of victims, but he knew he'd read somewhere about how, in many cases, it resulted in a lack of interest in sex. Conversely, in a considerable number of other cases, victims would exhibit sexual promiscuity. This latter, it was theorised, could be taken as a need for approval in the only way the victim could understand.

'Aslı, did she ever mention any names of friends to you?' Eylül asked.

'No. I knew she lived over on the Asian side somewhere for a time, but I don't know who she was living with.'

That was, they now knew, Neşe Bocuk.

'One of her dad's friends was all she'd say,' Aslı continued. Then she frowned. 'She did sometimes talk about a girl called Suzi.'

Eylül wrote it down.

'What about Suzi?' Kerim asked.

She shrugged. 'She was very glamorous,' she said. 'Not like me.'

'And did you ever meet this woman?'

'No,' she said. 'Or rather not that I know of. There were hundreds of people at her engagement party and she introduced me to no one. I'm not important. Oh, but there is something I do know about Suzi . . .'

Mehmet Süleyman sat apart from the uniformed officers on the launch back to the city. They were talking about football, a conversation to which he could add precisely nothing. Also he wanted to be alone.

He'd found nothing at Atila Avrant's apartment to suggest that Sümeyye Paşahan had been there. He hadn't heard from either Kerim Gürsel or Ömer Müngün so far, and so it looked as if the whole operation had been a failure. Ozer wouldn't be pleased and Alibey, whom he had effectively cut out, would probably faux commiserate for months.

In his head, Süleyman went right back to the beginning of his involvement with the Paşahans. The previous year he'd investigated the death of the prostitute Sofija Ozola. He'd interviewed Paşahan and his then accuser Zuzanna Nowak. Within days Nowak had retracted her evidence and Paşahan had left the country. Ozola's remained an unsolved murder. They happened more than the general public liked to think. Süleyman had moved on.

Then Alibey had asked him to go back over his evidence pertaining to Paşahan with a view to possibly extraditing him back to Turkey on a murder charge. But events in Cihangir had intervened. Now what?

He took his phone out of his coat pocket and looked at all his missed calls and messages. A lot of the missed calls were from Çetin İkmen. They were probably about Kerim Gürsel. He called the older man back.

'Çetin, how are you?'

'Fine, because I'm out on my balcony,' İkmen said. 'I've just fed the cat, so he's in love with me again. On the down side, Samsun has brought home a fellow Albanian and so they're inside talking at the tops of their voices in a language I don't understand. Oh, they're also ignoring some dizi on the TV.'

The İkmen apartment had a sort of magnetic pull for the city's waifs and strays, and so Süleyman wasn't surprised that Samsun Bajraktar had felt entitled to bring an Albanian version home. He was tired, but that word stuck in his head. Albanian . . .

'I've been trying to call you,' İkmen continued.

'I know. Sorry.'

'Want to run a name by you again,' he said. 'Enver Yılmaz.'

'Kerim Bey's neighbour? Why?'

İkmen talked about his recent pursuit of Mr Yılmaz while Süleyman watched the lights of İstanbul grow closer as the police launch cut its way through the choppy waters of the Sea of Marmara.

'Apart from the possible identity theft I told you about, I know no more. Been busy,' he said. And then that word came into his head again.

'Çetin,' he said, 'talking of Albanians, did you ever find out anything about that Albanian demon or whatever it was you saw in Cihangir?'

'The dordelec? No,' İkmen said. 'You?'

'Didn't pursue it very much, to be honest,' Süleyman said. 'Just an act on a night of carnival.'

'It's a warning, you know,' İkmen said.

'The dordelec?'

'Yes, a signal to keep away. It tells people that somewhere is owned and they can't come in unless they want to risk raising harmful spirits.'

'A warning?'

'Mmm.' There was a pause, and then İkmen said, 'What are you thinking, Mehmet?'

'I'm not really sure. But it just came into my mind, just now . . .'

'What did?'

'Görkan Paşahan comes from an Albanian family.'

He couldn't get through to Süleyman, and so Kerim Gürsel called Ömer Müngün.

'Still at the Dölen apartment. When we got here, we discovered the father died this morning.'

Ömer said, 'That's tough.'

'I feel like a ghoul. Anyway, wanted to run something past you. Aslı Dölen has told us that Sümeyye Paşahan had a friend called Suzi. Does that name mean anything to you?'

'No. But we were investigating her father then, not Sümeyye.'

'Thought I'd ask. What about the brother?'

'Says he's not seen her. Hates her.'

'I know. I didn't think it was an act.'

'I don't either.'

'She doesn't sound nice,' Kerim continued. 'Aslı says she bullied her. Apparently Sümeyye uses people. Which, given her provenance . . .'

'Have you heard from the boss?'

'No.'

'Unless he's found something, he's not going to be happy. I can hear Alibey crowing from here.'

Kerim laughed.

There was a pause, after which Ömer said, 'Suzi, you say?'

'So a dordelec in Cihangir means . . .'

'Could mean keep out of Cihangir or keep out of that particular street,' İkmen said.

'Doesn't make sense. Paşahan wasn't in Cihangir, he was abroad,' Süleyman said. 'Anyway, I'm too tired, and when I get tired I get stupid.'

'I always did my best work when I was about to drop,' İkmen said.

'That was you.'

İkmen laughed.

Süleyman said, 'You know, this is the first time I've really had a chance to look at Galataport from the sea. Whatever objections I may have had about it in the past, it's quite impressive.'

The new development known as Galataport had been opened in 2021. A vast complex of museums, shopping facilities, hotels and eating venues on the side of the Bosphorus, its main function was as a port for cruise liners. But it had been built at the expense of the old port of Galata, which had been partially derelict for many years. It was still not without its detractors. Çetin

İkmen was one of their number and so ignored Süleyman's observation.

'Have you read Gonca's prediction for today yet?' he asked.

'No.'

'I suggest you do so, and at least send her an emoji to acknowledge it.'

'I will do. I've heard nothing from Kerim or Ömer, so I imagine that we are no further forward in our search for Sümeyye Paşahan. Which means I'll soon be going home anyway.'

'Well just do it,' İkmen said.

'I said I will.'

'Make sure you do.'

İkmen was pressing the point rather more vigorously than he usually did when it came to what Süleyman should and should not do.

'Çetin,' Süleyman said, 'is there any reason you're so keen for me to see this message?'

'I want Gonca to be happy,' İkmen said and then he cut the connection.

While not often given to bouts of self-pity, Mehmet Süleyman did wonder how long it would be before people, especially İkmen, stopped reminding him, obliquely of course, that he'd had a wild and not always laudable romantic past. He'd slept around for decades. Married or single, and even when Gonca was his mistress, he'd taken sexual pleasure wherever and whenever he could, with little regard to the consequences. However, all of that had stopped when he'd married Gonca. Not only was he, for the first time in his life, truly in love, he had also begun to fear a lonely old age. And Gonca adored him. Beautiful, sexy, artistic and fiercely intelligent, even in her sixties she caused men around him to envy him his remarkable bride. İkmen, maybe, was just making sure he never lost sight of how lucky he was.

And so he brought up his messages and was just about to select

Gonca's latest prediction when the launch bumped against the side of the jetty at Karaköy. He walked towards the prow of the vessel preparatory to disembarking and put his phone back in his pocket. As one of the uniformed officers jumped out of the launch and began to tie the vessel up, he noticed that on shore there were a lot of familiar faces looking at him.

Chapter 23

The cat had not appreciated being moved from İkmen's lap. But when Samsun had offered her guest, an elderly Albanian woman called Maxhide, a bed for the night, first the woman and then Samsun had retired. This enabled İkmen to return to his own living room and switch on his computer. As soon as it had booted up, Marlboro, with a warning growl, returned to his lap.

'It's all right, I won't push you away again,' İkmen said as he attempted to pull his fingers through the beast's dirty fur. 'When I go to bed, you can come with me. I've not got that woman you hate coming over tonight, more's the pity.'

Marlboro didn't like Peri, mainly because she objected to sharing a bed with him and his fleas.

İkmen looked at his screen saver, which consisted of a photograph of what remained of the wooden house in Üsküdar where he'd been born: namely the original black wooden veranda at the front. Around it had been built an elegant modern home, all glass and steel. İkmen and his brother Halıl used to play out on the veranda while their father marked his students' papers by candlelight inside.

Once again he searched for the name 'Enver Yılmaz', and once again the search engine threw up so many entries it made his head swim. Not even narrowing his search by limiting entries to Turkey and 'crime' made much difference. There were loads of them. Bakers, hoteliers, police officers, actors – even apparently a fashion house in Izmir.

It was possibly an alias anyway.

He leaned back in his chair. Marlboro dribbled in his sleep. Could Enver Yılmaz have something personal against Kerim? Was he perhaps a former lover? Surely, though, Kerim would have recognised him. But then to act so viciously against someone, if indeed he was right about this man, one had to have a strong reason. İkmen needed to look elsewhere. Jealousy? Again, though, a person tended to know who was jealous of them, and why.

Did Kerim know what Yılmaz was doing? He couldn't. He loved Sinem and wouldn't allow her to suffer if he could help it. Another man having sex with his wife would also dishonour him.

'What's this?'

Ömer Müngün, Kerim Gürsel and Eylül Yavaş had been waiting for him. It was cold, and they all had their overcoats wrapped tightly around them as a sharp wind blew in off the Bosphorus.

'Boss, this may be something and it may not be,' Ömer said.

Süleyman took his phone out of his pocket. 'Just give me a moment. I must reply to a message.'

The three officers watched him as he scrolled down to Gonca's text: *Follow the money*. He sighed. What did that mean? The trouble with predictions, in his experience, was that they always seemed to be generic. It could be argued that he followed the money every day of his life on account of the fact that he worked. But he sent her a heart emoji to keep her happy and then put his phone away.

'Well?'

'We've not found Sümeyye Paşahan,' Ömer said.

'Nor me. I suggest—'

'Boss, Aslı Dölen told us that the only friend she knows Sümeyye to have in the city is someone called Suzi.'

It didn't mean anything, so Süleyman said, 'And?'

'And although we've nothing but this name, Suzi, it took me back to Zuzanna Nowak. You know, the woman who ID'd—'

'I remember her,' Süleyman said. 'We were in the process of going back over that case when Cihangir happened. I know there's no connection to Sümeyye, but . . .'

'It's something,' Kerim Gürsel said.

Süleyman frowned, took his phone out of his pocket again and looked at it.

The city was beginning to fall asleep. It did that in the winter. Back in the 1970s, when Çetin İkmen had first patrolled the streets of İstanbul, whole areas of the metropolis had been dark and silent during the winter months. It had been a strange, monochrome world of coffee houses lit by hurricane lamps, and small subterranean bars filled with smoke, where hookers in hot pants prowled for custom among nylon-suited men who drank hard and guiltily. The past what it had always been, desperate. Just like the present.

Marlboro was snoring now. İkmen, still staring at his computer screen, changed tack. Enver Yılmaz had to have presented the landlord of the Poisoned Princess apartments with ID before he could rent his place. Or not. As İkmen knew, for a consideration a lot of red tape could be avoided, particularly in the rental sector and especially in a place like Tarlabaşı.

He turned to the name of Yılmaz's non-existent company, Mahzur IT Solutions. Mahzur, meaning sad, was a rare male name. Why would you call your company 'sad'? Why would you call your child 'sad'? Maybe Enver Yılmaz, whoever he was, was one of those people who glorified suffering – always in others – underneath a veneer of apparent goodness. There were a lot of those.

In the summer, the pretty Bosphorus village of Bebek rocked to the sounds of numerous nightclubs until the early hours of the morning. However, in the winter, this prosperous İstanbul suburb languished in the more muted atmosphere of coffee shops and restaurants that closed their doors by midnight.

When Süleyman and Kerim Gürsel and their two sergeants arrived in the village, it was 11 p.m., and so most of the district was all but deserted. Pulling into the road where Zuzanna Nowak now lived, Günaydın Çıkmazı Sokak, Kerim identified her building, the Papatya, which was on the right of the heavily wooded turning.

Süleyman said, 'I interviewed her briefly last year. But she didn't make a great impression on me. However, I think I saw a picture of her earlier tonight.'

'Where?' Eylül asked.

'At the home of Sümeyye Paşahan's fiancé. He's an artist. Claimed he created it from a photograph taken at his engagement party.'

'Why would Nowak have been there?'

'Good question.'

As Süleyman's car turned into the lane leading to the Papatya apartments, all the lights in the building went out.

'Power cut,' Kerim Gürsel said.

Süleyman stopped the car and looked around. 'In just one apartment block?'

Çetin İkmen leaned back in his chair and stared at the screen in front of him. Sometimes unusual names were hard to track down, but where someone with such a name had committed an offence, that could become much easier.

While the cat snored on and occasionally dug his claws into İkmen's thigh, he read:

Suspected killer Mahzur Açar was finally arrested today in Yalova. Açar (35) had been on the run since Tuesday when the body of a woman

308

believed to be his wife, Dünya (25), was discovered in the basement of his apartment block in Kadıköy. Arresting officer Inspector Kerim Gürsel gave this statement: 'Mahzur Açar was arrested this morning during a dawn raid in Yalova on the house of an 80-year-old woman, believed to be Açar's aunt.'

The report, in *Cumhuriyet*, was dated 20 June 2020, at the height of the pandemic. Trapped indoors almost all the time during that period, İkmen had only managed to speak to his 'boys and girls' still in the police from time to time. As well as helping to make the streets safe from the kind of opportunist criminal who saw the pandemic as a business opportunity, officers were also tasked with making sure people obeyed the rules as well as carrying out their usual functions. Almost inevitably in a city of seventeen million people, murders had continued to happen, of which this was just one.

Following up on the 20 June report, İkmen discovered that Açar had been found guilty of his wife's murder the following spring, when he'd been sentenced to fifteen years in prison. His crime, for which he pleaded mitigation due to his wife's unfaithfulness, had nevertheless been premeditated. Further, the officiating judge had found no evidence of any sexual misconduct on Dünya Açar's part, and had consequently handed down a tough sentence.

A rather more conservative daily had then followed Açar's sentencing with an opinion piece stating that a tariff of fifteen years while 'a question mark remains over Dünya Hanım's behaviour' was too harsh and that the Açar family were going to suffer unduly for Mahzur's 'alleged' crime.

Apparently Mahzur, a lawyer, was the financial patriarch of a large family of unskilled workers who originated from the northern mining city of Zonguldak. At thirty-five, he was young to have been responsible for rent on two large Kadıköy apartments where he and his relatives lived. But when he was convicted of murder, the extended family had to downsize considerably, and the paper had caught up with them in a leaky old house in Tarlabaşı. They had, his mother told the publication, 'suffered endless harm from the unfair judgement against my son. Unable to find work, my husband took his own life. The shame of it kills every one of us.'

Tragic if the family had suffered, tragic that Mahzur's father had died, but had İkmen been in the judge's position, he too would have handed down a long sentence. In spite of numerous campaigns against femicide, the awful truth was that this phenomenon was not going away. Some men still felt, it seemed, that as not much more than property, their wives were disposable. Not that the rights and wrongs of the case had bothered İkmen unduly at the time.

What he wanted to know was whether Enver Yılmaz was in some way related to Mahzur Açar. And he wanted to know this without alerting Kerim Gürsel to what he was doing. He tried to call Eylül Yavaş, but her phone went straight to voicemail.

The kapıcı was standing on the doorstep of the building, composing a text on his phone, when the officers arrived.

Kerim held his badge up. 'Police.'

'Just let me . . .' The man looked up. 'Oh,' he said. 'Just telling my ladies and gentlemen to stay in their apartments, and that I've called the power company. The lifts are out and the stairs are dangerous in the dark. We've all had just about enough of this for one day!'

'What do you mean?'

'They came this morning,' he said. 'Maintenance work. When they left, everything was fine. Now this. Anyway, what do you want? I didn't call the police.'

'We've come to see Zuzanna Nowak,' Süleyman said. 'I believe she lives in the penthouse.'

310

'Polish woman, yeah,' the kapıcı said. 'She's in, I think. What do you want her for?'

'We need to talk to her.'

'Oh. Well, I suppose you can go up. But be careful on the stairs. You got torches?'

'Yes. Is there just one entrance to the penthouse?'

'Yeah.' He stood to one side. 'I'll carry on trying to get some sense out of the power company. It really isn't good enough.'

The four officers pushed past him and entered the building. The stairs were directly in front of them.

'OK,' Süleyman said. 'Kapıcı thinks she's in. We're only dealing with one entrance and the lift is inoperative.'

'So do we all go?' Eylül asked.

'I'd like to have eyes on the outside of the building ideally.'

'What? In case she rappels down on a rope?' Eylül said. There was a sharp tone to her question that wasn't actually a question. But she had a point. Zuzanna Nowak was not, as far as they knew, the type of woman given to daring feats of bravery.

Süleyman said, 'Look, I know how it sounds, but I want eyes outside.'

'I'll take outside,' Kerim Gürsel said.

Süleyman paused for a moment. 'All right.'

Eylül smiled. While not exhibiting overtly sexist views, Mehmet Bey was, she knew, the sort of man who really preferred the assistance of other males. She liked him but thanked God that she didn't have to work for him.

Once Kerim Gürsel had left, Ömer Müngün shone his torch up into the centre stairwell. Four galleries led off into four apartments on each floor. In the middle of the stairwell hung a vast chandelier consisting of long cables dressed with crystals that reached almost to the ground floor.

'That's . . .'

'Ugly,' Süleyman said. He turned towards the kapıcı, who

311

appeared to be fighting with his phone. 'How does one access the penthouse?'

'Eh?' He looked up. 'How am I supposed to report a fault if their emergency line doesn't work?'

'You dialled correctly?'

'Of course I did!' He sighed. 'What did you say?'

'The penthouse,' Süleyman said. 'How does one access . . .'

'There's a door to the right of Apartment Fourteen,' he said. 'There's no number on it, just go through. It's the emergency stairs. It'll take you to the hallway beside the lift, then the door to the penthouse is right in front of you.'

'Thanks.'

The kapıcı went back to his phone and Süleyman led Eylül Yavaş and Ömer Müngün up the marble staircase.

'Edith?'

She groaned. Who the hell was calling her at this hour? In the summer, yes, when she was rolling around the clubs until the early hours, but in the winter?

'Who is it?' she asked. 'It better be urgent, waking me up in the middle of the night.'

'It's İkmen,' the caller said. 'I need you to do something for me.'

'İkmen? What?'

'I need you to go out tomorrow morning and take Melda with you.'

'Why?'

'I want to speak to Sinem Hanım alone,' he said.

'Why?'

She heard him sigh with impatience. 'Do you want me to get to the bottom of what's happening with the Gürsels or not?'

'Yes . . .'

'So listen. Leave the apartment as early as you can . . .'

'Sinem doesn't usually get up before ten.'

'Then go out at eight.'

'Eight! You forget about Kerim Bey. He doesn't usually leave until eight thirty.'

'OK, go out just after he leaves. I'll be outside in the hallway,' he said. 'As you and Melda leave, I'll go in.'

'What for?'

'As I said, to talk to Sinem. Trust me. In order to do anything about what's happening, I need her to listen to me. Believe me, Edith, I wouldn't drag you out of bed so early unless it was urgent.'

İkmen was not generally one to do anything without a reason, so she said, 'All right. The kid's usually up at six or thereabouts. I'll tell Sinem I'm taking her over to my sister's.'

The crystals on the enormous chandelier tinkled in the breeze as the officers walked up the four flights of stairs. Ömer Müngün whispered to Eylül, 'I couldn't live with that.'

She smiled. Up ahead, Süleyman shone his torch towards the door on the right-hand side of Apartment Fourteen. From there it was a short climb up the emergency stairs to the internal hallway in front of the penthouse door.

Once the two sergeants had joined him, Süleyman pointed his torch at the door. Like all the other front doors, it was plain white with what looked like brass fittings.

Ömer Müngün said, 'So what now? Are we going to—'

Süleyman put a finger to his lips to silence him. 'Listen . . .' he whispered.

There wasn't much to hear from inside the apartment. The sound of creaking, faint. Occupied homes were never entirely silent, even when their residents were asleep. Furniture, often wood, settled, cooling cookers could make noises, fridges hum. But this was something more . . .

Süleyman moved closer, which was when he saw that the front door was ever so slightly ajar. He beckoned his officers to show them.

First Süleyman drew his weapon, then the others.

There was a roof garden that went all around the penthouse. Kerim couldn't see much of it because it was dark, with all the lights having failed, and he was loath to use his torch in case it alerted the occupants to the fact that they were being pursued. He wanted a cigarette, but he ignored the urge for the same reason. And yet . . .

What were they actually doing? All this was based on the tenuous connection between Sümeyye Paşahan and 'Suzi', who might or might not be Zuzanna Nowak. Why would Sümeyye befriend someone who had indirectly accused her father of murder? Maybe Mehmet was right and it was revenge. He'd said, 'Görkan Paşahan is a public figure. He's also ruthless and powerful. How does a child abused by such a person make him pay?' By siding with his enemies? By killing the child he'd foisted upon her?

The kapıcı, who had been engrossed in his phone ever since Süleyman and the others had left for the penthouse, sidled up to Kerim and said, 'What's the point of giving out the number of an emergency line if it doesn't fucking work?' He handed the phone to Kerim. 'Can you have a go? I'm an old man, maybe I'm doing something wrong.'

'OK.'

He gave Kerim a piece of paper with a number written on it. People usually just put new numbers directly into their phones, but this kapıcı obviously preferred to write things down.

Kerim keyed the number into the phone and put it up to his ear. A spoken message told him that the number he'd called was incorrect and asked him to try again. He did, but got the same result.

'You sure you took the number down right?' he asked the kapıcı.
'I thought I did.'

The man took the phone back. As he began to walk towards the apartment block, Kerim saw a brief flash of light from the penthouse.

Chapter 24

It was definitely a woman. Lying flat on the floor at the end of the corridor, she wore a nightdress, pulled up above her waist, exposing the undersides of her breasts. Her pubic area was covered in bloodied banknotes. She didn't have a head.

The three officers froze. Now there were no noises anywhere. Ömer Müngün stuffed his fist into his mouth, stifling a heave from his stomach. Süleyman killed the light from his torch as he remembered something the magician Buyu Hanım had told him.

As he drew his pistol, he whispered, 'They're still here.'

In common with the hallway outside the apartment, the corridor was matt black. They stood with the iron tang of blood washing over them, their ears straining for any slight noise. None came except Ömer's rapid breathing, their feet rooted to the spot by the horror in front of them. Sweat, gathered at their hairlines, began to snake down towards their eyes, and a primal fear of a space with no frames of reference made their hearts thunder in their chests.

It was unbearable, and for Ömer Müngün and Eylül Yavaş, the fact that Süleyman was as helpless and immobile as they brought with it an existential dread that peopled the darkness with demons from fairy stories told by elderly relatives long, long ago.

Eventually, unable to take it any longer, Ömer Müngün said, 'Boss . . .'

Would what happened next have worked out differently had he not spoken? It certainly gave direction to his assailant when the shot was fired. He fell to the ground as the bullet crashed through his shoulder, ripping apart bone, muscle and sinew. The pain took his breath away. Gasping as Süleyman shone his torch into his face, Ömer felt something or someone disturb the air beside his head, and then he saw Eylül run for the door.

It was just a moving outline. Even with her torch shining right at it, the figure was as black as its surroundings. Only when it opened the door that led to the staircase could Eylül hear it, grunting as it pulled the handle. Pistol in one hand, phone torch in the other, she flung herself after it, her feet almost flying above the treads.

The door at the bottom of the flight swung open and she caught it just before the figure arrived at the fourth-floor balcony. And although Eylül knew that a little more light from outside the building had permeated into the stairwell, she still couldn't make out any details of the fleeing figure. Was it male or female? Who cared? Could she catch it?

'Stop! Police!'

The figure didn't break stride. She flung herself forward, touching it with just the very tips of her fingers.

It stopped, turned to face the railings that ran around the stairwell. Eylül opened her hand to grab hold of its shoulder, and missed . . . dammit!

And then it launched itself into the void. Four storeys up, limbs flailing . . .

Jerked backwards by her own fear of the stairwell, Eylül hit the floor as the figure's hands grabbed at and fastened around the cables that made up the chandelier. Breathless with fear, she watched as it clung with its arms and legs like a monkey. And while she didn't see its eyes, she could feel them on her as it turned its head just prior to loosening its grip slightly and then sliding down the cables at dizzying speed.

As it made its way to the ground floor, hundreds of crystals popped off the cables, making its descent look as if it was happening through a rain storm. When they hit the marble of the entrance hall they shattered, and when Eylül looked for the figure again, she saw that it had gone.

'Kerim! Call an ambulance! Ömer's been shot! And call it in!'

Mehmet Süleyman flung his phone on the floor so that he could concentrate on maintaining compression on Ömer's shoulder wound.

'Boss . . .'

'It's going to be all right.' Then he added, 'İnşallah.' If God wills. Shaking in spite of himself, Süleyman wondered how God could possibly will any other outcome.

'The body, it's got no head,' Ömer said.

'I know. I know. Shh. Try not to talk, but keep your eyes open.'

Ömer was very pale, deathly. Süleyman felt a sudden spike of guilt. The four of them had come to this place with no backup, largely at his request. Not that any of the others had objected. They'd all wanted to get their hands on Sümeyye Paşahan, whatever the cost, because she was the only person who could answer their questions about the baby, about Cihangir and about the possible whereabouts of her father.

The door opened and Süleyman glanced behind him. Eylül stood there, torch in hand, then dropped to her knees beside him.

'How is he?' she asked breathlessly.

'I am here, Eylül Hanım,' Ömer said. 'I'm not dead yet.'

'I'm assuming you lost him?' Süleyman said as he pressed still harder on Ömer's shoulder.

'Don't know whether they were male or female,' she said. 'But they were athletic.'

'Outran you.'

'No, sir, they jumped over the railings into the stairwell and then let themselves down the chandelier like some sort of ape. I've never seen anything like it.'

'They've gone?'

'Yes. Don't know where, didn't see them leave the building. Sorry.'

'Don't be. Kerim Bey's called an ambulance. Can you carry on compressing Ömer's shoulder while I go and make sure our athletic friend hasn't left any colleagues behind?'

'Yes, sir.'

She pressed on Ömer's wound through his rapidly reddening overcoat and said, 'How you feeling?'

'Light headed.'

'Keep your eyes open. What do you want me to talk to you about?'

Süleyman picked up his phone, switched the torch on and opened the door to his left.

Several lights, probably from torches, began to move around in the penthouse. Having called an ambulance, Kerim Gürsel was pacing outside the apartment building, wishing he could go in to help his colleagues, knowing that he couldn't. When he passed the front entrance to the block, the kapıcı came running out to speak to him.

'Hey,' he said, 'all this shooting . . .'

'We've a man down up in the penthouse,' Kerim said.

'What? That Polish woman . . .'

'I don't know whether it's anything to do with her. There's an ambulance on its way, and police reinforcements. Have you managed to get in contact with the power company yet? Some light would be helpful.'

The kapıcı threw his arms in the air. 'Used the old number I rang last time in the end.'

'And they answered?'

'On their way now. Funny thing is, they say they don't know anything about that maintenance work we had done this morning. Do you ever get the feeling that the right hand doesn't know what the left hand is doing, Inspector?'

Kerim did. But not in this particular instance.

It was a bedroom. Pretty and feminine. Had it belonged to the dead woman? On the bed, the duvet had been half pulled back, as if someone had just got up.

Süleyman opened the curtains so that he caught any stray light from outside. A dressing table crowded with bottles and jars, a wardrobe. He looked at the floor, which was covered by a large flowery carpet. In the corridor Eylül was talking to Ömer about her one long-ago visit to the Tur Abdin, his home district. In the distance he could hear the sound of a siren. He hoped that was the ambulance.

After opening the wardrobe and looking inside, he unlocked the patio doors leading onto the roof terrace and went outside. He was still shaking slightly, and the cold wind made his teeth chatter. He walked quickly to get his blood moving, passing a few sad plants in terracotta pots and, on the opposite side of the terrace, a leaf-strewn hot tub. There was another door, from the living area, but when he tried it, he found that it was locked. Returning to the bedroom, he was just about to step back through the glass door when something to his left caught his eye. He ran towards it.

In spite of the kapıcı's texts, residents of the Papatya building, some attracted by the sound of gunfire, were beginning to come out onto the balconies around the stairwell.

'What's going on?' one man shouted down from the fourth floor.

Kerim Gürsel held up his badge and called out, 'I'm a police officer. Please go back into your apartments.'

'Why?'

'Because I'm a police officer and I'm telling you,' Kerim said.

'What's happening?'

The siren he'd heard in the distance a few minutes ago had got much louder, and he could see red and blue flashing lights outside.

This time he yelled at the Papatya's residents in anger. 'Get back in your apartments! We have a situation we are in control of, but if you get in the way, you could get hurt!'

A man on the first floor said to his wife, 'Is he threatening us?'

Kerim, now beyond patience, stepped aside as the ambulance crew ran into the building with a stretcher. He directed them to the penthouse, then called out to the man on the first floor, 'Yes, I am! Get behind your front door – now!'

Once the last residents had disappeared back into their apartments, he wondered what he should do next. He wanted to see for himself that Ömer Müngün was OK, but he knew that one more body up on the top floor would only confuse matters. Even with torches, it was going to be difficult to see in that utter blackness, and as far as he knew, it was still uncertain as to whether whoever had killed the woman and shot Ömer had actually gone. He'd seen no one leave the building, so it had to be assumed that the offender was still *in situ*.

The kapıcı came in from having a cigarette. 'These engineers are taking their time . . .'

He needed help. Whoever was on the roof terrace was fast moving, and although Süleyman had seen a second door, that had been locked. The implication was that whoever this person was must have followed him out of the bedroom door. So where had they been hiding? He sent a text to Kerim Gürsel:

Am out on penthouse terrace. Think I'm not alone. Need your help. Approach via door on the left from apartment corridor. Eylül will direct you. Proceed with caution.

Nothing moved. Standing in front of the bedroom door, he could hear muffled voices inside the penthouse – presumably the paramedics. If Ömer died . . .

His phone vibrated and he looked at the screen. Kerim had responded: *On way.*

Good. He stood and waited, his back to the bedroom door, looking from side to side, hoping that this person was not as athletic as the other one. The penthouse roof was not high, so he realised he was also vulnerable from above. Time lengthened, and he heard some sort of electronic device beep behind him. A medical monitor attached to his colleague. What was he going to say to Ömer's wife, or rather his sister? Any grip on the Turkish language Yeşili Müngün had would disappear as soon as she realised her husband had been shot. Peri, he knew, would be all business, a nurse to her core. But underneath she'd be screaming. The two of them were close, the older sister fiercely protective of her brother.

He felt a hand on his shoulder and turned his head to look into Kerim Gürsel's face. Süleyman nodded and then pointed to his right.

As soon as the paramedics had arrived, Eylül Yavaş had moved herself out of their way. Ömer Müngün had lost a lot of blood, in spite of her efforts, and when she finally managed to look down at herself by the lights the paramedics had brought with them, she saw that her clothes were soaked in it.

He had lost consciousness just before the team arrived. When they'd come through the front door, she'd been trying to revive him by slapping the side of his face. But to no avail. The paramedics had fired questions at her:

From what range was he shot?

When did he last speak?

What type of weapon was used?

Words tumbled out of her, but she was barely aware of what they were. Then a cuff was placed around Ömer's arm, one of his hands was swabbed and a cannula fitted, a drip bag was produced, the cuff inflated and then deflated, and one of the team called out, 'Ninety over forty-five.'

Eylül wasn't medically trained, but she knew this was a blood pressure measurement, a low one. More numbers were called out: 'Eighty-six over thirty-six. BP dropping!'

Eylül could feel her eyes filling up, and stepped into the room Inspector Gürsel had gone into earlier.

Kerim couldn't find anything or anyone. He even pulled himself up onto the roof, but still there was nothing. Süleyman looked over the balustrade to see whether he could spot any ropes or ladders. When Kerim returned for the second time, he said, 'Are you sure you saw someone?'

He had been, but now he wasn't so sure. He'd seen a retreating foot, but had it been a foot? Could it have maybe been a cat? Given the anxiety he was feeling, had what he'd seen simply been a trick of the light – or lack thereof?

But then another thought occurred to him. When he'd first set off in pursuit of this 'person', he'd left the door back into the apartment open. Only for a few seconds, but . . .

He put a finger to his lips and turned back into the pretty bedroom. Out of the darkness and against a backdrop of noises emanating from the corridor beyond, Eylül Yavaş's white face loomed out of the darkness at him, eyes staring, lips trembling.

She was not alone.

'Eylül . . .'

Neither Süleyman nor Gürsel could see who was standing

behind the sergeant, but whoever it was shoved something into her back and Eylül grunted.

'She's got a gun . . .' she said through a constricted, terrified throat.

The unseen figure behind Eylül didn't speak. All they knew was that it was a woman. Zuzanna Nowak? Sümeyye Paşahan? Or someone they'd never come across before?

An arm snaked around Eylül's waist. It was slim, its nails long and talon like. Eylül was red from her breasts down. Ömer Müngün's blood. It was a disturbing sight.

Süleyman said, 'If you kill my officer, you will never leave jail.'

Beeps and cries from outside in the corridor punched worrying holes in the silence that ensued.

'Lift him up, we can't work on him here!'

'He's dropping again!'

Beeeeep . . .

'Just let me leave.'

It was a female voice, light and, Kerim Gürsel felt, a little bit silly.

'Who are you?'

'Let me leave and that'll be the end of it,' she said.

Eylül's eyes, looking into Kerim's, flickered in the torchlight, then dropped to the floor. Was she trying to tell him something? She looked down again, and then her arms came up as though she was confused and every muscle in her body appeared to go limp as she slipped through her attacker's embrace. The woman behind her, a small one, maybe even a girl, tried to cling on to her, but the weight of Eylül's body pulled her and her gun forward.

As she headed towards the floor, she pointed her weapon at Kerim Gürsel and pulled the trigger.

With the electricity in the building still out, the paramedics couldn't use the lift to get Ömer Müngün down to the ground floor and into the ambulance. Even holding torches above the stretcher, it was slow going as they carried him and their equipment down the five flights of stairs.

Mehmet Süleyman took the woman's gun away from her.

'Unfortunate for you it wasn't loaded, Sümeyye,' he said.

Eylül had pushed her to the floor when she'd failed to fire the gun and was now cuffing her. When she'd finished, she pulled her to her feet. She wore a thin silk nightgown that emphasised her large, clearly enhanced breasts, and her eyes sloped downwards.

'Where's your friend?' Kerim Gürsel asked. 'The one Sergeant Yavaş chased?'

She said nothing.

The sound of cars arriving outside the building down below signalled the coming of either the electricians or police reinforcements, or both.

Süleyman took the woman's chin between his fingers and looked into her eyes. 'You may be silent now, but we have a lot to talk about.'

Chapter 25

When Peri Müngün received the call from Mehmet Süleyman, she assured Ömer's wife Yeşili that there was nothing she could do except look after Gibrail, then went straight to the Gayrettepe Florence Nightingale Hospital in Besiktas. On arrival, she stood outside for a moment to gather her thoughts.

When her brother had failed to come home again, she'd been angry with him. Although she didn't suspect him of having an actual affair, she had been wondering for some time whether he was sleeping around. He hardly spoke to Yeşili these days, and the girl had admitted to Peri that she had not become pregnant again after she'd had Gibrail because 'nothing is happening'. The Ömer Peri knew was enthusiastic about sex, and so, she reasoned, he had to be getting it somewhere. But in spite of all that, he was still her beloved baby brother, and the thought of him with a bullet inside him made her want to scream. On this occasion, it seemed, he really had been at work.

She walked into the hospital and gave her name at the reception desk. The receptionist looked at his computer screen and said, 'Your brother's in surgery.' Then he pointed to a bank of seats partially occupied by an elderly covered woman and a middle-aged man who was crying. 'Wait there.'

Peri did as she was told. It was strange being on this side of the health system. Sometimes when patients complained about the brusqueness of non-medical staff, Peri and her colleagues just rolled their eyes. Now she reassessed her perspective. It was cold in the waiting area, there was nothing to drink, and the feeling of despair was overwhelming.

Female custody officers found two kimlik identity cards on the woman, one in the name of Canan Turk, the other Sümeyye Paşahan. A routine breath test found that her blood alcohol level was high, and so the decision was taken to put her in a cell to sober up before questioning began the following morning. Süleyman had scheduled her interview for 11 a.m. to give her time to call her lawyer. A search of the Papatya apartments for Ömer Müngün's shooter was ongoing under an incident commander from Uniform.

Although covered in now drying blood, Eylül Yavaş was too tired to do anything except go home. The same applied to Kerim Gürsel. Even a sofa was better than falling asleep in his office at headquarters. Süleyman alone made the trip over to the Gayrettepe Florence Nightingale Hospital, where he found Peri Müngün sitting on a hard chair in the noisy reception area next to a man who was dribbling in his sleep.

'Peri Hanım,' he said, 'what's—'

'Ömer is in surgery,' she said. 'They told me to sit here.'

Süleyman walked up to the reception desk and showed a studiedly unimpressed man his badge.

'I want to know the status of my colleague, Sergeant Ömer Müngün,' he said.

Wordlessly the receptionist looked at his screen. 'In surgery.'

'Yes, I know. I'm here with Sergeant Müngün's sister.'

'You'll just have to wait.'

'Of course, but is there any way Miss Müngün could wait somewhere quieter?'

The receptionist shrugged. 'This is a public hospital, what do you expect?'

Tired, worried and now riled, Süleyman said, 'Compassion

might be nice, but then that's just me.' A man in a white coat walked behind the reception desk. Blinded by fury, Süleyman didn't see him. 'I'm not asking for anything for myself, you know,' he continued. 'I'm just asking for a bit of kindness and respect for this lady, who is a nurse, by the way, though she's too modest to say so. My colleague, her brother, is a police officer, as well you know . . .'

'Mehmet!'

The voice, which he didn't recognise, came from the small white-coated individual behind the receptionist. Süleyman looked up. The man was about his own age and appeared to be a doctor.

'Excuse me?' he said. 'Do I know you?'

The man smiled. 'You don't recognise me, do you?'

'I'm afraid . . . Look, are you a doctor? My sergeant came in a few hours ago, gunshot wound, he's in surgery . . .'

'You're police!' The man laughed. 'God, Prince Mehmet we used to call you! You've hardly changed!'

Süleyman felt cold. Who was this?

'Bülent Saka,' the man said. 'Dr Bülent Saka. We used to go to chess club together at the Lisesi.'

Then he remembered. Bülent Saka, son of a cotton baron from Anatolia. He'd had money and had never let anyone forget it.

He made himself smile. 'Saka, yes,' he said. 'Well, a doctor . . .'

'Public medicine, as you can see,' Saka said. 'Someone has to do it.' He laughed again. Then he said, 'Gunshot wound, yes. What's the problem?'

Süleyman looked at Peri. 'I'm here with Sergeant Müngün's sister. I'd like her to be somewhere more comfortable while we wait for news.'

'Of course!' Saka beckoned Peri over. 'Madam, it's like an animal house in here, I know. But if you come with me, I can take you somewhere quieter.'

'It's no problem . . .' Peri began.

'No, please, come with me,' he said. 'Can't have relatives of our brave policemen sitting out here in this hell.'

Peri looked at Süleyman.

'You don't need to stay, Mehmet Bey. You must be exhausted.'

'I can't leave Ömer.'

She put a hand on his arm. 'I'm not going anywhere,' she said. 'And now that this nice doctor . . .'

'And tea,' Saka said, 'I'll get you tea. You can sit in my office. Mehmet, we can catch up!'

It took all Süleyman's powers of restraint not to hit him. He was almost ignoring Peri, who was clearly distressed. However, he was offering her a quiet place to wait, and for that Süleyman had to thank him.

'I take your point, Peri Hanım, and I'm sure Dr Saka will look after you well.'

Peri took his hand and squeezed it, then turned to Saka. 'Doctor, I should like to pray in private, if you can accommodate that.'

Saka, now less excited because Süleyman was not staying, took Peri's arm. 'Of course, hanım. I will bring you tea and then I will leave you to your devotions.'

Süleyman thanked him and left. Back at school, Bülent Saka had not, to his knowledge, been a religious boy. But if he had known to whom Peri Müngün was going to pray, Süleyman wondered whether he would have given her the use of his office so readily.

Dark deeds required dark surroundings. Gonca had allowed herself to sleep until eleven, and then she had taken the envelope containing Neşe Bocuk's hair into the small Byzantine cistern in the garden. Although he didn't know it, she'd seen Mehmet look at it before he had left her in the middle of the previous night. He'd read the name on the front and peered inside before replacing it on her bedside table and going out. He'd not been back since.

What he'd made of it, Gonca didn't know. She did know that he disapproved of curses, but she had promised Büket Teyze, who was frantic with worry about her business, that she would do it, and so she had.

Hours of work had been invested, and now that she was finished, Gonca sat alone in the dark, wondering why her husband was still out. Had her magic worked quickly? She'd picked up a rumour from her son Rambo that Neşe Bocuk had been arrested, but he'd had no details. With difficulty, she pushed herself up off the cold dirt floor of the cistern, using her bare feet to cover up any last traces of her work and stamping them into the ground.

When she emerged, she was surprised to see Mehmet exiting from the back door of the house.

'I looked for you in bed,' he said. 'What are you doing out here?'

She walked over to him. 'You know I can't sleep without you, baby.'

'Yes, but the cistern?'

He didn't know that she used it for her darker workings. She smiled. Wrapped in a ratty full-length mink coat, she was dressed for the cold, even if her feet were bare.

'You know I like it in there,' she said as she put an arm around him. 'Makes me feel close to the old Byzantines.'

He snorted. 'Bunch of murderous—'

'Shh.' She put a finger on his lips. 'You seem wound up, baby. What's the matter?'

He kissed her finger and then said, 'It's Ömer.'

'What about him?'

'He's been shot.'

'Oh darling! How?'

He said nothing for a moment, then, choking on his fear, 'I put him in harm's way.'

She stroked his hair. 'No,' she said, 'you wouldn't do that.'

'I did!' His voice was shrill, almost hysterical, and she felt him begin to shake, so she led him back into the house and up to their bedroom.

'Gonca . . .'

'Shh.'

She undressed him and made him get into bed. Then she went downstairs to the kitchen and made a drink from rakı and juice from herbs she had steeped in sugar in the summer. Back in the bedroom, she sat beside him and gave him the drink.

His voice shaking, he said, 'Don't you want to know about it? How I messed up?'

'No,' she said. 'I want you to drink this and go to sleep.'

He looked at the glass, then sniffed it. 'Rakı? Gonca, Peri Müngün is going to call me, and anyway, I have to get up for work, I've people to interview . . .'

'At what time?'

'What?'

'Interview at what time?'

'Oh, eleven,' he said. 'But I must get to headquarters for nine, I've things to do.'

She tilted the glass towards his mouth. 'Drink.'

Out of excuses and ideas, he did as she asked. Soon she wouldn't have to listen to any more of his garbled self-flagellation. She knew nothing about what had happened to cause Ömer Müngün to be wounded, but she was sure that her husband hadn't either sought or accidentally instigated the young man's injury. She pulled the duvet up to his neck and kissed his lips. They tasted of valerian and aniseed, of passionflower and skullcap and of the slightest whisper of atropine to slow his racing heartbeat.

When she was certain he was asleep, she went back out into her garden, where, under the early-morning stars, she made a plea for Ömer Müngün's life.

*

331

When the engineers finally managed to restore power to the Papatya apartments, the full horror of what had happened in the penthouse that night was laid bare.

Scene-of-crime commander Superintendent Fahrettin Uysal, who had now been joined by officers from the forensic service, looked down at the headless body in the corridor that ran the length of the penthouse and let out a long, slow sigh. According to the engineers, the generator supplying electricity to the building had been vandalised, which was why it had taken them so long to restore power. Part of Uysal wished they hadn't.

'Sir?' A member of the forensic team, head to foot in white coveralls, approached him.

'Yes?'

'We've found the head.'

'Good. Where?'

'Bathroom,' he said. 'I think that's where she was attacked.'

So why was her body laid out in the corridor?

The whole apartment was alive with activity – people moving furniture, taking photographs, talking. By contrast, the central corridor was a place of whispers. Uysal watched as Dr Fuat Kartal, a new young pathologist, gently teased banknotes away from the victim's pubis. The superintendent thought he looked about fifteen.

'Good news about the head,' the doctor said as he laid another banknote out on a sheet of greaseproof paper on the floor.

'Yes,' Uysal said. 'All we have to hope now is that it fits this body.'

The doctor looked up. 'Grim.'

'Welcome to Scene of Crime,' Uysal said.

'Oh, I'm under no illusion that my career will be anything other than grim,' Kartal said. 'Look at what I'm doing now. Pulling hundred-lira notes out of a dead woman's vagina.'

Uysal winced. 'So it's . . . er, they go right up . . .'

332

'Pushed in by force,' the doctor said. 'Cervix has split. Classic Mafia revenge hit, if you ask me.'

Three women Süleyman had put down in the cells. One old, one middle aged, one young.

Custody officers had a reputation for violence, as well as a deeply black and also bitchy sense of humour. But then dealing with the mad, the bad, the drunk and the drugged on an everyday basis gave one a view of humanity that was most certainly not pretty.

Constables Ece Deniz and Hakan Öder could be particularly acerbic. Deniz, who was in her mid forties, had taken rather a fancy to her twenty-five-year- old male colleague some time ago, and so the exchanges between them were also tinged with flirtation.

'Do you think Mehmet Bey's making himself a harem down here?' she said as she chewed on a new piece of gum.

Öder laughed. 'Can't do that with the witchy wife back home. She'll curse him, turn him into a cockroach.'

'He's got it coming,' Deniz said.

Öder frowned. 'Don't you like him? I do.'

'Why?'

'Good at his job.'

'Yeah, but he's a maganda,' she said. 'Behind all that Ottoman stuff, he's like the dirty old uncles you see guiltily watching strippers on the TV and calling them whores.'

He laughed. 'Mehmet Bey's not old!'

'He is compared to you.'

Öder looked uncomfortable.

'Here, have either of you looked in on the girl and the old woman recently?' Their superior, Sergeant Ataman, came into the guard room and sat down. 'Mehmet Bey wanted them checked on every half-hour.'

Deniz got wearily to her feet. 'Why?'

'Because the girl was drunk and the falcı's as old as rock. Go on.'

Deniz left. When she'd gone, Ataman said to Öder, 'She still chasing you, is she, boy?'

Embarrassed, Öder reddened.

Ataman laughed. 'Divorced women.' He shook his head. 'What can you do with them? Trailing around after young men like bitches on heat. It's not natural. She's got a son only a few years younger than you. We need change in this country, and I think you know what I mean.'

Öder did. The sergeant was one of those officers who espoused a very puritanical form of Islam to which he felt everyone should adhere. Öder described himself as a Muslim, but he didn't agree with people like Ataman.

Alerted by the sound of running boots, Öder stood. Deniz, breathless, put her head around the door of the guard room. 'Call a medic! The old falcı, she's collapsed.'

It was five o'clock in the morning when Dr Saka and another man walked into Saka's office, where Peri Müngün had been pleading to her goddess, the Şahmeran, for her brother's life. When she saw the two men, she stood up, white and shaking.

Saka introduced his colleague. 'This is Dr Nacar. Burak Bey, this is Sergeant Müngün's sister, Peri Hanım. She's a nurse.'

'Well?' Peri wasn't interested in polite introductions.

'Please sit down, Miss Müngün,' Saka said. 'Dr Nacar is your brother's surgeon.'

Peri sat, almost in tears now.

Nacar was an elderly man with a heavily lined face and a huge, unruly plume of grey hair. He smiled. 'Miss Müngün, I am happy to say that Sergeant Müngün has come through surgery

334

successfully – for which we thank God – and I see no reason why he shouldn't make a full recovery.'

'Oh!' Peri put her hands up to her mouth. 'Thank you! Thank you!'

'Thank God,' Nacar reiterated. 'However . . .'

Now she was afraid again. What was he going to tell her? What was this 'however'?

'However, there has been considerable damage to his right shoulder,' the surgeon went on. He pointed at the area between his own right shoulder and his neck. 'There is a bundle of nerves here called the brachial plexus. It controls motor function to the right arm. Damage to this bundle may cause loss of function in the affected arm.'

'This is what has happened to Ömer?'

'Yes,' he said. 'Until his recovery is under way, we won't know how much function has been lost, but I do have to tell you that it is my belief it will not be inconsiderable.'

'Oh . . .'

'Sergeant Müngün is also right handed, and so this may impact more profoundly upon his life than if he were left handed.'

'But he will live?' Peri asked.

The surgeon smiled again. 'Like the rest of us, Sergeant Müngün began to die the moment he was born. However, I fully expect him to leave hospital sometime in the next two days. He won't be able to return to work for some weeks, however, and it will be important that he rests.'

'Of course,' Peri said. She stood up and took the surgeon's hand, then kissed it and pressed it to her forehead. 'Thank you for saving my brother's life, Doctor Bey.' Although she was an educated woman and a nurse, Peri Müngün was still, behind all that, a peasant woman from the east who expressed her gratitude in the same age-old manner as her forebears had done.

The surgeon squeezed her shoulder. 'With your expert care,

Miss Müngün, I am sure your brother will have a better than average chance of making a full recovery.'

Alone with Dr Saka, Peri thanked him too, then picked up her handbag. 'I'll go home now and let my sister-in-law know what has happened.'

'Of course,' Saka said. 'And, er, Mehmet Süleyman, don't forget, or do you want me to call him for you?'

'No,' she said, 'thank you. I think I'd like to tell Mehmet Bey myself.'

As she left his office, she saw that Dr Saka looked disappointed.

Chapter 26

Kerim Gürsel, followed shortly afterwards by Enver Yılmaz, had left his apartment almost an hour before Madam Edith and a very excited Melda, to whom Edith had promised both chocolate and a ferry ride, went out, leaving the Gürsels' front door open for Çetin İkmen. İkmen waited a further fifteen minutes before he went inside and closed the door behind him.

Standing in the hallway, he saw Sinem leave her bedroom and begin to cross towards the bathroom. She froze when she saw him.

'Çetin Bey?' she said. 'What are you doing here?' Her face was white with fear, but before he could speak, she said, 'You know, don't you?'

'Yes.'

She held herself stiff and straight for a moment, and then she slumped. İkmen helped her into the living room and sat her down in an armchair. Outside, he heard the sound of Rambo Şekeroğlu pulling up the metal blinds that protected his bar overnight.

Noting that the samovar in the kitchen was on, he got them both tea and then sat down opposite Sinem.

'Do you mind if I smoke?' he asked.

'Kerim and Edith do, why not you?' she said. 'There are ashtrays in the kitchen.'

He helped himself to one and lit up.

'Sinem Hanım . . .'

'Does Edith know?' she asked. 'She must have left the door open for you or given you her key.'

'No,' he said. 'But it was Edith who alerted me to your unhappiness. She wants only to help.'

'And Kerim?'

'Kerim knows nothing,' he said. 'And if we are to sort this out in the way I propose, he never will.'

Mehmet Süleyman had three messages on his phone. The first was from Peri Müngün, informing him that Ömer had come through surgery and was now recovering in hospital. The next one was from Custody Sergeant Ataman. Neşe Bocuk had somehow fallen over in her cell and temporarily knocked herself unconscious. A doctor had been called and she was now apparently fully recovered. She also wanted to see him as soon as possible. He wondered why. She'd never been keen to see him before. Had she found out that Sümeyye Paşahan was now in custody too, or did Gonca perhaps have something to do with it? But then that view had to be predicated on the notion that Gonca's curses worked, and he couldn't believe that. Or could he? The woman had taken a fall and become unconscious. Had she experienced some sort of epiphany as a result of the blow?

Gonca placed a glass of tea down in front of him and then wound herself around his shoulders.

'Baby, are you sure you don't want anything to eat?' she said.

'No. I'll pick up some simit on my way in.'

'That's not very much.'

'It's fine.' He smiled. 'I had the best sleep I've had for a long time last night, albeit a short one.'

'Good.' She kissed his neck.

'What was in that rakı, Gonca?' he asked.

She laughed. 'Secret,' she said.

It was only after he'd left the house and was in his car outside that Süleyman picked up the third message. The young boy the police had found behind the dustbins outside Neşe Bocuk's apartment block had been interviewed by uniformed officers late the previous night. At first Süleyman had rolled his eyes at the idea. Uniform? Really? What did they know? But as he listened, he was surprised. The boy, called Ata, apparently, had identified Sümeyye Paşahan as 'that maid from the penthouse'.

'How did it happen?' İkmen asked.

Sinem sipped her tea. 'He moved next door just before COVID really took hold in spring of 2020. So we were only aware of him as an occasional presence in the hallway for two years really. But he seemed nice, always said hello, that kind of thing. As you know, because of my health problems we were more cautious than most when it came to going out and mixing with others. Kerim continued to work, of course, but for much of that time we lived fairly separate lives in case he brought the virus home.'

A lot of people had lived like that. İkmen's daughter Çiçek, who had worked delivering food and other supplies to the elderly and infirm on behalf of the city authorities, had kept herself separate from her father and Samsun during that period.

'I suppose I must've actually met Enver Bey for the first time last summer,' Sinem continued.

'How?'

'In the hallway,' she said. 'On good days I go for walks along the corridor, sometimes up onto the roof. It began when he knocked on the door to ask whether we had damp in our apartment. Everyone here has damp, and so I told him it was quite normal. I thought nothing of it when he asked, some weeks later, whether he could see ours.'

'When was this?'

'Last autumn. September,' she said. 'Looking back, I shouldn't have let him in while Edith and Melda were out, but he seemed so respectful, and also when your husband is a police officer you do just think that other people will be too scared to attack you or anything. But I didn't know he had an agenda.'

'Which was?'

She began to cry. İkmen offered her some scrunched-up tissues from his pocket, which she took.

'You're charged with possession of a hundred milligrams of heroin,' Kerim Gürsel said to Meryem Kaya as he released her from her cell. 'Taking evidence from your neighbour Merve Karabulut into account, there is also the issue of intent to supply,' he continued. 'But for the time being, you can go. Needless to say, do not leave the city.'

'Where would I go?' she asked.

'I've no idea, but don't go there,' he said.

He watched her sign for her belongings with the custody officers and then told the young plain-clothed constable who had just joined him to follow her.

The small amount of heroin possessed by Meryem Kaya was, they all knew, just a tiny sample of the wares sold by the dealer Meryem would not name. Now with her home in ruins and no obvious source of money, and with this unnamed person clearly deeply in her debt, the dealer was the only source of finance the police team could discern. And so it was with this in mind that she was being followed and recorded now.

Everyone and anyone with whom Meryem Kaya made contact now was a person of interest.

'He touched my breast,' Sinem said once she'd managed to stop crying. 'I was so shocked! I pushed him away and told him that when my husband got home I would tell him. But he just laughed. Then he did it again. I was really scared now, but I couldn't push him away this time, I didn't have the strength.' She shook her head, her eyes closed, clearly trying not to relive her ordeal. 'He raped me.'

'Sinem . . .'

'On this floor, here in my own apartment, he raped me,' she said. 'I'm so easy to overpower. He put a hand over my mouth to stop me from screaming, told me that if I struggled he'd kill me. When it was over, I cried. I've never felt so dirty in my life! I scrubbed and scrubbed my skin in the bathroom after he'd gone, I threw my underwear away, but I could still smell him! I still can. Every time he does it . . .'

İkmen leaned across the table and took her hand. 'You mentioned an agenda . . .'

Sniffing, she wiped her nose. 'Yes. But he didn't tell me about that until the next time. About a week later. In the meantime, I couldn't look Kerim in the eye. I wondered what I'd done to tempt that man, and so every time Kerim tried to get close to me, I pushed him away. The next time I was alone in the apartment, he came in uninvited through the balcony.'

'It was his balcony door being open when I visited that gave me the first inkling that he might have just left you,' İkmen said.

'He came that day, yes,' she said. 'But back in the autumn, that second time he came to me, he told me why he was doing this. He said he knew about Kerim, what he was, he knew all about Pembe! If I didn't have sex with him, he'd tell the police and end Kerim's career. You can imagine how scared I was. Of course I denied what he was saying. I said that Kerim wasn't like that and that I was going to tell him. But he just laughed again, and because I knew that I was lying, I capitulated. I tried to offer him money to go away, but he said all he wanted was me because I was so "beautiful" and "helpless". He also said that Kerim didn't deserve me, that what I needed was a real man. He has degraded me for months. I have betrayed Kerim and I wish I was dead.'

'You haven't betrayed Kerim,' İkmen said. 'You've tried to protect him against an evil man who is, I believe, a relative of a

341

murderer called Mahzur Açar. Kerim arrested this man for the murder of his wife. This is revenge, Sinem, and it stops now.'

'But how can it?' she said. 'He will tell everyone and then—'

'He will not,' İkmen said. 'But in order to defeat this man, you have to do something that I know you will find very hard.'

'Which is?'

He took a deep breath. 'I promise you that together with one other person I will not name but who cares very deeply about both of you, I will get this man out of your lives. We will do it without involving or alerting your husband.'

'But I have—'

'You have not betrayed Kerim,' he said. 'You are a victim of a very wicked and cynical crime which he must never, ever know about. Because as you will know, Sinem Hanım, if he should find out, he would, as your husband and the father of your child, be bound to punish this man. He may even kill him. Now I don't want Kerim to spend the rest of his life in prison because of this piece of filth, and so you must never say a word. Do you understand?'

She began to cry again. 'But how do I live with that?' she said. 'How do I subject Kerim to my dirty, violated body? I can't do it! I can't!'

İkmen went and sat beside her. 'He loves you,' he said. 'And you love him. Sinem, I don't know what your arrangement was with Pembe . . .'

'That was different! We agreed!' she said. 'We loved each other, all three of us, we . . .'

'This man goes today,' İkmen said. 'It will be as if he never existed.'

'But I've not allowed Kerim near me for months!' she said. 'How can I now . . . I love him, it breaks my heart . . .'

'And because you love him, it will get better,' İkmen said. 'You've done nothing wrong, Sinem Hanım.' He squeezed her hand. 'Always remember that, and leave what must now be done to me.'

Mehmet Süleyman had been in his office for less than a minute when Inspector Mevlüt Alibey flung the door open and bore down on him.

'What the fuck was that last night?' he yelled.

Süleyman looked up from his computer screen. 'What the fuck was what, Inspector?'

Alibey was red in the face, and as he spoke, spittle shot out of his mouth towards his opponent.

'Sümeyye Paşahan is in custody,' he said. 'Do you know what you've done? A whole year of work up in flames because of you!'

'I don't know what you're talking about.'

He was aware of the fact that Eylül Yavaş was standing outside the open door. Just briefly, their eyes met.

'Mevlüt Bey, if you would care to close my door and take a seat . . .'

'I do not care to do anything recommended by you!' Alibey yelled.

'This is most—'

'Don't give me your Ottoman gentleman act! It doesn't work on me!' He hurled himself across the desk, his hands aiming for Süleyman's throat. Süleyman pushed himself backwards in his chair and watched as Alibey fell onto a pile of papers, scattering them across the floor.

'Sir, this is not how to behave!' Eylül Yavaş dragged Alibey away by his collar and flung him into the chair in front of Süleyman's desk.

Alibey looked up at her. 'You . . .'

'Do not abuse Sergeant Yavaş!' Süleyman said. Pulling himself towards his desk again, he looked at Eylül. 'Thank you, Sergeant.'

'Sir.' She took her hands off Alibey.

'Please tell no one of this incident, Eylül Hanım. I will speak to Inspector Alibey alone now. And close the door behind you.'

'Sure, sir?'

'Absolutely,' he said. 'And thank you.'

She left the room, leaving the two men glaring at each other.

'Where's Mehmet Bey?' the old woman asked Custody Constable Hakan Öder.

Rather than collapsing the previous night, Neşe Bocuk had, so she said, slipped on 'your filthy floor' and hit her head against her cell wall. Now sporting a gauze dressing held in place by a blood-ied bandage, she had quickly returned to her usual belligerent state and had been demanding to speak to Süleyman since the early hours.

'Busy,' the constable told her. 'You can speak to Kerim Bey if you want.'

'I don't,' she said. 'I've things to say to Süleyman and only him, not least about this wound to my head.'

'You fell over,' Öder said. 'You told us that yourself.'

'Ah, but I didn't tell you why I fell, did I?'

'You slipped.'

'And why, young man, do you think I slipped?' she asked.

He shrugged. 'You're old?'

Neşe Bocuk shook her head. The young could be so rude! But she ignored him and just said, 'Look, I've information for Mehmet Bey that will be advantageous to him. Tell him that and get him here as soon as you can. As you so acutely observed, I am old and may die at any minute. And if I do that, Mehmet Bey will never know the truth.'

'About what?' Öder asked.

'Never you mind,' she said. 'But he will know, and if he knows what's good for him, he will act accordingly.'

*

'The first time Görkan Paşahan travelled to Italy, it piqued our interest,' Mevlüt Alibey said to Süleyman. 'The decision to contact our counterparts in Italy was made way above my head. Officers from Rome travelled down to Reggio Calabria and confirmed to us that Paşahan had arrived as the guest of an elderly man called Giovanni Grecko. Apparently a humble owner of a small gelateria, Grecko is also one of the most lethal godfathers in the southern Italian 'Ndrangheta organisation. And while neither the Italians nor we were privy to their conversations, when Paşahan returned to Turkey he immediately began to make plans to move abroad. However . . .'

'His daughter . . .'

'I'm coming to her,' Alibey said. 'We don't know how Paşahan left the country, but I think it's safe to say that his new Italian friends helped him. At the time we couldn't understand why he left his pregnant daughter, his favourite child, with Neşe Bocuk. Now of course we know that the child she was carrying was his. So while he and Bocuk put word out that Sümeyye was in London, she was actually with the old witch, who, when the time came, would deliver the child, for a price. We don't know what that price was, but I imagine it was not inconsiderable.'

'So when did you make contact with Neşe Bocuk?' Süleyman asked. 'And why?'

Alibey leaned back in his chair. 'How do you know we made contact with her?'

Süleyman had no intention of betraying the confidence of Ömer Müngün's fellow Mardinli in Organised Crime, so he said, 'I just know.'

'Don't play games!' Alibey hissed.

They stared at each other for a moment, then Süleyman said, 'Continue or not, it's up to you. This is your story to tell, not mine.'

Alibey cleared his throat. 'We warned her that Paşahan was getting involved with people he couldn't control, and that if she

345

cooperated with us by telling us about any contact Sümeyye had with her father, we could make it worth her while. She denied everything and told us to fuck off. So we watched her.'

'Apart from the obvious lure of money, why did Paşahan want to get involved with the 'Ndrangheta? He's a gangster, surely he would know how dangerous they are? And why were they interested in him? He'd not even established himself in İstanbul . . .'

'Oh, they weren't interested in him,' Alibey said. 'What interested them was what he knew about people in power. The 'Ndrangheta have been keen to move into Turkey for decades. They like our beautiful country – it's much bigger than their own, with a huge coastline from which one can get easily to Russia, the Middle East and the Balkans. If you remember back to when Paşahan started his teasing broadcasts, a lot of people dismissed him, but not those his broadcasts hinted at. Unnamed but thinly disguised ministers, community leaders and soldiers involved in corruption, immorality and the like. Explosive stuff even if not true. But more importantly a clear signal from the 'Ndrangheta that they were going to use Paşahan to make inroads into organised crime in Turkey like they'd never done before. But what they, and we, hadn't counted on was the fucked-up dynamic between Paşahan and his daughter.'

Kerim Gürsel looked at his watch. It was 10.30 and Sümeyye Paşahan's lawyer had only just arrived. Her interview was scheduled for eleven, but a combination of the tardy lawyer and the fact that Sümeyye was extremely hung-over from the previous night could make for a difficult conversation.

He looked across his office at Eylül Yavaş. 'Do you know what Inspector Alibey went to talk to Mehmet Bey about?'

Although she'd told Süleyman she wouldn't tell anyone about Alibey's attack on him, she had mentioned to Kerim that she thought the two of them were having a difficult discourse.

346

'Not really,' she said. 'Although I did pick up that Inspector Alibey was less than impressed by our actions out at Bebek last night.'

Kerim shook his head. 'Probably jealous,' he said. 'That or afraid we've trodden on his toes.'

Eylül was now accustomed to the view many had of organised-crime officers – that they were almost by definition corrupt. She could see what people meant. When she had raised the spectre of Paşahan's possible involvement with Italian crime families, Alibey and Sergeant Güllü had been quick to shut her down.

But then surely if that were the case and Alibey's team were in bed with organised criminals from abroad, the inspector wouldn't be talking about it to Mehmet Bey now?

'We had no idea that Paşahan had got his own daughter pregnant until Gürsel requested DNA tests on the Kağıthane baby. We didn't even know that Sümeyye had given birth. But when the DNA came back showing that Paşahan had an incestuous relationship with his daughter, a lot of what had happened fell into place.'

'Like what?' Süleyman asked.

'Like Sümeyye's involvement with meth,' Alibey said. 'Why would she move into the production of meth while living in the apartment of one of her father's allies?'

'Did Neşe Bocuk tell you about that?'

'No.'

'So how did you find out?'

'We were watching the place and we work closely with Narc. You don't usually find meth coming out of penthouses in places like Bostancı. We let it happen.'

'Why?'

'Because we wanted to find out whether Görkan was behind it. Then suddenly Neşe Hanım contacted us and told us something very interesting. Sümeyye was actively challenging her father. We looked into whether the two men in her life – Emir Kaya and Zekeriya Bulut – were behind it, but it seemed they weren't. Kaya was a nice kid, genuinely in love with Sümeyye as she was genuinely in love with him – or so the old woman reckoned. I don't know whether he knew about the meth, but I think she planned ultimately to go away with him using the money she'd made from cooking.'

'What about her baby?' Süleyman asked.

'Ah, well here is where it gets interesting,' Alibey said. 'And so because I've been told that old Neşe is keen to see you, I think we should go and speak to her together.'

'I don't know about that,' Süleyman said. 'From what you've said so far, it appears that we have inadvertently helped Organised Crime in quite a few areas.'

'Oh you have,' Alibey said. 'Except for the most important ones.'

'Which are?'

'Keeping the innocent parties slandered by Paşahan safe and making sure the 'Ndrangheta don't move in on the Turkish crime scene. In those respects, Süleyman, you have failed.'

Chapter 27

Given the opportunity to describe himself, Mansur Nebati would always choose words like 'dull', 'logical' and 'unimaginative'. It was therefore a new and not altogether pleasant experience when the lawyer went to meet his new client, Sümeyye Paşahan, and experienced something he could only describe as intense dread.

He had acted for Sümeyye's father on a couple of occasions back in Uludağ. He'd known what Görkan was right from the start, but in common with many defence attorneys, he had taken the decision to believe his very rich and powerful client. Mansur Nebati had done good work for Görkan Paşahan. But he'd never met either of his children.

Now that he had, he wished he hadn't. Sümeyye Paşahan was sexual rather than beautiful. Every attribute – breasts, bottom, lips, cheeks – was enhanced and exaggerated. And in spite of having been drunk the previous night, the resultant hangover only made her more menacing than she already was – which was a lot.

'Sit down, Mansur Bey,' she said as he entered her cell.

He tried to smile, but couldn't. Her eyes were dead. He'd only seen eyes like that once before, when he had defended a man who had dismembered his own father. But he did as she asked and sat down.

'Well,' he said, 'I think—'

'I did not kill the woman in whose apartment I was staying last night,' she said. 'That is all you need to know. That is all Inspector Süleyman needs to know.'

Blunt. Mansur looked down at the few notes he'd taken when he'd been assigned the case and said, 'Zuzanna Nowak was a Polish citizen. The inspector will want to know how you knew her, why you were in her apartment. As will I. It is my understanding that Miss Nowak identified your father at a crime scene last year. She later retracted her evidence.'

He'd seen seething before, but not like this. She hardly changed her expression at all, but her eyes wanted him dead.

'My relationship with Nowak and my father's are entirely separate,' she said.

'Yes, but because you are related to your father—'

'Separate.' She held up a warning finger.

Mansur changed tack. 'There's also the issue of the production of methamphetamine,' he said. 'Traces of the drug as well as constituents for making it were found in the apartment of a woman called Neşe Bocuk, with whom you were staying.'

'Ask her about it,' she said. 'I don't know anything.'

'The scene-of-crime team—'

'Tell Süleyman he'll have to prove it,' she said. 'And he can't.'

'How do you know?' he asked.

'Because what Neşe Hanım did was off her own bat.'

She had an answer for everything so far. But would she have an answer for the other charge against her?

He said, 'And the baby?'

Here she appeared to be stumped.

'The police have DNA-tested a child they discovered drowned in a stream in Kağıthane. That child is yours, and its father was your father.'

She turned away.

'Miss Paşahan,' Mansur said, 'obviously I do not know how this came to be, but I do need to inform you that an unnatural act of incest perpetrated by your father can be held in mitigation if other offences are to be taken into account.'

She looked at him for a few seconds, then said, 'You must know, Mansur Bey, that I am admitting to nothing.'

'Yes, but where something is fact—'

'Haven't you heard?' she said as she tossed her hair across her shoulders. 'Nobody who is anybody deals in facts any more.'

Süleyman had wanted only Kerim Gürsel to join him when he interviewed Neşe Bocuk, but Mevlüt Alibey had insisted on being present too. So while Sümeyye Paşahan instructed her lawyer, the three officers went to speak to Neşe Bocuk in Interview Room 3. However, there was a problem.

As soon as she saw Alibey, the old woman waved him away, shouting, 'I told you I want to see Mehmet Bey! I want to see him alone or with that other one! Not you, Alibey! Not you!'

After a few moments' argument, Alibey left, and Süleyman and Kerim Gürsel sat down opposite Neşe Bocuk. Süleyman asked where her attorney was.

'I don't want him to hear,' she said.

'Why not?'

'Because you never know who you're speaking to these days.'

Süleyman went to switch on the recording equipment, but the old woman said, 'Not that either.'

'We have to.' He turned it on.

Neşe Bocuk retreated still further into her scarves and muttered. But Süleyman didn't stop the recording.

'So, Neşe Hanım, the difference between myself and Inspector Gürsel and your lawyer, Sinan Bey, is . . .?'

She sat back in her chair. 'I hate you, Mehmet Bey. You put my son and my grandson away, so I wish you dead every day of my life. You, Gürsel, I don't care.'

Kerim raised his eyebrows.

'But,' she raised a gnarled arthritic finger, 'for better or worse,

351

you two tell the truth. You say a thing, then you do that thing. You are the law and nothing else, not like him.'

'Him?'

'Alibey.' She shook her head. 'A man of two faces, a man who serves three masters.'

Süleyman frowned.

She said, 'The law, those who break the law and himself. Mainly himself.'

'That's a very serious accusation, Neşe Hanım,' Kerim Gürsel said. 'Can you back it up?'

Like Süleyman, Kerim Gürsel had heard gossip concerning the honesty or otherwise of Organised Crime for years. Alibey and his sergeant, Güllü, were names that came up repeatedly.

'I can,' she said. 'But I won't.'

'So why—'

'Look,' she said, 'I was a fool to let my son take over the business all those years ago when his father died – should have done it myself. But did I learn from that? No. When Görkan Paşahan came to me and asked me to look after his pregnant daughter while he spent some time abroad, I did it again. I should have known he was going to do something dangerous when he insisted I keep the girl a secret.'

'But he paid you?' Süleyman asked.

'Of course he did. I'm not a complete fool. Or rather I am,' she said. 'It was the promise of real money later that hooked me in.'

'Real money as in sixteen million lira?' Kerim asked.

'That money never passed through my hands,' she said.

'And yet a large building in Beyoğlu was bought in your name.'

She narrowed her eyes. 'Büket Erkek is a fraud,' she said. 'I've heard stories! When I set up in business again, I would take all those İstanbul falcıs out! Why do you think Büket Teyze asked your wife to curse me, Mehmet Bey? Why didn't she do it herself? Because she's nothing and no one!'

Kerim looked at Süleyman, who avoided his gaze. The recording equipment was running and now suddenly they were in personal territory.

'I'm right, aren't I, Mehmet Bey?' she said. 'I am under your wife's curse. I knew it when I had my "accident" last night. That's why I'm talking to you now. Tell your gypsy to lift it.'

'Madam,' Süleyman said, 'your deranged beliefs about people entirely unconnected to this case are not germane to our interview. Please limit yourself to the facts.'

She smiled. 'I bet you wished you'd turned off that camera thing now, don't you?'

'Tell us everything,' Süleyman said. 'From the moment Görkan Paşahan came to you to ask for help right up until today. And no baseless connections via fortune telling or contact with the dead.'

'Everything? A person who loves God doesn't lie, Mehmet Bey. I will tell you what I can. But I think you already know where I will stop, don't you?'

If Sümeyye Paşahan had lived with the old woman for some months, then she probably knew that her father was in Italy – and with whom. Also if Paşahan was in the process of giving the 'Ndrangheta information about his former allies, the sixteen million lira seemed like a good down-payment. But what would she say and where would she stop?

Süleyman said, 'All right, tell us what you know, hanım.'

'About what? Please, Mehmet Bey, be exact, and no straying into any odd beliefs you might have, because living with Gonca Şekeroğlu, you must be at least a little bewitched.'

And then she laughed.

Eylül Yavaş picked up her phone.

'Çetin Bey,' she said, 'it's nice to hear from you.'

'I know you're probably busy . . .'

353

'I am,' she said. She told him what had happened to Ömer Müngün.

İkmen sounded shocked. 'Peri Hanım told me nothing!'

She heard the hurt in his voice and said, 'Peri Hanım was at the hospital until this morning. I expect that once she knew her brother was going to be all right, she went home.'

'Yes, yes, of course. Don't listen to me,' he said. 'Not everyone has the time to keep me in the loop, and that's just fine.'

It wasn't.

'Çetin Bey,' Eylül said, 'did you want something?'

'Ah, yes,' he said. 'It's a little bit, well, delicate, and you're busy . . .'

She smiled. İkmen wasn't good at being humble. She put an end to it.

'Çetin Bey, Inspector Süleyman and Inspector Gürsel are interviewing suspects from last night's incident. I am basically formalising my own account. But if you'd like to meet me for lunch, I will be free in just over an hour. There's a new coffee shop across the road from headquarters. It's almost as good as Starbucks.'

'I thought she'd had it on her own,' Neşe Bocuk said.

'The baby?'

'Yes. Tough as steel, that girl. Or so I thought.'

'What do you mean?' Kerim Gürsel asked.

'She had the baby elsewhere. In a hospital.'

'I would hope so,' Süleyman said.

She leaned forward. 'I was supposed to deliver that child! That was what Görkan Bey said. That was why she came to me! But when her pains began, she left.'

'Which hospital?' Kerim Gürsel asked.

She shrugged.

'You don't know?'

354

'No. Anyway, she came back without it, said it had died.'

'And had it?'

'What do you think?' she snarled. 'And don't think I'm going to pretend I didn't know about the baby over in Kağıthane. I may be an ignorant woman, but I can put two and two together.'

'You think she killed it?'

'I don't know. What I do know is that she had two men in her life – that artist in Cihangir . . .'

'Emir Kaya.'

'If that's his name. And that groom from Gedik Stables, Zekeriya. He was a meth taker, that one.'

'So Sümeyye cooked for him?'

'If she did, it wasn't at my place.'

'Oh, come on, Neşe Hanım . . .'

'I swear!' she said.

'We have evidence!' Süleyman told her. 'Constituents needed to make methamphetamine in your bedroom, traces of meth on your kitchen surfaces.'

'Nothing to do with me.'

'No?'

'Prove it!' she said. 'That girl did just as she pleased, and what pleased her most, or so it seemed to me, was aggravating her father. What sort of person doesn't respect their father, eh? As God is my witness, I tried to look after her, just as Görkan Bey instructed, but she was beyond me. It was as if her whole life was one big attack on her father. And yet he gave her money, had her taken care of . . .'

'Raped her,' Süleyman said.

Neşe Bocuk just sat.

'Inspector Gürsel had the sad duty of recovering Sümeyye's dead baby,' Süleyman said. 'We didn't know to whom it belonged . . .'

'Well, to her,' she said.

'And her father. Standard DNA tests performed on the child's body resulted in the inescapable fact that the father of Sümeyye's baby was Görkan Paşahan. So while not approving of the killing of this child by Sümeyye or someone around her, I have to say that I can see why she might not respect him.'

The old woman was quiet for quite a while, taking in what she had just been told. Then she said, 'I let him know the child was dead – Görkan Bey. I said he had a right to know seeing as he'd paid me to take care of it. Sümeyye begged me not to.'

'But you did anyway.'

'He was paying me,' she repeated.

'And so what happened after you told him?' Kerim asked.

'Cihangir was what happened. The events of the darkest night, when Sümeyye lost her soul.'

'Meaning?'

'Meaning it was her father and . . . They took that Cihangir boy and then they killed him. I thought Sümeyye would die.'

'You are referring to Emir Kaya?' Süleyman asked.

'Yeah. She loved him,' she said. 'The other lad, the horsey boy, he was taken with her but she treated him like shit. No, it was Emir . . .'

'But Görkan Paşahan wasn't in the country on Bocuk Gecesi,' Kerim said. 'Or was he, Neşe Hanım?'

'I don't know. But those he's put himself in with were.'

'And who might that be?'

She looked up. 'You remember, Mehmet Bey, that I told you I'd stop at some point. Now is that point. I've a notion you know why. And let me tell you that you can do what you like to get it out of me, but I won't break. I daren't.'

Arto Sarkissian rather liked his new colleague, Dr Fuat Kartal. He was young, enthusiastic and attractive – things that would not have necessarily endeared him to the Armenian – but he was also deeply cynical. Arto imagined how much his friend Çetin İkmen would approve.

He sat down beside his colleague at his bench, in front of the corpse of the woman Kartal had been called out to the previous night.

'Dr Kartal . . .'

'Well, she was drunk, which is a mercy,' Kartal said as he tipped his head towards the body on the trolley in the middle of the room.'0.35 blood alcohol content,' he continued. 'I doubt she even knew she was dead.'

'Defence wounds?'

'None, which also bears out the toxicology so far,' Kartal said. 'She was dead drunk, but was she dead drunk in order to enable her killer? That's the question.'

'What about the other woman found in the apartment?'

'She was drunk too,' Kartal said. 'Mehmet Bey's interviewing her.'

Arto shook his head. 'I heard that Sergeant Müngün was injured, though I gather he's recovering.'

'For what it's worth, I think this was a Mafia hit – and I mean the Italian Mafia. Or if it wasn't, it was a copycat.'

'Does Inspector Süleyman know that is your opinion?'

'Yes,' Kartal said. 'He seemed unsurprised.'

Arto raised his eyebrows.

The two men went straight from interviewing Neşe Bocuk to, finally, confronting Sümeyye Paşahan. Of course they'd both seen her before, back at Zuzanna Nowak's penthouse apartment. Now confined to an interview room with her lawyer, Mansur Nebati, she was, if anything, even more unnerving than she'd been the previous night. Hooded downturned eyes viewed them with contempt.

Süleyman got straight to the point with no preamble. 'Miss

'Paşahan,' he said, 'we have much to discuss and so I would like to begin by addressing the issue of your child.'

'Mehmet Bey,' the lawyer said, 'my client, quite reasonably, is unwilling to discuss a personal matter with you at this time. Suffice to say the child was stillborn.'

'It wasn't,' Süleyman said. 'The child drowned. It was held down by force in a tributary of the Kağıthane Stream until it, a little girl, died. Where did you give birth to your daughter, Miss Paşahan? Was it at the home of Neşe Bocuk, or did you give birth in a hospital?'

She said nothing. Nebati took a sheet of paper from his briefcase and put it on the table.

'As you will see, gentlemen, the child was born, dead, at this clinic, the Empress Elizabeth Maternity Clinic in Nişantaşı.'

Süleyman took the document from the lawyer and read it, along with Kerim Gürsel. Then he put it back on the table. 'I will scan that and check it,' he said. 'Personally I've never heard of such a place.'

'My client, as you will see, opted to take the child away with her.'

'Which I understand,' Süleyman said. 'But Mansur Bey, while having some interest in where the child was born, my main concern is what happened to it between the time of its birth and its death in a stream in Kağıthane.'

'My client doesn't recognise your assumption that her child and the one in Kağıthane—'

'DNA evidence from the child's corpse has informed us that your client was its mother and her father was its father,' Süleyman said. 'Are you and your client asking us to ignore the reality of that evidence, Mansur Bey?'

Sümeyye Paşahan laughed.

They'd gone to interview the rancid little bitch now. So it was, in part, going to be her word against Sümeyye's.

358

Neşe Bocuk thought about the old music shop in Beyoğlu and wondered whether she would ultimately have to kiss that good-bye. Why hadn't the girl simply had the child and then given it to its father? Neşe Bocuk had grown up with stories of incest in and around her village just outside the great city of Antakya. Such children were frequently damaged, many idiotic, but if Görkan Bey had fathered a child on his whore of a daughter, that was his business.

Why had Sümeyye set out to challenge him? He'd tried to keep her out of harm's way, and yet she had started to undermine him way before he'd had that stupid little junkie killed, that artist she claimed to be in love with. The girl was a witch, Neşe was sure of it. She knew the signs. Multiple lovers disappeared under her spell, although whether that boy from the stables was bewitched by her or by her easy access to crystal meth, she didn't know.

Neşe drank some water and then lay down on the pallet they'd given her. She was to blame too. Any opportunity to take back all that money and power she'd lost when Esat had been arrested. But she wasn't going to die for this. She might have to go to prison, but if Mehmet Bey thought she was ever going to tell him any more, he was mistaken.

She'd heard the guards talking about what had been done to the Polish woman. That wasn't happening to her. And Neşe Bocuk knew it was them and not Sümeyye, as one of the grunts had opined at some point, because even Sümeyye wasn't that vicious. Anyway, money shoved up the cunt meant something. It meant that you were a greedy whore.

They stood in the car park, smoking. Süleyman had called for a break and now he and Kerim Gürsel were talking about what had happened so far.

'She can't deny the facts for ever,' Kerim said. 'Even if Eylül does get this Empress Elizabeth hospital to confirm Sümeyye's story, we know the parentage of that child and we also know that people lie, particularly if they're in thrall to big players.'

'It's Görkan Paşahan who's made contact with the Italians, not Sümeyye, as far as we know,' Süleyman said.

'Yes, but Mehmet, last night . . .'

'Last night Zuzanna Nowak was falling-down drunk. Pathologist said her blood alcohol level was at 0.35. Sümeyye's, by contrast, was 0.06. A bit unsteady, clearly aggressive, but not out of her mind. And she survived and threatened us. Why?'

'You think she could've killed Nowak?'

He shrugged. 'There's a fury in her you don't often see, and she wanted to get away.'

'The old woman said that her father killed Emir Kaya, whom she loved.'

'Yes, but how, Kerim? He's not here. He's somewhere, but not here.'

'Italy?'

'We've no proof he actually went there to visit the 'Ndrangheta. Just hearsay. And yet . . .'

'What?'

'And yet I have the urge to ask her straight out. I want to see her face when I say their name.'

'Logically she should oppose them,' Kerim said.

Süleyman sighed. 'Yes.'

'And we don't know who else was in Nowak's apartment last night, do we?'

'We don't. But what we do know is that Nowak was blind drunk and Sümeyye wasn't. We know that Nowak died and Sümeyye did not. If one of Görkan Bey's allies was in that apartment, why did he or she kill Nowak? She withdrew her statement putting Paşahan at the scene of Sofija Ozola's murder.'

'Maybe he or she was actually after Sümeyye. Made a mistake. Maybe Paşahan intended to kill her for getting rid of his baby.'

Süleyman said nothing. Kerim changed the subject to something else that had been bothering him.

'Mehmet,' he said, 'what the old woman said about Gonca Hanım . . .'

'Oh.' Süleyman shook his head. 'Families, eh? My wife lays curses. I know she does it, but what can I do? Officially I will deny all knowledge of Neşe Hanım's superstitious opinions, but . . .'

'What?'

'Büket Teyze was getting that boy to go through Neşe Hanım's bin for a reason,' he said. 'That is all I will say. But I won't be interviewing Büket any time soon.'

'Understood.'

He looked up into the slate-grey sky. 'We have to up our aggression, Kerim. Sümeyye Paşahan is a crime lord's daughter, she won't crack easily. There's a lot at stake, not least of which is the spectre of the 'Ndrangheta taking an interest in the affairs of this city. And of course there is Ömer Bey. He's alive and I thank God for it, but if his arm is substantially weakened after this, he won't be able to function properly, and I resent that with my entire soul.'

When Süleyman and Gürsel went for their break, Sümeyye Paşahan's lawyer, Mansur Nebati, also left to, as he put it, stretch his legs. Sümeyye requested a comfort break. She was taken to the lavatory by Constable Ece Deniz.

Later, when questioned about what happened next, Deniz would tell Süleyman and Gürsel that Sümeyye Paşahan's request to enter the actual toilet cubicle alone was one she found reasonable.

'She was on her period,' she told the officers and their superior, Commissioner Selahattin Ozer. 'For the sake of modesty . . .'

'Of course,' Ozer said.

Süleyman, however, was in no mood for niceties. 'Are you insane?' he asked Deniz. 'Or did you assist her?'

361

Gürsel, equally furious said, 'Or did you do it? How much were you paid?'

Ozer was incensed by his officers' apparent lack of control. 'Enough! Mehmet Bey, Kerim Bey, control yourselves!'

Ece Deniz wept.

'There will of course have to be an investigation. But for the time being, there is nothing to be gained from pointing fingers. Constable Deniz did what she thought was right at the time.' He sat back down in his chair.

Süleyman glared at Deniz. 'This isn't over. The officer you left outside the toilets heard what he described to me as choking from inside. He said he called out to you but you didn't answer him.'

She looked away.

Before he left with Gürsel in his wake, Süleyman addressed his superior. 'Seems like a good day for some, doesn't it, sir? Sadly for us, it would also seem to be a good day for Italian crime syndicates.'

Chapter 28

The old woman wasn't shocked.

'Anything is possible,' she told Süleyman when he informed her that Sümeyye Paşahan was dead. 'Did she tell you anything before she . . .'

'Not a lot,' Kerim Gürsel said. 'She denied she killed her child.'

'Can't help you with that,' Neşe Bocuk said. 'I don't know.'

The two men looked at each other. Both witnesses and perpetrators of what had become a murderous crime wave in the city were dying around them, leaving not much more than this old woman, who, by the look of the smile on her face, knew that this gave her some strength in the situation. And while they hadn't told her about the manner of Sümeyye Paşahan's death, they both knew that she was also probably frightened. The two men certainly were.

Just as Constable Deniz had told them, Sümeyye Paşahan had asked to enter the toilet cubicle alone because she had her period. Deniz had left her colleague, Constable Hakan Öder, in the corridor and positioned herself outside the cubicle after Sümeyye went inside. She said she'd told Sümeyye not to lock the door behind her, but the girl had disobeyed. She'd then asked her politely to comply, after which she'd hammered on the door until she broke it down. Between her polite request and the hammering on the door, Öder claimed he heard choking noises. Then Deniz screamed for a medic, but by the time the duty doctor arrived, Sümeyye Paşahan was dead.

Nobody yet knew how she had died. The only evidence, beyond that given by Deniz and Öder, was bruises on the dead woman's neck and arms and two broken teeth.

Süleyman stood.

The old woman looked up at him. 'Going so soon, Mehmet Bey?'

'Yes,' he said. 'A thought. Come along, Kerim Bey, I think we need to be somewhere else for a while.'

'Unfortunate,' the commissioner said.

'Tragic.'

'Indeed, Inspector Alibey.' Ozer shook his head.

'But at least it would seem that this may put a stop to Görkan Bey's rantings about certain people,' Alibey said. 'The loss of a child I believe he loved very much will, I think, take up most of his time for the foreseeable future.'

'Which nevertheless leaves us with a series of unexplained deaths,' the commissioner said. 'And as you know, Inspector, there are some amongst our ranks who are keen to obtain answers.'

'Given that our priority is to ensure that someone like Görkan Paşahan never puts our city at risk again, I would say these unfortunate, truly regrettable homicides are a small price to pay.'

'Are they?' the commissioner asked. 'I wonder.'

'Sir . . .'

'And we do still have the old woman in custody, I understand.'

'Yes, but only until the end of the day.'

'Mehmet Bey and Kerim Bey continue to pursue that avenue . . .'

There was a knock at the door.

'Come.'

The door opened and Süleyman and Gürsel entered.

Neşe Bocuk had been allowed to keep the pack of tarot cards she always had about her person. Now she spread them out on the dusty floor in front of her and narrowed her eyes. It wasn't good. But then she didn't need the cards to tell her that.

However, the overwhelming message from the spread was about truth, and she didn't know that she was ready for that. Certainly not until and unless the gypsy Gonca Şekeroğlu's curse was lifted. And Mehmet Bey Efendi could arrange for that to happen, if it pleased him. Long ago, when she'd been friends with Büket Teyze, the scruffy old bitch had told her stories about the magic that Mehmet Bey Efendi exerted over the gypsy. Fearsome sexual things that had made Neşe recoil in horror and marinate in envy.

But Mehmet Bey Efendi was also in thrall to Gonca, and he was the law. He would never allude to magic. He had denied even the possibility of his wife's curse. How different it would have been had that witch's son İkmen been questioning her. Back in the days when her son Esat had ruled the Asian side of the city, he'd come up against that wily old man on several occasions. The stupid boy had been bested by him every time, even though it had ultimately been Mehmet Bey Efendi who had arrested him. Neşe had never come up against him herself, but she knew that if she had, things would have been different. The witch's son knew how to co-exist. Mehmet Bey Efendi knew only how to fight and win at any cost. But then he was an Ottoman, schooled by five hundred years of empire to get what he needed by force.

Well, this time he was going to lose. She was never going to talk now, because talking meant certain death.

'Ömer Bey!'

What looked like a vast floral arrangement burst through the door of Ömer Müngün's hospital room, leaking snowdrop heads and black tulips. Ömer, had he been alone, might have thought this vision had come about as a result of the morphine he was being given, but then he heard his sister say, 'Gonca Hanım!'

Depositing her flowery offering on his bed, Gonca, all rose

perfume and tangled hair, kissed Ömer on both cheeks and then sat down in the chair beside him.

'From Mehmet Bey and me,' she said as she nodded towards the flowers. 'He is so sorry he can't be here.'

'Gonca Hanım, we understand,' Peri said. 'And this is so, so kind of you! I will go and see whether I can find a vase big enough for your wonderful flowers.'

When she'd left, Ömer tried to sit up, but Gonca wouldn't have it.

'No, no, no!' she said. 'You must rest. My husband would be furious if he thought I had disturbed you. As I say, he would have come himself . . .'

'Boss has to close this case down, Gonca Hanım,' Ömer said. 'I do appreciate you coming to see me.' He knew that Gonca was often unwell these days, although he didn't dare allude to it.

'Is there anything you need?' she asked. 'I know that Peri Hanım and Yeşili Hanım will be looking after you very well, but if there is anything you want that I can get you, you only have to ask. If you want food from a particular place, I can send my son to get that and bring it to you.'

The thought of Rambo junior breezing into the hospital with a cigarette hanging out of his mouth made Ömer smile.

'Because a man has recently moved to Balat from . . .' She thought for a moment and then said, 'I don't know, somewhere in the east. Anyway, he makes mirra coffee and I know that is an eastern thing and that you all tend to like it.'

Mirra, a thick, bitter brew from eastern Turkey, was a very powerful version of the already strong Turkish coffee.

Realising she was not to be denied her own generosity, Ömer said, 'Thank you, Gonca Hanım, that would be wonderful.'

Her eyes shone with glee and she pinched his cheek as if she were his mother. Ömer's occasional sexual fantasies about Gonca Hanım dissolved in that moment.

*

366

'You know what I think about unorthodox methods,' Commissioner Selahattin Ozer said.

Kerim Gürsel cut in. 'Sir, I agree with Mehmet Bey. The old woman is all we have now that Sümeyye Paşahan is dead. She has to know what happened . . .'

'I have initiated an investigation into Sümeyye Paşahan's death.'

'Good. Thank you, sir,' Süleyman said.

'If there has been influence from Italy . . .'

'I believe there has, sir. I believe this is why Neşe Bocuk isn't talking to us. Further, I believe that Sümeyye's death has hardened her resolve to keep quiet.'

'Mehmet Bey, you are aware, I know, that Inspector Alibey holds you responsible for the failure of his investigation into Italian influence.'

'Alibey enlisted my help, which initially I gave,' Süleyman said. 'Further, when asked about possible 'Ndrangheta influence vis-à-vis Paşahan, he denied—'

'His mission was classified.'

'I don't care!' Süleyman roared. 'He and I, we are supposed to be on the same side!'

'Are you impugning Inspector Alibey?'

'Yes! He's a—'

Kerim Gürsel put a restraining hand on Süleyman's arm. 'Commissioner Bey, Neşe Bocuk has information that both Inspector Süleyman and myself believe will lead to the apprehension of at least some of the people who have brought chaos and misery to our city over the past two weeks. However, Neşe Hanım is of a particular superstitious type who believe in irrational unseen forces.'

'I've heard about the interview where the woman cited your wife, Süleyman.'

'Because my wife is Roma.'

'Quite.' Ozer didn't want to discuss Gonca and neither did Süleyman.

367

Kerim continued. 'Sir, if the 'Ndrangheta are involved, as we believe, then if Neşe Hanım spills everything to us, they will kill her.'

'If she is in prison—'

'Sir, with respect,' Kerim said, 'the jury is still out as to whether they got to Sümeyye Paşahan here at headquarters. Her corpse isn't even cold!'

The commissioner looked down at his desk. 'You know, gentlemen, when I was a young man, I went to Italy to attend a conference about organised crime. It was held in Naples, which was then the centre of intense Cosa Nostra activity. Our small Turkish delegation was escorted everywhere. I still remember how shocked we all were to see how heavily their courthouses and police stations were guarded. I heard stories told by men whose colleagues had been tortured and murdered by the Mafia. I thought about how I would feel should such a powerful criminal organisation take over cities in Turkey. And now—'

'Sir . . .'

'Hear me out, Süleyman,' Ozer said. 'I met Görkan Paşahan once . . .'

Süleyman and Kerim Gürsel looked at each other, wondering what he was going to say about the one-time establishment golden boy turned traitor.

'I was taken in, I will be honest,' Ozer said. 'I knew he had a past, but he showed every sign of having reformed. I do not know the exact circumstances around his sudden change of heart, but I am aware of rumours that Görkan Bey did not, it is said, get his way on a certain issue.'

Süleyman had heard he had been denied a lucrative building contract. Had his exalted friends discovered what he had done to his daughter? Or had there been something else?

'However, if he has enlisted the help of the 'Ndrangheta, he has to be stopped.'

368

'It may be too late, sir,' Süleyman said.

Ozer sighed. 'Yes.' He cleared his throat. 'However, answers. We need them, now.' He straightened his shoulders. 'So do it. Do your unorthodox thing and let's have done with it.'

Çetin İkmen didn't hold with the new coffee place that had opened up opposite headquarters. For a start, getting hold of just an ordinary sweet Turkish coffee had proved to be a minefield. Sweet? How sweet? Sugar or artificial sweetener?

Did he look like a man who had to watch his weight?

But at least the place had given him somewhere to meet Eylül Yavaş in partial privacy. They'd found a table in a nook over by some weird fake fireplace and had concluded their business away from prying eyes and ears. Not that anyone in there knew İkmen. When Eylül had gone back to work, he'd sat outside with a tall glass of sahlep, to people-watch, smoke and hide in his overcoat. He'd seen only young kids in uniform, a few sharp-suited graduate recruits. Soon, he reckoned, one or other of them would move him on, threatening to charge him with vagrancy. He rather looked forward to it.

'Çetin Bey!'

He wasn't often caught unawares, but this time he was. Probably because it was so cold and he was half asleep.

'Eh?'

Kerim Gürsel shook one of his shoulders. 'Are you asleep, Çetin Bey?'

'Asleep? No!' İkmen sat up. 'Kerim! How lovely to see you. I . . .'

Kerim was pulling him to his feet.

'No time to explain now,' he said. 'But we need you.'

'Need me? For what? Don't tell me we've gone back to doing identity parades! Had I known, I would have rolled around in the mud for half an hour.'

369

But Kerim wasn't listening. Pulling İkmen across the road and into headquarters, all he would say was, 'We need your magical brain, Çetin Bey!'

It was strange to be in his office without Ömer Müngün. He felt lonely and guilty and bereft. Hopefully Kerim would find İkmen still at the café over the road, although quite why he'd been meeting there with Eylül Yavaş, Süleyman didn't know. He didn't care. All he wanted was the truth about the seeming slaughter of innocents that had taken place in his city on his watch. Sümeyye Paşahan's baby, magician Nuri Taslı, Emir Kaya, Zuzanna Nowak. Maybe even that meth addict Zekeriya Bulut. Now Sümeyye Paşahan too. He thought about her father. Did he know she was dead? Did he care? Love and hate were such close friends, especially in criminal circles.

His phone rang. It was Gonca.

'I took flowers to Ömer Bey,' she told him. 'I got a lot. When I told Didim what had happened, she gave me a good price.' Her sister worked as a flower seller in Taksim Square.

'Thank you. How was he?'

'On morphine,' she said. 'He asked after you. I told him you were working. He was very concerned that you don't worry about him.'

'How can I *not* worry about him!'

'Shh, Mehmet,' she said. 'I know you when you have the bit between your teeth, but stop shouting.'

'I'm sorry . . .' He rubbed his brow.

'Anyway, I saw Peri at the hospital and she's making sure they take good care of him.'

'What about his wife?'

'Didn't see Yeşili or the little one,' Gonca said.

They both knew that the relationship between Ömer and his wife was all but dead, but neither of them spoke of it.

'Anyway,' Gonca went on, 'I got a text this morning from my

370

Cengiz. He's arriving this afternoon from Bucharest. Rambo will go to the airport to pick him up and then we'll have a party.'

There was a lot to unpack here. Gonca wasn't always good at providing context. Cengiz, he seemed to recall, was one of her brothers. He was fairly sure he'd never met him. He said, 'Your brother?'

'Yes!' she said. 'You know! He plays the violin!'

He didn't know, but he said nothing.

'Didim is cooking now and Erdem has gone to buy rakı.'

'Darling, do you feel well enough for a party?' Süleyman asked. Although she sounded animated, he knew that she was still heavily afflicted by her post-COVID stiffness.

But she brushed his concern away. 'Of course I do!' she said. 'It will be wonderful! Cengiz is the best dancer in the world! Everyone will come to our house. It will be like the old days!'

He had no doubt that it would. When he'd just lived with Gonca, as opposed to being her husband, before COVID, her family had come to Balat for parties all the time. He'd watched Gonca dance for hours without a break. Clever, sensual dances during which, sometimes, she would take his hand and pull him onto the floor with her. He'd always started out hideously embarrassed and ended up pinned by his own passion to her undulating body. In many senses the way she moved mirrored that of her pet, Sara.

A knock at his door allowed him to end the call, and there was İkmen, looking like a beggar, alongside Kerim Gürsel. Now maybe they'd get somewhere.

'She died in front of me.'

Commissioner Selahattin Ozer watched Mehmet Görür's interrogation of Constable Ece Deniz from the viewing room. Görür, together with his much older sidekick, Sergeant Ufuk Pulak, was not pulling any punches.

'You know as well as I do that there are no cameras in the toilet cubicles themselves,' he said. 'However, provided the door to the cubicle is left open, it is possible to see what the person inside is doing. Other people were being prevented from entering the toilets. It was just you and Sümeyye Paşahan, so why did you close the door of the cubicle once she had gone inside?'

'To give her some privacy. She was on her period.' Deniz's eyes were wide and glassy. Sergeant Pulak would later state that she looked as if she'd taken cannabis.

'The footage I have seen shows you briefly shutting the door behind you with Paşahan in the cubicle,' Görür said. 'Why did you do that?'

'I was searching her, sir.'

'Why? You searched her before she entered the toilets.'

'Sometimes suspects secrete weapons inside themselves,' she said. 'Typically in the anus.'

'Did you inspect Paşahan's anus?'

'Briefly. It was clear.'

'And then you came out and closed the door on her. According to you, she locked it.'

'She did.'

Görür looked down at some paperwork in front of him. 'You proceeded to try to force the door, is that correct?'

'Yes, sir. You can see it on the footage.'

'Yes,' he said. 'You appear to push hard.'

'It was difficult.'

'I've no doubt. It *is* difficult to open a door you are actively holding shut with one hand.'

Silence swept into the room. Ozer had seen that on the footage too. Deniz had held onto the top of the cubicle door while apparently barging it with her shoulder.

Deniz said nothing.

Görür continued. 'And then we come to the report submitted by your colleague Constable Hakan Öder, who claims he heard choking noises coming from inside the toilet.'

'I don't recall any choking noises,' she said.

Görür looked at Ufuk Pulak. 'So we come to preliminary forensic evidence, Sergeant Pulak.'

'Yes, sir.' Pulak put on a pair of spectacles and looked down at his tablet computer. 'According to attending police pathologist Dr Sarkissian, when he arrived at the scene and got down close to the dead woman, he was struck by a strong smell of almonds. This could be indicative of the presence of potassium cyanide. In addition, two of the subject's teeth had been knocked out. Can you tell us what you think about that?'

Deniz swallowed.

Görür took over. 'Now while I'm aware that during the Nuremberg trials of senior Nazis in 1946, it is said that Hermann Göring took his own life using a poison capsule secreted underneath a tooth, I believe this story may be apocryphal. That said, I am prepared to accept that this method of suicide is not unknown. However, it is rare, and I am not aware of such a phenomenon in civilian life.'

'Sümeyye Paşahan was a gangster's daughter,' Deniz said.

'She was. She was also the victim of her father's sexual abuse.'

She said nothing.

Then he struck. 'However, you did not report anything about missing teeth in the aftermath of the event.'

'I was shocked!'

'Not shocked enough to attempt to conceal the plastic gloves you had been wearing at the time, which have, I am assured, tested positive for potassium cyanide.'

She turned her head away.

'I understand that you are a single parent, Officer Deniz,' Görür said. 'And times are hard. Yet whatever they paid or promised to pay you for this service will, I think, prove to be insufficient to the need for legal counsel you will now require.'

Tears began to gather in the corners of her eyes.

'However, you can help yourself by telling us who "they" are . . .'

It was then that, through the tears, she began to laugh.

Chapter 29

It was after the two men had explained what was going to happen, while Kerim Gürsel went down to the cells to collect Neşe Bocuk, that Çetin İkmen struck a deal with Mehmet Süleyman.

'He enjoys parties,' İkmen said. 'You might care to embellish by emphasising how much Gonca Hanım would appreciate his presence.'

Süleyman frowned. 'What are you plotting, Çetin?'

The older man shrugged.

Süleyman shook his head. It was useless to ask. 'OK,' he said. 'Because it's you, I am assuming it is something that is beneficial to Kerim Bey . . .'

But İkmen would not be drawn.

Süleyman's office door opened and Kerim arrived with the short, wide bundle that was Neşe Bocuk. İkmen stood.

'Ah, Neşe Hanım,' he said. 'Always a pleasure to spend time with one of our esteemed Antakya falcıs!'

Kerim settled her in a chair and placed cushions at her back.

She looked up at İkmen and smiled. 'I'm going to have to be careful, aren't I?'

'Careful?'

She watched as the two younger men left the office and İkmen sat in Süleyman's chair.

'Of you,' the old woman said, 'and your magic. My son—'

'With respect, Neşe Hanım,' İkmen said, 'you are not your son, are you? You are someone of far greater intelligence and skill.'

Neşe Bocuk began to laugh. İkmen offered her a cigarette, which she took.

'Now,' he said, 'you and I are going to have a talk.'

He put an old-fashioned dictaphone on Süleyman's desk and pressed record.

The old woman narrowed her eyes. 'Not with that thing on!' she said. 'I'm not saying a word with that thing on!'

'Dear lady, I am not a serving police officer. This talk we are having is off the record – at the moment.'

'Yes, but—'

'I know why you are so reticent to tell us what you know,' he said. 'I would be too. But we just want the truth – for ourselves and for the families of all those who have died in the past few weeks. If you are afraid we will put you in the firing line of people—'

'Don't say it!' She cringed.

İkmen took a piece of paper from Süleyman's printer and wrote a word down on it. She looked at the word and said nothing. But she nodded.

'I will write key words down on paper so you don't have to use those words,' he said. 'We all understand, Neşe Hanım. You came into contact with something way above anything we have experienced locally. Way above your son, above his enemies, something entwined with crime and politics all across the world. I would be afraid.'

She looked down at the floor. 'And what about Gonca Şekeroğlu's curse? What are you going to do about that?'

'Ömer!'

'Boss!'

Süleyman and Kerim Gürsel were standing out in the cold, grey car park when Ömer Müngün rang.

'Your stepson has just brought me mirra,' Ömer said. He was

376

shouting and sounded very 'up'. He was clearly still on morphine. 'And Gonca Hanım brought flowers. I'm fine!'

Süleyman put his phone on speaker. 'I'm very relieved. I'm so sorry, Ömer . . .'

'Don't be! I'll be OK. The doctor says I'll need some physiotherapy but I'll be back before you know it.'

Süleyman and Kerim shared a look, and then Kerim said, 'We miss you, Ömer Bey.'

'Kerim Bey! I miss you too!'

'I will come and visit you in hospital as soon as I can.'

'I'd like that,' Ömer said. 'Peri's here and she's really looking after me, but I want to know what's going on.'

'Nothing to report yet,' Süleyman said. 'But as soon as we have news, we will let you know. Whoever shot you will be punished.'

'Good!' And then Ömer lowered his voice a little, as if suddenly deflated. 'When it happened, it was agony. I thought my heart was going to stop.'

'You're in good hands,' Süleyman said. 'And you're tough.'

They heard him laugh. 'They make us strong in the Tur Abdin.'

When the call was over, Süleyman said, 'I do hope he's right and he makes a full recovery. But it's by no means assured.'

Kerim shook his head. 'It would have to be his right arm.'

Süleyman changed the subject. Mindful of İkmen's request, he said, 'Kerim Bey, my brother-in-law Cengiz Şekeroğlu is arriving from Romania this afternoon and so my wife is having a party for him tonight. She has asked me to ask you whether you'd like to come. She noticed how much you enjoyed the Romani music played at our wedding. Apparently Cengiz is an accomplished violinist.'

'That's a very nice offer, Mehmet Bey,' Kerim said. 'But I should probably go home . . .'

Thinking on his feet, Süleyman said, 'Bring Sinem Hanım and

377

Melda. You know how Romani parties are, everyone is welcome.'

'Mmm.' Kerim looked doubtful. Things were obviously not good in the Gürsel household – not that Süleyman could allude to that.

'Gonca Hanım would be so pleased if you would come. And so would I. I am likely to be the only gaco at the party, and so it would be nice . . .'

Kerim put a hand on his arm. 'Then of course I'll come,' he said. 'But won't Çetin Bey be there?'

'No.' Süleyman smiled. 'Apparently he's busy with other things tonight.'

He took the old woman's hand in his and said, 'Start from the beginning, Neşe Hanım. As I told you, any names you do not want to utter, I will write down and bring to your attention.'

'Then you'll burn the paper, yes?' she asked.

'Yes, as agreed. Now, how did Görkan Paşahan come into your life?'

He'd got her to agree to the dictaphone, and that if and when a written statement was needed, he and he alone would write it for her. However, what had really persuaded Neşe Bocuk to speak was the ceremony he had performed to lift Gonca Şekeroğlu's curse. He'd made it up as he'd gone along – a lot of spitting away the 'eye', of elevating his own magic above that of Gonca. But then what else were spells but words uttered with absolute belief and intent? And İkmen knew his magic, and his psychology, well.

Neşe Bocuk said, 'He came to the city at the end of 2021. He bought property that had belonged to my Esat. But it was he who sought me out, not the other way around. He suggested we could help each other.'

'How?'

378

'I know people, Çetin Bey,' she said. 'People my son and I could trust. I made some introductions. Such a powerful friend to have at that time, Görkan Bey! He had everyone's ear, as you know. Maybe if I did him some favours he would help me to restore our fortunes. Maybe he would also help me take revenge against your friend . . .'

'Mehmet Bey?'

She smiled. 'I met Görkan Bey's lovely daughter. We became close. Last year he told me that he was about to do a really big deal that would provide a lot of opportunities for me as well as him. I waited. I can wait. Görkan Bey's visits became less frequent, until this spring he came to me to tell me he was going abroad.'

'Why was he doing that?' İkmen asked.

'He said those who had promised him great things had gone back on the deal. He said he now had more powerful backers abroad. He was about to take his revenge.'

'Where abroad?'

She stared at him, and so İkmen wrote the word 'Italy' down on the sheet of paper he had taken from Süleyman's printer.

She looked at it and nodded before continuing. 'The one worry he had was Sümeyye, who was pregnant. He didn't say who the father was and I didn't ask. He wanted me to help him by looking after her when he left the country. The child, he said, had to be born in Turkey. He gave me money and told me I would be rewarded in a big way later. I had no reason not to trust him. Sümeyye came, and right from the beginning, much as I liked the girl, I knew she was going to be trouble.'

'Why?'

'Because first she used my apartment to cook up meth. She said her father didn't give her enough money and this was how she was forced to live. There's a big appetite for meth in this city, and I will be honest, she gave me money to buy my silence. She bad-mouthed her father every day. Admittedly by that time Görkan

Bey was broadcasting, threatening people here at home, and I was not comfortable with that. But he carried on paying me . . . However, then there were men. Her pregnant and there were men! One in particular she told me she loved, the boy from Cihangir . . .'

'Emir Kaya.'

'That's him,' she said. 'Never slept with him, so she told me. Of course I didn't believe her. Told me she loved him and didn't believe that either. But when that boy died, all the demons inside her came out and she went to war with her own father.'

Sinem Gürsel looked down at the text on her phone and said, 'I wonder where he's really going . . .'

Madam Edith, who had been reading, looked up from her magazine. 'Who, lovely?'

'Kerim. Says he's going to go to a party at Mehmet Bey's house tonight after work. Says it's a Romani thing. But everyone knows that Gonca Hanım is sick.'

'Yes, but she's not dead,' Edith said. 'She's a gypsy, any excuse for a party. Anyway, I've heard her brother Cengiz is back in town, so it's probably connected to that.'

She also knew that İkmen was up to something. She didn't know what, but she surmised he wanted Kerim out of the way for some reason. Madonna had told her that Cengiz Şekeroğlu was indeed back in İstanbul and the gypsies were preparing for a big party, but there were also rumours that the city was at a precarious point in its history. It was, it was said, under attack by foreigners. This was often a trope used by those in charge to consolidate the people – it always had been. However, this was different. This didn't come from politicians or their acolytes, but from street people – falcıs, pickpockets and prostitutes – whispering that local godfathers were withdrawing into their great mansions on the Bosphorus, unable to sleep . . .

*

380

'I didn't know the child was Görkan Bey's,' Neşe Hanım said. 'I never asked whose it was. All I knew was that I was supposed to deliver it when her time came. But then she went to the hospital. I never saw it. She told me it had died. There were phone calls between her and her father, angry ones, but I didn't know what they were about. Then the boy disappeared and she went mad.'

'How?'

'Screaming, swearing, cutting herself. Of course Görkan Bey was enemy number one by this time and I was scared, I admit it. It was when the boy . . .'

'Emir Kaya?'

'. . . when he was found dead, she told me everything. Her father had abused her from a child. I was horrified. I know men do that. I grew up in a village. One of my uncles had my cousin Defne and then killed her when she became pregnant.' She shook her head. 'Görkan Bey wanted the child. Wanted to start again with a new son, or so he hoped.'

'What about his existing son?' İkmen asked.

'The carpet dealer? He didn't know, doesn't know. It was always Sümeyye and Görkan. That boy completely misread the situation, felt rejected by Görkan Bey. Jealousy of his sister made him leave the family. Anyway, Sümeyye told her father, like me, that the child had died. It was one of the meth-heads she dealt to who told me otherwise. Obsessed with her – and of course her product. He killed the child for her out in the fields where he worked around Kağıthane.'

Süleyman had told him about a horse groom called Zekeriya Bulut. Now dead, apparently from the drug he loved so much. A lot of people involved in this story were dead . . .

'Çetin Bey,' the old woman said, 'you are sure that the curse has been lifted?'

'Yes.' He'd have to tell Gonca. Unless she already knew. If one believed that she could know . . .

'Neşe Hanım,' he said, 'what about the foreigners?'

'Everyone knows that Görkan Bey is abroad. Or do they?' she said. 'Sümeyye told me that the people who killed the boy Emir Kaya were from that country – all except one.'

'We're talking about the magicians who "disappeared" Emir Kaya on Bocuk Gecesi?'

'They were from that country.'

Italy.

'Except one,' she said. 'Only Sümeyye knew – or so she said. Her father's people were originally from Albania – like your mother.'

Suddenly İkmen felt cold. 'The dordelec? Görkan Paşahan was the dordelec?'

'If that is what the demon is called,' the old woman said. 'Yes. Sümeyye was in Cihangir. She saw him, so she said. He was sending her a message: *You killed our child, I will punish you.* And so of course she went to war with him.' She shook her head. 'But you know I don't think she did it because of the abuse. True, she hated the idea of the child, which was why she had it killed. *Had* it killed, couldn't do it herself. But was she jealous of it too, of it taking her father's affection and maybe his money away from her? She told me she would destroy him. She knew the woman he had bribed to change her story about him and some foreign prostitute just before he left Turkey. She told me this woman, another foreigner, had pictures on her phone that would prove he killed that hooker. I don't know, but Sümeyye was convinced.'

'So she told her father she had this evidence?'

'No,' she said. 'She contacted the foreigners, her father's new partners.'

İkmen wrote another word down on his piece of paper. She looked at it and said, 'Yes. That's them.'

He felt the coldness creep into his every bone and muscle.

'She said to them that when her father told them he could

382

provide them with a strong foothold here in the city using information about those at the top of the food chain, he was lying. Only she could do that.'

'How?'

She laughed. 'She was lying, Çetin Bey! She had nothing! A spoilt, abused little girl who had lost the only man she had ever loved – what could she have? She had threats, that was it! And here is where my story becomes shameful to me – at least that's what I think, may God forgive me.'

İkmen leaned forward. 'Tell me.'

'I made her go,' she said. 'And I was right to do so, because when the boy at the riding school died, I knew that Mehmet Bey would soon be knocking on my door. The boy came to my apartment and the two of them got so high I thought Sümeyye might die. I didn't think the boy would.'

'He died on his way home,' İkmen said.

'Yes.' She sighed. 'So I asked her to go – Sümeyye. She said she was going to stay with a friend, I didn't know who.' She swallowed hard. 'They came for her . . . they killed her friend. They're not stupid, they know that Görkan Bey is their real asset. They protected that asset. And now Sümeyye's dead because . . .' She put her head down.

'They're already here,' İkmen said.

Nothing moved. The old woman said, 'I am dead. I am dead and so I will say their name. Mafia. There.'

'Neşe Hanım . . .'

'Bring Mehmet Bey back and write my statement,' she said. 'He cannot protect me, or you, or anyone. They call İstanbul the city of the world's desire, and it is. There is too much here for them. Now that they have arrived, they will not leave.'

Chapter 30

'Baby!'

She was dancing, hips swinging, stomach undulating. She looked beautiful and so, so happy. If he hadn't been exhausted, Mehmet Süleyman would have run to his wife and picked her up in his arms. But it had been both a terrible and a wonderful day. Neşe Bocuk had confirmed what they had suspected about Görkan Paşahan and the trail of destruction he had brought about in the city. And it wasn't over. Far from it. His 'friends' the 'Ndrangheta were here now, and they weren't going to let go of either Görkan Bey or the inroads into the city he had allowed them to make.

But that was for later. Now he and Kerim had come to the party to celebrate the return of a tall, handsome man who was dancing while playing a violin with lightning speed. There was no doubt this man was Cengiz Şekeroğlu. Like his sister, he had strong, hawk-like features, a body that moved almost bonelessly through space, and eyes as black as sin.

Gonca danced over to her husband's side and kissed him. She pointed to the violinist. 'That is my Cengiz,' she said. 'Isn't he wonderful?'

'Yes.'

A large fire burned in the middle of the garden, around which Gonca's daughters and grandchildren and their many cousins danced. A table set with food and drink – mainly rakı – had been set up outside the kitchen, and the fairy lights Gonca had strung across the trees illuminated the scene in flashing rainbow colours.

384

Gonca's eldest daughter, the lawyer Asana Şekeroğlu, sidled up to Kerim Gürsel and took his arm. They knew each other through their mutual love of drag shows. Mehmet had told his wife he was going to bring Kerim to the party, and why, and now Gonca looked at her daughter with a frown on her face. Asana had never made a secret of the fact that she desired Kerim even if he was gay.

'Asana!'

She looked at her mother, lazily letting smoke from her cigarette ooze out of her mouth.

'Mum, Kerim Bey is a friend,' she said.

'And always welcome here,' Gonca said as she squeezed Kerim's arm.

Then she said something to Asana in Romani, and the younger woman kissed Kerim's neck and sauntered away.

Eylül Yavaş knocked on the door and said, 'Open up! Police.'

Not a sound issued from inside the apartment, and she looked nervously at Çetin İkmen, who whispered, 'Maybe in bed. Try again.'

It was one o'clock in the morning and so it was quite possible that the man had gone to bed.

'Police! Open up!'

Eventually they heard the sound of shuffling feet on carpet, and a middle-aged man in pyjamas opened the door. İkmen recognised him immediately.

Eylül held up her badge. 'Enver Yılmaz?'

'Er, yes . . .'

'Police.'

She barged past him, with İkmen in tow. The latter noticed that Madam Edith had briefly poked her head outside the Gürsels' apartment.

Once inside, Eylül turned to a bewildered Enver Yılmaz. 'What do you know about a company called Mahzur IT Solutions?'

He frowned, said, 'Nothing,' and then looked at İkmen. 'Who are you?'

İkmen sat down in a chair and lit a cigarette. 'Me? Oh, I'm no one. Answer the officer's question. Truthfully this time.'

Yılmaz said, 'I did!'

'No you didn't. A friend of mine, Halil Tatar – remember him – made an appointment with you regarding Mahzur IT Solutions. He even, poor man, went to their offices in Maslak to meet you. But of course neither you nor Mahzur IT Solutions was there, because the company isn't real, is it, Mr Yılmaz?'

'I . . .'

'We don't like companies that don't exist, Mr Yılmaz,' Eylül said. 'Rightly or wrongly, we associate such phenomena with scams and money laundering.'

Yılmaz sat down, and now so did Eylül.

Apart from multiple computers – on a desk and on the floor – the Yılmaz apartment was spare. No photographs, books, ornaments – just scruffy elderly chairs, a TV set and a small plastic table. Everything about the place seemed to point towards it being just a temporary home.

'These computers,' Eylül said, 'if I asked to look at what is on them . . .'

'Get a warrant!' Yılmaz's face was now flushed, his teeth gritted.

'Well, let's not get ahead of ourselves, shall we?' İkmen said. 'Mr Yılmaz, what does the name Mahzur Açar mean to you? Is he a relative of yours? A good friend, maybe? Possibly a lover?'

'I am not an LGBTQ pervert . . .'

'Kimlik.' Eylül held out her hand. 'You know that if a police officer asks you for your kimlik, you must show it. If you don't, we arrest you.'

'I haven't got it on me! I'm in my pyjamas!'

'So get it,' she said. 'Where is it?

386

He looked around the room, blinking. Was he trying to remember where he'd put it or wondering what he could do to convince them he'd lost it somewhere? İkmen saw a bead of sweat begin at Yılmaz's hairline and fall down his face.

'Mr. Yılmaz?'

They all looked at each other, and then Yılmaz said, 'What do you want?'

'Your kimlik,' Eylül said. She put her hand inside her coat so that he could see her shoulder holster and her gun.

'Why do the Italians want to be here? Why now?' Kerim Gürsel said to Mehmet Süleyman.

The two men were sitting in garden chairs watching the gypsies dance to unfamiliar tunes played on the violin by Cengiz Şekeroğlu. Süleyman hadn't even been introduced to the man, but he could see in Cengiz's eyes the same lack of trust Gonca's older, now dead, brother Şükrü had always shot his way. Romani men had never liked their women marrying out; they probably never would.

Süleyman said, 'I can only theorise.'

'Oh?'

'Someone in the 'Ndrangheta saw an opportunity in Görkan Paşahan,' he said. 'I don't know why those Paşahan was in bed with decided to cut him out of whatever business he was in line for, but it must have been big. I mean, walking straight into the arms of the Mafia is a bold statement.'

'And so much for his patriotism,' Kerim said. 'In effect, selling his country.'

'Gangsters only use patriotism when it benefits them,' Süleyman said. 'And look at the man! A murderer, an incestuous abuser. We still don't know whether he ordered his new friends to kill his own daughter. We probably never will.'

Gonca appeared in front of them with her brother. Süleyman

387

looked around to see who was playing the violin now, and saw a small boy, his eyes closed, performing like a maestro.

'Cengiz,' Gonca said, 'this is my husband Mehmet and his friend and colleague Kerim Bey.'

Cengiz Şekeroğlu was a heavily lined man, his face almost as brown as the soft felt hat he wore on top of his waist-length black hair. Had Mehmet not known that he was one of Gonca's younger siblings, he would have thought he was older than she.

Cengiz bowed slightly. Süleyman went to stand, but the gypsy motioned for him to stay seated.

'I am glad to meet you, bey efendi,' he said. 'You make our Gonca happy. You take care.'

There was a slight accent, probably because of the many years he had spent in Romania. Also his use of 'bey efendi' was in no way subservient. Cengiz Şekeroğlu was a proud man, respectfully acknowledging another man he deemed worthy of his attention.

'Thank you, Cengiz Bey,' Süleyman said. 'That means a lot to me.'

The gypsy nodded and then allowed himself to be taken by his sister inside the house. When they'd gone, Süleyman said, 'Speaking of Sümeyye Paşahan's death . . .'

'Do you think Constable Deniz killed her?' Kerim asked.

'It's possible,' Süleyman replied. 'As a target for bribery, or threats, she's a good example. Single parent, not much money, no man in her life. But if the 'Ndrangheta are involved, she won't talk, she's got children.'

'How did they get to her?'

'They didn't,' Süleyman said. 'They got to someone else, a long time ago.'

'Alibey?'

'Maybe, although while I don't entirely trust the man, I think that may be too easy an answer. Do you remember how just before

388

the pandemic we worked on a case involving the death of a jeweller over in Vefa?'

'Fahrettin Müftüoğlu, yes,' Kerim said. 'He produced copies of religious artefacts for rich people. We never found out who.'

'Three of our officers were implicated and dismissed. Our art expert died while investigating the role an Italian aristocrat's daughter may have played in Müftüoğlu's business. We were warned at the time that was just the tip of the iceberg.'

More details were coming to Kerim now. He said, 'That's right! Müftüoğlu made a copy of the Ark of the Covenant!'

'We think it was a copy, yes.'

'It had to have been! Where is it now?'

'I don't know,' Süleyman said. 'But it makes you think. Who would have been powerful and knowledgeable enough to orchestrate something like that?'

'We stopped it, though.'

'We stopped that, yes. But if a criminal organisation is really determined to get a foothold somewhere, they're not going to give up, are they? They'll try again, maybe using another method.'

They sat in silence for a while, looking into the dying embers of the fire. Eventually Süleyman said, 'You're welcome to stay, Kerim.'

'What, with Gonca Hanım's family here?'

Süleyman smiled. 'Oh, they will party until dawn,' he said. 'And even if they do sleep, they'll just lie down on the floor. Her sister Didim stayed for a few weeks before we got married and didn't use the bed we gave her once. They're very honest about doing things their own way and I respect them for that.'

'All right,' Kerim said. 'I've been drinking, so driving home would not be a good idea. And anyway . . .'

He stopped. Süleyman looked up. 'Anyway what?'

Kerim shook his head. 'Nothing.' Then he smiled. 'Thank you, Mehmet.'

*

Eylül Yavaş looked at the identity card Yılmaz handed her and then passed it over to İkmen, who said, 'Whatever you paid for this, Mr Yılmaz, you were robbed.'

Yılmaz, sitting again now, said, 'I don't know what you mean.'

'Give us your real kimlik,' Eylül said. 'Or I will arrest you. Then you'll have to come with us to headquarters, where you'll be obliged to answer questions about ID forgery. Do you want that?'

Yılmaz raked a hand through his hair. 'What do you want?' he asked. 'I don't believe you're here about the company. If you were, you'd have some uniformed gorillas with you so you could beat a confession out of me.'

'Oh, we don't want to beat you, Mr Açar,' İkmen said.

Yılmaz paled.

'Because that is your real name, isn't it? Your mistake was naming your company after Mahzur. I know it's tempting to honour someone in that way, but it's hardly wise.'

When Yılmaz spoke again, his voice was soft, clearly contained using considerable effort. 'He is innocent.'

'Our prisons are full of innocent people,' Eylül said. 'Ask any prisoner whether they are guilty and they will tell you they're not.'

'Your brother . . .' İkmen began. 'Mahzur is your brother, isn't he?'

Yılmaz said nothing.

'Well, anyway, he was arrested by Inspector Kerim Gürsel, wasn't he? Your neighbour. Serendipitous, wasn't it, you obtaining the tenancy on this apartment. I wonder whether you knew back then what you think you know about him—'

'He's a filthy homosexual!' Yılmaz hissed, unable to contain himself any longer. 'He fluttered his eyelashes at me! And you people trust that . . . *thing* to arrest the right person!'

İkmen put one cigarette out and then lit another. 'I,' he said, 'chain-smoke. I don't apologise for it. But this isn't about me. Did

Kerim Gürsel sexually assault you, Mr Açar? I am going to use your real name because it's just silly not to.'

'You think I would allow that creature anywhere near me?' Açar said.

'You willingly had drinks with him on several occasions,' Eylül said.

'But that's not why we're here, is it?' İkmen said.

'No.'

'No.' He leaned forward in his chair. 'We're here because of what you have been doing to Sinem Hanım, Kerim's wife.'

'What?' Açar said. 'The woman next door? She's a cripple. What would I want with a cripple?'

'Sex?' İkmen flicked his ash onto the floor.

'Sex!' Açar laughed. 'Is that what she told you? In her dreams! Why would a man like me have sex with her?'

'Revenge,' Eylül said. 'My colleague here tells me that you were blackmailing Mrs Gürsel. Her sexual humiliation in return for your silence on the subject of her husband's alleged sexuality. Both mental and physical cruelty enacted on the body of a vulnerable woman.'

'Oh, and if that were so,' he said, 'if I were able to manipulate her in that way, that can only mean that her husband is an unnatural pervert.'

'Does it?' İkmen said. 'Mr Açar, you and I both know that we live in a time when even the slightest suggestion, true or not, about a public servant and impropriety will get that person dismissed. Truth can be entirely irrelevant.'

'So why didn't I just go to the police and tell them, then?'

'Because you are a psychopath,' İkmen said. 'Like your innocent brother, you do things on impulse and to gratify your own immediate desires.'

'I'm not—'

İkmen stood, threw himself at Açar and grabbed him by the throat. 'I can still move quickly for a very old bastard, can't I, Mr Açar?'

Açar, just about able to speak said, 'Who are you?'

'I told you, nobody. Just an interested citizen with the law on my side.'

'What do you want?'

Eylül Yavaş took her gun out of its holster and put it calmly against Açar's temple. 'We want you to go,' she said. 'I'm not interested in your fake kimlik or your fake company. My colleague and I will keep the first and you will shut down your company website tonight. You will also leave Tarlabaşı tonight and you will not return.'

'I could report you . . .'

'To whom?' Eylül said. 'Do you know who we are? No. Leave, never allude to this to anyone, and you are free to do whatever you like somewhere else. Trabzon maybe. That's where your family are originally from, isn't it?'

He looked at them both, from one to the other with frightened eyes.

'But this apartment . . . I've only just paid my rent!' he said. 'A month in advance!'

How mundane this had suddenly become, İkmen thought. A man sexually abuses a woman, effectively gets away with it and then bitches about his rent? The urge to punch Açar as hard as he could in the mouth was almost overwhelming. But instead he said, 'Go. We will help you pack.'

Eylül began to pick up Açar's computers, phones and attaché case. Opening his front door, she put them in the hall. Then she went into his bedroom.

To the sound of clothes being pulled off hangers, İkmen said, 'And if I ever see or hear about you again, I will kill you. Not my colleague, me. I will track you down, I will kill you and I will dance on your grave, because while I am not a psychopath like you, I am a very dangerous man who believes that bacteria in my gut has more of a right to life than you.'

And so it was that Enver Açar found himself walking towards Esenler bus station at three o'clock that morning with all his worldly possessions in two suitcases, wearing his pyjamas.

Chapter 31

The following week

They'd let him in with absolutely no compunction. They hadn't even given him a visitor's pass, because despite the fact that none of the young officers who patronised the new café opposite headquarters knew who he was, everyone in charge of letting people into the building knew Çetin İkmen.

When he got out of the lift on the fourth floor, Mehmet Süleyman was standing outside his office, waiting to greet him. The two men embraced.

Süleyman had invited İkmen to his office because it was one of the few places, at the present time, where they could be alone. Ömer Müngün was at home recovering from his gunshot wound, Eylül Yavaş was overseeing the transfer of Neşe Bocuk to Bakırköy women's prison and Kerim Gürsel had the day off to be with his family.

'I am surprised he's taken a day off, if I'm honest,' Süleyman said as he closed his office door and then opened the window. 'I don't know the details, obviously, but I do know, as you do, that things have not been easy for Kerim Bey at home lately. Maybe things are better now for some reason, though. Maybe he's sorted it out. Maybe you . . .'

İkmen shrugged. Although Sinem Gürsel had been unsure about whether she could keep what had happened to her a secret from her husband for all time, he knew that she was trying.

'Told Kerim Bey she was sorry she'd been such a bitch,' Madam Edith had told him. 'Told me and him it was the menopause. I know you know, Çetin Bey, but I won't ask. Just hope Mr Enver Yılmaz rots in hell.'

Süleyman offered İkmen a cigarette and both men lit up.

'So what are you going to do about Ömer Bey?' İkmen asked. 'Do you know how long he's going to be out of action?'

'No,' Süleyman said. 'As I'm sure Peri has told you—'

'I haven't seen Peri Hanım for a while,' İkmen said. 'She's been busy with the family, as you can imagine.'

Süleyman could. When Ömer had returned home, it had been his sister rather than his wife who had cared for him – while also doing a full-time job. Where the space for İkmen was, she and nobody else knew.

'So?' İkmen asked. 'What do you do in the meantime?'

'I've a graduate fresh from the academy. Not met him yet,' Süleyman said. 'Just temporary until Ömer is fit for service again. If . . .'

'He will be,' İkmen said.

Süleyman smiled. 'In your guise as the son of a witch?'

'Something like that.' But then İkmen's face dropped. 'You know, Mehmet, we all made it through Bocuk Gecesi, the darkest night, but considering what that night revealed, I wonder whether it is indeed the blackest night we will have to endure. This war in Ukraine haunts my nights. We moved out of the virus and into this, and this . . .' he shrugged, 'what does it mean for us? The Crimea is just across the Black Sea from here.'

'I'm rather more worried about Italian organised crime at the moment, Çetin.'

'I understand that,' İkmen said.

'I don't know whether I can trust Alibey . . .'

'They call it "omerta" in Italy, the silence that exists around their various mafias. But I wonder, you know, Mehmet.'

'About what?'

'About how close we are to Ukraine, about how "joined up" organised crime is in our Internet-connected world. The Russians have always wanted this city. When the tsars ruled their empire, they dreamed of praying in Aya Sofya. Does Mr Putin have similar aspirations?'

'What's that got to do with the Mafia?'

'Who knows?' İkmen said. 'But as I say, in our brave new world of interconnected crime syndicates . . .'

A knock on the door brought their conversation to a close.

'Come.'

A young man neither of them recognised walked in carrying a laptop computer.

'Yes?' Süleyman asked.

'Inspector Süleyman, sir, something's been picked up by technical that you might want to see.'

His voice was deep and husky and his thick black hair stood up from his scalp in waxed peaks.

He placed the laptop on Süleyman's desk and then looked at İkmen. 'Oh . . .'

'This is Çetin Bey,' Süleyman said without expanding on his description. 'Who are you?'

'I'm Sergeant Timur Eczacıbaşı. Sergeant Müngün's temporary replacement, sir.'

'Are you.' Süleyman looked him up and down. He was very smart and very, very young. 'So what's this?'

'The technical department found this online.' Eczacıbaşı pressed a key on the keyboard and all three men watched as a man restrained in a chair appeared to have his throat cut. There was no sound. Both İkmen and Süleyman winced, even though they knew that such things were often later discovered to be fake.

'On the Web, apparently,' Eczacıbaşı said. 'They thought you should see it because it appears to be Görkan Paşahan, sir.'

396

It did. The young sergeant played it again, and then İkmen said, 'If Paşahan has lost his usefulness to them, continuing to feed him will have become an unnecessary expense.'

'Which could mean that what he claimed to have for them was fake,' Süleyman said.

'Or not.'

Both Süleyman and Eczacıbaşı looked at İkmen, who said, 'More smoke and mirrors? I don't know. All I do know is that the magicians have it right. To fool all of the people all of the time is easy when you know how. It is finding the man behind the curtain that is the hard part. Especially when said man is actually many men and women whose only function is to fake what you have on so many fronts that you cannot, as the British say, see the wood for the trees. That is the real meaning of the darkest night, and the sun doesn't even have to have set for it to happen.'

Young Eczacıbaşı looked terribly confused, while Süleyman said, 'That's bleak.'

'It is,' İkmen said. 'Bleak is where we are. But it's not where we're going, not long term.'

'Why not?'

'Because we don't want to. And because we have the truth on our side.'

Süleyman leaned back in his chair. 'You know that Sümeyye Paşahan told her lawyer that no one cares about the truth any more.'

'Did she?' İkmen smiled. 'What a sad life that poor abused woman must have had. What a warped set of values she was raised with. I can see what she meant, but it's just an illusion, my dear Mehmet, Sergeant Eczacıbaşı. Everyone cares about the truth in the end, even those who seek to conceal or manipulate it. And that is because without it nothing works – not even, ultimately, our illusions.'

Then in typical İkmen style he changed the subject. 'And how is Gonca Hanım getting on with her Bocuk Gecesi artwork?'

'It's finished,' Süleyman said. 'There will be a viewing tomorrow night, to which you are invited. And, of course, a party.'

'Good.' İkmen nodded. 'Have you seen it, Mehmet?'

'Yes.'

'And how is it?'

Süleyman smiled. 'Magnificent.'